The Lieutenant of San Porfirio

* * *

Joel D. Hirst

The Lieutenant of San Porfirio

This is a work of fiction. All of the characters, names, incidents, organizations, and dialogue in this novel are either the products of the author's imagination or are used fictitiously.

iUniverse books may be ordered through booksellers or by contacting:

iUniverse
1663 Liberty Drive
Bloomington, IN 47403
www.iuniverse.com
1-800-Authors (1-800-288-4677)

ISBN: 978-1-4759-3949-1 (sc)
ISBN: 978-1-4759-3950-7 (hc)
ISBN: 978-1-4759-3951-4 (e)

Library of Congress Control Number: 2012912914

Print information available on the last page.

iUniverse rev. date: 11/03/2015

Dedication

* * *

For those who seek freedom: may you never tire.

Acknowledgements

* * *

I would like to thank my lovely wife; for countless hours, discussions and ideas as this story took shape. I would like to thank all those who continue to fight for their freedoms against yet another generation of dictators; they are the inspiration for this story – and it is written for them. I would like to thank Caroline Alethia for her help in editing. And I'd like to thank the team at I-Universe for all their support.

1

＊ ＊ ＊

It was early morning in the Revolutionary Socialist Republic of Venezuela. Despite the hour, Lieutenant Juan Marco Machado found himself crammed tightly in the belly of an armored personnel carrier. He looked down at the new bars on his shoulder and repeated aloud his new rank. *Lieutenant.* He smiled a lopsided grin. *Much more commanding than Sergeant.* His meager worldly possessions—the bounty of decades of faithful revolutionary service—had been carefully packed inside four large black plastic garbage bags and crammed into the crevices of the APC. The rusting eyesore idling around him was a relic from the Second World War, sold to the Revolutionary Socialist Armed Forces of Venezuela (FARS for short) by the Russian weapons dealer Rosoboron Export for a song—and an expensive maintenance contract. Machado was on his way to his new life in San Porfirio de la Guacharaca, the capital. Clutched tightly in his left hand was his new AK-103, given to him only yesterday along with his medals and his promotion. He lovingly caressed the grip of his new weapon, feeling the smooth plastic and the clammy metal, and sighed. *I'm a soldier of the revolution, and I've finally been noticed. My years of guarding tollbooths and power installations have finally paid off.*

As he adjusted his unwieldy mass in the tight space, lifting the plain opaque bottle brimming with bootlegged whiskey that he'd been energetically attempting to empty since daybreak but whose contents never seemed to go down, he banged his war-injured ankle on a large pile of unused shells that had rusted firmly to the metal floor.

"Oof!" Remembering his pain, and the source of his medals, he gave himself a salute and a grin. He was lifting the sweating bottle for another toast when he heard an unwelcome order intrude over his loudly idling metal bar and pierce the alcohol-induced buzz he'd been nurturing.

"*Teniente* Juan Marco Machado," one of his superior officers, a captain, yelled down into the belly of the aging weaponry.

"*Si, mi Capitán.*" Machado's voice cracked as he emerged sheepishly from his tank, squishing his expanding gut through the hatch and trying to balance himself unsteadily on the small platform. Behind and in front of him, the line of APCs and jeeps was assembled, ready to ferry chickens and goats to feed San Porfirio's starving poor.

A ray of sunlight from the bright equatorial sun hit Machado directly in the eye, making him squint. The tangy saltiness of the sea and the pungent smell of fish wafted from the docks as the early morning fishermen returned with their night's catch. These smells, to the lieutenant the smells of Venezuela, mixed easily with the humidity and lush vegetation of the jungle—punctuated by diesel fuel from the idling convoy. Through the morning sunlight he saw the Caribbean turquoise sea glistening, giving way immediately to the deep green of the jungle. The small garrison town he was leaving, forever, was nestled between the two on the perfect white beach. A dirt road cut the dejected town in half. The steeple of the centuries-old Catholic Church, the only construction higher than two stories, grasped desperately toward heaven as if trying to escape the squalor around it. Santo Tomas was a miserable town. Its only value was a deep-water port that, being the closest to San Porfirio, made it of strategic importance.

"Aghem." Teniente Machado cleared his throat. "At your orders." And he threw the well-practiced, crisp revolutionary salute—his middle and index finger making the sign of *V* for victory while tapping the back of his wrist to his forehead—attempting to look his new part. Machado had never been fully satisfied with his appearance. He was several inches shorter than he would have liked and was what some people described as "stocky," though he preferred "big-boned." His brown skin was a salute to his mixed-race heritage—black slaves from the Caribbean, Indians from the interior, and white landowners who spread their seed around lasciviously. He had short-cropped, curly black hair—*pelo malo* as they offensively called it in Spanish—and a well-groomed mustache.

"Congratulations on your medals and your promotion, young soldier. Stand straight and tall so that they shine in the Venezuelan sunlight," the garrison commander, a captain, said. "Let me see." The captain squinted as he leaned upward. "Ah, yes, one for courage in action and one for injury in the line of duty. You are truly a testament to the revolution."

"*Si, señor.* Thank you, *señor,*" Machado said. "I am but a faithful servant of El Comandante."

"We shouldn't have left you alone to guard that bridge," the captain said, his right hand stroking his silver-streaked goatee. "These things get out of hand. You're lucky you weren't seriously injured by those students."

"Yes, sir, these student marches are becoming dangerous," Machado said, thinking at the same time, *Thank God nobody was there to see me fall out of my tank trying to buy that empanada from a street vendor.*

"*Así es.*" The captain nodded in affirmation as if to a silent prayer. "We are grateful for your sacrifices for the fatherland."

"The honor is mine, for the glory of our invincible revolution, and I am thrilled that my superiors have seen fit to increase my responsibilities. I will seek to forever be a humble servant of El Comandante." Machado was anxious to return to the sweltering comfort of his private party, and as his well-tended buzz began to lose its edge, he was becoming slightly irritated.

"Is there anything else, sir?" He shifted his weight off his injured ankle, which responded in relief with a strange popping sound.

But the garrison captain wasn't done dispatching the convoy; it being the only thing he had on his agenda for the day, he wanted to talk.

"Someday, Machado, we will fight a real war. We will finally use these weapons that El Comandante has seen fit to trust us with. We may be patient with the enemies of the revolution, young Machado, but we have our limits." Emphasizing the point, on the last word he slapped the chamber of his AK-103, causing the clip to fall to the ground and the weapon to discharge the chambered round in Machado's direction. Machado had reached down to zip up his fly—he'd realized he'd left it open after relieving himself through the small APC window a few minutes earlier—and the stray bullet whizzed through the air where his revolutionary salute had been a split second before. He paled.

The captain's face flushed bright red. "Errghm, carry on then." He turned and walked quickly away.

"Yes, Captain …"

Machado watched the captain stroll down the line to the next vehicle, spraying a burst of machine gun fire at a spider monkey that was attempting to wrestle a coconut from a palm tree on the beach. The angry animal cursed at him in its own prehistoric language, giving him the middle finger before leaping to the jungle and plunging into the interior of the canopy.

Finally, the convoy started to move.

For the next several hours the procession snaked slowly forward, Machado fighting to keep his APC going in a straight line while continuing to empty the bottle of whiskey, when all of a sudden the line rattled and screeched to a sudden halt. A large plume of thick black smoke drifted above the convoy. Annoyed, Machado popped himself out of the inside of the canister and leaned out dangerously over the road, holding tenuously to the barrel of the 30-mm gun as he craned his neck to see what had happened. He realized immediately that the explosion had originated from one of the troop transports several vehicles ahead in the line, one that was hauling the livestock. As the dust cleared, Machado saw pieces of the ruined transport lying haphazardly on the asphalt. Goat parts were strewn in bloody mayhem across the road, and a white cloud of chicken feathers floated down on the procession like a tropical snowstorm. The dismembered head of a billy goat was stuck like a hood ornament to the business end of the cannon. The red lifeblood of the animal dripped onto the ground in a macabre spectacle.

A group of hungry peasants, their ribs showing through their emaciated chests from years of revolutionary sacrifice, charged out of their roadside hovels with shovels, plastic plates, and large black cauldrons to scoop up the shredded pieces of massacred flesh lying in moist piles on the road, across the guns of military vehicles, and over tree branches. They chattered together excitedly, amazed at the good fortune in their opportunity for a dinner of fresh meat.

Machado was unfazed; explosions were becoming more common in the FARS as the equipment disintegrated into the jungles and the oceans for lack of maintenance. So far nobody had been hurt—at least, nobody he knew. Besides, it wasn't his responsibility—he wasn't in charge of maintenance, which was somebody else's problem. In the new FARS it was best to keep your head down and focus on your job—and hope for a little bad luck for somebody else—if you wanted to advance.

"Something seems to have exploded," said an ancient woman matter-of-factly from a homemade rocking chair where she was selling small plastic cups of a dark, fragrant brew. The convoy had stopped in front of a wide spot in the road as it curved around the mountain. A few miserable makeshift houses, belonging to the emaciated peasants, clung desperately to the cliff above the jungle below.

Getting up from her chair, where she'd been engaged in an animated discussion with a shirtless man selling bananas, the oracle brought Machado a thimbleful of the drink. The aromatic elixir cleared the last remaining cobwebs from his booze-addled mind.

"You're looking mighty shiny, *mijito*," the old lady said, gesturing with a skeletal finger at his polished medals.

"Thank you," Machado said as he reached down for a refill. "For heroism," he said looking at the road ahead, hoping he sounded sufficiently nonchalant.

"*Si, muchacho*, it must take real valor to sit up there all day," the lady said as she deposited the hundred-Asno coin Machado had handed her into her the left cup of her brassiere—but not before she spat on it and wiped it clean with a brown handkerchief she pulled from a tiny, multicolored purse at her side.

"Listen, *vieja*," Machado said, annoyed by the slight, "It's our duty to protect and advance the revolution, for your benefit."

"What benefit? I was sitting here selling coffee before this *muchacho* took over." She gestured to the banner that hung down the side of the APC and prominently figured a life-sized image of El Comandante. "And I'll be here selling coffee after somebody else throws him out. For us, here, things don't change."

The old woman slowly creaked back into the ancient leather of her protesting chair. Since the day her enthusiastically wayward husband had left her for a brilliant misadventure in the capital that had cost him his life and her livelihood, the old woman could be found stationed unwearyingly from dawn to dusk in front of her house, which was made of cardboard, plywood, and sheets of tin for a roof. Beside the structure, five or six scraggly, naked children played with an underfed dog, whose ribs thrust through its paper-thin skin in a silent appeal for basic human decency. Occasionally, the children screamed as they poked the dog with a stick and received a snap in response.

"You aren't privy to all the information. That's okay; it's not your job. But you should know, the empire has agents behind every tree. You need us to keep your children safe. I should know. I've been promoted to head the intelligence service." Oops, he'd let it slip out.

"Ooh, military intelligence," she said with feigned respect. "Kind of like saying 'honest politician,' or 'healthy whiskey,' or 'free, quality health care' …"

"Hey, boy." Machado, attempting to divert the conversation, which was taking a direction he didn't like, yelled down to the banana salesman. "How much?"

"Only eighty Asnos, *compadre*."

"Throw me up one," Machado said.

"*Claro, chamo.*" The banana salesman grinned up at Machado, showing a row of blackened teeth, and pulled a banana from the bunch, tossing it up to the sitting lieutenant.

"*Adónde vas?*" the banana man and the oracle said in unison, the idle conversation of the underemployed adding flavor to their long days in the sun.

"I'm headed down to the capital. I've been promoted." Machado beamed almost as brightly as his new medals. He would be heading up the FARS intelligence unit responsible for the *whole* capital area, *and* the main international airport. Machado thought about the change. He was so used to the backwater barracks in one miserable hole after another; the capital would be a welcome improvement.

San Porfirio de la Guacharaca. It was hard for Machado to get used to the new name. Upon arriving to power, El Comandante had issued a decree renaming all the cities and states of the country. This had wreaked havoc with tourism, zoning, and even the ability of some to find their homes. The authorities were still discovering the burned-out shells of buses that had lost their way, the remains of their human cargo showing signs of cannibalism. In the same decree, El Comandante had reorganized the nation's geography, moving several mountain ranges and rerouting the powerful Great River. This had seriously affected the nation's transportation infrastructure, but in the process had unearthed a large silver mine that had become the lifeblood of the nation after all the oil wells were filled with dirt and garbage by revolutionaries who had feared that El Comandante would lose one of the endless elections he planned so his people could constantly prove their loyalty.

San Porfirio was a heated, energetic, vibrant South American capital. Around the old historic district, high-rise bank buildings shimmered in glass and steel. Two large highways slashed viciously through the city, filled constantly with the high-pitched beeping of motorcycles and the frequent motorcades of diplomats and ministers rushing to and fro on their important business. Circling the capital were the *barrios*, those orange brick neighborhoods that grew organically like mold up and over the hills that ringed the center. Machado loved the nightclub district and the red-light district with its seedy hotels beside a walking street where he could buy anything from switchblades to knock-off brand name watches and clothes.

"Congratulations," said the banana man. He was seconded by the oracle, who unenthusiastically interrupted the lieutenant's reverie. "Lots of movement on the road these days. Just yesterday, I saw a whole line of tanks going that way." And he took his finger out of his nose long enough to point in the opposite direction—back toward the barracks and the desperate church.

"*Si, mi amigo*," said Machado. "We were returning from the parade. I just came back to get my things." He dug into the APC, pulling out the garbage bag to prove to his audience of two that he was telling the truth. The banana man nodded, and as Machado tried to replace the bag, the plastic ripped and his used clothes spilled across the pavement at the foot of the APC.

"Which parade would that be?" The oracle spoke up. She rocked back and forth, swatting at a large fly that had come to rest on her shoulder.

Machado was surprised; these peasants obviously didn't have up-to-date information—or, worse, they were subversives. He would have to start watching out for those things; he was in *intelligence* now. He climbed down from the APC and started to collect his things.

"Don't you follow our revolutionary holidays here?"

"Can't seem to keep 'em all straight," the oracle said with a frown. The banana man had pulled a banana from the large bunch lying beside him on the asphalt and peeled it, and he was trying to cram the entire piece of fruit in his mouth.

Undeterred, Machado explained, "Yesterday was Revolution Day, the day we celebrate the ultimate sacrifice of the martyrs who were killed during the bloodless coup that brought our glorious Comandante to power. It was exhilarating …"

"What was exhilarating?" the man asked, looking up.

"Revolution Day," Machado said more loudly, climbing back into the APC while balancing his goods in his left hand.

"Oh, right."

"There were throngs of people …"

"What for?"

"Revolution Day," Machado huffed. "They were all wearing bright red shirts imprinted with El Comandante or El Che and lining both sides of the *avenida*. They waved their flags high as they cheered us on …"

Throughout the exchange, Machado had been resisting the siren call of the opaque bottle that was sealed with a dirty rag and lying on its side in the sweltering interior of the APC. A part of him deep down knew that an intelligence man had to hold his liquor, but that had never been one of Machado's strengths. One time while on leave he had gotten so drunk that he had woken up draped over a booth at the local fast food restaurant missing both his pants and, more seriously, his sidearm. He remembered in fits and bursts having pulled his weapon to demand that the capitalists also sacrifice for the revolution as he had—by providing him with a free meal. He'd spent the better part of the next day flitting from shadow to shade, tracking down his missing gear.

Losing the battle with the triumphant thought, *today I'm celebrating*, he ducked down into his APC for another mouthful of what was now very warm whiskey. He sputtered and choked as he downed the poison. Out of the corner of his eye, he saw the banana man root around under his pants, trying to relieve an inconveniently placed itch while he thought nobody was looking.

Popping back up, Machado continued in midsentence, "first came El Comandante's Youth, all dressed in their finest new uniforms and holding, instead of weapons, brooms. You see, this is symbolic of the cleanup that is being done to the great fatherland after centuries of oligarchic corruption." Mistaking apathy for stupidity, he was talking loudly and slowly.

"Following were the special revolutionary reserves." He looked down at the banana man. "You, man, should join the reserves."

"What reserves?"

"The *Special Revolutionary Reserves*," Machado repeated. He was becoming frustrated. He'd never been very good at figuring out when he was being made fun of or when he was genuinely outsmarting people.

"Oh, right. What for?" the banana man asked.

"All of us have to do our part in defending the revolution and reporting on subversive activity. I bet you see lots of subversive activity here on the road …"

Just then, a car full of young girls in bikinis honked as it tore past his APC and around the curve in the road. One ugly girl leaned out of the window and threw Machado a kiss. He stuttered, temporarily losing his train of thought.

Recovering his idea, he recalled the line of overweight and toothless seniors stretching the buttons of their ill-fitting uniforms. He chuckled a little. "While it's true they seem a little old, they are still valuable to our peaceful revolution."

"Ya, maybe. How much does it pay?"

"You get a uniform and a gun and the honor of serving the *madre patria*. What else would you want?" Machado asked.

"I'll think about it," the man said. "Would I get medals like those?"

"These, comrade, are for special acts of bravery. You would have to do something extraordinary." Machado took a deep breath, trying to expand his chest so his medals protruded more noticeably, "After the reserves were the elite paratroopers—huge muscles, very scary."

The banana man, probably sensing he was in for a long discussion, started to get to his feet, hefting the large branch of bananas onto his bare back. Machado realized he was losing his audience and rushed to finish. "Finally, I came leading the armored tank division. Of course, we went last because we didn't want to get any soot or grime on the new white uniforms of the officers. The only problem in the whole event was that my tank broke down—again, but only for forty-five minutes this time."

Refocusing his wavering attention for a brief moment, the bananas perched perilously now on his head, the banana man asked, "Ya, but where'd you get them medals? They real gold?"

"*Paciencia*. That is the best part. El Comandante himself called out my name, '*Sargento* Juan Marco Machado.'" Machado allowed sufficient time for the banana man to be impressed. "He is actually shorter than I thought. But very friendly. He gave me a smile; you could see he was pleased. He took my lapel in his hand and pinned the medals onto this fine new uniform—I haven't taken it off since."

Finally, the tank line started to move. "Heed my words," Machado yelled at the banana man, trying to sound heroic and commanding, and threw his old Soviet APC into gear. The banana man was opening his mouth to respond when a burst of black smoke belched out of the side of the APC, covering his tongue and the inside of his mouth with a thick coat of soot and ash.

The foot soldiers had pushed the remains of the offending vehicle over the cliff and into the jungle below, saving themselves the bother of attempting any repairs and setting a group of golden macaws squawking and flapping. As the convoy surged forward, Machado realized he was enjoying the ride. The hillsides going down to the beaches were covered with thick forests. He could hear the parrots gossiping busily and saw a family of toucans flying overhead. The occasional monkey jumped from branch to branch, ridiculing the sloths who were slowly making their careful way across the telephone wire strung above the roadway. The dark green canopy that reached above the road to form a translucent tunnel was heavy, laden with the rapidly fading remnants of the morning mists. The sweltering day increased Machado's sense of mystery and purpose. He was going to his new job. Now, finally, he was important. He threw the banana man and the lady a revolutionary salute, and they responded in unison with a corresponding one-fingered acknowledgment—but only when Machado was well out of sight.

2

*** *** ***

"Clarita, coffee, I need coffee," Doña Esmeralda de la Coromoto Garcia demanded in desperation as she stumbled from her room, wrapping her frail, thin fingers around her temples in hopes of silencing the pounding in her head.

Clarita's face froze in horror.

"Uh, *señora*," she said, pointing, "Um, you—well, your …"

Esmeralda quickly put her hands to her head, remembering that her wig was draped over the fake plastic skull on her nightstand and her teeth were still in a glass of blue liquid beside her bed. Her makeup had rubbed off onto her pillow, leaving a lifelike mask impressed on the Egyptian cotton—and leaving her looking like the mummy that a group of French archaeologists had found on a summit of the Andes mountains only last summer.

She rushed back into her room. As the years had gone by, Esmeralda had been taking more time to prepare herself for the scrutiny of the outside world (which in her mind included, unfortunately, her maid). Though she had never been a large woman, her physique had become yet more frail and dainty, making her increasingly vulnerable to the stiff Andes breezes. Her wispy white hair was so thin she was forced to wear that infernal wig, and too much time inside had turned her already pale skin into a ghostly white. The only thing that reminded her of the beautiful, rich young girl of yesteryear was her sparkling blue eyes; they somehow retained their intoxicating shimmer of youth. Doña Esmeralda emerged from her chambers half an hour later straightening her wig and looking almost human—having liberally applied an extra layer of makeup for good measure.

"Do you have my coffee ready?" she asked, the vodka-induced racket in her head making thought difficult. Clarita was watching TV, again. Today's program was a histrionic summary of the revolutionary government's youth socialist agenda, outlining in larger-than-life terms the multiple successes of the meetings they had hosted over the years and outlining the agenda for the next conference that would be taking place the next week. *I wish she wouldn't watch state TV. It is always such vulgar propaganda*, Esmeralda thought.

"The coffee is finished, ma'am."

"Again?"

"Yes, it goes quickly." Esmeralda secretly believed that Clarita was stealing coffee—she was one of *them*, after all—but couldn't prove it; and, frankly, she was afraid that if she did prove it, she would be forced to release Clarita, something that was unthinkable.

"I bought some tea. It's all I could find." Clarita gave an apathetic shrug.

"That's fine, why don't you just prepare me a ..." Esmeralda stopped. "*Que diablos es eso?*"

A heavy, pounding noise had exploded all of a sudden, coming from the direction of the large steel gate at the entrance to her *quinta*. "Who would be making that racket this early in the morning? I swear this neighborhood is going to the dogs." Her tiny Yorkshire terrier frowned at the reference and pranced back into the bedroom.

"It's almost noon, *señora*," Clarita said through the din. She received in response a withering glare from the bloodshot eyes of her mistress.

Followed closely by Clarita, Esmeralda rushed to the double doors that separated her from the outside world. The locks and alarms were still in place from the night before, and in her hurry Esmeralda punched in the wrong code. Immediately, an earsplitting blare laid itself over the pounding, causing her little yorkie terrier to emerge from under the ornamental bed that had been a gift from her ex-husband's family on their wedding day and add her shrill yapping to the cacophony.

Legend had it that the liberator had spent his wedding night in the very same bed, and sometimes when they had been making love Esmeralda had sworn to her now-deceased husband, Gonzalo, that she could feel the presence of that great man. She had secretly hoped she was right, and that if they conceived in that bed their child would be blessed with the liberator's qualities—a prayer that had gone terribly wrong when their baby had suffered, like the liberator, from a congenital birth defect, but unlike the great man had died shortly after birth.

The ornate telephone on the coffee table beside the door exploded into life, adding to the symphony. Already delicate from a late night of reminiscing with Gonzalo, Esmeralda thought her head was going to explode. She rushed to the telephone, trying to make out the caller's words through the brilliant noise. "Yes?" she screamed.

"This is the security company—your alarm has been activated," said the voice on the other end of the phone. "Is there a problem?"

"No, it's fine, just my mistake."

"Can you confirm the password?"

"Yes, it's 'Gonzalo.'"

"We'll turn it off from here." The noise stopped immediately. "Is there anything else, madam?" the man asked.

"Yes, there is. Somebody seems to be banging on my gate," Esmeralda said.

"Ya, I'm sorry, ma'am, but there's nothing we can do about that," the guard said.

"What's that supposed to mean?"

"They are from the government, ma'am. Have a nice day." Esmeralda was about to ask who they were when the line went suddenly dead.

"Damn mercenaries," she muttered as she unlocked the multilock and the padlocks and pulled back the prison-like iron doors that kept her safe from the *subversivos* who lived on the hills above her gated community and who, she was sure, were always conspiring to steal her things. She ran down the little brick path beside the small pond with its trickling stream and around the swing set that Gonzalo had built so many years ago for their son—she'd never had the heart to pull it down—and to the main gate. Outside, a young man wearing a red T-shirt was banging on the gate with a small hammer and a bent nail. His forehead was furrowed, and he stuck his tongue out of the side of his mouth, concentrating his efforts in the attempt to attach a cardboard poster he held in his left hand.

"What are you doing? You're going to ruin the paint."

The young man continued the incessant pounding.

"I asked you a question … answer me," Esmeralda said.

"I'm here from the Ministry of Social Housing," he said, addressing the gate. Apparently assuming that explanation sufficed, he continued trying to drive the nail through solid iron.

"So? What are you doing here?"

The red-shirted man had his hair greased back into a thick, shiny black helmet and had on a pair of jeans, army boots, and a gold watch. A strand of solid hair had fallen into his eye, and he stopped to reattach it behind his ear. That accomplished, he looked up from his hammer and said offhandedly, "You, or more accurately your house, has been targeted for the government's new social sharing program."

"For *what?* What the hell is that?"

The young man rasped a deep, paternalistic sigh, put down his nail, and pulled a clipboard out from his backpack, which was lying on the ground beside the gate. He started flipping through a few pages, looking for something.

"Right, here it is. According to our records, you've got seven bedrooms. Is this correct?"

"Yes."

"And you're single. Is this also correct?" the boy asked.

"Well, yes, *now*," Esmeralda repeated. "But …"

"So you only use one of the rooms." It was a statement, not a question.

"No, the others …"

"Okay, let's try it this way. Each of these seven rooms has a bed, correct?"

"Well, yes," Esmeralda said.

"Do you sleep in all the beds? Do you rotate from room to room, using a different bed each night?"

"Of course not."

"Does your maid sleep in any of the beds?" the man asked.

"No, she has her own quarters out back." *And how do you know I have a maid?* Esmeralda thought. Clarita was nowhere to be seen.

"So, you have six empty beds. You can easily show your solidarity to the revolution and your fellow countrymen by sharing your huge house with those less fortunate. If you hadn't noticed, we have a housing crisis in the country right now thanks to decades of lack of investment by the previous governments—I'm guessing *your* governments."

The boy bent down to put away his clipboard, picked up his small hammer, and continued nailing the cardboard into the metal.

"Share my house …?" Esmeralda was dumbfounded.

"Don't worry," he said between hammer strikes, "it's only temporary while the revolutionary housing projects ramp up their work. Then the families you host will be given their own homes."

"Families?" Esmeralda said, more to herself now than the bureaucrat.

The young man at last stepped back, looking at his handiwork, and grinned. He gave Esmeralda a revolutionary salute, picked up his backpack, and walked down the block. She ran out onto the street to read the sign. It read, "In two weeks, you will receive formal notice from the Ministry of Social Housing indicating the individuals you have agreed to support in collaboration with the revolution. El Comandante thanks you for your act of solidarity."

"Hey," she turned and yelled at the rapidly disappearing socialist. "Come back here, you. I said come back here!"

But the young man just turned a corner and vanished from sight.

"And that's it?" Esmeralda asked Clarita, who had mysteriously reappeared beside her on the sidewalk. "No phone number? No complaint box? Who do I talk to about this?"

"Maybe I should start getting the rooms ready," Clarita said. Esmeralda shot her an angry glance. She ripped the cardboard sign off her gate and threw it as hard as she could into the street. She walked back into the house with a sinking feeling of desperation. She would have to do something. But what? Whom did she know? She'd never felt so powerless, even when they'd taken her companies. Her mind was spinning as she frantically tried to formulate a plan.

3

* * *

Freddy bounded down the stairs and plopped himself down at the breakfast table.

"Hey, there's my high school graduate." His father's eyes, just visible over the morning edition of the *New Socialist Daily*, glistened with pride. The paper came down, and he grabbed for his cup of organic, fair-trade coffee.

"What's for breakfast?" Freddy said, looking pensively at his dad. His father's ponytail was long gone, but Freddy could still almost make out the hole in his left ear from which a golden peace sign had dangled years before. Now he was a balding, middle-aged man wearing a wrinkled hundred-dollar suit and working as a manager at a construction company.

"Eggs and bacon," his mother said from across the room. "How does it feel to be finished?"

"Oh, pretty good. I was getting bored; high school wasn't ever for me. But I'm really excited about my trip."

Freddy had graduated from high school only the night before and was finally an adult. But under the pale blue gown, his old feelings of insecurity were still very much with him. He had taken a long time to develop, and still at eighteen years old he felt frustrated. The thick, manly beard he had hoped would replace his peach fuzz had never appeared. He'd left it as long as he could, but had shaved it off the previous year hoping it would be replaced by the iron stubble of manhood. It hadn't. Instead, Freddy's one and only shave had left his face as smooth as a baby's behind; that is, besides the acne, which had never cleared. His straight, greasy, shoulder-length hair looked like a horse's mane, and despite the hours of physical training and weight lifting he still looked like a larger, pudgier version of his grade-school self. The thick glasses that made sight possible also made his eyes bulge from his head like an insect's.

"Yes, son," his dad said, "you're in for an exciting summer. It's been a long time since your mom and I had that kind of excitement."

His appearance notwithstanding, Freddy also had a mean, judgmental streak that had only gotten worse with time. "Dad, how do you do it?" Freddy looked down his nose at his dad.

"Do what?"

"I don't know. You know, do the nine-to-five gig. Didn't you ever want to do something else?"

His father folded the newspaper pensively, thinking about the question, and said, "Of course, but we all do our small part in our own way. You know, son, for your mom and me, life interrupted some of our more ambitious plans. But I don't feel bad about that. We host a voting station in our garage, volunteer when we can, buy our food at the local cooperative, and give money when we can to our politicians. We are, as they say, concerned citizens," he said with a twinkle in his eye. "'Sides, it gave us a chance to raise you right."

"But don't you feel like you're wasting your time?" Freddy'd had this conversation before with his dad many times—it always helped him feel better about himself to point out his father's failures.

"Dude, we can't all be Michael Moore. A lot of us have too many responsibilities." Freddy's dad liked to say "dude," probably thinking it proved he'd never fully embraced the establishment.

Freddy knew what his parents were talking about. He'd heard the story often. They'd been of the "progressive" persuasion since they had found enlightenment, and each other, over a bong and a song at Woodstock. The feeling of ecstasy and superiority had stayed with them long after the marihuana-induced high had faded. But "responsibilities," as his father put it, were the unanticipated product of their love during the days of passion—namely, Freddy's brother Vince, who was studying for his MBA at a state university on the West Coast. Vince, much to their dismay, was a Republican. Realizing too late their catastrophic error in their lack of more direct tutelage of their first son, they had embarked on a more deliberate and healthy progressive diet for Freddy.

"It's not that we're not proud of Vince," they would often say to Freddy, sometimes with Vince in the room, "but it's just a shame that he doesn't share our values."

Vince had stopped coming home for Christmas. Last year, as a sign of contempt, he had signed their father up to host a local pro-life seminar when a famous speaker came through town—a fact that Mr. Gilroy only realized when a group of fifty other "concerned citizens" appeared at his door with signs reading "stop the massacre." It had taken him half an hour to realize it was not an environmental rally, and by the time he did they were already through half of his coffee and some cookies that his wife had rushed out to buy at the supermarket.

Freddy picked up a piece of bacon and folded it into his toast, making a sandwich. *I wonder what Venezuela is like*, he thought. *And I wonder if the girls are hot.*

Freddy had arrived indirectly at the decision to do what some right-wing commentators offensively called "revolutionary tourism." It had all started with one of the many progressive events his parents organized to fill him with the liberal sense of ever-impending globe-altering doom. This time, only a few weeks ago, the featured guest had been one of Freddy's uncles, who was a humanitarian relief worker.

"In Africa," his uncle Dave had said, "The real problem is that the rich countries refuse to give enough money to make sure that Africa gets on its feet. In the scramble for the resources of the continent, the natural owners of the wealth get trampled by the big corporations. We owe it to our African brethren to give more of *our* money so that they can receive their natural human rights like education, housing, and jobs." They had just finished dinner and were sitting around the living room.

"Want a drink?" Freddy's dad had asked Uncle Dave. Freddy sat on the sofa drinking a soda.

"Scotch on the rocks with a twist. I only drink this in the States; the cost of this drink in Africa is criminal—especially with so many people living on just one dollar a day."

"But what if I don't have any money to give?" Freddy asked. He always took his uncle's advice seriously. Unlike his parents, whose screw-up had landed them in what Freddy considered the prison of Midwestern suburbia—a fate that filled Freddy with terror—his uncle had used his experience as a Peace Corps volunteer as a jumping-off point for work that Freddy always believed had more meaning.

"Well, you can volunteer, you can write letters to Congress to convince them to give more of the government's money. There are lots of things …"

"It's kinda overwhelming," Freddy frowned. "You know, I'm graduating high school in a few weeks. I need to decide what to do over the summer." *And it should be something important.* He was still lost, and it was becoming something of a family emergency.

"Son." Gravitas seeped into Uncle Dave's alcohol-slowed voice. "Each of us must find his own way—I'd suggest you take some time off after high school and see some of what I'm talking about. That's the only way that you'll really be able to make the right decisions. Take a trip, visit some poor people, and see some of the damage America does to the world."

"All right, I'll give it a shot." Without anything else to do and no better solution in sight, Freddy eagerly embraced his uncle's advice. His education and exposure at home had been important. However, his way forward would come just the next week from, ironically, the very high school that Freddy was so anxious to escape.

* * *

"This Friday, we are going to have a special event." Freddy's senior social studies teacher yanked a scrunchie out of his long, conditioned hair and rebraided it while giving his lecture.

"Like the fighter for social justice whose image is on my shirt, the famous Che ..." His teacher pointed to somebody that looked like Van Morrison but with a funny sideways hat, some Italian guy named Che Guilvairee, or something, but Freddy wasn't really listening. He liked the social studies teacher enough, and he knew that he was a member of the anarchist party in town, which met at a diner every Saturday evening to plan the week's random occupations.

The more closely graduation approached, the more acute Freddy's feeling of urgency was. His Uncle Dave's words echoed shrilly in his mind—"go see some of the damage America does to the world." *How do you find it? How do you get in? What do you look for?*

He continued zoning out until he heard, "The consulate of Venezuela in Miami is sending their cultural attaché, who will be talking about the peaceful, social revolution that is happening in that country. How they are trying to right the wrongs of two centuries of injustice."

Freddy immediately snapped to attention. "I have heard of Venezuela," he said out loud. All the eyes in the class turned to him. "Sorry."

"And so please arrive sharply on time," his teacher continued, giving Freddy a dirty look. "We don't want to keep such an important guest waiting. He even has a special request from the president of Venezuela that he's going to deliver in person."

"Dad." Back home that evening after school, Freddy was peppering his father with questions. "Cable news said this afternoon that Venezuela is a dictatorship."

"Ah, son, you know you're not supposed to watch those channels. And it isn't true, anyway. That poor, backward country is only trying to right the wrongs of centuries and redistribute its natural resources to the people, and that is threatening the interests of the politicians and the rich."

"Oh."

The week was endless as Freddy waited for the messenger who would deliver the words that would set him free. Freddy passed the time looking up articles about Venezuela's charismatic president, whom the people called El Comandante, and his trouble containing what he called the "oligarchs" and the "empire."

"Sounds like *Star Wars*, but it all seems very exciting and very important," Freddy commented to his dad over dinner one night.

"Yes, they are really trying to shake things up down there. I hope someday we'll have a leader like that in our country—really hold those conservatives' feet to the fire," he said, grinning.

The big day found Freddy in the front row, anxious to not miss anything. The bell rang and in walked his social studies teacher wearing faded jeans and a shirt with a large hammer and sickle on it. "Students," the teacher said, "I'd like to introduce you to the emissary from the President of Venezuela."

Another man walked through the door. Freddy sucked in his breath. The man had dark, caramel skin—visibly Latin. He had a thick black beard that was touched with just enough gray to ooze sophistication. His slick, shiny black hair was also touched with white at the temples, his dark brown eyes glinted with humor, and his straight white teeth shone as he smiled with calm maturity. As he came closer, Freddy smelled an intoxicating mix of cologne and tobacco. The emissary was of medium height and build and was wearing jeans, a red shirt, and a tan vest with the national flag on one side and large letters across the back that read "Reading is Freedom" in Spanish. He carried with him a large box, which he set at the back of the room, and a backpack out of which he withdrew a stack of laminated brochures.

"*Hola, mis amigos.*" He greeted the class in Spanish and then switched to English. "I bring you greetings from the independent *República Revolucionaria y Socialista de Venezuela.*" His accent was so thick that Freddy was having difficulty understanding him. Freddy leaned closer and adjusted his thick glasses to better read the lips of the emissary—he didn't want to miss a word.

"Today we in Venezuela are facing the historic challenge of providing social justice to the people of our impoverished country." His voice was intoxicating, as smooth and silky as his hair. "We are on the brink of social revolution, when we will finally shrug off the weight of the capitalists and the *oligarquia* and deliver our people into revolutionary socialist equality."

"*Revolution.*" As Freddy muttered the word out loud, even quietly, his eyes closed, and he allowed the sensation to reverberate. He rolled it around his tongue and bounced it off the back of his mouth, bringing it back again with a flair. It filled his mind with ideas, and his fingers twitched and tingled. There was new power in that word; there was also somehow safety and comfort. And there was hope.

"That is why, my new friends—" the visitor was still speaking. Freddy snapped back to the moment. "I would like to make a special request to you from our *Comandante*, the freely and democratically elected president of Venezuela. He is holding a special socialist youth summit, where *la juventud socialista* will come from all over the world to learn the lessons of our *Revolución Pacífica.*"

Freddy's heart skipped a beat. He looked up into the dark brown eyes of his new hero and was sure that the message was for him alone. "Please, come. Take a *folleto*, and if you are interested, follow the instructions to sign up." And with that, the presentation was over.

The first to jump out of his seat, Freddy accosted the speaker with questions. "Can I take several brochures? How many days is the trip for? How long is the flight? How much will it cost?"

The emissary handed Freddy several brochures. "You take these to your parents. Please, take a *camisa*." The man handed him one of the T-shirts with Van Morrison wearing a weird hat.

The class started to clear out, and the emissary kept handing over T-shirts and pamphlets to the seniors. Nobody else seemed interested, but Freddy made up for it with his enthusiasm. They talked for a long time about the government, the political organization, and some history. Finally, Freddy asked about the student movement he'd seen on TV. "They talk specifically about this one girl …"

Immediately, a light-skinned young man with dark hair and a thick accent barged angrily into the classroom. "How dare you? What do you know about it?"

4

✳ ✳ ✳

Standing in rapt attention in the hallway of his adoptive school, a temporary solution by his family to keep him away from Venezuela under the pretense of taking a high school English class, Pancho Randelli—political exile from Venezuela and leader of the student movement, famous nationwide for both his charisma and lack of self-control—had been listening with flashing rage at the conversation between somebody with the telltale Venezuelan accent and a fat kid Pancho had never seen before but already hated.

"I've been reading in the news some of the stories from the students in the student marches. They make it sound like they are really being harassed." The stupid kid's voice drifted out into the hall.

"*Si*, they've adopted the traditional 'soft coup' approach that oligarch students have used in other countries that are trying to increase social justice. They march, chant slogans, make it seem like they are being persecuted. It's pretty much a media stunt."

"They say it's like Iran, or Syria, or Cuba."

"*Primero*, all those countries are resisting the dictatorial pressure of privileged saboteurs funded by the empire. Those places have a different culture and are much less tolerant of treason than we are, as is their right. While we will never judge our brother revolutionaries, we have decided that *our* revolution will be totally peaceful," the emissary said. He continued, "Have you ever seen us repress a march?

On the contrary, they march till they are exhausted. We just make sure order is kept. They shouldn't have the right to disrupt the lives of ordinary, faithful citizens."

"But what about some of the student leaders being killed? They talk about specifically this one girl—"

The Venezuelan cut the fat kid off in midsentence. "Yes, I know. This was a tragic case. Our intelligence services investigated. In fact, we believe that she was raped and killed by the students themselves to try and blacken our peaceful revolution's reputation with the international capitalist press."

"Wow," said the fat kid. "They are animals."

Pancho had had enough. His emotion got the better of his common sense, a recurring problem he couldn't seem to control, and he turned on his heel and marched into the classroom, "How dare you? What do you know about it?" he said in a low, trembling voice to the fat kid.

"Huh? Who are you?" said the kid, obviously surprised.

Pancho, a good-looking kid, stood breathing heavily. He was in his mid-twenties and had dark, flowing hair and an olive Mediterranean complexion dusted with freckles. He was thin and tall, with the fit body of an athlete that had been honed first on the soccer team at a Catholic university and then in the endless student marches he had led. He was always quick with a smile, but his obsidian eyes flashed just as quickly with undisciplined anger.

"You Americans are all the same. The slightest hint of a south-of-the-border accent and you'll believe anything."

"We were just talking about the advances of the revolution in Venezuela. I've been invited to the youth social forum. And I'm excited to see the changes in that country ..." the kid said, still confused.

"*My* country," Pancho said.

"Our country," the older Venezuelan corrected him. "We are all partners in building our powerful new Venezuela." Pancho had seen the logo on the pamphlets and knew the man was from the Venezuelan government.

Pancho looked at the diplomat, about to respond, but thought better of it.

"You stay out of *my* country," he said instead to the gringo. "You let us fight for freedom on our own if you won't help us. But don't make things worse."

"You can't tell me what to do," the fat kid with the thick glasses said. "It's a free world."

"That's what you Americans always think and always say. For you it may be true, and you're lucky. For us it's not—not anymore."

"That's not what the government says," the gringo responded, "and that's not what he's been saying."

He pointed to the diplomat. "You have elections, right? Aren't governments in countries with elections always representative of its majorities? Isn't that so?" The gringo was smug, apparently pleased with his logic.

"It is, my young friend," the Venezuelan diplomat said. "But, as you are seeing, not everybody agrees with our project."

And he turned to Pancho. "Can you honestly say that your opinions are the majority?"

Pancho turned red with anger, but before he could respond, the gringo said, "You should let your government work, give them the opportunity to try. From what I've read, you've had your shot, and evidently you didn't do a very good job. Now it's their turn. It's only fair."

Pancho turned to face him head-on. "Listen, *gringo de mierda*, stay out of our problems. You're only making things worse for us. And you, a student of all people, should side with *us*, not the crony, thieving bureaucrats."

"That's what I want to do," the fat gringo said with a spark in his eye. "The emissary here has just been telling me about a group of socialist youth who are defending the poor. That's obviously not your concern." He grinned up at the older Venezuelan. "But there are others in your country who seem to be trying to do the right thing."

"I'm the son of immigrants," Pancho tried again. "And we arrived with nothing. We built what we have …" but he was interrupted by the fat kid.

"I'm sure the color of your skin helped …" the kid said, looking at his superiors, evidently thinking he'd said something clever.

"You'd better run along." The social studies teacher saw that things were getting out of hand. "There's plenty of time to have this sociological debate elsewhere. This isn't the place."

Pancho knew he was defeated. "Just don't go …" he begged the gringo before turning around to leave. As he headed for the door, he heard the gringo say sarcastically to the diplomat, "I wonder if it wasn't him who killed that girl. He seems like the type—angry."

Pancho couldn't contain himself any longer. He spun on his heels and charged toward the gringo kid. "You shut up. Don't you talk about her."

Buoyed by his two defenders, the fat kid raised his voice. "You don't come to my country and threaten me."

Pancho gave the gringo a shove.

"Don't you *shove* me," the gringo said, he looked around making sure he was well protected before he shoved Pancho back. The diplomat was leaning carelessly against the teacher's desk and said, "You see the violence that is inherent in our system? It's what we always have to put up with. You can tell who the people with the real ideas are, and why it's been so hard for El Comandante."

Pancho felt the cord in his head snap, as it had many times before—as had happened before Susana was killed. This was dangerous. He knew that he would pay for what was happening, but he didn't care anymore.

The room was spinning.

Pancho watched as his hand reached up slowly and slapped the gringo hard across the mouth. "Watch what you say about Susana."

Stunned, the fat kid seemed surprised when his own hand reached up to punch Pancho in the neck. It was a flimsy, feeble punch that landed with a *thunk* on the side of Pancho's collar bone.

Pancho looked down at the hand and up into the face of the pimpled boy who was grinning and raising his hand for another limp blow. Pancho responded first, and hard. He stepped back onto the ball of his right foot and, building momentum, laid both hands into the flab that was the gringo's chest. He caught the fat kid off guard, and Pancho felt the satisfying surge as his new enemy flew into the air and crashed down onto one of the desks. The desk overturned under the weight, and the boy tumbled headfirst over the back of the desk, smacking his head on the cement floor with a loud *crack*. Blood exploded from the back of his head, running down onto his shirt collar and pooling on the floor. The social studies teacher—stunned by real violence—finally reacted. He grabbed Pancho in a bear hug and pulled him in the direction of the principal's office. The last image Pancho saw was the diplomat lifting the kid up and patting him on the back, saying something to him in a sweet reassuring tone.

5

Doña Esmeralda de la Coromoto Garcia stared into her crystal glass, which was filled to the brim with expensive imported gin mixed with a locally produced tonic—one of the few things that was still made in their *communist* companies. She lifted it slowly to her painted lips in contempt, taking a delicate sip—then rethinking and draining the glass in one enthusiastic draught. She slammed the empty tumbler down on the glass-and-gold-painted metal coffee table in front of her. She looked out the window of her hilltop mansion and across San Porfirio de la Guacharaca, the capital city of Venezuela.

My city, and now my house too?

Esmeralda's house was a relic from Venezuela's colonial past. It was perched upon a hill that had been a bastion for the ruling families from the days that the Spanish colonizers had established a foothold in this resource-rich, agricultural colony. From their perch at the center of the colony, they had commanded control of the entire country, including the naturally growing coffee plantations around the base of the Andes mountains that produced thousands of tons of the flavorful bean, the grasslands upon which lived the cattle of an empire, and the robust fishing industry that took advantage of the colony's two thousand kilometers of shoreline. These stolen treasures had been loaded in cargo boats and sent back to feed the imperial tastes of successive monarchs in the old country.

The house was large and square, designed to provide the colonizers with memories of home in this vast new tropical land. Large rectangular windows gazed watchfully down into the valley, toward what had been the center of town during the colonial times. The open courtyard in the middle of the house was filled with tropical flowers, painstakingly procured from all over the country and brought by their gardener to adorn the estate of the oligarchs. The tree in the courtyard was a huge *ceiba;* planted as a sapling, it had grown tall and strong with the passing of the years and the tender care of the generations of wealthy owners. The tree's massive roots had started to lift the heavy, ancient multicolored tiles surrounding the courtyard. The old tree was rumored to have been planted by the last lover of the liberator—a final memory for the country she could no longer endure—before she died of a broken heart when she discovered that, in the ultimate act of betrayal, the great man had fathered a child with a local Indian woman during one of his campaigns against the Spaniards. Legend told that she cursed her former love while planting the tree, stating, "For as long as this tree stands, the republic you are trying to build will only know war and suffering." In a fit of oratory inspiration, El Comandante had once even announced that the government would cut down the tree to free Venezuela from the cycle of instability, but he had subsequently realized that the violence served useful purposes for the new revolutionary government and quietly let the promise slide.

How is this possible? Lost in thought, Esmeralda addressed the life-sized portrait of Gonzalo Garcia, her long-deceased husband, that still hung on the living room wall above the old Victorian couch. The painting was suspended among the clutter collected during generations of wealth and surrounded by furniture brought from all across Europe. There were Napoleonic rugs, Teutonic wooden furniture, tsarist paintings, and Italian frescoes. Gonzalo's face looked oddly regal among the assortment—despite his humble birth.

"They took everything from us. Now they want our house? What can we do?" Senility, an old friend by now, was becoming a more frequent visitor. She shakily got to her feet for a refill—her third.

On the way to the small bar nestled beside the kitchen, covered in mirrors and glass, she walked past several pictures hanging in the hallway.

"There we were, Gonzalo, vacationing in Madrid. Where did that rich, powerful, sexy woman of thirty years ago go?"

"You're still sexy to me." Gonzalo's shadow stepped out of the painting behind her and approached. He gave her a flirty wink.

"I imagine you don't have much to compare me with on the other side."

"That's not fair." And the ghost evaporated in a puff of mist.

She kept walking. *I don't even know why I framed this one.* It had been taken last Christmas. Her plan had been to send cards to her friends. She'd gotten dressed up, gone to her lifelong photo studio, and had dozens of pictures printed—and then realized in dismay that she didn't have any addresses, or for that matter any friends.

"I can barely recognize that old hag," she said to her dead husband's ghost. The white hair, the sagging breasts, the crow's feet around her eyes—she still thought of herself as the beautiful young daughter of the powerful Coromoto family.

"Esmeralda, if you saw what I looked like right now, you'd be thankful you're still alive." Gonzalo had reappeared on top of the bar. His image, not reflected in any of the mirrors, made for an eerie guest. Esmeralda grimaced, thinking of her husband's body in the cemetery on the east side of the city, buried in the family plot alongside the long unbroken line of Coromotos. Being part of a matriarchal society, Esmeralda had even forced her husband to assume her family name—it being more important in Venezuelan history than his own.

"He does okay with my stomach and ass," she said of the photograph as she reached toward the large crystal decanter filled with the clear intoxicating liquid, "but every surgery makes my face look like those statues in the wax museum we visited in Washington."

She stepped back and almost crushed her tiny Yorkshire terrier behind her, who yelped in protest. She shrugged and continued pouring herself another round. "Who cares? It's all gone to hell anyway," she again muttered as she liberally splashed gin into the glass. She walked back to her perch in her nest overlooking the city and continued her musings.

"How did it all go so wrong?" she asked Gonzalo, each sip of her G&T increasing her anger until it again raged white hot.

"It wasn't our fault. We were the victims. Now, well, we must accept our fate."

"Easy for you to say," Esmeralda looked at the painting. "You're dead, and you're not going to have to stand in line with the riffraff competing with you for your own *bathroom*."

"I know, but my dear, take heart. We had a wonderful past. We should remember that."

This was true.

For generations, the Coromotos were the *Amos del Valle*. The lucrative *fincas*, along with the heavy taxes levied on the peasants— *for their protection, of course*, Esmeralda mused—had made the family one of the wealthiest in the country. The old widow looked across the city skyline at the offices of the telecommunications business, the large banks, the national mining industry, and the national electricity company. Now the buildings were crumbling, their fading façades lacking a coat of paint, the old marble turning brown, and all the areas within the grasping reach of the mobs defaced with angry red posters of El Comandante.

"Those used to be mine. *I* ran things here," she addressed the portrait on the wall.

"Yes, you did."

"They all owed their careers to us. Even this so-called Comandante took my money—before he stabbed me in the back."

"They all owe everything to you, and they're very ungrateful," the picture responded. Gonzalo could be very consoling and agreeable, especially in his present form.

"Then came those damn communists …" Doña Esmeralda was now spitting venom, night was approaching, and the city, *her city*, was descending into darkness.

"So *we* charged excessive rates for electricity?" she raged. "At least we could keep the damn lights on." And the sun plummeted below the horizon, plunging the city into the black abyss of night. Esmeralda heard the click and the hum of her generator kicking in.

El Comandante had appeared on TV. Esmeralda remembered that speech well. It had been, for her, the beginning of the end.

> Comrades. We are in a national power emergency, because the empire is sabotaging the power grid with the help of their lackeys in the industries strategic to the national defense. Therefore we are seizing the power grid and have implemented energy saving measures—with all power being cut at nine o'clock at night except to important national security installations.

Explaining problems had gotten simpler as the revolution went along. These so-called "national security installations" were, of course, places like El Comandante's house and the large Bingo in the center of the city where the revolutionary government's most senior bureaucrats drank eighteen-year-old scotch and bought expensive prostitutes.

Outside the night had become immediately black; the blackness was not simply the absence of light but also the obsidian obscurity of evil. *The night.*

Esmeralda had almost forgotten. She jumped unsteadily to her feet and ran through the house to the door, turning the multilock that sent bolts into the floor and ceiling, slamming shut the inner door that resembled a safe, and entering her five-digit code to activate the alarm. Since the arrival of the Revolutionary National Socialist Police of Venezuela, *her city* had become one of the most dangerous in the world.

San Porfirio de la Guacharaca had been the new name El Comandante had given to the capital city. It was, of course, named for the patron saint of the republic. According to legend, in 1654 Porfirio Lopez, a doctor, had emerged from his house early in the morning in the capital city of the colony, which was then called *Ciudad del Rey* due to the townspeople's dearth of creativity. As he walked down the street, a Guacharaca bird, known for being particularly loud and obnoxious, came to rest on his shoulder. Annoyed, Porfirio Lopez tried to shoo the bird away. The doctor took swings at it with his large leather handbag but succeeded only in pummeling himself in the face. The bird just hopped from one shoulder to the next, looking at him with intelligent, questioning eyes. After three hours and many stares as Porfirio walked down the cobblestoned street toward his practice, cursing at the bird and attempting in vain to brush it away, the bird began to speak. It told him, in perfectly pronounced royal Castilian, of an earthquake that would happen in the town that very day. Taking this to heart—and seeing it as the only way to rid himself of the bird—Porfirio went house to house, warning the residents of the town about the upcoming calamity. Upon listening to the words of Porfirio—the Guacharaca still on his shoulder, although now mute—the peasants believed, fled the city, and were saved. Porfirio had been canonized by one of the long line of popes centuries ago, and San Porfirio de la Guacharaca had been named the country's patron saint. In a pompous ceremony in front of a massive cement-and-iron Guacharaca bird specially crafted by the finest Belorussian artisans, El Comandante had announced the renaming of the city.

Back in those days, the country itself had gone by a different name, a name given by the colonial conquerors and approved by the king of Spain. That Spanish name had brought to mind memories of ancient Europe, of festive royal parties and elegant dinners of the depraved nobility. Upon assuming power in his bloodless coup, El Comandante had appeared on state television (now called RTV, Revolution TV) with an important announcement.

No longer will this great country bear the name of our colonial oppressors, and no longer will the whisper of it bring back memories of imperial debauchery and impunity. For too long we have been reminded of the empires, old and now new, that have decided for us even the very name of our country. No, we will now and henceforth honor the ideas that will make our country free. I hereby announce the renaming of our great socialist republic. Henceforth it will be called the Revolutionary Socialist Republic of Venezuela.

Following this announcement, the government had been obliged to give away free recordings teaching people how to pronounce the name of their new country. They also had to reprint the currency, the textbooks, and the maps, and the revolutionary bureaucrats were still discovering documents that arrogantly announced the offending colonial name. Demarches were prepared to each country with which Venezuela had diplomatic relations demanding that those countries reprint their textbooks and maps and go back into their archives to purge any mention of the previous name of the new socialist republic. All ambassadors to the United Nations were given special tutoring to introduce the new name. The related expenses turned out to be greater than anticipated, and the government had to issue treasury notes to pay for it—although no foreigners wanted to purchase the fake-looking notes with the strange new name and the ratings agencies advised investors to stay away from the currency for the time being.

When Esmeralda was again seated on the balcony of her castle, at the very least protected against the petrifying Venezuelan night, a rare moment of clarity brought her back to when it all had started going wrong.

"There was that uprising. You remember, Gonzalo?" She looked up. "On one of our farms. It didn't seem like a huge problem at the time. A young priest was killed. Terrible thing, that, but the peasants seemed to respond wildly. He was just a priest …"

Ever since that day, bad news had assailed the Coromoto Garcias in an unending, unbroken line. Those issues were, unfortunately, things of the past. This latest affront by the housing ministry was the final indignity. Esmeralda had wracked her mind thinking about what she could do, how she could finally fight back. This was the final assault, the long-feared invasion of the detestable, filthy communists into her home. As she sat there in the dark of night, desperation seeped into her heart. Then suddenly she remembered her friend, her long-lost friend and lover, and she knew. She would call her one remaining contact, the only person who might be able to do something. She went over to the phone, picking up the receiver to dial the numbers—numbers that would change her life forever.

6

✳ ✳ ✳

Lieutenant Juan Marco Machado was in a remote basement corner of the Air Force Academy carrying out his duties. These duties, he'd quickly learned, weren't as difficult as people had said. Sure, he'd had to toughen his stomach a little more, but with power came responsibility and with responsibility came following orders. In the military, a good soldier had to embrace the unsavory tasks as well. They were an essential part of protecting the revolution.

The buildings where Machado was working were located in the old industrial and warehouse section of town and had been a training academy for air force officers. They were set back from the road into beautiful gardens and expansive walkways. Upon assuming power, El Comandante had been given a tour of the facility as part of the stocktaking done by the new government. He had immediately seen the huge potential, of which being a school wasn't even remotely a part. The top floor of the administration building was luxurious and would serve perfectly for the more venerated role that intelligence operations would have in advancing their peaceful socialist revolution. But more importantly, the complex had a large and extensive network of basement rooms, planned by former dictators as a bomb shelter. The previous elected government had used them for storage, but the newly arrived and more forward-leaning officers of the FARS envisioned a better use for these underground, soundproof rooms.

"I have been informed by my sources that you were overheard making destabilizing comments." Machado was sitting backward on an old orange plastic chair, smoking a cigarette. He was wearing an old pair of fatigues; he didn't want to dirty his special olive-green uniform, and sometimes the work was messy. The room smelled of urine and body odor. There was a single dingy fluorescent light bulb hanging from the ceiling; which through the smoke from Machado's cigarettes threw the room into a sickly blue fog. After several months, Machado was getting used to the work and the venue—but still couldn't stomach the smells.

"You realize that conspiracy isn't only an act. It's also a state of mind."

"*Pero, señor.*" The man was facing Machado, sitting naked on a similar orange plastic chair, which looked greenish yellow in the bad lighting. He was the owner of a small kiosk downtown where friends would come for *cafecitos* in the morning or cold *cervezas* after work. "I don't know what you're talking about. I'm not a conspirer. I vote for El Comandante every chance I get." Sweat was trickling down his bare chest.

Machado opened a file, which was empty except for some blank sheets of paper—but the terrified kiosk owner didn't know that. "It says here that you said, and I quote, 'this ridiculous revolution has made the country more dangerous.'"

He put down the file. "Did you say that?" Machado was guessing, but his source *had* told him that the man complained about crime.

"*Si, señor*," the man said. "Everybody knows that crime is out of control. I wasn't the only person who said so. I meant nothing by it. I was just making a careless remark. The others agreed with me …"

"I know. You just need to worry about yourself. We'll get to the name-giving part of this little exercise later." Machado stood up and walked slowly around the room. He stopped directly behind the man, who tried to turn his head to look at Machado.

"Look straight ahead," Machado ordered. "I ask again, why do you feel it is your right to criticize the revolutionary police? Do you risk your life for your country? Are you trying to make our nation strong? Do you go out of your way to serve? Do you know the empire's plans?"

The man just sat looking forward and lowered his head.

"No, you sit back, drink your beer, and criticize. You disgust me." Machado spat. He was being careful to not lay a finger on the man. He had learned that the tense absence of physical violence was as terrifying to the common man as was a punch to the stomach.

"I'm sorry, sir. I meant no harm." The man was now shaking violently. "I promise I'll do better. I'll volunteer. I'll march more often. I always vote for El Comandante, I do, I promise."

"Do you conspire often?"

"No, *señor*, it was just that one time. I'd had too much to drink." The kiosk owner looked as though he was about to throw up. Machado backed away slightly.

"So you admit you conspired."

"No, I didn't mean that …"

"Have you ever thought about overthrowing the government?"

"*Nunca, señor,*" the man pleaded. "I am a faithful servant."

"Do you meet with others at night to plan your counter-revolutionary activities?"

"*Señor*, I don't know what you're talking about. I'm just a simple shop owner."

"Do you own a gun?"

"*Bueno …*"

"Do you? Don't lie to me." Machado raised his voice.

"*Si, señor*—everybody in Venezuela owns a gun. It's so dangerous …"

"You realize gun ownership is illegal unless you get your gun from El Comandante's military reserve program. Are you a member of the reserves?"

"*No, señor.*"

"I know you're not. So you own an illegal gun."

"*Si, señor,* but …" the man started to give an explanation.

"Do you realize that owning an illegal gun carries a penalty of five years in jail?"

The color drained from the kiosk owner's face. He didn't respond.

"Have you ever planned to use that gun in a coup? Would you be happy to see El Comandante killed?" Machado had completed his full circle of the shop owner and was again standing behind the man. He rolled up the file folder and smacked the man smartly on the back of the head. Machado had also learned that after a long period without contact, an act of violence was very effective. The man cried out and began to sob.

"I'll do whatever you tell me. I'll give you all the names. I promise I meant nothing by it. I have a wife and two children. Please, please, just let me go." The wailing was reverberating off the bare walls in the soundproof room, and Machado was starting to get genuinely irritated. It was time for the interview to end.

He walked back around and looked the man in the eye for a long moment, extending the time until it was uncomfortable for both of them and the man started to squirm. The man lowered his gaze into his chest and continued to weep slow, wracking sobs that shook his whole body.

"I am willing to believe you," Machado said. He was getting bored. "I trust you won't be caught making those statements again. I don't ever want to see you in here again; if I do, it will go worse for you."

"*Si, señor.* I'm sorry, *señor.* I promise you will never hear from me again."

Machado rapped on the solid iron door, and a private swung it open. The soldier had on a rubber apron and was holding a set of shiny, metal tools in his left hand. The kiosk owner shrieked. Machado turned back to the man. He had gone white as a sheet, which in the blue lighting made him look like the Venezuelan sky after a rain. "You are free to go. The private will escort you out. Before you leave, you will sign your full confession and you will give us a list of the names of the people you were conspiring with." He walked out of the small cell.

"*Gracias, señor*," the man said after him. "God bless you, and long live El Comandante." Machado sighed; tomorrow he was going to have to round up another ten people.

The lieutenant-turned-spy walked up the dingy stairs from the basement and down the long hall. He sauntered slowly, making his way back to his small office on the ground floor overlooking a small garden filled with birds of paradise and daffodils. He loved daffodils; they reminded him of his home, and they helped take the edge off his mood. And he was on edge increasingly often. Today, his annoyance was starting to slip into downright anger.

He'd been very busy during his time as intelligence chief. Although he was only in charge of the capital city and had to report on a daily basis to his superiors, he *was* given a great deal of latitude to work as he saw fit, as long as he kept producing the numbers and the confessions. In his short tenure, he'd caught hundreds of conspirators. Sometimes, a little force had to be used—which Machado discovered made him sick to his stomach. In response, he'd developed various excuses that allowed him to leave this unsavory task to his underlings. His superiors nodded with obvious pleasure at the steady stream of confessions he'd received, but he had yet to catch a true counter-revolutionary and was getting bored intimidating store clerks and hospital nurses. Last week, he'd had a nurse strip searched and thrown into a cold cell overnight—simply because he heard that after a night in solitary confinement, a woman like that would do whatever it took to get free. But when he'd gone to see her the following morning, she'd simply stood straight, naked as the day she was born, and in a dignified manner demanded her confession—which she signed with a flowing hand—and her clothes. It was disappointing. He'd never been very lucky with women, but he still couldn't bring himself to forced intimacy, like the other interrogators—a fact that made him even angrier because he felt it showed weakness.

He sat down heavily at his desk and looked at the old, cracked picture of his father in an expensive gold frame he'd received as a gift from a particularly guilty-looking antique dealer. It was the only decoration he allowed himself in his spartan office. During his first days, he'd thought a lot about his father, his past, and his duty. He especially remembered Ignacio. These thoughts served as a reminder of the depths of poverty from which he came and lent urgency to his drive for advancement. During the unsavory activities, these fears hardened his commitment to do the job well and make himself essential to the revolution so he could build for himself a healthy cushion to ward off forever the poverty that terrified him. And he remembered his father's words. "There aren't many opportunities for somebody like you," he'd rasped out in his dying breath. "Join this young comandante. See if he can't give you what I never could."

The revolution *was* proving to be a source of advancement, just as he'd hoped it would. He put his feet on the desk and thought about his past, so long ago, and his peasant home in the great plains.

Young Machado had been born in a rural village in the interior of Venezuela, on the great plains from which meat was exported to consumer nations across the oceans. His father had been a simple peasant who worked on the *finca* owned by a white family descended from the colonial conquerors. They'd held the land in perpetuity for over three hundred years, ever since they had received it as a reward for some forgotten act performed for the Spanish monarchy. The *finca* consisted of over thirty thousand hectares, which were sub-divided among a few hundred families who held and worked the land. For this honor, they paid huge percentages of their yearly earnings—"for protection," the landowners had always said, but Machado had never seen any protection and never understood what they were to be protected from. They had nothing that even poor thieves would want.

The Machado family home had been built with love and care by his father and older brothers. It had mud walls and a dirt floor that his mother constantly swept, hunched over with her old broom made of branches and the long, strong grass that grew prolifically in the surrounding marshes. In her futile attempt to keep a well-ordered house for her family, she harvested the grass as often as possible, being careful to avoid the huge old anaconda that lived in the deep pool at the end of the narrow path toward their garden. The Machado family plot had been given to them as a wedding gift from the overseer—who had taken it from another family when the father had become sick and unable to work the land. In the house were two large rooms. One was the living room, where the family of seven spent most of their time—when they were not in the fields or with the cows, of course. The second room was for sleeping. Machado recalled with nostalgia the feeling of warmth and companionship as they spread out together on the hard floor covered by blankets for their short night's sleep.

On the walls of the living area were old posters of the Virgin Mary and Jesus—the European version portraying them as blond, blue-eyed Caucasians. Given as a Christmas present by the landowner family, they served to remind the peasants of the true nature—and race—of the Holy Family. The room also contained some rough furniture made by hand by the elder Machado. These consisted of a few chairs, a table, and a bookshelf to hold the five-or-six book library they'd carefully collected over the decades. The roof was made of sheets of zinc, a thin metal that was fantastically loud during the long, powerful rainstorms that fell on the plains. During these downpours they would huddle together, using their two buckets to collect the rainwater that flowed freely from the holes in the roof that the elder Machado could never afford to fix. The whole house smelled musty, like the odor of an early mountain morning—earthy and clean. The kitchen, where *Señora* Machado spent most of her time, was out back behind the house.

In the late afternoons, when he was back from helping his father and brothers, the young Juan Marco frequently listened to the sizzling of his mother's cooking as she prepared inexpensive but nourishing meals assembled mostly from ingredients grown on the land by their own hands.

"Very soon we will get lucky. We will have a crack season when we birth enough cattle and harvest enough crops, and I'll buy a—" The elder Machado's planning would be interrupted by a bout of coughing, the early signs of the tuberculosis that, untreated, would seal his fate. "Eeeghem, we'll buy a small place in town. We'll even get a small TV and a car. Those will be the days, going together to get a cold *cerveza*, smelling the tangy sweetness and toasting to our freedom …"

He would turn and look toward the powerful mountains in the distance, eyes glazing over as he assumed the faraway gaze of memory mingled with hope and salted with despair. A much younger Juan Marco had cherished those moments when his family was seated together on the porch in the homemade chairs and looking across the massive plains toward the towering Andes—this was his home. A mist rose from the plains. Relieved as another scorching equatorial day released its hold on the land, the wild animals moved about more freely and openly. The mountains turned slowly red, then purple. The snow caps turned a fluorescent pink before the small pinpricks of stars came out, covering the sky in a blanket of shining diamonds. They would smoke unfiltered, hand-rolled cigarettes from tobacco grown in their little garden out by the kitchen. The sweet, pungent smell took them together to a different place.

"Here he comes." Often a mouse or a rabbit would run breathlessly through the compound. "He's only a few minutes away," the meadow creatures would say to Juan Marco, solidarity with their co-inhabitants of the land overcoming their natural timidity at talking to humans. They were, naturally, referring to Enrique, the overseer—whom they hated as much as did the peasants, for his cruel traps placed to catch unwitting rodents for his evening stew.

"There you are, lazing around again. I pay you too much." Too often, their simple camaraderie was interrupted by the dreaded snarling voice of the landowners' primary enforcer. Enrique lived in the small village at the center of the *finca*. He'd been hired by the landowners to manage the *finca* and all *his* peasants, officially making sure that they were paid. But more importantly, he and they knew, though it was never formally written, that his primary job was to make sure that the peasants were registering each calf born and each kilo of crop harvested—protecting the compounding wealth of the landowners.

Machado remembered Enrique as a brutal, hard, dark man with thick black hair and a thick black beard whose own parents had been peasants but who had curried favor with the landowner family through his excessive loyalty tinged with fanaticism and his unjust sense of justice. He often went beyond the call of duty, making a habit of going around to each of the peasants' households and demanding an increased share of their crops—for himself, naturally—and oft-times even a "private moment" with one of the peasant's daughters in exchange for giving a good report back to the landowners in the capital.

"I've come to inspect your *finca*." Enrique never cared at what time he came to the Machado home. "But that smells good. I think I'll join you for dinner first."

He didn't care that there was barely enough food to feed the large family, either. "Then we can go look for the cattle. I heard, of course, that you have some new ones. I wanna make sure you're branding them correctly." Enrique stormed past them into the hut. Young Juan Marco Machado had hated Enrique, and his hatred extended out to the landowners and beyond, to all those unseen but complicit in his family's misery.

The village at the center of the *finca* was small, a few ramshackle houses placed randomly along a muddy road. At one end of the road was the large, fantastic *estancia* house, where the landowners could come to supervise their holdings and interact with *their* peasants— although Machado could not remember a single time that this beautiful, massive complex with its pool and stables and bars and courts had actually been used. It sat empty, an army of employees keeping it clean and tidy, the fresh, clear pool surrounded by fences while the peasants walked two kilometers for water, and the satellite television dish always turned off while the peasants tuned their cheap radios in the desperate attempt to find news of the outside world.

The village also had a small store where the Machados exchanged the vouchers they received from Enrique in payment for their crops and livestock for soap, clothes, pots and pans, shoes, and other basic needs of poverty-stricken peasant life. They weren't ever able to leave; Enrique didn't allow public transportation to or from the village. Machado had no way of knowing, until he finally fled that fateful day, about the inflated costs Enrique placed on everything in the store.

There was a small bar, a dark tavern of a place that smelled of urine and local brew, where the malicious bartender plied the peasants with drinks on credit, and where the so-inclined could further indebt themselves by picking up a vice that would eventually leave them in ruin. And there was a Catholic parish where they could atone for this vice and receive assurances from the local priest, a good friend of Enrique, that their status was all of their making, a penalty for original sin and for the color of their skin upon birth.

Growing up, Machado's favorite place had been the small school. It was planned as a place where the peasant children could learn basic reading and writing, which would enable them to better themselves should they ever manage to pay back the debt that the death of their parents passed on to them. This was where young Machado had found his solace. In between planting and harvests and after extensive chores, he would walk the three kilometers from his house to the school, which was run by a young, socially conscious Jesuit priest, Padre Ignacio.

His days as an indentured farmer filled with toil and hardship, young Machado embraced the teachings of Padre Ignacio with zest. The history lessons focused on the French Revolution, the American Revolution, and the Bolshevik Revolution and were full of exciting names like Sandino, Farabundo Marti, Fidel Castro, Karl Marx, Vladimir Lenin, Simon Bolivar, San Martin, Tupak Katari, and Pancho Villa.

"Jesus came," Padre Ignacio assured the young students when classes started, always sharply at ten to allow the students enough time to walk to the school, "as it says in the Bible, to set the captives free. Jesus came promoting the liberation of mankind from our oppressors. The message of Jesus was addressed to the poor, not to keep the poor in poverty as the oligarchs and capitalists say, but to foment revolution, which will lead to our emancipation and our equality."

This message was exciting to young Machado. "How will we be free?" he would often query Padre Ignacio. "Who will come to set us free?"

"Ah, my young student, Jesus's message is also a message of personal responsibility. If you want to be free, you must free yourself," were Ignacio's wise words.

Sitting in his small office, surrounded by the files of hundreds of his countrymen, Lieutenant Machado thought of Padre Ignacio often, and with consternation. He was increasingly accepting of his new line of work, and he had convinced himself that it wasn't a betrayal of the revolutionary values he'd fought for. In fact, he remembered often that it was to Ignacio he owed his awakening. When he thought about what had happened to the priest at the hands of Enrique, his anger burned fresh and bright. And he remembered the day he had, as Ignacio always preached, freed himself.

7

* * *

Freddy returned home after school. He was still a little rattled by the unexpected confrontation, and his head hurt from the bump on the floor. But he was more surprised by his reactions. He'd never been a fighter; in fact, he had been bullied all his life. It had felt exhilarating to spar with, well, with whoever the *hell* that was. Even hitting his head on the floor hadn't been bad, especially when the emissary had congratulated him afterward for his noble defense of the revolution. He was more committed than ever—and was surprised by how much he liked the fight. *If Venezuela is like this—the passion, the conflict—then it's definitely the place for me.* Returning home, he waved the brochure in front of his parents, deciding to keep his altercation a secret.

"Can't I use my graduation money as I want? Isn't this just what it is for?" he said.

"Absolutely. I think it would be very good for you." His father was obviously pleased.

His mother, while putting on a positive face, quietly said, "But honey, isn't it dangerous down there?"

"Our son must grow up to be a fighter. And fighting sometimes brings danger."

"But he's just a child," said Freddy's mother.

"I am not," Freddy responded indignantly, "I am almost a high school graduate, and I've been specially invited."

"But we don't know the situation down there. Can't he do something closer to home that we can better supervise?" Freddy hated being talked about as if he wasn't in the room. But he had the good sense to let his father and mother discuss this themselves—his father always won these arguments.

"He'll be on a special guided tour. They do this all the time; I've seen ads for it in *Revolution Magazine*." Mr. Gilroy was a lifetime subscriber. "If they do it that often, they can't have lost that many kids."

His attempt at humor fell flat. "Have you seen the murder and crime rates? It seems really dangerous down there."

To that his father answered, "Don't believe everything you see on the TV."

And with that the decision was made.

* * *

"I'm sorry, Pancho, but you're going to have to leave," his host said to him when he returned from school that day escorted by the police.

"But sir, I only have a six-month visa, and it's going to expire anyway. I'm really sorry; I didn't mean to become a problem to you. I know that you trusted my parents." Pancho's host family had been friends with the Randellis since Pancho's dad had earned his master's degree in the Midwest—back before the electricity company had been nationalized and all contact with America had been forbidden. But their relationship had continued, and when Pancho had gotten into serious trouble during a student march that had turned violent—trouble that had eventually led to the death of his girlfriend, Susana—his parents had called in a favor from the only friend they had left to get Pancho out of the country until the dust settled.

"Besides, we only have approval from the Ministry of Social Currency to exchange Asnos into dollars for six months—and my family was counting on that money." The revolutionary government of Venezuela had capped the exchange of Asnos into dollars to control capital flight, sending the black market exchange rate into the stratosphere. The dollars Pancho's family would be able to save would give them a cushion against the insecurity of the Venezuelan labor market and against black market currency fluctuations that were sending inflation through the roof. "And I'm saving as much as I can here. Do you know what dollars are worth down there? Can't I just stay until it runs out? I promise I'll behave. You can do whatever you want. Ground me, make me stay in my room. But please, don't punish my parents."

"I'm afraid not. You're a good kid; I know that. But you attacked somebody at school. You're going to have to go. We can't risk getting sued," he said.

"But sir, I promise I won't do that again. It's just that they said terrible things about me. I had to defend my honor."

"You can do that without hitting people. Did you know that the principal called me? He asked that I not let you return to the school. You're gonna have to wrap things up and be on your way."

Pancho's shoulders fell.

The battle had been fought. Why couldn't he just control his temper? He was here in the first place because of his temper—that terrible, violent fight with the government officials over Susana's death. It had only been a few months, and the pain still ran deep. She had been raped and murdered—how could he have reacted any other way? But now he would have to go back. Were they waiting for him? Could he go back to college, studying law as he had before? He had planned to go into politics, but since El Comandante had restricted the political parties' fund-raising, he would have to get a job. But he still hadn't graduated, and becoming a lawyer in Venezuela was an increasingly tenuous choice given the revolutionary judges' indiscriminate interpretation of the just-as-revolutionary laws. More importantly, would the students accept him back into the movement, or had his leaving opened an unbridgeable divide? Pancho sighed and put aside his doubts. The die had been cast.

"It's fine. I'll go home," he surrendered. "It's my time to return anyway. I'm sorry to have caused you such a problem."

Venezuela and the revolution were again pulling him, unwilling and afraid as always, back into the fight.

8

✳ ✳ ✳

"Coño, pero Colonel," *Teniente* Juan Marco Machado said to his superior officer, "why do *I* have to babysit these gringo children? I joined the revolutionary army to advance El Comandante's glorious plans. I'm a professional soldier, and an important one." He'd been ordered that morning to relocate temporarily to the administrative offices of the military airstrip on the east side of the city for a special job. He'd spent the last several hours moving his key personnel and taking control of the base, but was outraged at what he feared could become the permanent interruption of his meteoric rise in the intelligence services. *Could it be I've been noticed by an enemy and sidelined?* Just as his father had advised, he'd seized his window of opportunity to make important progress for the revolution and his own well-being—and was aggressively protecting his small kingdom.

"Don't lecture me," the colonel said. "I know exactly what you do, and you still work for *me*."

"For now," Machado said, covering his mouth and disguising the words with a cough. He'd noticed that his behavior had been changing subtly in the recent months. He pressed his uniform harder each morning, polishing his medals and his boots with a surprising vigor. He woke up earlier, and he was even trying to lose some of his *empanada* fat. But, more telling, his smile had shifted—it was now more of a smirk and implied sarcasm instead of mirth.

Machado took a break from his discussion with the colonel to berate one of his subordinates. "Clean this shit up." While polishing Machado's AK-103, the new recruit had spilled gun cleaning solvent on the inside of the barrel.

"You must know that the revolution demands order and obedience."

The young cadet hung his head in shame. "*Lo siento, mi Teniente.*"

The colonel gave Machado an approving glance out of the corner of his eye. "Now go outside and run for thirty minutes—*backward*," said Machado. As the cadet turned to go, he received a brutal kick to his calves.

"*Teniente* Machado," his commanding officer went on. Machado snapped back to attention. "You have been handpicked for this assignment. El Comandante has let it be known that if you represent us well, he has something special in mind for you."

"But babysitting those children? What do we need them for?"

"Machado, you must understand." The colonel tried a less formal, more collegial approach. He leaned back in Machado's chair, poured himself a double shot of eighteen-year whiskey over some ice taken from the small freezer that was the first thing that Machado had brought from the academy, and lit a cigar. "So let me explain it to you."

He threw his feet up on the desk. "What was the one mistake that General Pinochet committed? It is the same mistake that was committed by Galtieri, or by *La Junta en Brazil*. Even today, it is the mistake our Iranian friends and even the Chinese are making—*think, muchacho.*"

Machado sat down on a sofa, the colonel having taken over his desk. The new, quiet approach made him realize with a sinking feeling, *I'd better tone things down.*

"They allowed people too much freedom?" Machado asked.

"No, they pretended they could hold onto power even when people got rich. So as the middle class grew and got *economic* independence, they forgot to whom they owed their livelihoods and started to demand *political* freedom—they started to conspire.

In response, those dictators increased the repression and isolated themselves. This model was tragically wrong. In truth, the real mechanism for social control is to give people all the freedom they want but take away their money." Machado was trying his best to pay attention. However, the bottle of whiskey had started to dance *merengue* around the top of the desk and at one point almost fell off, causing Machado to gasp.

"But now, compare that to Cuba's success. They repeat ad nausea words like socialism, social justice, community property, and even participatory democracy, and they do it while calling everybody who dissents a fascist. They have periodic elections and even allow the opposition to march occasionally. How does the world see them, even after half a century of privilege and power? As freedom fighters. And they still have powerful friends all over the world. Even the genocidal blockade that the Americans have inflicted upon our Cuban brethren has served its purpose: to blame those powerful enemies, the United States, for all the country's economic woes."

Machado was relieved that the colonel had not reacted negatively to his outburst, and he felt the need to rebalance the relationship. "*Sr. Colonel*, mind if I have a drink?"

Of my own whiskey, he thought bitterly. The bottle sitting on the desk had grown to the full size of a man and was doing coquettish curtseys in Machado's direction.

"*Claro, mi Teniente.*" Machado poured a shot. As he sat back down, his attention span and motivation improved.

The colonel drained his glass and went on. "So we follow Cuba's example, but we do it better. We make people poor by destroying private-sector jobs, nationalizing key sectors of the economy, putting everybody on the public tit, and forcing the rich to flee. All in the name of 'redistributive justice,' which the poor at home and the liberals abroad love. We beat that drum every chance we get, call all our work 'social justice,' gild our revolution in a layer of beautiful socialist freedoms, but take away their money. We bind them to each other using words like 'socialism,' and in the end, we bind them to us. But we are careful not to repress people. In doing this, we will consolidate power and wealth at home while receiving applause from abroad."

The colonel stood up from the leather chair with an air of finality, a smug look in his eyes. "And we rule *forever*. Who will oppose us if they know that doing so means we will starve their families?"

Machado nodded seriously, acknowledging with the receipt of this wisdom his induction into the brotherhood at the core of the revolution. He knew that it was moments like these that cemented his place, and he grinned a wicked smile. "Brilliant plan, *mi colonel.*"

"These young people may seem like a waste of time, but we bring them in by the thousands. We give them a T-shirt, some cold beer, and a speech by El Comandante, and we've made allies who will defend us when we need them."

Machado stood up from the cracked leather sofa and snapped the *V* of the revolution. "*Mis ordenes son claros, Camarada* Colonel" he said. "I will serve the young gringos."

9

* * *

"We are crossing into Venezuelan airspace," the pilot announced over the speaker system. Freddy looked expectantly out of the small, round airplane window at his first glimpse of paradise. The beautiful blue expanse of the Caribbean sea was behind them, and Freddy was watching the massive piles of sand and rock that are the Andes mountains as they crawled out of the water and stretched their arms to reach to towering heights. On both sides of the airplane, a large flock of golden macaws rose up from the green of the jungles below to greet the incoming aircraft, as if summoned by El Comandante himself to offer a tropical welcome to the planeload of hopeful revolutionaries. The macaws formed themselves into the national salute, a *V* for victory, and flew alongside the plane, their squawking welcome audible even above the pounding of the engines.

Freddy had finally worked up the courage to talk to the beautiful girl sitting beside him. "Hi," he said, "My name is Freddy."

"Mia," she said curtly.

Freddy pushed on. "I'm coming at his special request." He pointed to the emissary, who was personally leading the group of thirty revolutionary youngsters of which Freddy was a part. "We talked about it and agreed I should come down."

"Oh?" Mia said, unimpressed. "I've been sent by my father, who is also my political science professor at Harvard, to do a paper on

Venezuela and the social revolution. I'm hoping to get it published when I get back." Mia stared down her turned-up nose at Freddy. He had never felt so frumpy in his life and could almost feel the pimples on his face growing and glowing bright white.

"That's fascinating. You are very lucky," he commented, trying desperately to sound grown up. She gave him a sweet, patronizing smile.

Freddy grew silent, thinking about his destination. Venezuela is situated on the equator. On its northern shore, it is flanked by the Caribbean sea and more than two thousand kilometers of beaches. From the beaches at the center of the country, the Andes mountains start their long voyage down to the southernmost tip of the continent. The great plains west of the mountains are the bread basket of the nation, and southeast of the mountains the sweltering equatorial jungle becomes the mighty Amazon rain forest, which marches angrily into Brazil across an invisible border. A hard, beautiful, brutal land—a land of poverty and misery, but also a place of hope and dreams; to Freddy, it was like returning home.

They finally landed, and after what was to Freddy an interminable wait while fellow passengers took huge plastic bags of soap, toilet paper, shampoo, and other items out of the overhead bins, he stepped from the Boeing 727 and onto the roll-out stairway and stretched, reaching his arms up into the sky. He could feel the cool breeze wafting down from the Venezuelan mountains, refreshing on his skin and with a faint hint of salt from the ocean not too far away. He looked around. The macaws, after escorting their precious cargo to the ground, had disappeared in the direction of the sea. Immediately on his right was the main terminal to the International Revolutionary Socialist Airport of Venezuela. Titillating in huge red letters were the words *"Bienvenido a la República Socialista."* Three or four of the letters had gone out, and two others were flickering and buzzing on and off. Immediately below them was a five-story-tall picture of El Comandante giving the *V* for victory to an Indian soldier while embracing a baby. The terminal was painted a bright revolutionary red, but the paint was peeling in places from the hot equatorial sun. On one of the walls by an old hanger some graffiti read, "The American Empire Commits War Crimes."

"See," Freddy told Mia who had exited right behind him, "A relic from our inglorious past." He gave a wink in appreciation of his clever mind. Mia only nodded, still visibly groggy and slightly wobbly from the flight.

In the terminal itself, one entrance was illuminated by a yellow sign that read *"Entrada 1."* Despite the fact that the yellow sign was smudged and the door propped open with an orange chair, this appeared to be the primary gateway for visitors into the revolutionary republic. Freddy deduced this, noticing that the other entrance, which read *"Entrada 2,"* was closed off with yellow police tape. Sitting on an old school desk in front of the closed door was an overweight, aged soldier smoking a cigarette. The patch on his arm gave Freddy an opportunity to demonstrate to Mia his knowledge of the intricacies of the revolution. "That man over there, guarding that door, is part of El Comandante's special elite fighting force, which is safeguarding the revolution." He'd even read the speech when El Comandante had made the announcement for the creation of this militia:

> The constant conspiring of the empire and their lackeys have forced us to consider the very real possibility of invasion. To protect the fatherland, the revolution demands that all of us as citizens must be trained and armed for the national defense.

Immediately beside the main terminal was a large green hangar covered with a green camouflage tarp. In front of the building were parked three F-16s, two with their wings removed and one whose engine sat on the tarmac in front of it surrounded by a group of fifteen soldiers. Tools of all kinds and sizes were spread across a piece of plastic sheeting with a massive logo that read, "USAID—From the American People." The tarp had been donated, along with other relief supplies, by the US embassy during the last flooding, which had left thousands homeless. One lone man was sitting on the ground, covered in grease, attempting to bend a clothes hanger and wrap it around a piece of the engine. Beside the F-16s were seven brand-new Russian helicopters.

"Let's move quickly now," the emissary said. "Not that way."

Freddy had been marching resolutely toward *Entrada 1*. "You are special guests. Come this way, please." They walked quickly toward a military bus waiting at the end of the runway. The side read, "*Guardia Nacional Revolucionaria*," identifying it as belonging to the National Guard, whom Freddy soon learned were responsible for safeguarding the airport. As he stepped onto the bus, out of the corner of his eye Freddy saw another green bus filled with bearded men. Little did he know they had just come off an Air Iran flight. They threw hardened glares at Freddy as they drove on. The emissary, although following Freddy's gaze, offered no explanation.

10

* * *

Pancho presented his passport to the immigration officer with a flourish and a smile. *"De dónde vienes?"* asked a bored girl, barely over eighteen, with long fingernails and a low-cut shirt that showed her cleavage, as she snatched the passport from his hand and started flipping through the pages.

"I was in America," Pancho said.

The young girl looked at his passport again and said, "Six-month visa. What were you doing there all that time?"

"I was studying English."

"Why would you want to do that?" She looked at him disdainfully.

"It's important to expand our horizons," Pancho said. She looked at him, at his passport photograph, and back at him and then typed several numbers into the computer. She frowned at the screen.

"Please wait here," she said. Taking his passport, she walked out of the booth and into a small room a few steps away. Pancho craned his neck but wasn't able to read the screen. He waited as the seconds turned into minutes—five, ten, fifteen—he tapped his foot on the new tiles of the airport floor as the renewed anguish of life in Venezuela returned. Behind him the crowd of impatient passengers was beginning to murmur. "Always the young troublemakers. We should have chosen another line."

Finally, the young woman appeared out of the side room, applying some lipstick. Walking purposefully behind her was a dark mountain of a man with shiny boots and a short haircut.

"Pancho Randelli?" the man said.

"Yes?"

"You need to come with me."

"But why, sir? What seems to be the problem?" Pancho looked around for his passport.

"Come with me. You're holding up the line."

"But I've done nothing wrong."

"Listen, *carajito*, just follow." Pancho's shoulders drooped as he marched dejectedly behind the spy into the side room. There were no windows in this room, and the lighting was bad, emanating only from a desk lamp placed upon a chipped wooden desk with the words "help me" scrawled down one side in black marker. The light was illuminating the lower half of the face of a man seated erectly behind it. Pancho turned green. As he was escorted closer, the man's full face was revealed. He was an intentionally ugly man, with a sinister scar spreading between his mouth and his left eye, which was slanted at a different angle than the right. His jaws were sculpted and clean shaven. He wore a flak jacket even in the oppressive heat of the enclosed room, and holstered on his belt was a 9-millimeter pistol. Sitting evenly between his two clenched fists on the top of the desk was Pancho's passport, open to the American visa. Behind Pancho, the spy with the crew cut leaned back nonchalantly against the painted-over windows.

"Sit down," he said without looking at Pancho. "So, America."

"Yes, sir," Pancho said, almost panicking. "Can I help you?"

"Why do you want to enter Venezuela?"

Pancho tilted his head incredulously. "Sir, I'm *Venezuelan*."

"For now, maybe," the man said. "What were you doing in America?"

"As I told the woman in immigration, I was learning English."

"Spanish not good enough for you? You think our language isn't enough for us to be a powerful nation?" The man finally looked up from the passport and leered at Pancho.

"Of course I love Spanish, but it's important to speak more than one language." He was trying to sound convincing.

"Why?"

"Well, so that we can better compete in the world market."

"The market? The capitalist system run by the Americans?"

"Well, err, no. The international community."

"You weren't learning French. You weren't learning German. You weren't learning Portuguese."

Pancho was having trouble following the argument. "It's so that I can be a better Venezuelan and help make our country strong."

He thought he'd won a point, but the large man came back with, "Are you saying we are weak?"

"No, sir, of course not."

"Or is it, maybe, so you can better communicate with the CIA, *student?*"

Ah, so they did know who he was. He was back. He took a deep breath and firmed up his bowels.

"So I can better serve my country, so I can help rebuild."

"Rebuild what? Your people already destroyed everything. It's *we* who are trying to rebuild."

Oops, wrong word. He knew that having this argument, here, wasn't a good idea. "I just want to go home, sir. May I go?"

"Don't take that tone with me," the spy said. "I don't see your travel permission stamped into the passport. You had no right to leave the country."

"Travel permission? I don't know what that is."

"Don't get coy with us. You people spend all your time flying to Miami—you are well aware of the rules. Only last month the Ministry of Internal Affairs published resolution number 99563 in the gazette requiring an exit visa before *trying* to travel abroad."

"But I've been out of the country for months," Pancho said.

"That's not our fault. You don't have a travel stamp. You broke the law."

"But it wasn't a law when I left," Pancho said.

"Irrelevant." The scarred man leaned back in his chair, causing it to protest under his sculpted physique. He pulled the 9-millimeter gun from its holster, withdrew the clip, and looked at the bullets before ramming it back into place. He set the gun down on the desk and picked up the passport. He flipped through the pages, as the girl at immigration had done, but all of a sudden in an act of violence he ripped out the American visa, crumpling it and throwing it onto the floor. "You could have gone to our consulate in Miami or our embassy in Washington to bring yourself into compliance."

"But I didn't even know about it."

"Ignorance is no excuse for lack of compliance. You are in violation of the law. You are being detained."

Pancho's heart skipped a beat.

"Detained? I need to go home."

"You should have thought about that before you broke the law," the spy smiled wide.

"Come with us." The man standing behind Pancho pulled him up by his collar, and they took him through the next door. His passport was left lying on the desk where the spy had roughly dropped it. The second interior door closed with a menacing click. They marched him down a dark hall into a second room. This room was even darker than the last, and the floor was bare cement. It had the stench of a detention center and the evil energy of a place of sadness and violence. "Okay, strip."

"What?"

"I said, take your clothes off," said the spy again. "We have to make sure you aren't carrying any contraband."

The other man pushed him into the corner. "Like this," he said, and he pulled a small plastic ball out of his pocket.

It was cocaine, Pancho knew from the movies, the kind that mules swallowed. Pancho smelled the mold and sweat in the room as his own mixed into the concoction, the cold wetness filling his eyes and dampening his shirt.

"No, I've done nothing wrong," Pancho said. "I refuse."

"You are under arrest for violation of the exit visa laws. The punishment is up to a year in jail and a fine of fifty minimum salaries. You'd better do as we say. Strip and bend over," the second man said while he tossed the cocaine ball from one hand to the other.

"I won't. I want to speak to your supervisor." Pancho's voice was high-pitched in panic.

The man exploded in laughter. "Supervisor? Would you like a complaint card as well? Maybe our toll-free number to report us?" They both laughed heartily.

"I said strip, *hijo de puta*." The big man grabbed Pancho by the collar, ripping a large hole in his shirt.

"Or," the first spy said to the man with the scar, taking an offhand tone, "maybe if he's in such a hurry, he'd be amenable to paying his bail on the spot?"

"Well, I suppose that could work—we'd save ourselves some paperwork," said the spy, who turned to Pancho and said, "You have that option. The fine is one thousand dollars."

"What? I don't have that much," Pancho said, desperate to leave. He realized his mistake immediately.

"Well, how much do you have?" the spy asked. Pancho knew he had to give in. "I've only got six hundred dollars that I was going to …"

"Hand it over." Pancho reluctantly reached into his pocket, pulling out the wadded bills.

"Thank you for paying your bail in a timely fashion," the spy said. "Should you have any recommendations, please call customer service." And he shoved Pancho out a back door.

"But my passport …" Pancho protested. The door slammed shut with finality. The last thing he saw was the man's ugly, leering face. Pancho turned around. He was in the luggage area, and his bags were circling alone on the carousel.

He grabbed his bags and pushed through the throng toward his father, who was standing beside an escalator that had stopped working some time in the distant past, with the metal steps having been scavenged for a greater purpose.

Pancho froze. *How could only six months make such a profound difference?* He thought. *What could have happened?*

His father, never a picture of health, looked as if he had contracted a tropical disease. He was losing his once-full head of hair, and he had grown a spare tire around his midriff. But even more pronounced were the downward stare and the shuffling gait he had adopted as he perfected the magic tricks of powerless non-revolutionaries—to be invisible in broad daylight, to be unthreatening in a crowd and servile when alone. His voice came out mumbled and uncharacteristically low.

"*Bienvenido*, my son," his dad said, avoiding eye contact.

"*Gracias, papa*. How have you been?" Up close, he noticed his father's worry lines, his shirt stained with sweat from the previous day's work, and the smell of stale olives. Once, the old man had taken pride in his appearance. He was always smartly dressed, and—even though they'd never been rich—he'd always been careful in his outward presentation. He didn't seem to care anymore.

"The sun still rises, and the sun still sets," he said in a futile attempt at humor.

"Let's just get out of here," Pancho said, overwhelmed by his reentry. His heart was still beating at his brush with the immigration spies—but the fear was being replaced slowly by humiliation.

"It's good to be home, Dad. It's still our country," Pancho said while getting into the car. It was more a question than a comment. A bus full of bearded men dressed in pajamas drove out of an airport exit marked "Security Personnel Only."

The tragic irony of the Randelli family's going from dictatorship to dictatorship was not lost on them. Only last year, his father had made an emergency trip to Rome following a rumor that a lawyer there could recuperate their Italian citizenship. He'd gone to the man's office, located in a third floor room of a *pensione* in the rundown neighborhood of the *Piazza della Repubblica*, near the *Stazione Termini* in Rome's historic district. Upon arrival, the man, in a shiny, wrinkled Italian suit and smelling of wine and cologne, had demanded up front the full fee for processing the paperwork. When Mr. Randelli had objected, the man had shrugged and said he couldn't help if he didn't have the full trust of his clients. Mr. Randelli had handed over the wad of dollars that the family had painstakingly hoarded for years. The con artist, unbeknownst to Pancho's dad, was not a lawyer but a convicted fraudster who'd made a lucrative business from Venezuelan desperation. For months the man had continued to ask for document after document while Pancho and his family had waited anxiously—wiring money time and again out of their precious allotment of dollars—until one day the phone calls had ceased. Mr. Randelli tried in vain to reach the thief. When in a last-ditch effort Mr. Randelli sent a friend to visit the *pensione*, he learned that it was closed, with police tape draped over the entrance.

The car was nearing the toll booth, or what had looked like a toll booth only months before. Now the pillboxes were painted red and television antennae were sticking out of the windows. Dirty laundry hung from lines stretched above the cars. The inhabitants, dressed in their underwear, were still collecting tolls from the cars.

"Are people living in there?" Pancho interrupted.

"Yeah," Pancho's dad said. "That's the new tollbooth workers cooperative. It's best to just give them what they ask for." He fished around for a five-Asno coin.

The drive was long. It usually took an hour to drive back up the mountain to San Porfirio, but a collapsed bridge was causing traffic to back up all the way from the airport into town. The highway was one massive traffic jam with street venders going from car to car selling revolutionary apparel, including hats, buttons, T-shirts, shoes, and everything else the state-subsidized companies churned out to feed the voracious propaganda efforts of the government. One adolescent leaned over their car and replaced the windshield wiper with a red one that screamed, *"Patria, socialismo, o muerte"* as it swished from side to side. Mr. Randelli leaned out of the car and screamed at the boy, who threw the original wipers over the edge of the highway and demanded a thousand Asnos. Seeing the sky darken with the impending afternoon rainstorm, Mr. Randelli just paid the youngster. A shudder of desperate frustration rattled his body.

"Were you here when they *recuperated* the electric industry?" Pancho realized his dad had lost all sense of time, one minute running into the next in an infinite loop of survival.

"Of course, *papa*, that was long before I left. I've only been gone four months."

"Oh, right. But that day …"

Pancho knew this story—in fact, he had heard it many times and had even watched the fateful march from his window. But he quietly waited for his father to finish telling about the day his life was ruined.

"That day, El Comandante stood in front of the crowds bused in from all over the country, with the backdrop of that *huge*, ten-story image of El Che, naked and in the clouds, reaching out his finger to touch Fidel's." He tried to laugh, but the noises that emerged were shrill and hacking.

Comrades, the electric industry is in the hands of saboteurs and spies. The money that it makes goes into the pockets of the empire, and at any moment they could cut us off, leaving us with nothing. We must recuperate the industry in order to provide true service to the people in solidarity with their poverty.

"Since then, my life has been hell."

"I know, Dad. But like I've told you before, you don't have to take it. You should start playing by their rules. Make things as slow as you can, break things, or try to get in the way of their plans."

"I don't know what to do. They'd fire me—or worse. I can't lose my job or quit on principle. Not now. There's your school, your mother, our house. I need this job."

He added, "Son, it's been a nightmare. The first day of the takeover, when I came in, they'd posted the names of those they were firing. Those poor bastards didn't get anything—back pay, retirement, nothing. At least *I* got to keep my job, for what it's worth."

"But are they letting you do your work, at least?" Pancho asked.

"Not really. There is always interference. On Friday, management came into my office and yelled—they always yell—'We need one billion Asnos. It is our contribution to the revolutionary marches.

Find the money.' When I said there was no extra money, they just said, 'Don't bother us with details. We expect to have one billion Asnos by tomorrow morning.' I had to draw it from the maintenance budget."

"There's gotta be some way we can fight back. I can't believe you're just taking this without doing anything to stop it. That's the problem with Venezuela: nobody is willing to fight for their country."

His dad gave him a patient smile. "Every day, more demands. 'Everybody, drop what you are doing, put on your T-shirts, and meet us at the bus out front. We are going to protest imperial aggression in front of the embassy of the empire.'"

"Maybe we can together find a way to do a little planning of our own," Pancho said.

"Not sure what anybody can do." Pancho's father dismissed his suggestion. "And they keep making worse demands." Mr. Randelli laid on the horn as a motorcyclist cut in front of him. The man turned around and pointed at them, mouthing menacing words.

Randelli went on, "Stuff like, 'from these sectors of the city, we want you to cancel the outstanding debts.' When something breaks, usually because some idiot with four months of training from some new revolutionary university flips the wrong switch, I have to get approval from management for the repairs. For *every* part I need, it's always, 'No, we will not purchase that part—it is produced in the empire. We are to be freeing ourselves from imperial domination. They make the same part in Iran—we will buy it from there.' When I try and explain that the electric power in Iran is 220-volt and we use 110-volt, they look at me like I'm talking another language and just repeat, 'No, when the part arrives, you will make it fit our requirements.' It's been a nightmare."

Pancho's dad finally grew quiet, and they rode the rest of the way home in silence.

11

* * *

"Well, we already have something in the planning phase," the voice on the other side of the telephone said carefully, "but what we really need are resources. Let's plan to meet somewhere."

Doña Esmeralda had finally worked up the resolve to make the one phone call she hoped would save her home, her life, and maybe her country—in that order. She was talking to her old friend, the former minister of defense, General Gregorio Campos. Esmeralda was dressed up in a long, dark gray chiffon dress, with high-heeled stilettos that clasped in the back, and her gray wig was done up in curls with what looked like a Miss Universe crown adorning the top. On her fingers and ears and around her neck were emeralds, gifts from Gonzalo when they had visited Monaco.

She didn't have any plans that evening.

"I can't believe we're in this situation," she said after sharing the story about her house. The ornate, antique mother-of-pearl telephone was pressed firmly to her ear, and her hearing aid was turned up all the way. "I laughed at my friends when they said this would happen."

"Come with us," they had said. She remembered well the conversations before they had fled the country. "Sell everything and leave. We just bought apartments in Miami. You will still be a rich woman and can die in peace." But Esmeralda was stubborn, unwilling to take the advice of those she considered her inferiors.

Then came the currency controls, the expropriations, the restrictions on simple buying and selling—even her car—and she realized it was too late. And now they were going to take her house. *If I flee now, it would be empty-handed. At my age, I can't live like that. But I won't welcome the riffraff into Gonzalo's house. There must be another way.* And she'd called her friend the general.

"Okay, I know just the place." Doña Esmeralda took a swig from her glass of champagne. "Let's make it my club. You know the one."

"Fine," said the voice of her last friend. "Let me set it up, and I'll give you a call when it's ready." A perfunctory *click* marked the end of her only lifeline to the outside world.

The loneliness hit again as she realized she would be passing another long night with her yorkie and her drink, waiting for the phone to ring and talking to an old oil painting on the wall while staring across the city that she had once considered hers but to which now she didn't belong.

12

* * *

"Over here," Teniente Machado was instructing a cadet, "is where I want the tents. Under them will be the tables, covered with red tablecloths, where our revolutionary leaders will give lessons."

"Where should we put this?" Three soldiers were carrying a massive, three-level frosted red cake with El Comandante's face on it.

"Put it in the pavilion beside the mess tent."

"What about this cauldron?" Two other soldiers were carrying a massive black pot that looked like something for a cannibal's feast.

"That needs to go right here in the center of the tarmac."

The airfield looked like the camp of an invading army. Teniente Machado had embraced his assignment with the energy and enthusiasm that for him were close companions of naked ambition. Everywhere, foot soldiers in green khaki were scurrying around, putting the final touches on the preparations for Machado's first social forum. They were carrying crepe paper, hanging balloons, and setting up chairs.

Machado turned to a group of civilians wrapped from head to toe in cables. "Up there—" he pointed to the far end of the runway— "is where I want the stage set up. Make sure the microphones are well connected and that there are backup speakers. That's where El Comandante will address the crowd on Thursday."

In the parking area sat the buses and jeeps that would take their guests up into the barrios every day after they were finished. Using his intelligence files, he'd carefully selected loyal families with whom the young gringos would stay. Machado had organized an armed escort for each jeep. This had been frustrating, and he was angry.

"I wish the new Revolutionary National Police would do their jobs," Machado complained to his aide-de-camp. "This insecurity is getting old. If something happens to one of these gringos, it's gonna be my ass."

13

✳ ✳ ✳

After the long ride to the capital, the bus leaped over the hill and through a final tunnel, and they were spit out into the heart of the famous capital city of Venezuela, San Porfirio de la Guacharaca. Freddy was astonished at how quickly the city had snuck up on them. One minute, they were chasing a baby spider monkey off the hood of the bus, and the next they were in a city that exuded all the power and the glory of a sweltering Latin American nation. On each side, high-rises and skyscrapers reached greedily into the sky, forming a canyon of steel and cement. The drab browns of the buildings made Freddy guess that they were old—perhaps decades old—but the sheer number still cultivated the cosmopolitan image of progress. The skyline was dotted with advertisements for revolutionary products. In the center of town, the colonial buildings, remnants of the Spanish occupation, were still being used as homes. The flow of people down the side streets by the highway and onto the overpasses was astonishing, so colorful and beautiful that Freddy sucked in his breath.

On the top of the mountain overlooking the city was a statue of Christ. His arms, which had been outstretched providing spiritual cover for all the inhabitants of the city since the previous dictator had constructed the statue in atonement for a massacre committed in the jungles, had been sawed off and fixed into a deformed revolutionary salute. Somebody had painted a beard on his massive cement face, and his robes had been painted red. On top of his head El Comandante had placed—in preparation for the previous Revolution Day celebration—a massive red beret made of metal melted down from a walkway that used to span the highway (now the *barrio* dwellers had to take their chances sprinting through the traffic). The beret had been touted as the largest beret in the world, but it had been completed only the night before the event. During the heat of the hours-long ceremony, a careless glob of red paint had fallen from the huge headpiece and trickled down to the inner corner of the left eye, causing quite a commotion among the devout Catholics on both sides of the political spectrum. He was now known as the crying Jesus. Crying, according to the revolutionary literature, for all the wrongs done to his country—and according to the rest, for the misery into which the country was being plunged.

Finally the bus arrived at the airbase on the east side of town where the summit would be held. Their bus was one of the first of the hundreds said to be arriving from the airport, bringing socialist young people from all over the world.

Freddy stepped out of the bus, breathing the Venezuelan air of freedom, and sucked in his breath in a visceral gut reaction.

"Soldiers ..."

Through long breakfast lectures and boring peacenik movies, his father had instilled in him the progressive distrust of the military. He even remembered the exact words. "Soldiers are just dumb brutes who can't be trusted. We dealt with them during the riots. They would just as soon kill you as look at you. They are the last protection of an illegitimate regime attempting to retain power," his father used to say in the tone of finality and flourish with which he would end every debate.

Yet here they were, in the hundreds, *guarding the revolution.* All around the outside of the airstrip, APCs with national guardsmen dressed in riot gear patrolled the perimeter. The "whale," as Freddy would soon learn it was called—a large water cannon used by riot police—was flopped on its belly at the main entrance to the airbase. Around the periphery of the base, FARS paratroopers were standing at attention with handguns in their holsters and AK-103s in their hands. The entire scene resembled a movie Freddy had once seen about the wall between East and West Germany—complete with the barbed wire and the large German Shepherds. Written boldly in large red letters above the base were the words, "Fatherland, Socialism, or Death."

"*Teniente Juan Marco Machado, a su servicio.*" Freddy ran headlong into a senior FARS official. He quickly recovered and tried awkwardly to return the revolutionary salute. The military official was a dark, round man. He had the red eyes of an alcoholic, and his poise was at once too formal and too congenial. There was something in his smile that made Freddy nervous. He turned quickly, seeking some protection in his mentor, but the emissary was nowhere to be seen. *I wonder where he went to.* Freddy realized the back of the bus was open. Several students were leaving from the rear as well. *He must have gone out that way.*

"Please step this way," said the FARS officer in broken English.

"Yes, sir," was all Freddy could think of saying. He moved to the side to stand under a tree.

Hours passed as all the buses arrived, and night started to descend upon the city. Movement and preparations were reaching a fever pitch, and the hum of olive-green activity around them gave the impression of an impending war.

At long last, the military man who called himself Machado walked briskly to the center of the crowd. Using a large, old-fashioned wireless microphone, surrounded by hundreds of foreign students and upon a backdrop of olive green, he addressed the crowd. To Freddy, his words were both bizarre and somehow exhilarating.

"*Mis amigos,*" he yelled with formality, addressing the crowd. "Today we are starting the celebration of the Youth Social Forum, and you are special guests of Venezuela and her peaceful, democratic Comandante. I welcome you …"

14

✳ ✳ ✳

Doña Esmeralda stood up from the Victorian couch in the living room and walked to the old tree. Still dressed in her chiffon gown and emerald earrings of that morning, she took a tenuous step in the direction of the bar. Her yorkie issued a high-pitched whine. "I know, I know. I won't have another, at least not until after dinner. I'll just go take a nap." She changed her trajectory to pass in front of the kitchen on the way back to her large bedroom at the rear of the colonial mansion. The bright colors of the wall and the tiled floor were blurring together as she walked by the parlor, and she tripped on the Persian rug and stumbled hard into the antique organ that she'd trained her servant's children to play for dinner parties when she and Gonzalo hosted the cream of Venezuelan elite.

She smiled, remembering the laudatory statements that ministers, ambassadors, titans of industry, and the occasional president had lavished upon her and her husband. "You see, it's not that the peasants are stupid. It's just their ignorance, lack of schooling, and upbringing," she'd said so often to polite applause and murmurs of admiration for her humanitarian spirit in teaching the poor urchins a useful skill. "They play like angels, when they have the *barrio* trained out of them."

Those parties had gone long into the night. Gentlemen with stern countenances had engaged in important affairs of state while their ladies flitted about like butterflies from flower to flower, satiating themselves on the nectar of expensive European liqueurs.

Waiting for the phone to ring was proving unbearable. She picked up her small dog, the pink lasso held firmly on top of his head, and walked resolutely past the kitchen on the way to her bedroom.

In the kitchen, Clarita was preparing dinner and watching a soap opera on the TV. Clarita always watched the same soap opera, and she even held conversations with the characters as she sliced and diced in preparation for the evening meal. All of a sudden, the trumpet sounded and a charging donkey appeared on the TV. Since the passing of the democratic media law, the government had the right to "take over" the airwaves at any time—even during soap operas, which made people angry and had even caused riots. On one occasion, El Comandante had broken into the last episode of a very popular Portuguese soap about a slave trader who fell in love with his cabin boy to announce his decision to limit the use of these "takeovers" because of his love for the humble people. This had caused the humble people all across the city to rush to their windows with their pots and pans and bang as hard as they could. The entire city exploded into the sound of a great Chinese kitchen. Those who didn't have pots or pans simply threw their dishes onto the pavement below, resulting in serious injuries. The cacophony could even be heard in the background of El Comandante's speech, forcing them to return to the soap out of embarrassment just in time for the final credits, eliciting another round of banging.

"Is anything going on today, Clarita?" Doña Esmeralda asked.

"Not that I know of, madam. Would you like me to turn it off?"

"No," said Doña Esmeralda. Bored, she had to pass the time somehow. She sat down on a small chair in the kitchen beside the breakfast table. "Let's see what they have to say."

"This is an interruption by the Revolutionary Socialist Government of Venezuela," the little mule said. "Stay tuned for your important message."

The mule galloped awkwardly off the screen, kicking a Spaniard dressed in armor as he did so, and was replaced by the fuzzy, shakily filmed image of a large contingent of soldiers. They stood at attention and in a straight line.

"Turn it up, Clarita. I can't hear what they are saying."

"… students and young people from America and around the world," a fat, short lieutenant was saying. "We are here together inviting the youth of the world to celebrate our glorious, peaceful resolution with us."

The camera panned away to show hundreds of young people wearing red shirts, jeans or shorts, and tennis shoes. A man with a thick Venezuelan accent translated the speech into English.

"During this youth celebration, we will hear from our most senior revolutionary leaders," the fat soldier went on.

Esmeralda watched as he preened like a peacock, presumably thinking he was waxing eloquent.

"But most importantly …" and he paused for effect, "most significantly …"

"Who is this guy? This is where our country has gone, having these terrible peasants representing us—us who used to have the best diplomats on the continent?"

Clarita kept cutting the onions.

"We will have the honor of receiving El Comandante, leader of the revolution, savior of mankind, field marshal of the plains, chief of Andean Indian chiefs, destroyer of empires, chosen one of God for the liberation and freedom of his people." With these words and an accompanying flourish, the military man became silent and expectant as he awaited the scattered applause.

Esmeralda switched off the TV. The demand of liquid patience was instantly too great to be refused. "I need another drink. After that, I'm going to bed. You'll wake me for dinner?"

"Yes, madam," Clarita said.

15

* * *

Across town, Pancho had finally arrived home. Returning exhausted from his flight and frightened of the future, he was anxious to reconnect with friends. He thanked his father and went into his room, picking up the phone. His first call was to Carlitos Guzman. Carlitos was an old friend, a quiet young man who was also studying law at the Catholic university, but with greater devotion than Pancho. He had fallen unwillingly into the leadership role of the student movement during Pancho's self-enforced exile.

"Hello," said Pancho.

"Hey, welcome back," said Carlitos. "It's good you're here. You're back early, aren't you?"

"It's good to be back," Freddy said. "Ya. You'll never believe what happened to me."

"What?" Carlitos said.

"I got kicked out. Again. Got in a fight with some gringo *cabron*. Never mind, I'll tell you later. We need to meet."

"Ya—okay, let's meet in your and Susana's place." It was good to conspire with people you knew. If military intelligence were bugging the phones, Pancho figured they would have a challenge decoding the ciphers of extensive personal camaraderie. "We'll meet in a few minutes."

"It's good to see you, *amigo*." Carlitos gave Pancho a big hug upon seeing him. "You are looking fit. America has treated you well."

"You too," said Pancho. "It seems like the revolution isn't treating you too badly." They both laughed.

Pancho stepped back and held his friend's shoulders in a familiar embrace. Carlitos was short, with long brown hair touching his collar and a small goatee framing his small mouth and small white teeth. He had green eyes, unusual in people from Latin America. He was slight of build and quick with a joke but a contemplative, serious young man. He was wearing jeans and a new *guayabera*.

"So I see the military hasn't gotten you," Pancho said to Carlitos. Only two years ago, El Comandante had reinstated the draft:

We, as a country, have to prepare for an invasion by the empire. Our youth are too busy drinking alcohol and going to parties. The beaches are crowded with them, scantily clad and behaving in an appalling manner.

"Nope," Carlitos said, laughing. "Not yet."

They continued walking through the disintegrating park.

"This place is kind of in shambles."

"They stopped charging admission and opened it up twenty-four hours. So it's gotten dangerous during the day. But man, at night ..." Carlitos frowned, stepping over a used syringe. The small parking lot was full of car cadavers, stripped bare and rusting in the afternoon sun.

"Remember, it was just over there, my and Susana's place." Pancho returned, if only in his mind's eye, to relive again in painful agony his memories of her.

Pancho and Susana had been a legendary couple. Their romance had been born of forbidden passion, emanating from a harmony only possible through the marriage of destiny with providence. It had grown out of a place most people are fearful to discover, nestled deep inside the chosen few who are willing to look for it with courage and submission. For Susana was black.

Their love had started as a secret summer romance hidden from everybody except Pancho's true friend, Carlitos. During the summer between the fourth and the fifth and final year of high school, Pancho and Carlitos decided to embrace their last moments of youthful indiscretion together, without the stifling supervision of school sponsors or the nosy intrusion of parents. Full of their own mutually assured manhood, they hatched their plan. All year, the student body of *Colegio San Jacinto*, a Catholic high school run by Jesuit priests, had been buzzing with rumors of new islands discovered off the coast of Venezuela far to the east, where the Great River flowed from its mountain stronghold and through the jungles out into the Caribbean. These islands were said to have trees bursting with coconuts, jungles full of tropical fruit, and endless shores of sandy beaches bathed in the seclusion that can only be found in the unknown.

They would take Carlitos's car, packed with as much food and supplies as possible, and set out for these islands and adventure. They would hire a local fisherman to ferry them to their hideaway, where they would live off their food and the fruit they could find around the islands for as long as possible. They would fish the untamed oceans, hunt for boar, and eat the sweet meat of the conchs. It would be a summer of careless fun, of wind and water and the tingling of the Caribbean sun. They invented a story for their parents about a summer internship in the interior, forging documents on stolen letterhead to cover their deception, and set off.

For days, they drove the length of the country as the highway turned from four lanes into two, then one, and finally petered out into a marram road that began a tenuous exploration into the four-story-high jungle on both sides of the narrow lifeline. That night, they slept several hundred miles into the dark jungle. A heavy, pounding rain dripped through the steamy windows of the car. The wandering thunder that chased the lightning around the sky obscured the screaming of the monkeys as they fell prey to the black panthers that roamed with impunity in the jungle night. The next morning, Pancho and Carlitos stepped out of the car to see that they had sunk a full ten centimeters into the muck. The chassis of the four-wheel-drive lay flat on the sludge. Try as they might, the tires would not grip, and the duo decided to set out on foot. They were at the very edge of the country, and the solitude was palpable. They knew, from their spotty maps and the occasional waft of salty air that penetrated through the jungle mist, that the lifesaving Caribbean was close. They walked all day, making camp at night in the middle of the overgrown, unused road, building a bright fire to keep away the night predators.

They trudged forward for three days, not giving a second thought to their car, until at long last the enfeebled road coughed them out with its dying breath onto a beautiful crystalline cove framed by the extensive white sands of crescent beach. The water was aqua blue, like the color of the school uniforms they had anxiously cast aside, and they could see schools of fish swimming in perpetual play just under the surface of the calm waters. On the far end of the cove, only a kilometer away, the ramshackle homes of a small fishing village huddled together in comfort and protection, with seven or eight wooden boats pulled up in front of them on the shore.

The duo set up their tents on the opposite side of the cove, unwilling to disturb the pristine community. That night, they sang hymns to the blanketing stars and drank rum mixed with the milk of coconuts, gifts from the giant palm trees—impossible trees that exploded from the shoreline as soon as the salty sand gave way to green. The next morning, slightly simple from the festivities but immensely glad for the dull throbbing in their temples—because it proved their life—they walked together to the village, which turned out to be a bustling little metropolis of fifty families.

At the far end of a narrow, sandy road, the town's only artery, was a centuries-old, two-story plantation house. Brown from the passing of time and the jungle rains, its two-foot-thick walls had been chipped away, and the immense wooden beams that held the Spanish tiles in place were rotting, allowing the waterlogged roof to list dangerously above the heads of the bureaucrats who now used the home as municipal offices.

The house had been the plantation owners' home. Over the hill on the other side of the cove during colonial times had stretched one of the largest sugarcane plantations in the colony, carved out of the jungles by unwilling hands to feed the sweet tooth of the old world. On both sides of the road leading to the house were small shops selling tackle, nets, and other items for the fish trade along with a tiny, government-sponsored kiosk, painted red, for even here the revolution was making itself felt. The kiosk was stocked with the items identified as essential by revolutionary bureaucrats a thousand miles away in their plush offices in San Porfirio—basic items such as soap, sardines, coffee, and toilet paper.

Beside the kiosk was a bar. Its neon lights flickered as a generator behind coughed and belched black diesel fuel, foretelling its imminent demise. The buildings were made of wood stripped from the jungle and decorated with prizes taken out of the ocean. Mother-of-pearl and sea-glass murals plastered across the buildings' facades made them glisten like Poseidon's lost village. There was also a small church, this one Pentecostal.

The village had a small, government-run school and a clinic, and it served as the metropolis for the populations of silent families who still hid out of fear and unknowing in the surrounding jungles. Pancho and Carlitos instantly fell in love with the place and immediately gave up their hunt for the mysterious islands.

Everybody they saw—from the little children running through the streets chasing a terrified *coati* to the old men sitting drinking coffee on the plastic chairs in front of their houses, leaning their scruffy beards on fantastically carved canes—was black. Centuries past, Basque and Portuguese traders had imported thousands of black slaves from West Africa via Haiti, Cuba, and Jamaica to care for the prescient needs of the sugarcane harvests. They had lived for generations huddled desperately together behind—far behind— the plantation owners' estancia, and their short, hard lives were highlighted by work, disease, and death. Upon the independence of the republic and the slaves' subsequent emancipation, the sugarcane plantation had become unprofitable and was abandoned by the businessmen. The newly freed men settled around the colonial plantation owners' estancia, which they turned into the municipal government office for the new town of La Selva. From that day on, they made a pact that they would no longer work the sugarcane plantation for profit, deciding instead to try their hand at fishing the tremendous bounty of bass, sardines, squid, and other creatures that fetched such a high price in the markets of San Porfirio.

Pancho and Carlitos approached the bar and went inside, knowing instinctively that it would become an important part of their adventure. They found it surprisingly clean and neat, obviously well cared for by the owner and important in the daily travails of the locals. They were astonished to find it stacked from floor to ceiling with old colonial bottles that had long ago turned from their original translucent blue to the color of murky caramel and were filled with the only drink available: golden, locally brewed rum.

The rum, the elixir that buttressed daily life in La Selva, had been discovered by the slaves only after emancipation. Worried about *sus esclavos* picking up a vice that would make them worthless, the landowners had never allowed them into the private, privileged world of distilling, claiming when they had to that all the cane went for the production of sugar. While the freedmen were ransacking the estancia house, they found the secret stash of aging oak barrels stacked in the basement. Not being used to the taste of alcohol, they at first believed it an excellent fuel to light the fires that smoked their fish, creating a wonderful, sweet aroma that gave their catch extra taste and value. That lasted until one dark, moonless night, when one of the former slaves mistook a large glass of rum for one of coconut water beside it. From that day on, the residents of La Selva drank rum from morning till night.

As they left the bar approvingly, Pancho stepped out onto the wooden sidewalk and ran headlong into a girl. He was immediately stunned by her ebony beauty. "Excuse me," he said, to which she responded, "Oh, no, it's my fault."

Her twinkling voice filled Pancho with yearning, and he found himself gazing longingly at her smooth obsidian skin while she smiled at him carefully, her perfect teeth like pearls taken from the cove shimmering behind her full lips.

"Um, excuse me again," Pancho repeated, his mind racing. "We're here from San Porfirio, and we were looking for some work for the summer." The vision of the magical islands fled rapidly from his mind as an alternative plan started to form.

"Yes?"

"Yes, well, we'd like to try our hand at fishing. Your father isn't, perchance, a fisherman—is he?" Knowing her father could be nothing else, Pancho was laying his trap.

"*Claro.* We are all fishermen here."

"Do you think he could use two strong, but inexperienced, hands?"

"It's possible." The girl scrutinized Pancho's face. "But we are only simple fishermen. We have no money to pay you."

"No problem," both Pancho and Carlitos said in unison. "We would only ask to be able to eat some of the fish that we catch—prepared by your lovely hands, of course." Pancho winked.

"We can ask," she said. They went to her father's house and worked out the deal, the unsuspecting man smiling all along without realizing the true nature of their quest. The work was hard, and each sunrise found Pancho and Carlitos out on the water, a net held firmly in their hands as they tried to scoop up fish into the bottom of their wooden tub. Several times they even overturned the boat, losing their day's work, as they tried to haul a too-large catch of fish aboard. The evenings were filled with the stunning beauty of fragrant Caribbean simplicity, and in Pancho's mind they would remain the best days of his life. They would struggle back to the fisherman's humble shack just as the sun plunged beneath the shimmering waves. Weighted down by the day's catch, they would begin the hard work of preparing the fish and mollusks for the next day's merchant boat. While they worked, the girl they now knew as Susana de la Torre would take the prize fish and, accompanying her mother, begin the simple process of turning them into gourmet meals—shared in joy in the flickering light of the wood fire.

It was late one night, when Pancho and Carlitos had already walked back down the shore of the cove to their tents and were fast asleep, that Pancho was awakened by a rustling of the fabric on his tent door. Thinking it was an animal or large crab—Pancho was terrified of crabs—he switched on his small flashlight and shined it directly into the obsidian gaze of Susana's beautiful eyes. Anxious to not wake Carlitos in the other tent, Susana and Pancho spent a cautious night wrapped in each other's arms. Before she left, the predawn stillness all around, she gave him a silent kiss and whispered electrically in his ear, "I always knew you'd come."

From that moment on, they were inseparable. Trying to hide their relationship from Susana's father proved difficult, but the tension increased their excitement at an expectant touch or word with a double meaning. Carlitos seemed happy, remaining a stalwart friend to Pancho, and the threesome shared a glorious, carefree summer.

As the summer came to an end, they were finally forced to confront the truth. "What are you going to do when you graduate?" Pancho asked. Susana, like him, was one year away from graduating from the small government school on the other side of the village.

"I always assumed I would stay here and work the fish with my family," she said.

"But is that what you want?" Pancho probed deeply into her eyes, meeting no resistance.

"Of course not. I would love to go to college. We just don't have any money."

From that moment, Pancho had one goal. His own place at the Catholic university was assured through a scholarship. Once back at home, he made it his mission to get Susana into college. While she completed her final year, remaining as always a good student, Pancho worked every connection he knew, every angle he could think of, and every scheme he could invent. And it worked. Through the incessant badgering and his not-insignificant charisma, he was able to secure a scholarship from the university, which was woefully short of black students and considered the issue somewhat of an emergency as the government drew increasing attention, and criticism, to the imbalances.

The first day of college arrived, and finally, at long last, they were together again. As they greeted each other at the bus station, the spark from their first touch ignited the passion that burned as brightly as ever. They celebrated their first day at university by a night on the town. Pancho used the little money he had been able to save to show Susana around San Porfirio, eating at the most expensive restaurant they could afford. They had finished the night by joining the other students at a campfire organized by the school at this very park he was now returning to with Carlitos. Arriving late, they had quickly been absorbed into the group and, after a long night of singing, had sneaked off behind the crop of trees for a kiss. Since that day, this place had been Susana's place.

"I took her by the hand, and we just walked and walked, right through there." Pancho paused and pointed to a spot behind a hillock upon which grew a cluster of eucalyptus trees.

"That was before they had her killed …" His voice trailed off.

"She was great," Carlitos said. "You were lucky to have her. You never deserved her."

"I know. I see that now. I wonder if we could have protected her …"

"You can't start that—you've been down that road, and it leads nowhere," Carlitos said.

Pancho coughed the words out in a sob: "I wonder if they raped and killed her in those trees …" Pancho turned his full gaze upon Carlitos. "*Hampa comun* my ass. I wonder which minister ordered her murder." Rage was beginning to make his voice quiver.

"It *could* have been an express kidnapping …" Carlitos interjected.

"Come on, you know as well as I do it was no coincidence. She was a student; if it was an express kidnapping, what did they think they could get from her? And right after El Comandante named her *specifically* on his damned radio show?"

Carlitos responded, "One day, my friend, one day there will be justice. One day the books will be opened, and they will have to answer for what they are doing."

Pancho said, "I'm not sure I have the patience for *one day*. But you're right. We'd better get moving. I've been lost for too long in the memories of her." Carlitos only nodded. Pancho knew that it would take much more than six months for time to heal his wounds, but at least the sweet sting of loss was starting to fade, replaced by a dull ache that was, shamefully, becoming easier to bear.

The park where they walked had been renamed by El Comandante to *Parque de la Revolución*. It was laid out in a circular pattern, with walking paths winding around in conjoining circles that intersected occasionally. There were groves of trees brought by the original city planners from all over the world. All were draped ornamentally with pink, yellow, and purple bougainvillea flowers.

They approached the lake, where the summer before Pancho and Susana had rented a small paddleboat and spent a quiet Saturday morning in each other's company. The water was toxic green and filled with grime and garbage—the ducks were gone, and dead fish floated in the shallows by the shore.

Carlitos and Pancho walked around the lake, sidestepping a drug addict lying face down on the steps. "So how's the student movement going?" Pancho asked. "I tried to follow from America."

"It's slowed down a bit," Carlitos said, "You shouldn't have left. After Susana was killed … That really discouraged people."

"I know, but I needed some time."

"You got scared and chickened out," Carlitos said.

"That's not fair, and you know it."

"Fair or not, we needed you more than ever. You weren't the only person that lost somebody. We all lost people. Remember, there were three that were killed," Carlitos said.

Pancho was silent for a moment.

"Well, anyway, after you left, I kept things up. We kept marching, organizing, and raising money. It became more difficult. But we knew we had to—we didn't have the luxury of middle class money to study *English*," Carlitos said. "Most of us can't run away, especially people like Juanita."

Pancho didn't respond.

As they talked, Pancho looked around and saw behind them a small, dark man with close-cropped hair who was walking along just within earshot, smoking a cigarette and reading a newspaper—upside down. The newspaper was *La Navaja*.

La Navaja—*I haven't thought about that paper for a while.* He was transported back to the meteoric rise of the student movement. El Comandante had appeared on TV.

Today, I am announcing the rescue of *La Nación.* This newspaper has printed its last lie—its last slander. In its place, we will print a revolutionary magazine that will speak only the truths about our glorious revolution and demonstrate to the world that we can, indeed, make our laws be respected. It will be called *La Navaja,* a knife that will cut through the oligarchs' lies.

"He's crossed the line this time," Pancho had angrily proclaimed to a vocal chorus of murmurs and acclamation. "First fining the paper, then trying lawsuits for defamation, revoking the owners' citizenship, and now just outright seizure? This isn't *his* private country. This is *our* country, and we will fight to defend our freedoms." And the student movement had been born.

La Navaja ... Pancho was thinking too much about the newspaper to pay attention to the small man who kept walking, holding his newspaper to cover his face, as the two friends sat down on a bench far enough away from the lake that they would not have to smell the stench.

"Listen, this is the way it has been," Carlitos said. "They've infiltrated our network. I don't even know who to trust. And they are on to our activities. We march, and they know where. We protest before the parliament, and they've given themselves the day off. We organize a rally; they have a bigger one somewhere else. They seem to know everything we're going to do, and they use that to deflate our message. I've been thinking about this for a while. We need some good press coverage. Somehow we *must* get heard by the outside world. The first few months were fantastic, so much support—but we have become lazy and predictable. Even the money has started to dry up."

"Sounds like you have a lot of work to do."

"You?"

"Yes, Carlitos. I'm not sure I can do it again. I've lost too much. And my dad has made it clear that he doesn't want me to get involved. He's worried about our family."

"But we need you now more than ever," said Carlitos.

He added angrily, "We were getting to them, but we were also careless. Now we know they are deadly serious. But we can be deadly serious, too." A glint appeared in Carlitos's eyes.

"Then why do you need me?"

Carlitos looked long into Pancho's eyes, breathed deeply, and said the words that Pancho could not resist: "To lead."

Pancho had a crease in his forehead and was deep in thought. They stood up again and continued their walk through the park, the smog that filled San Porfirio making it hard to breathe. They came to a chain-link fence that had rusted out and been cut to allow people to come and go unobserved. Beside the hole was a pile of used needles, and all of a sudden Pancho was angry. "How many universities are still on board?" he asked. They had started with sixteen universities across the country, the most important being the Catholic University of Venezuela.

"I think we still have about ten. The others had student elections, and we lost. El Comandante is spending a lot of money trying to swing these things. But we can still mobilize a good crowd, for something special of course—the incessant marching is getting to everybody," Carlitos said.

"Like I've said in the past, if folks just keep pushing, we'll finally rip open the old wounds. Then we will start to win."

"You're right: we need to find that energy again," Carlitos said. "Only then can we make ourselves heard."

"I'm still not sure," Pancho resisted for one last moment.

"I know you aren't. Neither am I. But what's the alternative? Do you want Susana to have died in vain?" Carlitos said, playing his trump card.

The decision was made.

"You know," Pancho said, allowing himself finally to think strategy, "as I was driving home I went by the airstrip in town. Looks like they are preparing for some big event. Do you know anything about this?"

"Indeed, come to think of it, I think it's some youth social forum that starts today or tomorrow" said Carlitos.

"Hmm," Pancho said, "I bet they've never seen a counter-revolutionary rally before …"

A grin spread across Carlitos' face.

And as they turned from the fence where they'd been gazing out onto the highway, Pancho noticed a large rat jump off the bench behind them—where he'd been crouching on top of a copy of La Navaja right where the tiny man had been a second before. Pancho shrugged, and they walked back to the car.

16

* * *

At first she thought it was the aftereffect of too much gin—her head felt like it was splitting open. But even as Doña Esmeralda spread her eyelids, cautiously testing the front lobe of her head where the alcohol had settled, the shrill chirping continued relentlessly. Finally, she realized through the haze and fog that the telephone was ringing.

She got up from the ancient bed and staggered to the mother-of-pearl telephone, grabbing the expensive, antique phone that Gonzalo had bought her on a trip to Russia when he had met with one of the representatives of the Tsar, or the Communist Party, or somebody. She screamed into the gold-plated receiver, "What is it?" only to be greeted by silence. For a full minute she waited, gaining control of her senses, until her patience ran out. "If this is some sort of a joke …"

The voice on the other side of the line simply said, "It's arranged—meet us tomorrow where we agreed," and hung up. Doña Esmeralda realized slowly that this was the call she'd been waiting for. She was finally going to put that money of hers—devaluing in a revolutionary bank—to some good use.

17

* * *

"All aboard." Finally, the hours of waiting were over. Freddy had been surprised that there wasn't anything planned while they waited, but he'd used the time to think about Mia and the revolution. They were at last leaving for their hosts' homes. Freddy was going to be staying with a revolutionary family in *La Vieja*.

"This *barrio*," the driver of his jeep lectured them as they got in, "is about forty-five minutes away. It's one of the most dangerous in the country, so when we drop you off at night you must make sure to stay inside your host family's house." Five soldiers with flak jackets mounted immediately behind the visiting youths, cramming them in like Venezuelan chickens. The soldiers held their Berettas and shotguns at the ready, their eyes barely visible under the riot helmets. Each had a belt of grenades around his shoulders. All of a sudden, Freddy felt naked.

Freddy's transport rattled over a single-lane bridge made of two rails of iron set across a small river that was dark brown and smelled of raw sewage. Immediately afterward, they leaped into a thirty-five-degree incline. The military officers were hanging out of the back, ogling the girls as they drove past. "*Epale, mamacita, do you have something for tu papito?*"

The slope was made of cement and graded so the tires of the jeeps—the only vehicles that could take the hill—would not lose their grip on the steep hillside during the torrential rains. Freddy held on tightly as he looked out the window for a better view of the orange brick buildings that made up the barrio. The buildings that sped by around him were four and five stories tall and over engineered by the peasant farmer turned slum dweller. Each one had cement and iron poking out of its sides, and the roofs were of rusting zinc. Wires spread like a spider web from house to house, and satellite dishes had been installed at regular intervals and manipulated to give free TV to everybody, as long as they agreed to watch the same channel. The revolutionary committee even had weekly meetings to vote on the shows and movies they wanted to watch. Of course, they had to turn quickly to El Comandante's speeches when they came on.

Everywhere Freddy looked, he saw the people's tributes to their revolution plastered on the walls of this man-made canyon. Posters, stickers, murals. On the side of one building were three large placards—side by side—of the Van Morrison dude (whom Freddy now knew as Che Guevara, an Argentine revolutionary), El Comandante, and Pancho Villa. Each picture was full size and depicted these important revolutionary leaders in some of the activities of daily socialist life.

Freddy also noticed murals that covered entire walls.

"We encourage the people," the driver said, "to express themselves and their solidarity with the revolution and their rejection of savage capitalism."

Of these displays of solidarity, one was a mural of Uncle Sam dressed up in a huge green suit made of dollar bills sucking oil from the ground with a huge straw from a famous American fast food restaurant chain. The next one was a picture of a US warplane dropping bombs on poor people in the form of diseases. Another one showed El Comandante sinking an aircraft carrier with a traditional Indian blowgun.

Freddy smiled approvingly. "Wow," he said as the tires hit a slick patch and started to spin, the acrid smell of tire smoke punctuating the air.

"Watch out!" Freddy yelled as the top of the jeep almost snagged one of the electric wires.

"Get out of the way." The driver honked at a group of children playing a form of baseball with bottle caps and broomsticks.

The sun was reaching the horizon, setting between two large antennae that were at the heart of the conurbation, laid there long before the no-man's-land had been claimed by the urban poor. The barrio residents, elegantly dressed, were filling the road to overflowing as they anxiously pushed upward through the crowds returning from work in the valleys to their hovels on the side of the hills. Freddy couldn't understand how they found their homes among the myriad of paths and stairways that tunneled around the hillside haphazardly. As the jeep passed, they yelled, "*Ustedes, gringos*, with your bodyguards …"

The jeep honked its horns threateningly.

"Why don't you come and spend the night up here with us? Why go rushing back down?"

The taunt, delivered to the military, bothered Freddy. The terrifying night of the Venezuelan barrios was falling quickly. "*Epa, gringos, una cerveza?*" yelled a group of young men boldly, all standing up in unison from their repose on the corner in front of a liquor store. As they rose, Freddy saw their jackets bulging suspiciously around their waists. Their swagger reminded him of the gangsters at his high school. Those bad days seemed long past, and the memory unsettled him.

The jeep slowed in front of a small stairway that squeezed through a narrow crevice in a solid, self-engineered wall. Homes after homes were attached to each other for comfort, protection, and stability.

"Get out, fast," said the driver to Freddy. The soldiers jumped out of the vehicle, deploying in protective position around the street. "Go three houses in, up a flight of stairs. Turn left, go seven houses down, through the side passageway, and up an incline until you see a small kiosk. Turn left and go five houses in and ask for the Mendoza family. *MOVE.* They know you are coming. Don't dally. This barrio is controlled by the *Putamaros*."

"But, wait, what the …" Freddy didn't have time to ask anything. Even the flak-jacketed military looked scared. Freddy sprinted through the narrow crevice in the canyon wall. Behind him, the tires of the jeep protested as it peeled away.

Right, then left, Freddy thought. *No, left then right. Wait, straight then right then left.* He was totally turned around. *Up the stairs, no down these stairs. Let's see, walk five houses, then turn left.* By an act of God, he found what he thought was the kiosk.

"Mendoza family?" he asked the kiosk owner, who was puffing on a hand-rolled cigar that was clenched firmly between his blackened teeth. He pulled a solid iron sheet down over the stale bread and old pasta that were his wares. "*Cuál? Juan Carlos Mendoza? O Heriberto Mendoza?*"

"Huh?"

"There's more than one," he said, giving Freddy a hard look, "But judging by your looks, you're probably looking for Geronimo Mendoza. Go that way." He pointed left, down another narrow alley. "*Pero apúrate!*"

"Is this the Mendoza family?" Freddy rapped energetically on a metal gate before what he desperately hoped was the right house. All the neighbors peered anxiously between the iron bars on the floors above him.

The gangsters he had seen in front of the liquor store swaggered into the narrow alley behind him, stalking him slowly and patiently as predators do the world over. It was almost dark now, and Freddy could barely make out the outline of their clothes—and their guns. They just stood there for a second, watching him and muttering jokes to each other, guffawing and slapping each other on the back. The leader had a bandana pulled low over his forehead. He yelled something in Freddy's direction that Freddy didn't understand.

"*Todo bien*," Freddy yelled back in his painfully accented Spanish. He pounded harder. "Mendozas, please." Still no answer, but this time he could hear the sound of shoes on the stairs as someone made his way up.

Then he heard something click.

Shit, he said to himself, and he looked back. One of the men had taken a 9-millimeter out of his pocket and cocked it. His smile showed sinister in the fading light. From above, he heard voices saying, "You need to run" and "What are you doing *here*?" He just pounded harder.

"*Epa, gringo*, what do you want up here in *La Vieja*?" the lead gangster yelled out.

"Please answer," Freddy whined. Through the door in front of him came a hoarse whisper. "This is not the Mendozas. Go down five doors, take a left, and go down the stairs. Now. Do you want to get killed?"

Freddy turned. The four gangsters were closing the distance slowly. Like Andes mountain foxes cornering a cowering *quis*, they all knew that the game was over. Where could he go? All of them now had their handguns out and were playing with them like toys, banging them on the sides of the alleyway and cocking and uncocking them.

Freddy grabbed his bag to run and was stopped cold as it snagged on a piece of rusted metal poking out from the door he'd been pounding on. He pulled as hard as he could, to no effect. He kneeled down, trying to see in the fading light if he could undo it with his hands. His nervous fingers fumbled to find the problem, stumbling around the canvas and the metal. The gangsters were closer now. Freddy could clearly make out tattoos on their faces and hands, and the smell of their overpowering cologne wafted toward him on the barrio winds. He stood up and made one tremendous yank, and the bag came free with a powerful ripping sound. Freddy ran.

"Stop there, gringo," said one of the predators of the perilous night. With no other option, Freddy ignored the order and bolted down the alleyway. Every step, every turn, and every stairway took him deeper and deeper into the unknowable heart of the barrio.

Behind him, the stalkers came steadily on.

"Mendoza?" Freddy said desperately through one door.

"No." Not even a face this time. Freddy started to despair.

"Mendoza?" he yelled up to a woman staring through iron grates from a window three stories up.

"No, keep going. Hurry up."

Running, running, running, Freddy stayed just ahead of the gangsters. They picked up their pace, their new white sneakers smacking on the cement, slapping an occasional puddle of refuse thrown from the second floor of one of the houses. They closed the distance between Freddy and themselves. His clothes kept spilling onto the ground through the large, gaping hole in his bag, falling unnoticed in his desperate flight to safety.

Freddy broke into a full sprint, his feet pounding down the bare cement. He wasn't even stopping to ask for directions. His only thought was to put as much distance between himself and the gangsters as possible.

He looked behind him. One of them stopped to light a cigarette, and the bright point of orange light flashed, illuminating the sinister eyes of the *malandro*.

Thirty more feet down the darkened canyon, his foot suddenly caught on a metal stud that was protruding from the side of an unfinished house. He went down hard, arms and legs flailing in all directions as his bag flew high in the sky to fall ten feet away. He flipped over and watched them advance, slowing down as they realized they had captured their prey, savoring their moment of triumph. As they arrived and leaned over him, light from the windows glinting on their gold teeth, the iron door beside him squeaked wide open, throwing a square of welcoming yellow light into the alley. He saw the outline of a tiny, hunched old woman silhouetted in the bright light—her hair was in curlers, and she held a cane in her hand. She stepped out into the alleyway, and Freddy noticed in a disjointed fashion that she was wearing slippers from a modern American cartoon series.

"Mendoza?" Freddy moaned desperately from the ground.

"*Si, mijito.*" The ancient oracle bent over to help him to his feet.

The gang leader, revolver in hand, put his other hand on Freddy's shoulder menacingly. Immediately, the miniscule elderly women reached her arm up high above her head, cane in hand—it was a wooden cane, elegantly carved, with a large bird on the grip—and brought it down hard onto the crown of the gangster's head. A crisp crack echoed through the alley, bouncing back and forth as it sought to escape into the night air above.

Freddy was stunned. "We're going to die," he said to the old lady matter-of-factly in English.

"Miguelito, what do you think you are doing?" The matriarch scolded good-naturedly. "This boy is our guest."

"Sorry, *tía*."

"Now you apologize to him," she ordered.

"*Lo siento, gringo*," the gangster mumbled, his shoulders lowered from the reprimand.

"Good, now go do something useful," she said, and the young ruffian turned and walked back toward his friends.

Color began to fill Freddy's face again, and his heartbeat slowed to normal. He looked thankfully at the old lady, resisting the urge to give her a hug and kiss. "Hi, and thank you," he said.

"*De nada*, and welcome," she said. "They didn't mean any harm. They are good boys, just sometimes a little rough."

Freddy's savior was only about four foot three inches tall. Her wrinkled face looked like a prune, or like she had been underwater too long, but there was a kind, playful twinkle in her eye. "Come on in, *mijito*," she said, and they went inside.

Freddy breathed deeply, waiting a few seconds before sheepishly poking his head back into the alleyway. The gangsters had disappeared around the winding stairway that led down and out toward the main road. The alleyway was filled with the hissing sounds and greasy smells of freshly cooked food being deep fried. Laundry hung from one neighbor's window to another's in the communal approach to solving individual needs. Raw sewage was running down the alley floor toward the steps. He slammed the steel door shut with finality and turned to address the old woman, who had brought him an empanada and a glass of juice.

"You are welcome to our home," she said. Freddy grinned at her and sat down in exhausted triumph in a small plastic chair by the door. "I am *really* here now, aren't I?" he said and reached out for the empanada.

18

* * *

Pancho arrived at home, his shoulders already sagging. Tomorrow, he knew, he'd make a phone call that would set in motion a plan that would inevitably lead to real danger and maybe even death, for his friends and strangers alike. The weight of renewed responsibility tugged at his heart strings, and he thought of Susana, knowing they could do nothing more to him. Anger boiled up in his stomach like a reflux, and he swallowed hard to contain it. He lay in his bed, trying to sleep, and gave a silent prayer for the soul of his sweet Susana.

* * *

Freddy was in a warm bed, disturbed by a day that he hadn't expected and a revolution that looked very different from inside. He laid his head on the pillow beneath posters filled with slogans, gestures, and commands and listened to the echoes of automatic gunfire that bounced around the *barrio*.

* * *

Doña Esmeralda had drunk herself to sleep, her spirit locked in conversation with Gonzalo. She could only reminisce about things lost, painful and bitter memories that left her exhausted and brimming with an uncontained hatred and an uncontrolled agony. She wouldn't let them take her house—not after everything they'd done. Her only solace came from her plans; tomorrow she would finally set in motion the triggers that would renew her position, her respect, and most of all her sense of self-worth. "*Buenas noches, Gonzalo,*" she said, and hugged her pillow tight.

* * *

Teniente Juan Marco Machado was pensive in the dark night. He was drunk on expensive booze, a mixed drink of whiskey shaken together with his future plans of revolutionary glory. He chased this cocktail with a large dose of the rising arrogance and sense of invincibility that is always bred by authority bereft of accountability. He had come so far; he would not let anybody rob him of the position he'd achieved. He would do *whatever* it took to show his commanders, and El Comandante, that he could be trusted to safeguard the revolution.

19

* * *

"Good morning, *papa*," Pancho said cheerfully to his father as he appeared from his bedroom. He felt well rested, no longer tired from his flight. The problems of the last weeks, and the last months, felt diminished. His energy had returned, and along with it his desire to fight.

"*Hola*, son. How did you sleep?" Even first thing in the morning, Pancho's dad looked worn out—a shadow covered his face despite him being well shaved.

"Very well. Nothing like sleeping in my own bed."

"Go take a shower. I'll make some coffee."

"Okay, *papa*." Pancho whistled as he stepped into the shower, turned on the hot water, and soaped himself up. He had just lathered his hair with a thick layer of green shampoo from the massive, unlabeled bottle and had a reassuring coat of suds covering his body when the water stopped.

"Dad," he yelled, "Come here."

His father pushed his head through the door. "What's wrong?"

"I don't know." Pancho squinted through eyes that were starting to burn. "The water shut off."

"Oh, sorry, I forgot to tell you. The government claims we are wasting water—which is a, let me think, what did they say? Oh, a 'strategic good that belongs to the people and shouldn't be put to the service of only those who are lucky enough to live in apartments.' So a few months ago, they went door to door fixing these timers on all our showers. We are only allowed to take three-minute showers."

"Really?"

"Yes, and El Comandante then took over the airwaves and showed us all how to bathe in three minutes, Indian style, using a gourd." Pancho's father smiled, showing a rare moment of humor from a defeated man.

Pancho was dumbfounded. "They went into every house?"

"Yes, son, every house," his father said. "Wait there."

"Where else would I go?" Pancho said. His dad returned with a bottle of water from the emergency stock of food and supplies that all Venezuelans accumulated. Fear of water or electricity outages—or government-decreed martial law because of a fabled foreign invasion—were a daily reality, so most families had cupboards full of canned food, candles, and water.

"Here" he handed over the bottle with a shrug and walked out of the bathroom.

Pancho stepped into the kitchen after his "shower," frowning as he was reintroduced to the travails of living in the new Venezuela. "Where's the coffee?"

"Well," his father said, "It's rationed, too. I'm allowed one bag per trip to the supermarket." His father grabbed a bag of coffee grounds from an old garbage bag on a shelf above the counter.

"I couldn't find coffee this week. But I usually reuse the grounds. After I make coffee, I dry them in the oven, when there's power. I can usually do this three times. I will probably find more next week," he said as he brewed a pot of reused Andean coffee. Pancho smelled the fantastic aroma of that dark brew. Even reused, the musty, earthy, and pungent smell reminded him of his childhood.

"Not bad for a rerun."

"Nope. I'll go shopping in a few days when I pick up my ration cards from work. I have to stop at three or four markets these days; it usually takes me all day. Wanna come?"

"Sure, maybe." Pancho finished his coffee. "Well, Pop, gotta go." He went back to his room to start making phone calls.

"Benito, I'm back. Same place at noon," and "Fernando, it's me. Come meet us. We gotta talk."

One by one he called the student leaders from across the country, summoning them to a rendezvous with the future, toward a destiny all of them knew would hold danger. Pancho knew they would come. They would come because Pancho had been their leader, and the call of his voice, even after his betrayal, was more than they could resist. They would come because they were scared for their future and hungry to do something—anything—that could make a difference for themselves and their children.

And then the call he'd been dreading all morning. "Juanita?"

"*Hola*. I heard the rumor you were back. You should have stayed away."

"Don't be like that. You know it wasn't my fault," Pancho pleaded.

"Not your fault? Whose fault was it, then? Surely not those of us you abandoned, who don't have rich families who can give us dollars?" Juanita said.

"It would have been worse if I'd stayed. They were gunning for us. Me leaving took some pressure off."

"You think so? So it's all about you? You think they just forgot about us when you were out of the picture. Boy, you are arrogant," Juanita said. "Well, it hasn't been easy, for your information. But Carlitos filled in where you failed. And now, we're supposed to jump at your command? Okay. *Si, señor, a sus ordenes*."

"Come on, I know you're pissed. But you gotta come. We need you. And you know as well as anybody that Carlitos can't do what I can."

"How do you know what Carlitos can do? You never let him do anything."

Sigh. "Will you come?" asked Pancho.

"Of course I'll be there. I, unlike others, can be counted on." And she clicked off the phone.

Finally, the last call, to the student leader from the beach. They discussed the meeting place and the time later that day. Pancho was about ready to click off when he noticed a slight problem. "Amigo, I think your phone isn't plugged in right. There's a weird buzz."

20

*** *** ***

Freddy woke up a little rattled. The incessant gunfire and occasional screams had kept him up late. After each burst of heavy fire, it had taken him a long time to fall back asleep—only to have it repeat. "How do you sleep through all that?" he asked the twenty-something boy he found trying to make coffee with an old sock and a pan of boiling water. He rubbed his eyes, trying to get them clear.

"All what?" said the boy.

"The gunfire. I dreamed I was in the middle of a war movie."

"Oh, you get used to that. That's why we put you in the inside room. Didn't want you to get freaked out by a stray bullet," he said, diligently working on his coffee.

"My name is Geronimo, by the way. Nice to meet you." He stuck out his hand containing a cup of black coffee in greeting. Geronimo was, very obviously, a young revolutionary. He was dressed in one of the ubiquitous red T-shirts and had a red bandana tied around his head. "I'm going to be showing you around. Just one of my many important assignments for the revolution and the barrio," he said and gave Freddy a wink.

"Nice to meet you too, and thanks for taking me in." Freddy yawned, clearing his head to better absorb the day-to-day reality of a true barrio revolutionary. "What assignments are you talking about?"

"Oh, lots of stuff. I'm on the barrio water committee, the barrio electric committee, the committee in defense of the revolution, and a bunch of others."

"Sounds fascinating."

"We basically keep our eyes and ears open up here and report out if we hear something we don't like. I'm also a member of the Communist Party and president of Young Communists for El Comandante. When I'm not doing all of that, I pick up a march here and there."

"But don't you have a job?" Freddy asked.

"You think doing all those things isn't hard work? I have a bunch of jobs."

"Well, I mean, you know. You don't have a full-time, nine-to-five thing at a business or something?" Freddy realized that his idea of employment had been preprogrammed by American capitalist ideas, something he'd have to work on.

"No. Those things are hard to get here."

"So, um, well, how do you pay for stuff?" asked Freddy uncomfortably.

"Oh, well each of the committees gives a stipend—they're taken from the profits of the natural resources that El Comandante recuperated for the fatherland from the hands of the oligarchs and the lackeys of the empire—no offense."

Freddy wasn't offended.

"Also, I'm a member of the Committee for the Redistribution of what is Rightfully Ours—the CRRO for short—and we run the revolutionary kiosks, so I get food for free with my card." He pulled a red ID card out of his pocket. "Between my six or seven different committees and the extra money I pick up on the side marching, I do okay." And he gave Freddy a lopsided grin.

Geronimo was short, no more than five foot six. He was dark, had long black hair, and was wearing many necklaces and bracelets colored in the green, red, yellow and black of Rastafarian Jamaica.

"Why did you join the revolution?" Freddy asked.

"You met my grandma last night, right?"

"Yes, she saved my life."

"Oh, right, sorry about that. I was supposed to pick you up on the curb, but a water pipe burst up the hill and I had to go fix it. I forgot to let my cousin know you were coming. He can be a bit protective of *his* barrio—likes to control the comings and goings," Geronimo said.

"No prob, I wasn't worried," Freddy lied.

"Anyway, my grandmother used to work as a maid in the house of one of those *malditos ricos* all her life. When she got too old and couldn't work sixteen-hour days, they fired her—just like that. No warning, no severance, no pension. After the thirty years of work, she'd been able to finish this house—thank God, or else we all would have been out on the street. When my father abandoned us, my mother started working as a maid too. I didn't have enough money to go to university. So sometimes I'd go and help them with their work. I saw those houses. Those people are no better than we are—yet they have mansions and treat us like garbage. I am Venezuelan too. I deserve some money. Why should they have it all? El Comandante has promised to take some of it from them and give it to us, and I say it's about time."

"But you still live here?" Freddy said. He pointed at the house around them. It was small, with only two bedrooms where the family slept together—poverty is no friend to privacy. A tiny living room separated them. A small hall led to a narrow kitchen with a hole in the back where they kept a small washing machine. A clothesline stretched out the window, heavily laden with damp clothes—it had rained last night, which meant that they would have to wait another day for their clothes to dry. They had a small refrigerator of the hotel minibar variety. The small living room had a TV set and plastic furniture draped with doilies and hand-sewn cushions. On the simple red brick walls hung unframed posters of Jesus and Mary. In one corner on a small stand was a small shrine to Maria Liberia, a tiny statue surrounded by candles and medallions of important saints. The floors were cement, but clean and well-polished, reflecting the light from a naked bulb hanging from a wire in the middle of the living room. The place smelled clean, of bleach, and was well cared for—but the poverty spoke with its own voice.

"Well," continued Geronimo, "El Comandante's obviously having trouble, no secret there, but he is trying. And I'm committed to do my part to help him succeed."

Freddy nodded in agreement, looking down at his watch. "I think it's time to go."

"Okay, let's go." As they climbed down the stairs and through the alley to stand on the curb, waiting for the jeep that would take them back to the airstrip, Freddy overflowed with the anticipation of the secrets the day would reveal. He was convinced that this was an important step toward becoming the man he wanted to be.

21

* * *

"I did as you ordered, *mi Teniente*," said the slight, dark man. Like any good intelligence agent, this man was in every way unremarkable. Those who met him at a gathering or party could never be quite sure if he had really been there at all. Even Machado, try as he might, could never remember what he looked like. The conversations were like talking to a memory, or a shade—or a demon. "I traced the call from the phone of the one named Carlitos—the one who's given us so much trouble lately. He set up a meeting with a student, one who just returned from overseas. They set up a meeting at the park. I followed them there."

"Could you catch what they were saying?" said Machado.

"Not very much, *mi Teniente*, but they did say they are meeting again first thing this morning to continue their discussion. They seem to be planning something."

Machado hated talking to this spy. The room darkened when he entered, and the intercourse left Machado feeling sullied. He always had the impression that his defects stood out more starkly, his gut expanding and his yellow teeth becoming more prominent the longer they spoke. He knew the little man was taking stock of the surroundings, making Machado more self-conscious about the bottles of whiskey on the desk and the disheveled sheets on the cot where he had passed another fitful night. He slipped his hand through his greasy hair and sucked in his gut, attempting to transport the paunch from his midriff to his chest. He had to reassert authority.

"Then *que diablos* are you doing here?" Machado said in his best menacing voice, which unfortunately came out instead in a squeak. "Follow them and figure it out. Details, I need details—what, when, where, how many. You know the drill. Move." And the little man quickly saluted the revolution and rushed out of the little office at the airport.

Everybody I work with is an idiot. Teniente Machado had a hangover, which always made him irritable, and he started rifling around the office for some coffee. He also was thinking about the long day he would spend with the gringo children and their incessant questions. He was already losing his patience. Almost an hour went by while Machado cleared his head, finally resorting to a stiff belt of whiskey to calm his trembling hands. The young people had started to arrive, and he had to prepare the day's events.

22

* * *

"First, we need to pick up some stuff from the store," Carlitos was saying to Pancho. "Then we'll go to our secret hideout. You called the others, right? They might not have come if not for your call. Morale is pretty low." It was midmorning, and Carlitos was picking up Pancho in his old, beaten-down four-wheel-drive truck.

"Man, I love this car." Pancho inhaled deeply of the aroma of his past, embracing the nostalgia, always a stalwart friend in difficult moments, and returning to the carefree days of his first years of college.

During the summer between their first and second years of college, the bond that held Carlitos, Pancho, and Susana together had led them to a corner of the country that was unknown to the boys and only a rumor to Susana. It was an exciting place of ancient mystery and modern misery, and their joint imagination trembled in anticipation of the discoveries they were sure were just over the horizon. They packed up their truck, as they had two summers before, and drove south from San Porfirio, hoping only to lose themselves in each other and in the sacred bosom of the country they loved. The long journey took them into the sweltering heart of the vast jungle, through which the last dictator had bravely forged a path, clearing the way for an indomitable highway.

The highway had survived decades of assault from the elements and the angry power of *La Pachamama*, desperate to destroy the only gateway to her realm and thereby keep her kingdom secret and inviolate. Yet the power of the creative human mind that had for so long held back the jungle's onslaught, safeguarding access to the domain that remained the lifeblood of the country, had surrendered under the mindless mismanagement of the revolutionary bureaucrats. Now the trio, traveling slowly along the imposing infrastructure, took care to avoid the potholes that had grown to the size of a car. Once, Carlitos almost ran into an arm-thick tree that had found fertile ground in a crevice in the asphalt and grown, splitting the pavement around it. Another time, as night grew near, their car almost slammed into a rock that somebody had placed as a warning in front of a huge gash in the shoulder. At long last, *La Pachamama* was finding an unworthy adversary, and the tide of the battle between the forces of nature and the strength of the mind was turning.

When the sun rested beneath the lush green jungle cover at the end of each day, the trio would stop and wait out the impenetrable darkness. The once-powerful lights that had brightened the road for nighttime travelers in days past had fallen across the highway and been scavenged by locals elated at their good fortune in obtaining some metal to prop up their decaying mud houses. None of these inconveniences bothered the trio; the exquisite company made the travails seem a most exotic adventure. During the long, dark nights the musketeers would regale each other with illusory tales of future grandeur. They were impetuous, full of the carelessness of youth and the excitement of now. Outside the impossibly thin windows of the car, jungle predators—seeking sustenance as they had for eons from the lifeblood of the jungle—would stop in curiosity and listen to the gales of laughter and the flickering lights coming from the metal beast. They contemplated the possibility of this new life form in their unchanging world briefly before pressing on in their eternal effort to preserve life.

The drive through the sweltering jungles led the trio to the foothills of the *Cordillera de los Andes*, a great mountain range that takes its first stumbling steps in Venezuela and continues from there, grasping hungrily toward the sky as it becomes the backbone of a powerful continent. Hidden away in the folds of the hills, a surprise *quebrada* appeared, carved by an eons-old river powered by the runoff from the ageless glaciers crowning the tops of the distant peaks. It sliced through the Andes Mountains like boiling water through a massive pile of golden Venezuelan sugar and burst onto the plains below to irrigate the jungles and feed the Great River on its way to the ocean. When the government had discovered the silver mine, they had built a dangerously winding road that clung precariously to the side of the canyon above the river, starting from the jungles to finally emerge onto the plateau where at twenty thousand feet three thousand hearty miners lived, worked, drank, and died in the increasingly frequent accidents of revolutionary incompetence.

Pancho, Susana, and Carlitos drove lazily through the jungles with no thought to their destination until, surprised, they stumbled upon the canyon entrance. Taking a deep breath in quiet expectation, they plunged into the underbelly of the Pachamama. Immediately, they left the mystical creatures of the Venezuelan jungle behind them—the puma, the anaconda, the large rodent that fed on the children of inattentive mothers, and the dangerous unnamed things that lived in the murky waters of the Great River.

As they powered upward, the topography changed radically, and instantly. "Isn't this fantastic?" Pancho said, throwing the car into four-wheel-drive and feeling that thrill as it grabbed hold of the gravel road and pulled them upward into the austere landscape. The green was suddenly and violently replaced by the dirty brown of the Andes, with the hills on both sides a Technicolor celebration of the minerals still waiting to be found and put to the work of building the nation. They continued on for days, watching as even the trees fell away to be replaced by cacti and then by small shrubs. They slept in the car at night, huddled together for warmth, and told stories they had heard from their parents about this most remote of places. Occasionally, they would pass side roads with faded, green, rusted-out signs written in the Indian language.

"I wonder what that says," Pancho said, looking up at a sign in front of an intriguing path that led off to the right, climbing unsteadily around a hill out of the canyon, becoming lost at last as it turned around a bend behind a cliff. Taking out their dictionary of the local Indian language, Carlitos started to read. "It says 'beware.'"

"Maybe that's it?"

"Maybe," Pancho said.

"Maybe it's what?" Susana asked.

Pancho, always the leader even among the three, told her of the legend.

Since childhood, all misbehaving children heard stories from their parents of a secret Indian road to a lost valley somewhere in the mountains. A beautiful, verdant valley thick with elephant grass, heavy with fruit and vegetables, and crawling with the ancient animals of prehistory; a valley where the descendants of the first men of the mountains—large, powerful men more closely related to the cavemen of old than to the Indians or the Spaniards—still lived. They were the original inhabitants of this land, and sometimes, when the rains ceased to caress the lushness of their highland stronghold, they would abandon their secret mountain to plunder the animals of their newly arrived Andes neighbors. They were said to be a cruel people, a thankless, hard tribe who gave no thought to the plight of their victims and survived as prehistoric champions upon the weakness of their adversaries.

Susana shuddered as Pancho squinted through the darkening late-afternoon sun—for night came more quickly in the canyon—and said the words they were all thinking, "We'd better go."

Grateful, Pancho said, "As you wish," and they peeled away from the entrance into the mountains. They powered down the road, eager to put as much distance as possible between them and the Neolithic hunters they were sure were following them before nightfall.

Before they were a bastion of revolutionary rage, the Andes Mountain Indians had been fiercely independent and freedom-loving people, desperate to hold on to their language and their customs against the overwhelming power of modernity. Pancho, Susana, and Carlitos, all studying sociology courses that required field work, spent that long, glorious summer in communion with the increasingly revolutionary Indians, learning their customs and their history. They worked together on their alpaca or llama farms, learning to birth the newborn *crias* and shear the valuable wool. In the afternoons, they took language classes in the villages, and at night they chewed coca leaves to acclimatize to the altitude, drank *mate* to ward themselves from the cold, and drank *aguardiente* to enliven the revolutionary debates with their hosts that were, at the time, simply the academic exercises of adolescence. This last act always made waking in the early hours of the morning much more of a challenge—but their strong young bodies took the liquid abuse as they surrendered themselves to mountain life. Susana had loved the summer. Being from the Caribbean coast, it was difficult for her to imagine that there was such a place within the confines of the national geography. If she hadn't been there, she would never have believed it. As they had driven back to San Porfirio, Susana had leaned close to Pancho, caressing his shoulder, and said, "Thank you—I'd always dreamed of traveling before I died." That memory was like an open wound in Pancho's heart, one of so many others.

"I hear things are really changing up there," Carlitos said, somehow reading Pancho's thoughts. "Recently, El Comandante has put more effort into controlling the mine. So he's sent lots of his minions up there to brainwash the Indians. They say it's even getting dangerous—lots of drugs up there, too. Seems the *narcos* have found the Indians' coca."

"Kind of a shame—I hope they can keep their culture," Pancho said. "We sure as hell are losing ours …"

They were silent for a while.

"Man, I thought my political career was going to be different. I figured it would be straight politics, not this shit. Boy, was I naive," Pancho said. "I really miss those times when I felt I loved everybody in the country. I wish we could go back to those days. I wasn't afraid of the Indians back then, or the poor for that matter—I hate how things have changed."

Hatred—a defining emotion for the unwilling participants of the new, revolutionary Venezuela.

"I guess it's up to us to change them back, then," Carlitos said. "Either that or join the revolution." They both grimaced. They passed old cars belching smoke and ancient American school buses used as public transport as they went first to the large hardware store, to purchase the weapons of peaceful protest, and then on to the supermarket. Pancho glanced behind through the cracked rear-view mirror. A small, fluorescent green car caught his attention before they passed around a bus and lost it in a belch of burned oil.

"*Chamo*, where's the food?" Pancho asked when they entered the supermarket.

"You heard about the rationing," Carlitos respond, slightly distracted. He rifled through the packages of chips, trying to find one that had not been already opened and half the contents siphoned off.

"Ya, but there's *nothing.*" Pancho signaled to the empty shelves.

"Here we are." There were six eggs left on the shelf, two of them broken. Alongside the eggs were four bags of milk. Pancho picked up one of the bags.

"Expired," he said.

Carlitos shrugged.

"I was here first," screamed a lady, obviously from the barrios, right in Pancho's ear. He almost dropped the milk. She gave him a furious push, sending him flying to land flat on his back in the middle of the aisle as she wrested the bag of expired milk from his grasp.

"This is my milk," she screamed over and over, grabbing the other three bags. Her greedy fingers were accentuated by long, grotesque fake nails. Pancho tried to get to his feet, but just as he did, another woman lunged over him to grab a bag of sugar from the almost-empty shopping cart of his first assailant.

"You can only have one—I'm taking this."

"Hey, give that back," the first woman screamed. She dropped the four bags of expired milk into the shopping cart and grabbed for the quickly vanishing bag of sugar. One of the milk bags burst open and showered Pancho in a rancid mist. A tug-of-war ensued over the sugar. Finally, the bag split in two, exploding over Pancho's head. The sugar and milk mixed, leaving him looking like a large glazed donut. The two women went down on their knees, scooping sugar into their pockets.

Together, Pancho and Carlitos picked up several large bottles of vinegar, some bottled water, some expensive canned food, the last bag of rice, a tiny chicken imported from Brazil, and a bag of coffee they found hidden behind a box of tampons that cost 50,000 Asnos. Finally, Pancho picked out an expensive bottle of rum. "Tonight, we celebrate. For tomorrow—who knows …" and they walked toward the register, Carlitos picking up some candles and matches on their way out.

23

*** * * ***

The military man Freddy knew as Machado stood up again at the microphone. Around Freddy were assembled the young activists, eager to hear about the days' activities. "Young people, among you are passing the soldiers of the revolution with our implements of protest. You must become familiar with these, for they are as important to our peaceful revolution as are the guns and the bombs of the empire. Please take a marker and a piece of cardboard, for today we are taking our peaceful protest directly to the heart of the empire. Today is Minority Resistance Day, the day when we celebrate the historic revolt that our minorities continue to lead against their oppressors and occupiers. We used to call this day Columbus Day, but we changed the day and the name in honor of our Indians and their fight *against* those colonialists whom in the past we celebrated with such thoughtlessness to the plight of our Indians, for whom the coming of Columbus meant destruction."

"Last year," Geronimo had appeared by his side as if by magic, "We held a rally where El Comandante gave a speech to us, the community organizers, *alone*. It was the first time I had been so close to him. There were only about ten thousand of us standing in front of the Casa Naranja. It was so personal, so intimate. That day, we went to the center of town where there was a plaza called Columbus Square that hosted a statue of Christopher Columbus standing holding a sword. We held a trial for Columbus, a criminal prosecution for genocide. We called witnesses from the indigenous community. We even subpoenaed the oligarchs, so they could defend themselves. Of course, they never showed up. Finally, in an act of revolutionary justice, we sentenced Columbus to death. We ripped down the statue, hanged the iron Columbus in effigy, and spray painted what we thought of him and his kind all over the base. He still hangs there today, a reminder for the oligarchs who think they will be back," Geronimo said resolutely.

Encouraged, Freddy redoubled his effort to make his sign more meaningful. With their implements of battle drawn up in their own hands and gripped as firmly as any sword or gun, the visiting activists boarded the buses that had become chariots ferrying them to battle.

The buses moved in a convoy, pushing forward as if to deploy soldiers in a forward operating area. A gang of motorcyclists gyrated around them, lending increasing power to the onward motion of the buses as they came closer to their mark. The riders of the motorcycles honked their horns and screamed. They were echoed by hundreds of young voices exploding from the buses. Freddy himself led his troop in cheers and slogans all the way. Occasionally one of the motorcyclists would pull a revolver out of his belt and fire into the air, whooping and screaming.

Freddy was seated at the front of the bus, beside the driver, who turned to him as they drove onto an overpass. "See that down there?" He nudged Freddy and motioned below.

"Looks like the central plaza," Freddy said. *It also looks like anarchy.* One street vendor was blasting music from a large speaker system. He could hear the perverse lyrics in English all the way up on the freeway. The vendor appeared to be selling pirated CDs and DVDs. Beside this stand, another—this time covered with plastic sheeting—was hawking women's lingerie. Yet another tent was selling everything from 110/220 volt converters to switchblades. Across the plaza itself and in front of the cathedral was a large red tent selling revolutionary merchandise, including small puppets and dolls of El Comandante, the omnipresent T-shirts, hats, shoes, beach balls, and beach blankets all bearing the red of the revolution with the donkey of the national seal. Some had the swollen face of El Comandante and the disheveled, bearded Che. Across the front of the cathedral, built by the Spanish over four hundred years ago, were scrawled angry inflammatory words and crude, grotesque images depicting the alleged extracurricular activities of the clergy. On Easter Sunday one year, El Comandante had taken over the airwaves—exactly during the high mass—to show digitally edited images of the priests in the middle of unflattering and compromising activities.

> *Vea, mis hijos*, the activities of our so highly esteemed spiritual leaders. Look what they do when they are not taking your money in offerings or imprinting upon the young souls of your children their eternal damnation. Know now, my children, that we do not need them, for I am your father, incarnating the spirit of our great Liberator.

The priests had protested, demonstrating that the videos and pictures were doctored—but nobody was listening. "And that," the driver told Freddy proudly, pointing in the direction of the red tent, "is where 'the happening' took place. I was there."

"It was black like Venezuelan oil. A cloud had covered the moon, and the night air was so thick you could cut it with a machete. For weeks, the opposition had been marching and rioting. They were angry that El Comandante had nationalized the private schools and put in place a curriculum that reflects our nation's socialist values. You see, they had expensive private schools where they wouldn't let any poor student attend—and why should they alone have the right to a good education?"

"That's true—it's wrong" Freddy interjected authoritatively.

"But they could not accept it. They marched toward the parliament and down to the military bases on the beach. Each day the rioting increased and became more violent. A policewoman was raped; a soldier was burned to death by a Molotov cocktail. They overturned several of our buses going to a peaceful gathering at the national theater. They ambushed the military recruits that were coming to safeguard the strategic sites within the city, pelting them with rocks and bottles. It felt like the whole country was going to explode. Even the weather seemed angry. The days were unbearably hot and humid—there was no rain to calm the rioters down and force them indoors," the bus driver said.

"Sounds like an amazing time." Freddy was jealous he hadn't been there.

"The night before 'the happening,' they took over one of the plazas on the east side of town. They placed snipers on the tops of buildings, shooting at any of our police who tried to break through their barricades. Yes, they barricaded the small plaza using cobblestones from the century's old road and furniture they took from the buildings they broke into. Behind their impunity, they set up illegal activity. Loudspeakers powered with generators called for insurrection and violence, and for the overthrow of our Comandante."

"That's incredible," Freddy said. "To have lived all that …"

"Yes, but it gets worse. They started assembling, first hundreds, then thousands, then hundreds of thousands—spilling into the alleyways around the plaza. They draped themselves in our flag—held upside down to demonstrate their disdain—and stayed there all night playing their music. The next morning, El Comandante took over all the TV stations, closing them down in the national interest and running only peaceful programming. Nobody knew what was happening, and this only made the enemy bolder. Two revolutionary journalists from RTV were beaten as they tried to enter the plaza, their broken bodies thrown over barricades spray-painted with offensive words. At noon, El Comandante himself appeared on the screen calling to defend the revolution.

"As a leading member of the local CRRO, I went door to door mobilizing my community, and we all marched down the hillside from the barrio to the plaza. El Comandante had summoned; and we obeyed. We came in the thousands, maybe tens of thousands. We placed watchmen on the buildings to alert us to their advance. And we organized our defense. Even though El Comandante didn't appear—I'm sure he was busy with other important issues—we set in place the defense of the Casa Naranja."

"Why didn't he come? Where was he?" Freddy asked.

"I don't know. People said he was busy deploying the military and intelligence services—work that is vital but most times secret. We walked and worked all day, preparing to defend our plaza and our Casa Naranja, the place that El Comandante took from the oligarchs and gave back to us. Then just as darkness arrived on that hot, dark, sticky night, the lights in the city went off. We knew that was it. Back then, the oligarchs still owned the electricity company. We braced for the attack. It was too quiet, and in the pitch blackness we could hear the muffled shuffling of thousands of feet. They were coming quietly this time. They had wrapped dark cloth around their shoes to take us by surprise. No shouting or protest slogans—they were readying for a physical attack. We waited. Seconds turned into minutes. The air around us pulsated. Minutes turned into hours as we waited, the air turning to electricity."

Freddy was holding his breath.

"I was at the center, right there." The driver pointed. "In front of the church. I was smoking, and I'm sure the light gave me away because I saw a rock fly out of the darkness. I fell to the ground, but otherwise it would have hit me. With that they came. From the right, the mob tried to push us back. We fought in the dark with flashlights and sticks, clubbing and pushing. There was shooting in the air. But the line held. Then, they pushed from the west, and we threw rocks and bricks and pushed back. The darkness was overpowering, and all we could hear were the screams of our countrymen and the grunts of the aggressors. Reinforcements arrived from the neighboring barrios, but the lights were still off—the power station was still theirs, barricaded behind an angry army of their employees who chose their privilege over our need. But we lasted—all night, we lasted. By the time the morning light came, we could see dozens of our dead countrymen, with hundreds of more injured. But there were deaths on their side as well—they'd felt the bite of the revolution. Through the dark night, loyal military had been on the move, and by midmorning the power was back up and El Comandante had declared martial law. We were saved." A broad smile crept across his face.

"Their intention was to take over that plaza, then the house, and then the country. We pushed them out. And since then, we've established a twenty-four-hour presence here to make sure they don't try it again." Freddy looked down and saw that the large red tent was manned by several dozen people wearing red. Behind the tent were a half-dozen motorcyclists wearing large jackets and bandanas around their faces. There were also seven or eight Revolutionary National Police standing around. One was smoking a cigarette while playing a game of checkers with a stocky female officer with bleach-blond hair.

In the center of the plaza was what looked like the remains of a statue or monument. The shoulder-high pedestal stood naked and empty, its ancient stone decorated only with an identical set of iron feet rusting in the early afternoon sunlight. Everything above the statue's ankles, including a long sword that was bent until it was piercing the metal heart of the rejected hero was disintegrating into the uncut knee-high grass around the monument.

"Who sawed off that statue?" Freddy asked.

"Ah." The bus driver winked. "After that day, we tore down their statues, their idols, and their relevance—their celebration of colonial privilege. We erected a monument to ourselves, lest they forget what they did here and who won that fateful day." The massive nouveau-art sculpture replacing the bronze statue rusting on the ground had the body of David, the head of Fidel, and an upheld hand grasping a large book.

"And the book?"

"That's the new Venezuelan constitution."

Freddy nodded, energy brimming at the story and in anticipation of his own role in the next chapter of Venezuelan independence. He was so anxious to participate that he could taste the sourness of the adrenaline that flowed into his veins as he gazed spellbound at the plaza where everything had changed for this bold country and its exciting experiment.

As they drove above it, he gazed down into the plaza. On top of the ramshackle, makeshift stores were thick layers of garbage. Behind the stores was also garbage, piled in mounds and clogging the gutters. In fact, now that Freddy looked at it, he saw garbage everywhere. Through the open window of the bus he could even smell the refuse advancing in wafts alongside the robust, noxious smell of diesel exhaust from the old military bus. "For such an important place, its kinda dirty ..." he didn't want to sound judgmental but felt the need to say something.

"We don't oppress the people," the driver said, "like the *oligarquia* used to. We try to work with them and educate them without falling into the trap of violence. We don't burden people with expensive fines when they are trying to provide for their families. And, most of all, we don't discriminate against them and their use of their plaza. The oligarchs did this, holding ridiculous classical music concerts here. The people don't like classical music. We do things for their benefit, not for the benefit of those who disdain the people's simple pleasures. Because, remember, this revolution is of the people and for the people. It's *their* plaza, after all; they fought for it with their blood, and so we have to educate them, not oppress them. And if this is the use they want for their plaza, the people's plaza, who are we to say otherwise?"

For the remainder of the ride, Freddy was quiet. The young people at the back of the bus were screaming and joking, but he was steeped in the driver's story and the meaning of the making of revolution.

Arriving at the venue, Freddy surveyed the situation. The American embassy was a fortress set high on the hill overlooking the richest part of the city. Massive walls surrounded the complex that was itself out of sight. The brown walls were fortified by razor wire and security cameras. At the very front there was a massive iron portico that slid open and shut, through which people seeking visas or passports could enter—but only after passing through three rings of security.

The protest—which was to be their ticket to revolution—had already begun. Assembled around the main iron doors of the embassy were thousands of protesters wearing red. They were screaming and throwing rocks and bottles, fruits and vegetables. A dozen of them were off to the left scribbling something on the embassy's outer wall in red spray paint. Two or three dozen young people were screaming and yelling obscenities directly in front of a line of riot police. The mob was a living organism, expanding out toward the police to shout something and quickly collapsing in upon itself. At the very front of the protest were the riot police—hot and obviously tired—dressed in black, with body armor and night sticks and leaning on their huge plastic shields.

Behind the front line of radicals stood a forlorn group of midlevel bureaucrats, unenthusiastically mumbling slogans under their breath and quite obviously wishing they were somewhere else. At the far back of the mob, sitting on the curb or leaning against their motorcycles, was a group of thugs. They were dripping sweat onto their thick jackets, worn in defiance of the midday sun, and some had strange bulges in the back of their pants. They were wearing red bandanas around their mouths so they couldn't be identified and had on dark sunglasses.

"Check that out over there." Mia and Freddy were off the bus and walking through the crowd toward the front of the protest. Freddy looked in the direction of Mia's indiscreetly outstretched hand. Beside the bikers was a group of fifteen young, pregnant women standing in attention in a straight line. They were wearing army-issued black laced boots and camouflaged military pants. They had on tiny red tube-top shirts barely covering their bosoms. Over their mouths they also had red bandanas with El Comandante's face printed on them, and they were wearing army caps. Across their bare, swollen bellies were written in large, black block letters, "El Comandante's Revolutionary Children." They were chanting in unison a lyrical slogan laced with expletives and angry threats, and whenever they reached the end of the rhyme their bellies bulged as the unborn babies saluted their revolutionary father.

"Wow, kinda creepy," Freddy said.

"What do we do now?" a girl from Freddy's team asked.

"We are here to protest. To show our disfavor at the American government and the terrible things they do around the world. Do what is in your heart." Freddy felt very mature.

"But I've never done this before."

"Just follow the lead of the others." The group was now several thousand strong, from the forum, the *barrios*, and civil servants. They were holding up their placards and chanting in unison.

"Free Trashcanistan," shouted Mia, diving into the fray.

"America is terror," another student shouted.

Taking the lead, Freddy ran and hurled himself against the police line. "Move aside," he screamed, trying to break through a crease between two young, scared-looking rookies. The younger of the two rapped him on the hand with his wand. "Ouch," Freddy yelled, and he fell back. He repeated the effort, but this time the other one hit him on the head. He wailed in rage and ventured off in search of a more mature and measured policeman against whom he could vent his wrath. "Let me through," he screamed at an old policeman who was using his shield as a cane and taking a drink from a bottle that poked out of his armor. The policeman looked at him and just sighed.

"I said let me through!" Freddy wasn't really sure what he would do if they did, in fact, let him pass—secretly, he was counting on the human wall remaining firmly in place. For several hours, the protesters screamed at the two-story-high wall of the embassy, marching up and down with their placards. Sometimes they chanted in unison and sometimes they angrily threw water bottles at the police (making sure they were plastic, lest they be arrested by an angry officer). Still nothing.

As the melee reached crescendo, Freddy heard a scuffle break out behind him. He heard Mia let out a bloodcurdling scream, and he twisted around—water bottle in hand—trying to identify the problem.

"You give that back," Mia kept screaming. Freddy followed Mia's voice in time to see a leather-jacketed biker sprinting toward the back of the march, holding Mia's purse in his left hand while using his right to push protesters aside.

"Help!" Mia screamed as she looked around desperately for assistance. Her eyes landed on Freddy, who was anxiously looking for a way through the crowd. Mia pushed out in the direction of the biker, but to no avail. The man reached his motorcycle, hopped on the back and—gunning his engine—peeled down the hill and out of sight.

"That's not yours," Freddy screamed in Midwest-accented English at the back of the rapidly vanishing motorcyclist, marshaling his remaining strength as he tried to push his way through the crowd to dive in the direction of the now-disappeared biker. Mia had fallen to her knees in the scuffle and was getting shakily to her feet.

"Bring that back here," Freddy yelled again. "Hey!" He directed his panicked pleas to the police standing on the sidelines. The old policeman simply smiled, shrugged, and took another pull on his now half-empty bottle.

Finding himself alone in the mob, Freddy dove in between a woman holding a notepad and a middle-aged businessman who had pulled a red shirt over his dress shirt and wrapped his red tie around his head. "I'm coming, Mia." He pushed harder. Not seeing the foot sneak from the crowd in front of him, he tripped and smacked the pavement like a plantain, scraping the skin off his elbow. From behind, Freddy felt a push.

"What the heck?" Outraged, he tried to push himself to his feet but could feel more than see the hands that were pressed firmly against his shoulders, pinning him down. He tried to spin himself around but still couldn't worm out from under his aggressors.

"Hey, what the …" he felt a hand reach into his front pocket, where he'd carefully stowed his wallet upon the advice of Geronimo. "Hey, leave me alone."

A foot pressed down more firmly on the small of his back. All he could see were ankles and feet everywhere, a sea of dirty socks and scuffed shoes. "Let me up." All of a sudden, a heavy boot beside his head turned and clomped toward the edge of the crowd.

Freddy picked himself up off the floor, dusting off his arms, back, and legs. His hand passed over his pockets, where his wallet had been only a second earlier. "Have you seen my wallet?" he asked the red-tied bureaucrat standing beside him, who only shook his head. He bent over and looked under the people's feet around him, praying without hope that it had simply dropped to the pavement in the scuffle.

"You, did you get a look at his face?" Only shaken heads. "I really need that back," he said to nobody in particular.

Preparing for his altercation with the bikers who were still sitting on the curb, Freddy inflated his courage and walked determinately over in their direction. "Comrades," *maybe if they know I'm one of them, it will help things,* "I think somebody who was masquerading as a revolutionary has stolen my wallet. I'm sure you are appalled to hear that somebody would pretend to be a part of the process just to steal from others. Please, can you help me get it back? I really need it," he said.

"This wallet?" one of the thugs pulled out Freddy's brown wallet from his jacket.

"Yes, that's it. Oh, thank you!" He said gratefully.

"You must be mistaken. This is mine." The thug grinned.

"No, that's mine. Look, that's my passport sticking out of the side," Freddy insisted.

"Listen, gringo, are you accusing me of stealing from you?"

"Well, no. But, well, that's my wallet," Freddy said. "Give it back."

"No, I don't think I will."

"Listen, just give it back to me. I won't press charges." Freddy was reaching the limits of his meager command of the Spanish language.

"Charges?" one of the guys responded as he leaned against his bike. They all laughed raucously, a hacking sound without humor.

"Ya, I won't turn you in to the police."

"Those police?" The man pointed over to the old policeman, who was now curled up under a tree, asleep, the empty bottle held firmly in his iron alcoholic's grip. "I'll take my chances."

"Damn it all, just give me my passport, then."

"Don't know what you're talking about, kid. Maybe it just fell out of your pocket?"

Defeated, Freddy returned to alert the organizers, but nobody was listening. Finally, he sat down on the curb behind the march, frustrated. "Now what am I going to do?"

Mia popped to his side and said, "That's why that dumb-ass who stole my bag only got makeup. You're not supposed to walk around with important documents. Didn't you read the embassy's warning notice?"

"No."

"The crime rate here is pretty high."

"Well, what do I do? Without my passport, I can't leave the country."

"I guess it's your lucky day. Be thankful we aren't protesting the British embassy." Mia pointed to the large gate in front of the embassy. Printed on the front in big, bold letters, a sign read, "American Citizen Services—Open to walk-ins from 12:00 p.m. to 3:00 p.m."

Freddy looked down at his watch and shrugged, standing up from the curb and pushing his way back through the mob. They were still chanting slogans, but lunchtime was approaching, and the midday sun had sapped some of their fervor. He walked to the front of the line and addressed the line of riot policemen manning the barricade. "I need to get by, excuse me. That's my embassy." They gave him an awkward stare through the shields, but his new-found meekness convinced them of his genuine need, and they ultimately opened a crack through which Freddy could pass to the big, iron embassy door.

"Okay, all, it's time to go," the bus driver said. Relieved and exhausted, Freddy's post pubescent army mounted their buses to go back to the airfield; feeling less satisfied than they had hoped after their first day working the revolution. Freddy was already rewriting his version of their assault on the embassy, fine-tuning the details for telling when he returned back to America; he would tell the story with drama and suspense, using creative enhancement to make his family proud. But inside, he nevertheless was left with an empty feeling. Fatigue allowed Freddy to wondered why sometimes in this strange place some things were so magical while others, ones that should be important, felt simply bizarre—or worse, foolish.

24

★ ★ ★

The expensive gold clock on the mantle struck midday, drawing Esmeralda's attention to the ancient relic and reminding her of the trip she had taken to Buenos Aires, accompanying Gonzalo on a special diplomatic mission for the then-president of the republic, Adalberto Cifontes. Adalberto had been an old childhood friend of hers and Gonzalo's; they had played together in the tree house on his expansive family estate when their parents vacationed together in *San Vicente de las Anacondas*, the capital city of the great plains state and the place where Adalberto had been the owner of the largest ranch in the country. It had been a glorious estate with deep ponds to fish, broad rivers to swim, and a special stable for the nation's finest horses. Every year they had gone together to the *finca* to get away from the congestion of the city and—as their parents had said often—see how real Venezuelans lived. Adalberto had moved quickly up the ladder of power, graduating from Harvard and serving as a national assembly deputy, regional governor, and minister before he was hand-picked by the oligarchy to be the next president.

"Ah, Adalberto," Esmeralda sighed in distress. Her friend—like so many others—had left. He was now an old, lonely man living out his last days in exile in Madrid, wanted on charges of public fornication and bestiality after the revolutionary government had released a video of his head juxtaposed upon the protagonist of one of the outdoor shows that took place in La Asuncion, the largest port city in the country. La Asuncion had become an international destination of choice for corrupt sailors and paranoid transvestites, known for its lax regulations and its creative interpretations of the sex act. His daughter had remained in the country, still living in peaceful anonymity in the visitor's cottage at what remained of their ranch in San Vicente. After Adalberto had fled, the lion's share of the *finca* had been seized by the government and redistributed to El Comandante's mother to keep that notorious hag quiet.

Seeing the time, Esmeralda put down her book and struggled to her feet. She went back into her bedroom, sidestepping the liberator's bed and moving over to the closet to prepare for her three-minute shower. She still couldn't believe they'd come into *her house*. "You're going to monitor *my* shower times?" she'd yelled at the infant with the clipboard. But with the threat of a fine or, worse, having her water cut off entirely, she'd just given in.

She put on a smart gray skirt and a frilly pink blouse. She was going out, so she decided against her expensive emeralds of the day before, instead donning a plain gold watch and ring. Even these simple pleasures elicited chastisement. "Madam, it's too dangerous to wear those," Clarita told her as she headed toward the door. "You'd better just leave them off."

Ignoring her maid's advice, she ordered through the intercom for the driver to bring her car. The old, flowing town car pulled around to the front of the house from the underground garage that had once held Gonzalo's antique car collection. The collection had been recuperated by the government for the use of the nation, and occasionally she would see one of the ministers driving around in one of Gonzalo's award-winning cars, tires lowered and a new, expensive sound system pounding out vulgar *reggaeton* music. She got into the car, the only one the revolution had left her, and looked at the leather seats that had begun to crack and the paint that had faded and was peeling and wearing in places. "I thought we were going to get this car painted?" she asked the chauffeur.

"*Señora*, there is none of this color paint left. And the dealership shut down—couldn't get dollars from the ministry. Anyway, the workers went on strike last year."

"I don't remember that," Esmeralda said.

"Yes, ma'am, during the third wave of nationalizations. The workers demanded that the plant be worker-owned, and that they each receive a one-hundred-pound pig for Christmas. The foreign company refused, so El Comandante sent in the soldiers to take it over. But the plant was only an assembly line, and without the parent company sending the parts, the plant just went out of business."

"Right, I remember now. So how do you service this car?" She knew she should keep up on all of this, but the mundane affairs of life after the revolution always left her spent.

"Usually I can find used parts off other cars that are sitting around the junkyard. If not, I get them handmade—I have a guy."

The words that had come to epitomize the revolution, "I have a guy." In this new world, where not only goods and services but also influence was for sale, everybody seemed to need a guy.

"Odd that nobody really complained about that …" the driver just nodded.

"Take me to the club."

"Which club?"

The question made Esmeralda angry. During the height of their wealth, the Coromoto Garcias were members of four discrete clubs, each more luxurious than the last and sprinkled equidistant around the city for their elite convenience and pleasure. During the days of opulence, the *amos del valle* would fly in from around the country to play a round of golf at the club near the small airstrip that was now a military base. After eighteen holes, they would transact billion-Asno deals over a martini and decide the fate of tens of thousands of their peasants over range-fed steak from the great plains at the Michelin-starred restaurant in the main building. The golf course had, unfortunately, come under scrutiny when the management had expelled a high-ranking member of the new government.

One stormy night, the newly-arrived revolutionary bureaucrat had gotten wildly drunk on *aguardiente*, a fact that on its own angered the club owners, for the bar was not supposed to serve the common drink of *pueblo* drunkards. When the bartender suggested he'd probably had enough for the evening, the government man had beaten the bartender to death using a nine-iron stolen from the club's store after smashing the window with the empty bottle of hooch. When the bureaucrat came to the following morning, he was lying sprawled on the curb outside the main club building covered in his own vomit, with the bent and bloody nine-iron still gripped tightly in his hands.

In response to the negative publicity that ensued from the incident, he sued the club for defamation of character, claiming they had staged the whole thing in order to expel him from the club due to his skin color. After a fifteen-minute trial, the revolutionary judge had ruled in favor of the bureaucrat and awarded him the entire club as settlement. In a fit of revolutionary largesse, the bureaucrat offered the entire property to El Comandante, who had the land divided into small plots and held a lottery among the poorest citizens of San Porfirio for ownership of them. The rolling green lawns were now host to thousands of the orange, self-engineered *barrio* structures—and the stink of the raw sewage that ran down the once–bright green hillocks and into the street wafted up to the apartments that surrounded the once-pristine park. The clubhouse had been claimed by thirteen families who rented out the bathrooms and the spa to the community.

Nobody ever mentioned the dead bartender.

The second club was farther from the hustle and bustle of the city and therefore required a greater investment of leisure time from the elites, time that they greatly appreciated as an opportunity to rest from the stresses brought about by their position. "I am so thankful for this place," they would often say. "My life is so difficult and exhausting. My maid went on maternity leave again, and I have to clean the bedroom myself." Coming from the interior to spend a night away from their *fincas* and *sus indiecitos*, they could engage in a friendly wager and a chilled drink around their daughters' polo matches at the equestrian club.

Far up along a cobbled road, into a secluded valley in the mountains, the club had been a cavalry base during the thirty-year dictatorship at the turn of the twentieth century. Since the arrival of more democratic governments, the elites had commandeered the place for their private use. Through a special presidential decree, the base had been given over to an unidentified membership organization, which included all the most important donors to the new democratic president's campaign. A special fund, the national fund for the preservation of historic spaces, was also set up and given an earmark in the national budget for the elites to use to rehabilitate the base into a fully functional club. A much-younger Esmeralda had been on the revitalization committee. She had spent a great deal of time and energy making that club into a beautiful and mystical place unlike any other in the country.

For those who abhorred the long, bumpy drive, a helicopter landing pad was made available. The club consisted of a set of stables, a large polo field, a dozen well-equipped bungalows for those wishing to spend the night, and another Michelin-starred restaurant serving French food prepared by a chef that Esmeralda had insisted upon meeting after having the finest meal of foie gras, duck à l'orange, and cream of asparagus and crab soup at a restaurant in Paris. Upon meeting the cook, who was also young and charming, she had offered him an exorbitant salary from the national fund, and he had signed a lifetime contract to work for the *amos*.

After the arrival of the revolutionary government, the equestrian club had gone back to its predemocratic use. Upon takeover and as they surveyed their national wealth, the military had found the club. The stables full of prize Arabian horses fit their plans perfectly, and in a fit of historic glory El Comandante had sat upon a white charger and announced the reinstitution of the FARS Cavalry. What followed were months of training that left the "recuperated" horses thin and exhausted, the elegant prance gone from their steps and replaced by an ambling, dejected gait. Yet try as they might through periodic beatings and debilitating schedules, the FARS trainers were unable to endow the horses with the requisite skills to fit into modern warfare. Admitting defeat, they sold the horses to the surrounding population, who used them as pack animals to carry bags of rice or stolen electronics to the new barrio invasions that had popped up on the other side of the hill where the polo field had been. Occasionally Esmeralda would see one of her fine, sixteen-hand steeds walking down the streets of San Porfirio, thin as a mule, with a patchy coat and a defeated, angry look in his once-proud eyes. Her French chef had been forced by the revolutionary government, upon pain of prison, to honor his contract and was now the personal cook for El Comandante at the Casa Naranja, where he was denied any salary for fear he would flee. His passport had been seized for reasons of national security.

A third club, which Esmeralda had never visited, was the sports club. It had a gym and state-of-the-art facilities for tennis, racquetball, basketball, soccer, and all other sports the elite had envisioned. Upon learning of this facility, El Comandante had said:

> We will have the greatest revolutionary sports teams in the world, and will finally show the empire that winning at sporting events is not about money paid in exorbitant salaries but about the spirit of revolutionary nationalist pride.

The health club was renamed the National Revolutionary Olympic Training Facility. After fifteen years, it had failed to produce a single Olympian. Doña Esmeralda was still billed for her share of the maintenance of the three clubs.

Doña Esmeralda and Gonzalo had preferred the solitude of the last and, in her mind, most exclusive of the clubs. *El retiro*, as she fondly referred to it, was an old Spanish colonial mansion, formerly the house of a large coffee plantation owner, that had been converted into a place of serenity. Esmeralda considered herself lucky because while the other three had been expropriated, for some reason that defied logic they'd left her preferred club alone.

"*El retiro*, please," she told the chauffeur, and they drove in silence through the traffic.

El retiro had been identified by Esmeralda's great-grandfather when it was only the decrepit remains of an old hacienda that had, during colonial times, been an important source of produce for San Porfirio and coffee for the European markets. Back then, it had been a two day's horse ride from the small colonial town, down muddy lanes and through the thick forest that blanketed the valley in the first youthful years of the nation. The large estancia had a pool with tilapia for food and goldfish for beauty. It had walking trails through the green lushness of the valley into a garden where they had grown carrots, peppers, onions, tomatoes, and yucca. The original owner had been a great colonial rancher—a favored man in the Spanish courts who had inherited a large cattle ranch when the king of Spain had defiled his underage daughter and sent them both to the colonies to avoid repercussions from the court or the church.

But the owner had himself fallen on hard times after choosing the wrong side of a power struggle between one of the generals of the *Armada de Independencia* and his Indian concubine, a girl of eighteen years but such striking beauty that legend of her had spread beyond the borders of the colony to other parts of the empire. To witness this fabled beauty, men would come from all over the colony to dine at the general's house, an imposing structure of two stories on the central plaza in San Porfirio that was a place of importance in the colonial hierarchy. Thinking they came to see him and not his stunning mistress, the general came to believe he commanded such authority and power in the colony that he envisioned *himself* as the next king of a newly independent country and began to act accordingly, holding ever-more-opulent feasts and talking more freely of independence.

The rancher, hearing of the Indian woman's beauty, had also arrived to court her pompous husband in the hopes of a glance at this mysterious woman. At one such event, the rich rancher, still faithfully caring for the royal bastard, had met the brown-skinned beauty. With one mesmerizing whiff of her floral-scented youth, he'd fallen madly and passionately in love. Upon declaring his love to her quietly in erotic secrecy, he'd done what all foolish men do and impregnated her in the wine cellar below the colonial mansion. Now, the rancher was a dark man of Moorish descent, in sharp contrast to the general's white Basque origins. Their forbidden love was discovered when the general witnessed what he thought was his child emerge from the womb of his Indian princess with skin as black as the night sky. The general was so infuriated and humiliated that he ordered his nascent army to destroy the Moor's estancia, salt all the fields, set fire to the buildings, and slaughter all of the cattle and horses. These he used to feed his army, part of which he'd deployed to a neighboring colony after malicious slander about the infidelities of his mistress began to spread.

The Moorish estancia owner was hanged, and the Indian beauty fled, leaving the estancia house in ruins until its recuperation by Esmeralda's great-grandfather. Nobody ever saw the bastard baby again, but all the guests of the club swore to Esmeralda—who didn't believe in such things—that on dark nights during card games or on lazy rainy afternoons sipping gin, they had often seen a small moorish infant crawling through the shadowy areas of the building, an angry gleam in his almond eyes.

Esmeralda entered the estancia with practiced determination. She nodded in approval of one of the last areas in the country untouched by the riffraff. On her immediate left was the men's chamber, where Gonzalo used to drink whiskey and smoke Cuban cigars. It was a warm room of dark colors, wood, and leather with an imposing bar at one side and walls hung with animal heads from the hunts of different members. Often in days of yore they had set out into the tropical mystery of the great plains or up into the mist of the mountains looking for elusive and challenging game. Gonzalo himself had supervised its redecoration when they were only just married. Even empty, it smelled of tobacco and of wealth.

The next door on the left was hers, for when she wanted to use the spa and massage area and then slip into the adjacent tea room shimmering with ornate china and crystal. It sparkled with spectacular brilliance, the angle of the windows just right to catch the late-afternoon sun. It was a quiet place, a place of refuge, where nothing was overlooked.

The resort was staffed by several families of servants, who were most noteworthy for their being almost completely invisible. When he had taken over the property, Esmeralda's great-grandfather had had the foresight to choose the unwanted albino children of the superstitious peasants to serve as the staff. Through exorbitant salaries along with some good-natured threats, he was able, as any good *caudillo* should, to choose the spouses of the staff. He would make regular forays into the villages in his perennial search for the palest albinos he could find, offering these disadvantaged people a place of employ away from superstition and discrimination. Being rejected from society and thought to be cursed, they would quickly and gratefully accept the offers. He then proceeded to stock the servants' kitchen with only milk, white bread, light cheeses, and the like, forbidding the cook to give them any foods with tannins or other colorants, natural or artificial. Through this selective and visionary process, over several generations, he had rendered the retreat's staff invisible to the human eye. Occasionally if they stepped directly into a beam of sunlight or stood against a particularly colorful painting, Esmeralda could see an unnatural shimmer, but for the most part they remained completely unseen.

Esmeralda loved this place. She had come here with her husband on a regular basis to bask in the comfort of collective wealth. "People don't realize how lonely it is to be rich," they would often say as the invisible servants refilled expensive wine glasses. "It is good to have a place to come where we can commiserate without apologizing for ourselves all the time." Murmurs of agreement. "If only we could find something to do with that dreaded riffraff, so we didn't have to see them all the time," they would say as a translucent servant pulled the chairs away, helping them to stand as they moved to the five-course lunch.

Content in the memories of the past and pleased at least for one last place where she could leave her house and commune with like-minded people, Esmeralda approached her guests. They were in the foyer in front of the restaurant toward the rear of the main building. They stood as she approached, still deferential to the respect that she had commanded in bygone days. "Gentlemen," she said, nodding, and they sat down.

The foyer was host to a small lounge and bar for a cocktail before dining. The chairs were large and double-stuffed, designed for comfort, and upholstered in the subtle colors of the Venezuelan mountain scenery. Between them was a large coffee table upon which rested two golden-colored whiskeys, tinkling with ice cubes melting in the tropical heat. Large drops of condensation dripped down the outside of the glasses and pooled in perfect circles around the base of the untouched beverages. The lounge opened luxuriously into the gardens and became a part of the trees, birds, and afternoon sunlight. Around them was an explosion of tropical colors. The smells of the flowers wafted on the delicate afternoon air to tickle the guests, enticing them to relaxation. In the distance, the ornate fountains tinkled in respectful subservience to the environment of elegance. Even the large goldfish and trout from the mountains played their parts.

"Bring me a gin and tonic." Esmeralda demanded her normal drink in the direction of the bar. She straightened her dress, adjusted the top button of her blouse, and patted down her dust-colored hair. Everything in order, she greeted the man on her right. "Hello, Gregorio." Gregorio was from another old family and was a lifelong military man. He'd been minister of defense and still commanded respect among the armed forces for his valiant service and his fair treatment.

"No military uniform for you today, I see," she said, and the gray handlebar mustache that reached across his face turned up in a grin.

"I was told that since I was fired and thrown in jail, it's a *crime* for me to use it." He wore his elegant guayabera and panama hat, imported from Ecuador, with the same military precision.

"A crime? And what about that?" Esmeralda smirked at the general, who adjusted his shirt to cover an obvious bulge. "You know how it is here—can never be too careful. It would be very convenient for the government for me to suffer from 'street crime.'"

She switched her attention to the second man. "And you, my friend, how's the political scene?"

This man had once been a well-known politician. "*Hola Esmeraldita.* I'm afraid after being busy all the time, I'm still not grown accustomed to the leisurely life." He shrugged. "But I'm finding time to reconnect with my constituency. After so many years abroad, it's good to get a feel for the country again. Embassies can be very lonely places."

Maybe it was the nature of politics in Venezuela, but Esmeralda had never trusted this man. She had paid for many of his campaigns but had always kept him at arm's length—*I'm not even really sure why.*

"Are you running for national assembly next year?"

"Well, things are complicated. I guess you haven't seen the news, but I've been banned from politics. Something about a vehicle I bought while I was governor in the Amazon. Me and the other seven hundred people on the black list have taken the government to court—but you know how that goes ..."

"I'm sorry about that. I wish I could help," Esmeralda said unconvincingly.

"Ya, it's difficult. I'd do *anything* to get off that list," the politician said in a low voice, almost to himself.

Doña Esmeralda, the general, and the politician had known each other for many decades. They had attended one of the important boarding schools that trained the offspring of Venezuelan nobility, grooming them to assume the mantle of leadership and authority that was their birthright. After boarding school, they had gone their separate ways, the general joining the military academy, the politician attending the Catholic university, and Doña Esmeralda marrying and preparing for a life of hosting dinner parties and running social projects. She had even had her small intrigue, a brief—a very brief—affair with the general. But that was decades ago, and her husband, God rest his soul, had never found out. There was still tenderness and a twinkle in the general's gaze. Then Gonzalo had died, and she'd been forced unwillingly into the role of businesswoman—a role that she had never fully liked but that she knew she had to embrace. In that *machista* environment, she had learned tenacity, perseverance, and a quick eye for a con—traits that had made her less of a "catch" in the eyes of the conservative Venezuelan elite.

Esmeralda turned matter-of-factly to the last guest, a stranger. "I guess you are the reason we're all here."

"Yes, Esmeralda. I'd like to introduce you to Alejandro Fuentes—*Capitán* Alejandro Fuentes—of the Venezuelan battle cruiser *La Esperanza*." Several years ago, during one of his panic-induced weapons purchases, El Comandante had purchased five used battleships from the French navy. They were rusted relics, taken out of mothballs when the military attaché at the French embassy in San Porfirio smelled an opportunity. Although they were usually in La Asuncion undergoing repairs for serious technical malfunctions due to age and overuse, in his speeches El Comandante portrayed himself as the commander of a massive naval flotilla operational on two oceans.

"*Capitán Fuentes.*" Esmeralda nodded, looking him over. He was also in civilian dress: a pair of crisp new jeans, ironed because he couldn't break the habit, loafers, and a nice two-button shirt. His hard jawline, perfect posture, and formed muscles showed him to be an active military man and a sailor. He had the faraway, empty gaze of one who loved the sea because of its loneliness, not in spite of it.

Rudely ignoring the naval captain, she said to her friend, "*Pero Gregorio*, how do you know he can be trusted? I don't know this man's family."

"Esmeralda, I can assure you, I still have some connections, and I checked him out fully. Sorry, Alejandro. There is nothing to fear."

"We are placing our lives in the hands of a stranger," Esmeralda said.

The politician jumped in. "Our lives are already in the hands of strangers. At least this one is of our choosing."

"Touché," Esmeralda said. "I suppose it's too late to turn back now."

Capitan Alejandro had been watching this exchange with alacrity. Now, for the first time, he spoke.

"Doña Esmeralda." His voice was surprisingly high pitched, contrasting with his physique. He smelled of cheap drugstore cologne, not a bad smell but one to which Esmeralda was unaccustomed, so long had she lived among those with money and power. He was an attractive man, with light skin and blue-green eyes. As he was seated, she couldn't guess his height, but she assumed it was average. When he smiled, a rare occasion, he displayed a large gap between his stained yellow teeth. *Probably from too many cigarettes, a bad habit in the navy.*

"I understand your concern. You don't know me." Alejandro's sweet, high voice was somewhat enchanting. "I am third generation Venezuelan. My grandfather came over fleeing the Great War. When he arrived, we changed our names."

He slowed. "I'm now going to tell you our best-guarded secret—so you know you can trust me."

He swiveled his head behind him, trying to locate the sheen of the invisible servants, and leaned forward. The other three followed his lead reflexively. "Before coming over, when he was packed into a large boat looking for a harbor, my grandfather's name in the old country was Ezekiel."

Esmeralda nodded, understanding.

"We were welcomed into Venezuela those many years ago and have made it our own. But we have kept our traditions, peacefully and secretly, these long years. My grandfather told me the story on his deathbed. They were his last words, but they are our first motivations."

He took a sip of his whiskey, prolonging the moment. It was as if all urgency were put aside as he thought of his family and the long path to now. "And this is the story that my grandfather told. 'You, Alejandro,' he said to me, 'are a polish Jew.' We fled from Poland just before the country was overrun. The anti-Semitism was increasing, and for our family, and our people, things were hard. Every night the rallies filled the air with ever-more-virulent rhetoric. Our kosher butcher shop was burned down, marked with the swastika and the Star of David. On the streets during the day, hard men with foreign eyes distributed pamphlets pronouncing horrible accusations and advocating terrible acts. One night during a pogrom, my grandfather's sister was walking outside looking for some bread and cabbage to cook for dinner when she stumbled upon the mob."

Alejandro's voice cracked as he reflected on the ancient history of his family and his race. "She was wearing a traditional Jewish dress, for back then we did not hide. When the mob, whipped into violent hatred, saw her, they fell upon her. They used their sticks, their fists, their shoes—they beat her to death. But she didn't die immediately.

"When she didn't come back, my grandfather went out looking for her and found her bloody and broken body lying face down in the snow of the town square." Alejandro's only emotion was the clenching of his jaw. "As he turned her over and saw her disfigured face, she said one thing: 'Keep the family safe.' Those words stayed with my grandfather as an admonishment of his failure and a challenge to the future."

A single tear.

"At that moment, my grandfather decided that it was time to go. They started packing up, selling all the precious items collected over the centuries, hiding jewelry and precious gold in different places so the border guards wouldn't take them, and they began the long trek." He was gazing out into the garden at a small, yellow bird that had perched on the edge of the fountain and was delicately bathing its small body, ruffling its feathers in obvious pleasure. "They traveled the length of Europe. With nowhere to go, they marched, with hundreds of other Jews, until they came to the ocean. There, they pooled their money and hired a boat to go to America—they'd heard that there they could be free. But upon arrival, after months packed together in the hull of the only ship they found that would risk that perilous journey through submarine-infested waters with its dejected human cargo, they were refused entry. The Americans, as it turned out, were also racist. For four months they floated aimlessly around the ocean from country to country, seeking asylum. When they ran out of food, they would put into a harbor and exchange some of their jewels for food, water, and wine."

"Finally, they pulled up into La Asuncion. To their terror, a large crowd was waiting for them on the pier; word had gone out that a boat of Jewish refugees was searching the high seas for a welcome port. Here, as in so many other places, must be an angry mob screaming violent words to turn them away. However, when they pulled into the harbor to deliver the message, they were dumbfounded as, instead of insults and rejection, they found the people waiting on the shore for them with open arms. They had come from all over the country with blankets, food, and offers of lodging and even work. For my people, so accustomed to hatred and violence, the response was overwhelming. And we became proudly, steadfastly Venezuelan, forever grateful to this our adoptive nation."

Doña Esmeralda was wrenched back in time. She was an old woman now, much older than this young *capitán*. "I remember that," she said out loud, accessing the dusty parts of her mind. "I was only five or six, but my mother came in and told me to pack up dresses and shoes that I didn't need. I was so angry at being forced to give away my personal things. But I obeyed, and we made the long drive down to the port, stopping by the supermarket to buy food and water. They smelled so bad; they looked so tired and scared. We greeted one family with a blanket and a bowl of soup and even took a family with children into our servants' quarters, giving them a job and a time to get on their feet ..."

"And now," Alejandro said, picking up where Esmeralda left off, his high pitched voice shifting to a businesslike intensity, "it's happening again. El Comandante thinks we don't see the pamphlets that are distributed at his rallies, anti-Semitic propaganda that we're so used to and so watchful for. And he thinks we're fooled when he says publicly that this is the act of only a few. He thinks we don't see the malicious twinkle in his eye when they vandalize our synagogues and raid our schools. That we don't see these for what they are: carefully planned and sanctioned activities. When he screams out the word 'Zionists' at the top of his lungs, to appease his mongrel masses and his new Iranian friends while we suffer anew from stigma and persecution. We have seen all this before. We are not a stupid people, and we know where this leads."

Doña Esmeralda looked at him. "But, Capitán, this is dangerous. Don't you see what the repercussions could be?"

"Ah, but Doña Esmeralda, that is why *I* am perfect. We've hidden our identities and renounced our race—if only in public. It probably seemed like a betrayal to our people at the time, but it serves for moments such as these, moments we knew would come—moments we've watched for," he went on. "And besides, it doesn't matter. So many times in the past we have done nothing, just waited as Russian pogroms destroyed our villages and Nazi Aryans led us to our deaths. But the time to sit back and ignore the signs, while they plan and conspire for our destruction, is over. No longer will we go meekly into the night. The murder must stop, and it must stop here."

And the Capitán sat back and emptied his whiskey glass. He slammed down the tumbler on the coffee table in frustration but with a renewed resolve.

"Okay," said Esmeralda, convinced and moved by the story, "let's get to it."

25

✶ ✶ ✶

"Greetings, my friends—and thank you for coming." Pancho went around the circle, welcoming each old friend generously. "Benito, it's good to see you. How are your cows? Juanita, I hope you brought some coca leaves and *mate*. Fernando, looks like the jungles haven't swallowed you up yet?" He went one by one until all ten members of the Student Freedom Council had received a personal salute. Pancho had a special ability of making people feel as if they were alone among a crowd. They sat down together on the floor of the broken-down old chapel.

He got right to it.

"I know I disappointed many of you. I disappointed myself. There is no excuse. I was heartbroken, and I let you down. But I'm back now, and I'm ready to try again." His companions looked at him with skepticism. Camaraderie is easily broken and difficult to renew, for it only thrives like a parasite in its host—friendship. And from the faces, Pancho knew his work was just beginning. "I see I'm going to have to win your trust again. I understand—that's what I came back for, and I know it's gonna take time. But that is one thing we don't have the luxury of. So, meanwhile, we need to start. I want to thank you for joining me, on such short notice, in this place—our place. We've been meeting here for years—since we started to march and to plan and to make ourselves heard. This place has special meaning for us. Let's all take a moment to appreciate it, to let it welcome us again as it always has." Pancho grew silent and the small group let the memories of better times, of energy and life, fill the space. And with all those memories came the smiling face and carefree charm of Susana.

Back in days long past, their secret hideout had been the central point of worship for a large colonial coffee plantation, up high on a hill just northwest of San Porfirio. The now-bustling capital city of San Porfirio itself had been a village placed equidistant between the two largest coffee plantations in the Americas. The one out east had become a club, but this one had been totally forgotten.

The sophisticated infrastructure of production, processing, and distribution had wrapped itself around this small, delicate berry. Blanketing the hills as far as the eyes could see—the same hills that were now covered with barrios and the uncontrolled sprawling urban growth of poverty—had been the delicate green of the dainty coffee plants. These gentle bushes had spread out under the cover of the larger forest trees, and their tiny red beans—a tropical holly and ivy—decorated the forests and gave the mountainside a perennial festive atmosphere.

The main plantation complex had been a sprawling display of pre-independence opulence. It had an estancia house in which the plantation owner had lived with his family—a large, square structure with many rooms surrounding a central courtyard. The roof was of red tile, and the doors were made of a thick wood and iron. In the evenings, the sounds of the violin and the clinking of crystal that marked the merrymaking of the colonial elite would last well into the night. Rain pattered softly on the expensive tile, creating a warm, comfortable cocoon of luxury. Behind the mansion and over a kilometer away were the houses for the workers, ramshackle lean-tos made of sticks collected from the forest and tied together with homemade rope. The skeletons of the houses were filled in with a mixture of mud, straw, and cattle dung. The same battering of the tropical storms on the thin, tin roofs kept the inhabitants awake at night as they huddled together in the cold and the wet. They worked long days in perpetual bondage to the master, surrendering their harvests to him for a pittance and the protection of his mercenary Spanish forces.

Lying exactly halfway between the mansion and the shacks was a small Catholic chapel where the students had found a resting place. The plantation owner had it specially built to serve the spiritual needs of the poor and allow him the infrequent and sometimes unpleasant opportunity of interacting with his peasants. Two hundred years of abandonment had disintegrated the mighty Spanish structure.

"These ruins will bring us again together," Pancho said to his student generals, who were quietly assembled cross-legged on the floor among the ancient and cluttered ruins of the past, both near and distant.

"As when we used it for our first planning session, I think here we can find our stride again. Up there on the hill, not too far from where we sit this morning, were the homes of the slaves. They were the unwilling architects of their enslavement, because through their toil they made this place profitable. It can't be that over two hundred years later, we are still in bondage, our productivity stolen from us again to serve an overlord, an overlord of our own kind and of our own making, much closer to home—and for this reason more dangerous." Pancho had always been able to rally people to a cause.

But his friends were not ready yet; their bitterness stemmed from the unshakable feeling of abandonment.

"We know why you left," Juanita the Indian said, "but we still feel betrayed. We were gaining momentum, and you let them scare you."

Benito chimed in, his mouth full of spit and chewing tobacco. "Ya, you thought you were the only one they were after? Franco and Rafael were also killed, but that didn't stop us ..." and there were murmurs of approval.

"Fighting for our freedoms can't end when it gets hard," said the young fellow from the mining town. "In fact, when the pressure heats up, that's when you know you are finally making an impact. We had them on the cusp. They were starting to make stupid decisions. They were starting to crack. That's why they killed Susana. To get to you. And it worked ..."

"I loved Susana, and she's gone," Pancho said. "I know that. There's nothing that will bring her back. I have to deal with this fact every day. I wake up with it. I eat lunch in the emptiness of her absence. I sleep alone. It will be this way until I get old and surrender at last to the great black owl of death that comes from the Andes when we are weak to take us back into our final rest in the bosom of the Pachamama." Pancho looked at Juanita, who grinned sadly, understanding the reference.

"But that is my struggle. My cross, and my destiny. I shouldn't have let that affect the rest of you—that isn't leadership. And you're right. I got scared and lost my way. I know I let you down and let down the movement. I don't expect you to understand. Someday, if you forgive me, I'll try to explain what was going through my mind." He stood to his feet and walked one time around the backs of the students sitting in a circle. Juanita had pulled out a metal *mate* gourd with its elaborate metal straw, packing the herbs tightly as Pancho spoke—one layer of leaves, one of sugar, another of leaves, another of sugar until it was full to the top. She then extracted a thermos of hot water from her bag, filled the gourd, and after taking a sip passed it around the circle.

The *mate* that was passed around became a peace pipe.

Pancho stood up, followed by Carlitos, and then one by one they embraced again.

The past set aside, but not forgotten, they sat down.

"What, then, are we going to do?" Carlitos asked Pancho.

"I've been thinking about this a lot," said Pancho. "We gotta hit them where it hurts." Pancho held his breath for a minute, gauging the group.

"What are you thinking?" Benito said.

"They are having another one of these socialist youth exchanges. Let's see what the socialist gringo youth think about the water cannons and tear gas." They all nodded their heads in unison—but in their hearts, they were afraid.

26

* * *

Back at the airport in the center of San Porfirio, the foreign students were settling in for their afternoon events. Freddy was craning his head looking around for his mentor. Where was the emissary? He was starting to feel slightly offended—he'd been expecting the emissary to open up the revolution to him. He didn't like being simply one of the crowd.

"How did you enjoy your protest?" Over the speakers, the distant, diminutive figure of the military man named Machado addressed the conglomeration of youth from atop the stage, his voice reverberating across the distances and bouncing off the adjoining high-rise apartment buildings.

"I think that's the first time they had a group of gringos marching against them. Maybe we ruined their day." More cheers.

After an appropriate, if awkward, silence, the military man continued. "Now we have planned something historic, revolutionary, and spectacular. There are those that say that the revolution is just a peasant's revolt. They say that we are an unsophisticated mob, that we are simply out to steal from the rich to line our pockets. They scoff when we tell them we are fulfilling our sacred duty to free those who are oppressed and to redistribute the economic prizes from which we have so long been excluded."

The military man looked down at the ground. "But, humbly, we must carry out this sacred duty with sophistication and with creativity." He turned around, his back now facing the large group of students. "So, young people the world over, we are going to start this historic celebration with a historic achievement—as a symbol of the redistribution that we are so eager to carry out for those who are less fortunate."

Freddy looked at Mia. "What's he talking about?" he asked.

"I don't know, but they seem to be boiling water in the cauldron."

The lieutenant pointed at the cauldron. "Young people, we have a tradition in the Great Plains, where I come from. To celebrate special occasions, we go with family and friends to the river.— We take precious, life-giving water from our Great River, and animals and vegetables from our fertile land, and we have a soup—*locro*, we call it." He gestured with a flourish. "Today, I have had specially flown in on a helicopter water from the Great River, our life-giver. And today, together, we will make the largest pot of soup ever made in the history of mankind—and it will serve as our dinner, and a visual representation of our redistribution of all the land has to offer. And we will be proving that it is the largest, by submitting the picture and measurements to the Guinness World Records." He stepped back and bowed; a tremendous effort that almost caused him to fall over. Around him the students were applauding.

"Yuck." Ten minutes later, Freddy was elbow deep in raw chicken. "This is disgusting."

His stomach rumbled, and he complained to his companion, "I don't see how we can set this soup to cooking in time for dinner."

"Maybe we should just order a pizza," said Mia. She was standing beside Freddy with a large machete in one hand and a rope in the other. On the other end of the rope, tugging as hard as he could, one of the goats was bleating a bloodcurdling cry of despair. "What am I supposed to do now?" Mia asked Freddy, in obvious denial of her duty.

Freddy just shrugged.

Neither Freddy nor his team had eaten lunch—none of them had been bold enough to buy any of the mystery meat that was pushed through the bus windows at them as they sat in traffic.

"The revolution is sacrifice," he said, as a chicken breast slipped out of his hands and plopped with a sticky smack onto the tarmac. Mia had had an unfortunate encounter with ants earlier as she sat on the lawn in front of the embassy to rest. Now, she was suffering from angry red welts on her arms and probably other parts of her body. She was edging ever closer to the large open gate to the airstrip. Below the blazing signs demanding socialism or death, she carried out an emancipation of her own, letting go of her end of the rope and smacking the goat hard on its hind parts. She watched in satisfaction as the terrified animal ran out of the gate of the airport toward freedom. Smugly, she picked up a carrot and, taking her machete in the other hand, sliced a deep gash into her palm, eliciting a shriek of pain.

The hot equatorial sun was beating down on them, and the combination of their sweat, the overheated chicken, and fumes from the APCs that were constantly patrolling the perimeter behind them had combined to create an awful stench. It was impossible to describe and even more difficult to bear. Between that and the constant squishing of the raw meat in his hands, Freddy was beginning to feel peculiar.

A leg bone cracked, and Freddy dry heaved for several seconds before regaining control of his protesting stomach. The portable latrines were too close to the kitchen and fairground, and as their use increased, those smells were adding themselves enthusiastically to the concoction.

Mia had left and reappeared, looking forlorn, with a white handkerchief wrapped around her ant-bitten, sliced hand. Up above, something golden glinted from a window, and Freddy squinted up to see the military man smirking down over the crowd from the third floor of the administrative building. He raised a large burrito in a salute to Freddy and emptied a glistening bottle of beer.

After more than an hour, the work was almost done. Freddy's hands were swollen from peeling potatoes, cutting chicken, shredding those strange tubers and greens, and ripping the hides off of goats. He had never had such a hard, disgusting job in his life. But at long last he leaned back and surveyed his handiwork. The massive cauldron was full to the brim with river water, vegetables, and meat. Under the cauldron, were fragments from dozens of old-school desks, set ablaze with some jet fuel that one of the soldiers had siphoned out of the large helicopter that lay in pieces on the tarmac. More importantly, Freddy was convinced that they had passed El Comandante's first test. He lay down in the grass to wait, and several hours passed in boredom while the concoction boiled in the midafternoon sun.

"Thank God. The soup is ready. I was about to eat my shoe," Freddy said to Mia as the soldier who called himself Machado stumbled down the steps from his office and onto the tarmac. Freddy was so hungry that he couldn't even pay attention to the speech. He was also having trouble understanding the lieutenant, who was slurring his words heavily.

A dozen paratroopers immediately took their positions beside the steaming cauldron. With military precision, they unpacked, filled, and distributed little Styrofoam bowls brimming with the hot soup. El Comandante's special foreign guests also received a package of crackers and a plastic spoon. Terribly disappointed, Freddy slumped under the tree in the waning hours of the day and slurped his soup.

Yet as Freddy sipped the tasteless soup, his frustration strangely began to melt away. In its place, a strange euphoria started to take hold. He began to giggle uncontrollably. He lifted the tiny spoon to his mouth and dribbled the soup down his chin, and Mia exploded in raucous laughter. Around him his group of thirty companions was also laughing, trying not to spill their soup on themselves or their neighbors. The laughter spread around them into the rank and file of the military and to the thousands of guests.

"What a wonderful day," Freddy said between gasps to Mia. "And what a beautiful country." His soul was lifted up onto the wings of jubilation. He looked around at the band of brothers surrounded by the barbed wire fence and the barking dogs and felt a sense of unity, of camaraderie, and of peace. He looked at the kindly guards, no longer holding guns but instead bushels of flowers, and he smiled. His spirit flew farther over the mountains, where he watched the Indians living as they had for millennia, in perfect social harmony and love with themselves and their land. The llamas were speaking to each other in low voices, contented with their work as they climbed the impossible crevices in the mountains, transporting the lifeblood of commerce to even the most reclusive villages. And Freddy's soul flew on, down over the other side of the snow-capped peaks to hover over the Great River, where the fish frolicked and played, jumping enthusiastically into the nets of the overjoyed fishermen—willing sacrifices to the social well-being of this great nation.

Freddy felt in communion with them all. His spirit became part of the wind and the hills and the rocks, seeing through the eyes of the jaguar in the jungles and of the poisonous dart frog as it searched out its tiny prey. A yellow pastel humming bird flew up from the jungle floor to meet him, a tiny flower in its porcelain beak. It perched on his shoulder, nestling the flower in his hair, and whispered in his ear, "You are welcome here." This place, this paradise, was heaven.

Slowly, Freddy started to return to earth. He was finished with his soup, and those around him were also putting down their bowls to rest and feeling the tingling of the grass against the back of their bare legs as they let the wind caress their hair and massage their cheeks and foreheads. He was glad he had come. This place was special; he was sure of it.

"Wow," Freddy said to Mia. "That was amazing. This Great River must be quite a place." And as he drew his hands through his hair, a tiny flower fell to the ground.

"Tonight—" Freddy noticed through the haze that Machado was again on the stage. As the chatter settled down, the military man pulled out a wrinkled piece of paper from his back pocket. "Ah, yes. Tonight we are going to receive a special gift. We are going to have an evening of entertainment. There is a famous Cuban singer, a true communist, who has agreed to bless us with some of his revolutionary tunes. He has been sick, so has been for a long time in New York seeking treatment, but thank God he is better and is ready again to stand up against the empire and use his words and melodies again as his weapons in the fight to defend our glorious revolution.

This will be his first concert back." *Latin revolutionary music, finally.* Freddy had already forgotten his misgivings.

The sky began to get dark. There was to be a huge bonfire in the center of the runway, and several cadets were dousing the pile of broken-up desks and stray planks and boards that made up the wood pile with some of the jet fuel they'd siphoned from a helicopter. When the last drops of jet fuel had been poured over the odd assortment, one of the cadets threw his cigarette into the pile. The ensuing explosion was fantastic. The heat blast laid Freddy flat on the ground, singeing his eyebrows and melting the bottoms of his shoes.

"Young people." An old man had quietly struggled onto the stage to take his seat. "Welcome."

All eyes turned to the stage, and the carefree chatter quickly subdued. Freddy put down his tray to listen better. "We have a kind of *musica* here in *America Latina*. It's called *musica protesta*. It flows from the broken hearts of a powerless people. It has risen from centuries of domination, oppression, and poverty. For generations our people have struggled to be free and to embrace the birthright of humanity. In solidarity with each other, we have occasionally shed the chains of dictatorship and colonialism to come into a new dawn, at last to embrace our inheritance as free men. An example of that is here, among these wonderful people with their Comandante that has brought them the freedom they now enjoy. But these hard-fought victories have been few and short lived. Again we are falling under the slavery of another imperial domination, this time as serfs to the twice-damned 'free market' through savage capitalism, which warps the minds of your young people and destroys the planet through greed and selfishness. And we are preparing for another fight, this one as epic as anything we have fought before. For in the past we fought against internal dictators who oppressed and enslaved the bodies of our women and children. But this time, we fight against a more insidious enemy, an enemy both within and without who is trying to enslave our minds. And this battle has just begun. The outcomes are unclear—and the future does not look bright."

"Yet we as *latinoamericanos* are accustomed to the fight. It is in our blood, and it is in our heart, and more than anything else it has always been in our music. Through it all, we have always sung. When we were slaves in the sugarcane fields of the Spaniards, we sang to give each other hope. When we were serfs, working the land in bondage to the landowner, we sang to ward off despair and to encourage each other to keep dreaming. When we rotted in their jails because of our opinions or our friends, we sang to give each other strength. This music I am about to play for you is called protest music. We call it protest music because through the centuries of violence and slavery, around the jungle campfires warming our ragtag guerilla armies and over the Spartan meals of peasant poverty, we have uplifted our souls and joined together in a community of protest. As our rebel soldiers—seeking to free their families from the oppression of the nouveau monarchs that still dominate most of our countries—marched against the American-equipped armies of those dictators, we sang. As we fled in defeat from the airplanes and the bombs thrown against our villages and our farms, we sang. When they took our children, forcing them to serve in their armies, or stole our money to pay for their lavish lifestyle, we sang. We sang the protest songs to remind each other of our humanity, to steel our hearts for the difficult struggle and to ennoble our condition. And we still sing the songs of protest, to remind us of the past and the struggle, and to embolden ourselves to continue fighting until the last of our enslaved comrades are living in the glorious utopia of socialist freedom."

Freddy was crying.

"So without further ado," he started strumming his old guitar, "let's start with a song by Mercedes Sosa, *'Todavia Cantamos.'* Because we can still sing."

Freddy closed his eyes and listened to music—songs of passion, of struggle, and of love. Music that filled the heart and the soul with the age-old struggle for freedom and for justice of those desperately seeking to break the chains of poverty and oppression. The melodious voice of the singer mingled with the fire and the approaching night to create a feeling of solidarity and sharing.

Lieutenant Machado emerged from a tent leading five soldiers. "Bring them over here," he commanded, and the soldiers placed several kegs of local beer equidistant throughout the crowd.

"Let me get you one" the military man said and, much to Freddy's delight, sat down beside him. Together the lieutenant and the liberal enjoyed the beer and each other's unlikely company, listening to the music and watching the flames from the fire flicker.

"*This* is what I've been looking for," Freddy confided to Juan Marco Machado, the beer lending him confidence.

The lieutenant winked in return. "It's good you're here to experience and share in what we are trying to build." He gulped down the rest of his beer and got up, patting Freddy on the shoulder and walking back toward his office.

Today I'm a revolutionary, Freddy thought. The mix of the melody, the night sky, and the alcohol reawakened Freddy's soul, and he was sure that something special was happening to him in that small, poor, backward South American country.

27

✳ ✳ ✳

"We've thought this through extensively," Capitan Alejandro said. "Our biggest problem is that the top brass of the military are running drugs. The junior officers who aren't stealing have no leadership around whom to organize." They were sitting in the same places, deep in conversation. Alejandro, as a disciplined *capitán*, had kept himself to one whiskey. Doña Esmeralda was on her fourth G&T and beginning to slur.

"But there have to be some senior members of the army that are still loyal—" she almost said, "to me," but caught herself—"to the way Venezuela was." She turned to the general. "You must still have contacts you could call up?"

General Gregorio said, "Well, Esmeralda, even after all the purges, there *is* still a group of patriots in the Army. I've been in touch with them."

The late afternoon sun was glinting through the window, bathing everything with a golden glow. It was lovely, and in that setting Doña Esmeralda was lulled into a sense of confidence. But for the topic of conversation, she might have been meeting old friends for a late afternoon drink and then dinner thirty years ago. Things had not changed, Gonzalo was still with her, and she still owned her companies and commanded her privilege. The gracious, faithful hand of memory was leading her along a pleasant path, soothing her and reminding her of the endless possibilities the world had held for her. In her mind, for a split second, the world was as it should be.

She was snapped brutally back to reality by the politician's voice. "So what should we do?"

"We've worked up a plan. There are still people here who love freedom and who demand justice. Too often do our corrupt leaders die with impunity, and too infrequently do they have to face the consequences of their actions." Gregorio was pensive. "That must not be the case here. Impunity is rotting out the soul of the country—it cannot go unanswered. There must be justice."

All three nodded in agreement, and the planning continued.

"I understand. Do what you must. I'll get the money. It's late; while we were talking, night fell around us, and it's going to be dangerous getting home. Let's plan to meet tomorrow. Same place." They all nodded, their fates sealed.

28

✳ ✳ ✳

Lieutenant Juan Marco Machado looked sideways at the fat, pimply gringo sitting beside him drinking Venezuelan beer. He was indignant to think that *he* should have to lower himself and interact with this ridiculous American. A boy who in any other world wouldn't receive the time of day but here was an *honored guest of the revolution? What value could he really have to our pursuit for permanent power?* "It's good you're here to experience and share in what we are trying to build," he said to the stupid boy and watched his simple face fill with gratitude. Machado got up quickly and walked away.

In his office above the Russian helicopters, to the tune of the *trova* music and watching the students swaying in equatorial ecstasy, *Teniente Machado* began to receive his daily briefings from his spies. "What do you have for me?" he asked the small man. Authoritarianism breeds intrigue and makes espionage essential, and revolutionary Venezuela was no different.

When Machado had taken command, he thought that his biggest problem was going to be with the students. He had requested copies of all video surveillance of the marches. "That one," he pointed out a student in the opposition march. "What's his name?"

"I'll get it, *mi Teniente.*"

"I need informants." The conversations with his slight intelligence chief had gone on for hours. "Kids who can be bought, threatened, or manipulated. What about this one?"

"He's incorruptible—we've tried. This one has girl troubles," the spy said. He pointed to another. "This one can't pay his college bills."

They had gone one by one through the most visible of the leaders. Together, they had identified five or six, and each received a thorough review.

"At long last, we have him." One of the students, he found out, was addicted to heroin.

"Bring him into my office," Machado instructed.

A few hours later, face to face, he had told the young student, "I know all about your reckless habits, young man. If you do what I tell you, I won't tell your family, and I won't put you in jail for illegal possession of a controlled substance."

Broken, the boy had helped Machado with some information. It was, unfortunately, spotty. He had, however, learned the organizational structure, the names of the leaders, and their methods of coordination.

But he'd also discovered that there was no way into the inner core and that the movement was more centralized and more exclusive than he'd thought at first. His young drug addict could point him in the right direction. And, as it turned out, he'd been worth the effort.

"Our little addict called me last night and told me of the return of the fellow they call Pancho. He's called around to all the leaders. It was him I was following this morning. I followed them all the way to that old chapel outside town," the little man said. "They have been locked up in there all afternoon."

"Hmm," said Teniente Machado. "I see. What do we think they are up to?"

Machado thought, *If I were a student, where would I march to?* "Who were the other students there?" he asked.

"Sir, they were all there, the leaders from all the big universities— the Indian girl, the cowboy, the beach bum, all of 'em. Do you think we should arrest them? I could call in our elite squad and hold them all. Or I could organize a random motorcycle attack on their hideout—show them that we know what they're up to."

"No, you're always too overanxious. You miss opportunities that way. Let's play with them a little instead." Machado had in an instant become dangerous.

"Go back, find out what they are planning. If they sleep there, creep as close as you can without being discovered. Find out their thoughts. We have some time still. Go find out what, when, and where." And the interview was over. The spy chief flashed into a mosquito and flew out the window.

Next, Machado told his assistant to bring in the translucent bartender for a report on the tiresome oligarchs' ongoing conspiracies.

"There were four of them, *mi Teniente.*" Standing in front of Machado was the indistinct shimmer of the invisible bartender from the club. He'd called earlier in the evening, saying he had urgent information. "They stayed for hours," he said.

"Who were they?" Machado asked. The man handed him a small roll of micro-film from a tiny camera.

"Miria," Machado yelled, and in rushed a young girl with bleached-blond hair. "I need this back immediately."

"*Si, señor.*" She took the film and ran down the stairs to the portable lab they'd set up.

They waited, tensely. There was no small talk. Machado kept trying to see the bartender. He turned his head to try and find him out of the corner of his eye, but as soon as he moved his gaze, the man vanished. "Amazing," he murmured.

Finally, the woman returned. "Sorry for the delay. We had to warm up the machine," she said and handed him the pictures.

"I see," Machado said. "I know these three. Old counter-revolutionaries. This man used to be my boss, the former 'minister of defense.'"

He spoke with feigned respect. "He even spent time in prison for his conspiracies—no surprise here. I'm amazed he continues his intrigue after a stint in one of *our* jails." He gave a smirk.

As with the students, the *teniente* had figured out who was up to no good by watching all the places that the oligarchs conspired. Frankly, there weren't many he was worried about. The middle class was in such a desperate shape that they could be counted on to keep their heads down and out of trouble. But there were still a few people with enough money and influence to cause mischief. He'd identified these and had their watering holes watched—even gone to the trouble to bug some of their houses—but this was the first real, actionable intelligence he'd received.

"What were they saying?" He looked toward where he thought the bartender was, although only his eyes were visible above the large black-and-white prints in his hands. He was staring at each one intently and then flipping it onto a pile on his desk.

"Well, *mi Teniente*, they kept their voices very low, but I was able to stagger their drinks enough to hear a lot." Machado saw one of the pictures on his desk move slightly and realized the bartender was standing right beside him. "This one here, this old hag, seemed to be leading the meeting."

"That doesn't surprise me," Machado said. "I doubt they are capable of pulling anything off. Every week there are stupid, angry people who cross the line from disgruntled to conspirators."

Nevertheless, he made a special note of it; this Doña Esmeralda de la Coromoto Garcia—he knew the old hag's name well—still had a lot of money. "Thank you. You've done excellent work for the revolution, and you will be rewarded. You may go. But advise me immediately if they return."

Alone again, he looked at the four people in the picture and made a quick phone call, cryptic in its brevity but fully understood. "I see you're up to no good, again. Were you planning on calling me?"

The voice on the other side of the line started to respond. "Ya, sure," Machado cut him off. "Remember who is paying you, and don't think that you can outsmart us. I know everything. You know how to reach me. I expect an update." And he clicked off the cell phone.

He sighed as if exhausted and ordered Miria to bring him a small coffee. When it arrived, he drained it to the dregs and threw the little plastic cup out the open window, turning his attention to the last item on his to-do list. *This one's trickier, but much more important.*

Since he had taken command of the airport, he had finally come into the kind of opportunity his father had entreated him to watch out for. It was an opportunity too good to pass up—and one that would ensure his perpetual prosperity. Machado had inherited a monopoly on drug running through the airport. As soon as he had realized the extent of the network, he'd moved quickly to have his predecessor killed. This had not been easy, for the man had been his roommate at the military academy. Up until then, he'd only interrogated students, harassed some of the more attractive "conspirators," and physically abused a few old men.

But he'd never killed anybody.

After making the fateful call, it had been weeks before he could look in the mirror again. Weeks of nightmares, occasional nausea, and wild mood swings. He consoled himself that the man had died peacefully, bitten by a *cuaima* in the dark of night. That tiny snake rarely left a mark, and its bite was, he repeated often, painless. Finally, and amazingly—like with everything else—his guilt faded. After the panic-wracked dreams began to subside, he started to enjoy his power.

Emerging from his malaise, he'd replaced all the airport security personnel with his own loyal men. He centralized all the camera feeds and installed new ones—even in the ladies' lavatories, *this one just for fun.*

"I want this place totally locked down," he'd told the new security chief. "I don't want anybody to even sneeze without me knowing about it."

"*Sí, señor,*" was the reply.

"I want to receive the airline manifests and passenger lists for *all* the airplanes coming in and going out." He already had a dozen staff ready to scan the lists for the names of several hundred people whose movements he wanted to track.

"You have been letting people on the no-fly list leave the country. Last week it was one of their *so-called* human rights defenders on their way abroad to some conference to stir up trouble. These people must, conveniently, miss their flights." He'd received a dressing-down from the colonel and passed on his displeasure to his men.

"We have installed the new biometric systems and cameras you ordered. That won't happen again."

"See that it doesn't," Machado said.

"I won't fail you, *mi Teniente*."

Machado had also caught people entering the country with sizable stashes of dollars—trying to avoid the currency controls. He'd had the money seized and wired by his friend in the central bank to his account in the Gran Caymans.

"And lastly," he said in a low growl, "Somebody—and that somebody *isn't me*, is moving product through *my airport*."

"Tell me." Machado stood and walked over to the security chief, looking him directly in the eye. His breath stank of coffee and beer and cigarettes. Machado's bloodshot eyes burrowed deep into the man's soul. "How can this be?"

Machado held the man's gaze for a long, awkward moment. "Do you know about this?" he demanded. "There isn't anything that you are holding back, is there?"

"Nothing, *mi Teniente*." The security chief had started to sweat. Beads of cold perspiration were flowing freely down his pockmarked face and onto his collar. "We search all bags; we even put the dogs on it, although that's sometimes complicated because they bark all the time at everything …" He erupted in a nervous machine-gun laugh.

Machado frowned. "My people in Miami told me that there is product making it through, and they swear it comes from *my* airport. They are unhappy. If they are unhappy, I am unhappy. If I am unhappy, you, my friend, had best take note."

"*Señor*, nobody is more surprised than I am. We look at every *camera*, search every single bag, and place our own shipments throughout. If it's not one of our own, well …" the security man dropped off. "There is only one central baggage handling area, it can't be there …"

"Well, deal with it, *cabrón*. This is unacceptable. And this is how …"

The security chief leaned forward expectantly.

"I want *our* men positioned in the bonded warehouses, managing the Air Chef's packaged food, and dealing with the checked luggage. Each one of them knows their jobs; I've talked to them individually."

"*Sí, señor.*"

Machado nodded. "You may go." The man bowed in subservience as he slinked through the door.

Managing a drug network, Machado had learned, was dangerous—and tricky. But he had been wildly successful, more successful than even he could have imagined. A few weeks ago he had even managed to send several kilos of cocaine in the American Diplomatic Pouch—a feat that made him almost giddy with glee.

Machado collapsed into his chair and started twirling in circles. He hadn't planned to become a drug trafficker. When he'd joined the revolution, his idea was to fight for those less fortunate and defend the poor, lofty goals that had come from the teachings of his mentor, *Padre Ignacio*. He could still hear the last words Ignacio had spoken to him, "It's for the least of these—that is why we make revolution. Never for personal advancement have we sought to build a world for others." But along the way Machado had discovered in himself a new character trait, a trait that helped him get through the difficult times and the less savory tasks: pragmatism. Like many people who'd grown up poor, he'd found it hard to turn down an opportunity to become rich.

He was also very frustrated and anxious by his delay at coming into power, and he was keen to make up for lost time. He'd obliviously been foolishly guarding toll booths while his superiors had, unbeknownst to him, pocketed millions. It was now his turn.

And the more he learned of the scope of it, the more surprised he became. Up in the mountains, where the Indians still chewed coca leaves, the international mafias had set up drug labs for producing cocaine. But far more important, the lax laws and general anarchy of revolutionary government had thrown wide the borders, and drugs began to pour into Venezuela from all sides—from neighbors close and far—for repackaging and transport to the big markets of America and Europe. Machado, from his vantage point, had become witness to the dark underbelly of his peaceful revolution. He knew now the revolution's dirty little secret: everybody was involved. From government ministers to high military officials, from civil servants to the police force and even Supreme Court justices, all sectors of public life competed with each other, sometimes violently, to control the floodgates.

Lecherous gangs from Mexico, America, and Europe had waded into the fray. Russian mafia disenchanted with a post-communist fatherland seized a new opportunity. Chinese triads arrived looking to fuel their world takeover from ungoverned areas much closer to the west. The Salvadoran Maras, the largest gang in the world, who'd learned their trade on the perilous streets of Los Angeles, were also here. And as they all arrived, they fought a bloody war with each other that claimed thousands of lives, innocent and guilty, in an orgy of greed. They fought with each other for space, dividing the cities into turfs that they defended with a tribal brutality. They fought with their suppliers for an increasing share of the profits. They fought with their distributors in paranoia that profits were being missed. And profits were staggering. In their greed, they began to pay their minions in product and in turn fought with the junkies desperate for their next fix.

The violence spiraled out of control, inevitably reaching the morgue in Santa Eduvigis, on the outskirts of San Porfirio, where the bodies began to pile up. Every morning when the mortician, appropriately named Igor—he only had a first name—arrived, he would count the bodies that were dumped by the carload. Fifteen, twenty, thirty, all with bullet wounds, some with heads and hands cut off so they couldn't be identified. And he would carry out his grisly work of stitching together the pieces he could find, readying them for burial.

San Porfirio followed Spanish common law that outlawed the embalming of corpses, so as his workload increased, Igor hired assistants, day laborers taken from the streets and willing to carry out the morbid job for a pittance. For the unclaimed bodies, they set up a special cemetery by the city dump, digging the holes ten feet deep to protect them from the carrion-eating animals and dumping as many as thirty bodies in one bloody, messy heap. After work, Igor would purchase a bottle of *aguardiente* from his local Portuguese vendor and become blindly and violently drunk on a street corner outside his small, middle-class home. Each morning he would awake again and, holding his splitting head, go to dig out from under another night in the new Venezuela.

And the white river of drugs poured through Venezuela, using even the sacred waters of the Great River. Tightly wrapped packages went out on military airplanes. They were transported on mineral barges. They went creeping their way up the islands or the isthmus and into Mexico. They funded a private, secret air force that took the drugs far and wide through the ungoverned airspace of friendly countries. They were shipped on a private navy, via self-engineered submarines and in the hulls of fishing boats. And the drugs fueled instability as they pushed through, a life force of their own, seeking the path of least resistance to their final destinations.

They even funded coups in miserable African countries, setting up puppet narco-governments who followed the orders of their suppliers. Machado had himself participated in one such adventure shortly after assuming control. His promotion to the intelligence services made him a kingpin, and with that came the prestige and power only illicit wealth can bring. One day, he was invited by new friends for a private meeting. They gave him the address of the place, an elite club on the top floor of one of the skyscrapers that adorned San Porfirio's powerful financial district. Walking into the lobby, passing people wearing suits leaving the building on their way to their mundane lives, he felt important. He was greeted by three ominous-looking men with thick arms and sinister demeanors who took him to a back elevator that only moved with a key and a code.

Powering up to the fiftieth floor, he thought of his own meteoric rise and smiled at the simile.

The elevator door opened, and he was ushered into a room lit with rich, dark lighting and with a floor covered in plush purple carpet. On the walls between the ample windows that looked out over San Porfirio, shining like a jewel in the night, were nouveau-art paintings by unknown authors bought for exorbitant prices—the Asnos laundered by the same *capos* that managed this decadent den of drugs. All along the windows was a transparent crystal bar glinting with the rainbow sparkling of liquors brought from near and far to satisfy the exquisite taste of the kingpins. On the far side was a crystal stage where naked women shimmered as they danced—each behind translucent colored glass—spinning around in circles and gyrating as the *first sons of the revolution* looked on, occasionally launching onto the stage themselves to elicit a private dance and frolic in their power.

Machado was directed to a corner where three people were sitting, their watches glinting diamonds and heavy gold weighing down their necks. Their suits were silk and their hair greased, completing the effect as they too became glistening denizens of their shimmering world. Machado took a seat, ordered blue whiskey, and attempted to look the part of the *capo* he'd only recently become.

"We've identified a real opportunity," one of the greased suits said.

"What is it?"

"First, Machado, can you get your hands on an airplane? We need specifically a cargo plane, maybe the size of an Antanov or a C-130."

"It depends what for," he said, hopefully sounding sufficiently influential. The purpose, as it happened, was the transfer of forty tons of weapons to West Africa.

"Our people over there have identified a powerful, up-and-coming young colonel in their weak and dysfunctional army. He's willing to allow us to use his airports as long as we help him with what he needs; his country is on the verge of a revolution of its own."

"And what does our young friend need?" said Machado.

"To free his country? Not very much, some weapons and some hard cash—to pay off people too complicated to kill. Nothing that we can't handle, especially since El Comandante inaugurated our *brand new* Kalashnikov factory. Now the only things cheap in this country are guns and drugs." The *capo* laughed at his own joke. "We've agreed that we'll take an Antanov, fill it up, and send it off. But we need an airplane, the approved flight plan, and a plausible alibi. We figure something like 'a shipment of food in revolutionary solidarity for our poor brethren in Africa.' You can come up what sounds best."

"What do I get out of this?" Machado asked.

"A whole country at your service." And the *capo* leaned back, lit up a Cuban cigar, and grinned—his gold teeth gleaming in the semidarkness. Greed flashed in Machado's eyes, and he quickly agreed. He'd even participated in one of the flights. He wanted to meet this young African colonel himself and watch the arrangements as they were set up. It had been surprisingly easy; nobody monitored the airspace between Venezuela and West Africa, and the distance was short. The whole affair had taken less than twenty-four hours, after which, indeed, there was a small West African country that took orders from Machado and his new friends.

Machado looked at the full-length picture of El Comandante pasted hastily to the wall of his makeshift office at the airstrip. He did not know whether El Comandante himself was involved, although it was difficult to imagine that he wasn't aware. What Machado did know was that the revolution needed the drugs. The violence served to keep the opposition inside their homes, and it could be used to pick off the ones who became too vocal. The money served to pay the willing and sometimes unwilling participants of the revolution. And the dirt that was kicked up stuck to everybody, making trusting each other easier.

He stopped swiveling in his chair, his reverie over, and stood up to look out the window at the end of the concert. He needed to compose himself for his closing remarks.

Just one more thing to do. He called in Miria. "Spread these orders around. You see these four people?" he said, handing her the large black-and-white picture of the conspirators. "For these three, I have written down names. I don't know who the last one is, but by his build and haircut, he looks military. Find out who he is. Then have them all tailed. *Now, go.*"

Machado took a shot of whiskey and marched down the stairs toward the stage. As he walked, he looked at where the bonfire still had embers glowing from the large fire of the night. The heat from the jet fuel had melted a hole five feet wide and one foot deep right smack in the middle of the runway. *We'll have to fix that before El Comandante sees it*, Machado thought. He shook his head, continuing to the stage.

"Young people." He seized the microphone with energy. "I hope you appreciate the lengths this great singer went to, to give you this inspiring socialist concert. We thank our friend the *musico*." Applause. Machado liked to have the opportunity to practice public speaking; it was a handy skill in the new Venezuela. "I want to thank each and every one of you for your commitment to our glorious revolution, and I want to remind you of the important work that we are doing. Work that you yourselves must continue when you return to your home countries, building a world of social justice and equality where nobody is richer or more beautiful than anybody else. You have a lot to think about, and it's late—you must sleep. Tomorrow will come early, and we have more important work to do. Thank you, and have a wonderful night." And with that, the day was over.

Machado went back upstairs, still thinking about his drug network. He didn't consider himself a corrupt man. Corruption, according to his definition, meant to change the ethically accepted way of doing business for personal gain. This wasn't corruption; this was, in fact, the way things were done. *I was poor for a long time, a slave to those bastards. Now the revolution came—to spread around the wealth. Well, I'm sure spreading it around. Besides, how is anybody supposed to live on these military salaries?* His favorite adage, taken from a book he'd read about another revolution, was that African one, "A goat eats where he's tied." And based upon his excellent sense of timing, he'd tied himself to a fine spot. *Ah, there is money to be made there. And in the revolution, I am doing a little bit of redistribution of my own.* He smirked.

29

* * *

Freddy enjoyed the concert like nothing else he could remember. Plied by song and cold gold Venezuelan beer, he repeated often and to anybody who would listen, "I am, today, feeling very revolutionary indeed." He often looked up to the window where the military man was conducting revolutionary business and admired his dedication. His friend wasn't even taking a minute away from the business of running a revolution to enjoy the fruits of the labor; such was the commitment of these soldiers.

He lay back on the smooth grass under the tree, the individual blades poking his shoulders through his shirt, and let the music soothe him. The lyrics from "*Todavia Cantamos*" massaged his angry adolescent soul and built in his mind's eye a world of noble poverty, the honor of the desperate, and the futile fight for equality. He sighed and breathed deeply of the Venezuelan tropical air scented with revolutionary third-world smells of burning wood, gas, the bitter bouquet of the beer, and the soft sweetness of tropical flowers that fell into his lap from the tree above.

Then all of a sudden the music was over, and he snapped awake. All around him, people were getting up, brushing themselves off, and getting ready to leave. He realized, belatedly, that perhaps he'd been a little bit drunk and was thankful for the opportunity to clear the cobwebs from his head before he reached Geronimo's home.

Again he mounted his jeep with his military escort. He repeated the now-familiar journey deep into the hills to his host family. He was anxious to share in his musical experience and hear some of the stories of everyday life here. He jumped out of the jeep, his escort deploying swagger style beside him as he walked up to the house in the barrio. He'd told one of the military of his experience with the gangsters and they had agreed to accompany him to the door, saying, "We can't have anything happen to our gringo guests."

Geronimo received Freddy at the door. "Welcome, *hermano*," he said. "Glad to see you made it back here in one piece."

Freddy entered the small living/dining room area and immediately smelled something fantastic that Geronimo's grandmother was frying on the single range. The sizzling and the smells made Freddy realize that he was hungry again. "We'd be more than happy if you joined us," said Gernomio. "Just a late-night snack—waiting for my favorite part of the day."

The smells were coming from a fried cornmeal pancake, which they would eat with a locally made salty cheese, slathered in mayonnaise. A filling and cheap food, perfect for those who couldn't afford to eat more than once a day. With their patties on diverse and chipped plates, they sat around the living room. Freddy cut into the pancake and savored the mealy texture and the contrast between sweet and salty, giving it an energetic nod of approval accompanied by the requisite mumble between the mouthfuls of meal.

"Before the revolution," Geronimo's grandmother groaned as she folded herself into a creaking wood-and-leather rocking chair and started swaying back and forth, "There was nothing up here in the barrios. We were alone, abandoned. The government didn't care. The rich people sure as hell didn't care. The only medicine was down in the expensive hospitals in the valley. There weren't any social workers, any community mobilizers, or any social programs. Now we have volunteer doctors *right here* that we can see if we feel poorly, even at night. It's true that they don't have much equipment, training, or supplies, but we know because they're here that El Comandante cares for us—and they're doing what they can. Before, there was no money for us either; we had to depend on the odd jobs that the rich would throw our way. Now we receive our fair share for organizing our communities. Sometimes they even approve our community projects, like a new staircase or a new pathway between the houses." The ancient woman was more thoughtful this evening, less electric than the night before.

"That must have been hard." Freddy wanted to keep her talking, to hear the stories of their suffering and how their lives were being changed by El Comandante.

"Oh, *mijito*, you have no idea. I remember one night, when Geronimo was just a boy, he got sick. He was so hot, so very hot. It was late and the jeeps had stopped running. I didn't know what to do. I tucked him into a blanket and wrapped him in my arms, and we started walking. Down the hill we went. It was so dark outside, and I slipped—I didn't see a large hole—and I bloodied my hand and knee while trying to break my fall and protect Geronimo's hot little head." She presented her hand for Freddy's examination.

"It took me hours, but I finally made it down to the highway. Standing there on the side of the road with this little bundle, I tried to flag down a car. They passed me by—Mercedes, luxurious *camiones*—none of them would stop for me. They flashed their lights and honked, moving into the far lane. I walked for three more hours until I came to one of *their* clinics on the east side of town and asked if I could see the doctor. I was exhausted. It was so dark and damp outside, and the blood had hardened into a nasty welt on my palm."

"What happened then?" Freddy asked.

"Nothing. The beautiful nurse, all dressed up nice and clean, just looked at me as if I had fallen out of a tree and asked me if I had insurance or money. I said, 'of course not,' and she told me I must go to the opposite side of town to the *free* city hospital. I told her it was too far away to walk and I didn't have any money for a taxi, but she just shrugged and walked away."

Freddy had stopped eating and was listening, eyes moistened by the story.

"And then the strangest thing happened. I walked outside and sat down on the curb with my little hot bundle. I started to cry—I was so desperate. Just then a young taxi driver pulled up in front of us. He was wild and unruly, his dark hair was long and thick, and his smile glinted through the full beard. He said, 'My name is Enrique,' and then he asked me where I needed to go. I told him that I didn't have any money. He said it didn't matter, and he drove us all the way across San Porfirio to the *free* hospital. When I got out of the car, I asked him, '*Señor*, how can I thank you?' and he looked up at me through the window, turned down the music, and said only, 'Don't worry, *vieja*, revolution is coming.' And he just drove away. I often wonder what happened to that young man."

She was silent a long time and then said, "Before, we had nothing and watched the rich with their cars and their restaurants and their malls, and we were stuck here. At least El Comandante is sticking it to them, too; they are finally getting their payback." In this tiny, poor house nestled among countless others up on a hill overlooking an extensive valley, the unuttered word of the revolution *screamed* to be heard—revenge.

"In America, we are not too far from revolution," Freddy responded. "The fat cats in Washington have for too long ignored the will of the people. Soon they will find out about our wrath."

He was even beginning to believe that. The more they repeated the word, and the longer he stayed in Venezuela, the more he thought anything was possible. "I will be the first, me and my family, to usher in our own socialist revolution. We want everybody to be the same; we don't want any differences in our society."

"Well, my boy," the grandmother said, grunting as she stood, "Good luck with that. I must now be off to bed. Tomorrow will come early again for me." And with that, she was gone.

Freddy and Geronimo stayed up talking late into the night. They talked in sweeping, broad generalities about topics near and far—a conversation of youth and virility and anger. Freddy was astonished at how much more educated Geronimo was than himself and made up his mind to study further the great writers and important ideas. Finally, it was approaching midnight. "Watch this," Geronimo said. Onto the screen pranced the little mule, the nation's mascot, leading the national anthem. As the song played out, Geronimo and Freddy stood up, their hands over their hearts. Then, the announcer came on. "And now, the midnight cocktail."

Onto the screen came sixty seconds of the most brutal pornography that Freddy had ever seen. For one endless minute he witnessed things that would haunt him forever and leave within him unanswered and unaskable questions for the rest of his life. Then, as quickly as it came, it was over. "That," Geronimo said, grinning, "Is my favorite minute of the day."

Freddy said nothing. Stunned by the display he'd just witnessed, he only nodded and went to bed.

30

* * *

The students unloaded their cars with supplies needed for their night together in that musty, earthy old chapel. A few sleeping bags, a gas lantern, a gas range, some cans of food, several candles, even a guitar. Juanita pulled out a blanket woven by her grandmother from alpaca fur, resplendent in colors and wonderfully soft to the touch. She was about to lay it onto the dirty floor when Pancho asked, "What about your sleeping bag?"

"I don't own one," Juanita said shyly, looking away.

Remembering Juanita's poverty, Pancho asked, "Would you like to share with me?" and they made their nest using Pancho's sleeping bag covered with the beautiful blanket to protect them against the misty mountain night air. The earthen goodness of the land wafted in, filling the chapel until it was replaced by the delightful aroma emanating from the simple sizzling of their spartan meal on the portable gas stove. Carlitos pulled a bottle of rum out from his duffel bag and lit one of the gas lamps that would illuminate their vigil. They talked about the future, what plans they had. They talked about what they would do the next day, and the following. How they would free their country for themselves and their children.

Benito, the big cowboy from the Great Plains and by far the most musical of the students, pulled his guitar out of its case and began to strum the song aptly named "*Ojala*"—"I Hope." One by one, the students' voices rose in unison, uplifted in defiance against dictatorship and tyranny. Finally at the last chorus they all stood and belted out the song to the mist and the night. The owls that nested in the rafters above swiveled their heads and looked down at the small group. This chapel had seen this before—so many times. Groups of young people, angered, seeking revolution. Revolution that would bring them into long-awaited freedom. At that moment, they were connected back through time with the revolutionaries who themselves sang "*Ojala*" in defiance of their own dictators. So long ago, bands of people, of a different ideology and a different vision, had opted for freedom. The irony was not lost on Pancho that somewhere in these forests, maybe even in the same place, El Comandante himself had probably sung this song and dreamed of the moment he would chase away his enemies. And how telling that with the passing of the years the revolution, and he himself, had come to resemble all the things he claimed to have fought against. The song, this important protest song, came to an end—and there was silence.

"My great-aunt," Carlitos said after a while, "Was one of the rich people. Her family owned everything, even the electric company at one time. You know, where Pancho's dad works? She tells me stories about how things were back in the day, peaceful and serene with no violence or hatred—just the harmony of people building a country together."

"Don't you think that's maybe the memory of a nostalgic old woman?" Juanita asked. "We are poor now. But back then my family wasn't any better off. I don't remember Venezuela the way your aunt did. I remember a lot of suffering and misery. I am not here to return to those times. I am here because, on top of being poor and miserable, I don't want to lose my freedom too."

"My family," Pancho said, "Came over from Italy to avoid just this type of problem. We escaped Mussolini and lost everything in the process. Now, here we are. After three generations of rebuilding, we are plunged into another dictatorship that will probably leave us poor and hopeless again. It's more clear to me now than ever why people go to America—there at least you can build without the fear of somebody coming along to destroy all your hard work."

The inside of the chapel was narrow and musty, smelling of rotten wood and clean earth. Above, in the rafters, the barn owls settled in, hooting into the crisp cool night. The ten friends were strewn haphazardly around their lamp, nestled inside their sleeping bags on the cracked and crumbling stone blocks that made up the chapel floor. The altitude was high, and it was cool outside; and there were no bugs or mosquitoes to bother them. That night, the rum became their Eucharist, and their communion grew as they passed the bottle around, filling up coffee mugs, tumblers, and Styrofoam cups. That night, the sweet nectar of the sugarcane fields did not inebriate, and as they passed it around the euphoria produced was not a lessening of the senses but a heightening; like a miracle of old, the rum bottle never emptied but continued to dispense the exhilarating elixir long into the night.

Up above them in the rafters, one of the owls—one that was not like the others, for it was larger and darker—took special interest in the conversation and committed to memory the faces, names, and plans.

31

* * *

The lieutenant had said good-bye to the students and finished his affairs for the day, and he was finally settling in for the night. He had a busy day tomorrow, and had received bad news—there were student revolts and conspiracies, and somebody was interfering with his drug network. *Many people will suffer when I get through with them.* A malice that came more and more frequently soothed his anxious spirit, lulling him to sleep.

* * *

The old lady had returned home. She had caught the last part of the concert on television—the government had again taken over the airwaves, and since she had nothing left to do, she let the music that had been her music soothe her aching soul. "Remember, Gonzalo, back when he was a friend of ours?" she said as the old musician sang songs of revolution.

"Yes, Esmeralda." Gonzalo's ghost had been waiting for her upon her return home. "I remember the private concerts like they were yesterday. Right over there"—and he lifted a translucent finger— "the same songs. Then we would drink until the sun rose."

"Those songs meant something different to us back then," Esmeralda said. "Doesn't he see? Doesn't he know what they are doing to us?"

Gonzalo just shrugged.

She wondered if the singer ever thought about them and their enduring friendship that had faded. El Comandante's touch brought death and destruction, shattering even time-worn friendships, those deepest of friendships that are not born out of mutual agreement but of mutual respect. What would the singer say if he knew the government was just using him? But people were behaving *so* strangely when it came to the new Venezuela. She drifted off to sleep, relatively sober for the first time in a long time, and slept the sleep of the hopeful.

* * *

Young Freddy, finally sleeping, albeit in a foreign bed, in a foreign country, and after a long and strange day, was tired. He was tired from the myriad of emotions and the cruel contradictions that he hadn't expected. Something itched inside, a scratch he was afraid to soothe. This night, not even the sporadic gunfire of the perilous barrios disturbed his slumber. But disturbing dreams woke him often and energetically, dreams that would haunt him for a long time.

* * *

And Pancho snuggled close in his sleeping bag, sharing his precious space with his coconspirators—as he had done with Susana in the not-so-distant past. The mountain air descended, bringing with it a chilling but refreshing fog. The smell of the earth around the chapel was reinvigorating, and the grateful hooting of the owls transported him back in time. He didn't dream, instead choosing to allow his heavy spirit to lift the weights of responsibility and the duties at hand and embrace the young man that he knew he still should be.

And around them all, the power was again extinguished, as if the eyes of the city had been plucked out and devoured by the monster. The cool Venezuelan night blanketed the city below in darkness and terror. Those who could shut fast their homes and prayed for morning to come quickly. Those who could not prayed equally hard for their deliverance from yet another night of blackness. In the few installations of national security, the nouveau riche were busy gambling late into the night, drinking their expensive whiskeys. They toasted to El Comandante, raising their crystal glasses high over their heads as they selected the finest whores—some of them the firstborn daughters of formerly middle-class families. The smoke from the fine Cuban cigars wafted around their heads like clouds and into the rafters—and the revolution advanced.

32

✳ ✳ ✳

Freddy woke up refreshed from the overwhelming day before. He felt today less of an intruder, like at last he was connecting better with Venezuela. His sleep, however, had been plagued by nightmares—scenes cut from last night's midnight cocktail interwoven with memories of the lieutenant. They'd been sharp, disturbing erotic dreams featuring Geronimo's grandmother, which left him somewhat ashamed. "*Hola, mijito,*" Geronimo's grandmother greeted him as he came out of the room, making Freddy wince.

"*Hola,*" he said in return. He looked the other way, trying to escape a simple chat that seemed this morning indecent.

"Here you go." Freddy was relieved when Geronimo came out of the small kitchen and handed him a cup of steaming, black Venezuelan coffee, thick with sugar. "Our finest." Freddy sniffed the pungent, earthy aroma and was immediately refreshed and wide awake.

"You can't get this in the supermarkets anymore." Geronimo grinned his toothy smile. "Oh, and I've got some good news." I pulled some strings. This morning we will be working together on a project I'm working on, part of the *Iniciativas Sociales*. There are many different projects, all designed to advance our socialist vision, but I asked yesterday that you join mine so you can get a feel for some of the important work that I do."

"Sounds great," Freddy said. "Looks like we'll be doing some of the real revolutionary work today. That's kinda what I wanted to do, actually. I understand that this whole process isn't necessarily flashy, and I want to get a feel for some of the *plodding* that you have to do to make a revolution stick. I mean, don't get me wrong, the concert was fantastic. But you can't do that every day, right?"

Geronimo beamed. "You, my friend, have the makings of a great revolutionary. Let's go." They headed out, down the stairs and through the alleys to their waiting jeep—just in time to take the long ride back to the airfield, watching as the barrio stretched, yawned, and started to breathe again after the darkness. Through the awakening streets citizens were cleaning up from another frightful night. There were burned cars, charred bodies, and everywhere the pockmarks of bullet holes. Men in red shirts were hurriedly plastering over the holes with posters of El Comandante.

Freddy had put on his special shirt of el Che and was very pleased that Geronimo noticed it. "I see you are wearing the colors of a true freedom fighter."

"Yes indeed." Freddy beamed.

Arriving at the airport, they found the lieutenant already well into his morning announcements. "My young friends," he said, "today we'll be hearing first from the minister of social development, who will explain the importance of *Iniciativas Sociales* in the revolution's plan to reach the poorest people and advance the cause of peaceful socialism. Let us welcome him with a round of applause."

Up onto the stage leapt an energetic young man. "He's from the communist party, and he's kinda my boss," said Geronimo, explaining the unasked question. His shirt showed a large orange hammer and sickle, and on his hat was an embroidered image of Lenin.

"Greetings, comrades. My name is Nixon Bustamante, and I want to give you a warm revolutionary welcome." He looked to be about thirty years old and was in the early stages of trying to grow a goatee but, like Freddy, didn't have enough facial hair. The ensuing misfortune was a pubescent plume that made him look sheepish. Freddy immediately liked him. He had short hair, designer pants, and a red bracelet. He wore expensive sunglasses even at this early hour of the morning.

"Today I come to talk to you about my work. I coordinate the Ministry of Social Initiatives. El Comandante has embarked upon a program of social redistribution, finally recuperating the wealth of the nation through taxes and the nationalization of formerly privatized industries, especially extractive industries and the chain of production and distribution, and is creating through these equalization schemes the beginnings of a workers' paradise." He took a deep breath after that difficult run-on sentence and continued.

"When he announced the creation of these social initiatives, people said it would take away from the money going to the health and education ministries. But El Comandante has answered those criticisms and given us—good soldiers all—our marching orders. First must come equalization through the acts of, well, let's say leveling the playing field, after which the now-equal citizens can be organized into productive groups to combat the shortages that we are currently having. These shortages—be they in health care, education, food, medicine, or building supplies—are only hiccups, necessary speed bumps along the road to social justice. Finally, when the back of the capitalist machinery is broken, we will be able to assure that every poor, uneducated person is treated the same as every *rich*, or *intelligent*, or *good looking*, or *innovative* person." These words the communist spat out in sarcastic venom.

"Learning from communist projects across the world—" Freddy noticed with admiration that unlike other revolutionary leaders, this man did not avoid the word "communist," substituting the more soothing word "socialist"—"El Comandante first set in place social initiatives for reading and writing, where the adult and elderly are taught those basic rights."

According to Freddy's research, only about one or two percent of the population of Venezuela was illiterate. "The program must really be working," Freddy whispered.

"Then, emerging from illiteracy, people are organized into councils where they are given Asnos from the state for their own productive projects. Simultaneously, there are social initiatives that have set up small kiosks where poor people can buy food for subsidized prices. There are tree-planting initiatives. There are initiatives where people care for the homeless. There are initiatives where people band together to make their own electricity. And many others. These are an essential backbone of this peaceful revolution and are under my purview as minister." The young man smiled broadly with pride.

"Now let me introduce you to my nephew." A boy emerged from the crowd and walked onto the stage. "Smile wide for everybody," the communist ordered, and the gleaming metal wires of braces glistened in the morning sunlight.

"Through our social initiative for teeth, everybody has the chance to participate in a lottery for braces. For those who get the braces, life is improved. And for those who haven't won yet, their life is also improved through hope—real hope for a better future—and hope is the primary emotion of our revolution."

As the young boy left the stage, lips curled uncomfortably around the large wires, the communist continued, "It is essential, of course, that during this process we work closely with the sectors of the government that are tasked with enforcing the *fairness coefficient*. This is important. How else could we find resources for our political and social projects?" The question hung heavy for a moment in the air. "And without resources, what good is redistribution?"

Another important question, Freddy thought. The minister raised his arm for emphasis, and a morning beam of sun glittered off his expensive gold bracelet. "Because until that wealth is either destroyed or redistributed, there is no way to create an equal society."

Finished with his speech, he descended the platform and tripped on one of his bodyguards who wasn't paying attention. He dove headlong into his large purple sport utility vehicle and banged his elbow on the heavy armored door. His cursing was heard across the assembly as he ripped open the door, slamming it heavily behind him and peeling through the airport exit and onto the highway.

"Come this way." Freddy noticed that Geronimo had vanished for a few minutes, but had reappeared with a large red backpack for Freddy. "Like I said, you're with me today."

Freddy opened the backpack. "Light bulbs?"

"Actually, they're fluorescent, long-lasting halogen bulbs," Geronimo said. "As you probably figured out, we here in Venezuela are having a challenge with the electricity. The empire has laced the clouds with a special solution, so it doesn't rain. At the same time, they have engaged in asymmetrical warfare against our hydroelectric plant, shutting down ninety percent of the turbines. Our engineers can't identify how they did it yet, because they made it look like they just rusted shut and filled up with mud, but we know it was the work of the empire. El Comandante said so, and he's got the spies. So we, as good citizens, are fighting back." Geronimo's eyes gleamed. "These light bulbs were specially made in Cuba, and they consume much less power than the other ones that are so popular here—pushed by imperial companies."

Freddy unzipped the bag, selected a bulb for inspection, and pulled it out, reading the inscription around the band, "A Gift from the Revolution." It looked exactly like an ordinary light bulb, and he just shrugged, replacing it carefully in the backpack.

"So what do we do with 'em?" asked Freddy, truly at a loss.

"Well, we go house by house and offer to go inside and change their old light bulbs for them, replacing them with our better ones."

Seems a bit labor intensive, but I'll give it a try, Freddy thought. "Just one question. What happens if one burns out? How do they get a replacement—are these sold in hardware stores?"

Geronimo didn't miss a beat. "No, they aren't sold in stores. We can't give the capitalists that kind of control over our plans. But no worries, they are guaranteed to last a long time." He set off energetically toward the airstrip exit.

"There is one more thing," Geronimo said. He pulled out a sheet of paper from his jeans pocket as he walked. "We are targeting the middle-class neighborhood right over there."

He pointed to the other side of the highway. "And one of our jobs, to kill two birds with one stone, if I may, is a brief, informal census. We'll be gathering information on each house. How big it is, how many people live there, how many rooms it has, how many bathrooms it has, how many TVs it has, whether they have two refrigerators, and so on. This is truly important work, in case in the future, for some emergency purpose that nobody foresees—because the government's housing projects are just now getting on their feet after much sabotage by the empire, so we'll very soon be able to take care of our own—we need a temporary place to house patriots who need a place to live."

They maneuvered through the throng of red-shirted gringos all clamoring to get to the exit. Some had red brooms clenched tightly in their hands; others were straining under large bags of food. There were some with small seedlings and a few were following white-coated doctors who spoke with an accent Freddy could barely understand. They made it to the exit, set off down the street, crossed the highway, and entered a middle-class neighborhood. Having spent all his short time in the barrios, Freddy was stunned by the difference. The first thing he noticed was that there were almost no posters promoting the revolution. He had become accustomed to the posters, flags, stickers, and other accoutrements of the revolution—to be in a place that looked bare to him was strange. People were walking briskly, it was clean, and the shrubs and trees were neatly pruned.

The first building they arrived at was maybe thirty stories tall. There was a gate that was propped open; while there was no doorman, it did have an unarmed, uniformed guard walking rounds around the premises. The guard gave Geronimo a knowing wink and let him into the front door of the building. Inside the building there were was a neat foyer with plants and some comfortable chairs and a large set of intercom buttons. On one side of the foyer were two elevators, one for the odd floors and one for even ones. The stairs were barred by a large steel door. Geronimo pushed one of the intercom buttons. "Who is it?" the voice from the inside answered.

"Social Initiative for Revolutionary Light bulbs," Geronimo said into the microphone. "We are here to make sure you are compliant with the new decree number 134987, which instructs all Venezuelans to use only halogen light bulbs. I am here to provide you with the aforementioned bulbs for your convenience."

A short pause. "Go to hell, there are no communists here." The click was defiant.

Freddy was stung, as if by a bee, immediately hurt and a little angry.

Noting his chagrin, Geronimo said, "You get lots of responses like that. Don't worry."

"But what do we do if they refuse?" Freddy asked. But Geronimo was already buzzing back.

"Yes?" came the voice.

Geronimo continued as if uninterrupted. "If you are unwilling to follow the laws of the republic and collaborate with the revolution, you will be reported to the proper authorities for the appropriate administrative action."

"Kiss my ass, you bastard," and another click.

"What do we do now?" asked Freddy.

"Well, every building has a live-in property manager. We've organized them into Unions of Property Managers in Defense of the Revolution and put them on a stipend. They meet on a weekly basis to give information about the people in their building to the government. Stuff like who pays their bills late, who has women coming and going, who is cheating on their wife, who drinks too much, and who is conspiring. You know, stuff we can use if we need to. After we're done with this building, I'll give a report apartment by apartment to the property manager. The day will come when people will be targeted for redistribution, and those that were unhelpful will be first on the list."

"But what if the property managers refuse to cooperate?"

"We thought of that. We've made property management a civil service job, so we can screen and place the right people where we need them."

"Does that work?" Freddy asked.

"Most of the time. You should have seen one old hag with a stupid little useless dog. It was a few months ago, and I was installing the shower timers."

"Shower timers?" Freddy asked.

"Ya—that's another story. Anyway, she lives in a huge, rich house up on top of that hill." Geronimo gestured out the large window on the far side of the lobby. "Really fantastic old place. Anyway, she called me names, she threatened me. Told me she used to be famous or something. 'Do you know who I am?' she kept saying. I said, 'That's the power of the revolution, I don't know who you are and now I don't have to care, El Comandante has made us all the same.' Man, she went crazy. I thought she was going to hit me. I'd never seen anything like it."

"So you reported her." Freddy grinned conspiratorially.

"Yup, I put her on a special list, for urgent cases." He grinned. "She got the surprise of her life."

Geronimo buzzed the next apartment.

"Yes?" came the answer.

"We are here to make sure you are compliant with the new decree dictated by El Comandante, decree number 134987, which instructs all Venezuelans to use only the halogen light bulbs I am prepared to provide for you."

"Must it be now? I'm just out of the shower."

"I'm afraid it must, madam. Please let us in." Geronimo repeated the previous threat.

"Oh, well, come on up." She buzzed open the iron door on the stairs, and with that they were in the building. They climbed the stairs up to the first floor. Standing in front of the open door was the most beautiful girl Freddy had ever seen. Legs, busty, blond, and dressed only in a large green towel—Freddy was immediately in love.

"Do what you must." She frowned. Freddy was amazed at the power of the revolution to get into people's homes at even the most intimate moments.

"We'll start in *your* bedroom." Geronimo winked at her, and they marched without permission straight into the girl's bedroom. There laid out neatly and cleanly on the bed was her underwear, a blue thong and a lacy bra. Geronimo just grabbed them, throwing them into a pile on the floor as he stepped up onto the unmade bed to change the light bulb. To make sure it worked, Geronimo clicked it on, and a weak, sickly green light flooded the room. The vivid colors, the flowered wallpaper, the colorful hand-painted wooden armoire, and the rich fabric of expensive clothes became instantly distorted. The natural hue of white light was corrupted into an aberration, an abomination of color, and a depressing, oppressive pall fell across everything in the room.

"There we go," Geronimo said cheerfully, and they moved on to the next room. While Geronimo was changing the lights in each of the rooms, Freddy was counting the rooms, the TV sets, the refrigerator, and the washer and dryer. The whole process took them ten minutes. They finished and walked out to the living room. The beautiful woman waited impatiently beside the open door into the hallway.

"Thank you for your cooperation," Geronimo said professionally. He grinned and nonchalantly reached under her towel to give her a little squeeze. Her face immediately drained of all color. Geronimo winked again and turned to leave. Her shock quickly turned to fury, and she raised her hand, stretched flat, to slap Geronimo across the back of the head.

Geronimo stopped and slowly turned to face the woman, looking at her directly in the eyes. "Yes?"

The woman's uplifted hand shook as it fell slowly back to her side, and she retreated behind the flimsy protection of the green towel, as if all of a sudden realizing her position and her condition in front of these unknown men. "I thought so," Geronimo said, and a malicious smile, one new to Freddy, slithered across his face. "Thank you for your cooperation." He gave the young woman the party salute and walked out into the hall.

"I'll report you," she threatened, finally finding her voice.

"Ya? To whom? How?" Geronimo had turned around and made as if to reenter the apartment.

"I'm sure you have a boss."

"Do your best," Geronimo said. "How would you like me to come live with you? I live in the barrios, and I kind of like this apartment."

"How many extra rooms does she have?" he addressed Freddy, who looked down at the note pad where he'd been writing. The woman's face turned the shade of her towel.

"You wouldn't dare."

"Don't push me, ma'am. You don't know what we're capable of."

Freddy followed this exchange with awe. Violence was suddenly all around them. The seething undercurrents of the new power relationships in this people's revolution had all of a sudden been exposed into a sickly green light not unlike the that cast by the bulbs they were installing. *This is turning things on their heads for sure.*

The young woman recovered, slamming the steel door in their face with finality. Her expletives followed them down the stairway. "What was she going to do? We've got the power now." Geronimo answered Freddy's unasked question.

"Let's get to work. We gotta cover this whole block today." They went to the next apartment.

33

✳ ✳ ✳

Pancho woke up in the early morning, long before his coconspirators, who were curled together in a jumbled pile of arms and legs, snoring soundly and comfortably in the early-morning silence. Careful to not wake Juanita, he slipped out of the small sleeping bag he'd shared with her the whole night, cuddled together in a platonic embrace. He thought he'd take a walk to clear his head before they fired up their small gas stove to make some coffee and a simple breakfast. Predawn darkness stretched across the length of the *finca*. It was quiet—the intense and still quiet of those last moments of night when the sun is at once a vague rumor and a distant memory.

He walked from the little chapel and up the narrow, still-worn path toward where the peasant houses had been those many generations ago. The walk was only a few minutes, twenty at most, but for Pancho the time had no measure. All around, the silence of the forest engulfed him. The little coffee trees, now unattended and underutilized, were laden heavy with their ripe red fruit. Years ago, this farm had been *recuperated* for the people, and since then had been abandoned, nobody caring for its temperamental harvest. The refuse of precious wasted years, fallen unharvested to the earth, had disintegrated into a robust, sweet-smelling mulch that gave the entire forest the aroma of day-old coffee. Up above, in the centuries-old Caribbean Trumpet trees, he could hear the parrots chattering with each other in their incessant squawking. All around him rained the rejected seedlings, bare of fruit after parrots stripped each bean of its meat. The occasional bat zoomed above his head, blindly seeking a last cicada before hiding itself away for the day.

Pancho stopped and breathed deeply of the musty, oxygenated air of the forest. He liked the sound of the birds and the rustling of leaves in the wind. He bent down and picked up a handful of rich earth, savoring its texture and its smell. He heard the trickle of water and abandoned the safety of the path to seek the source of the sound. Down he plunged through the dense foliage until he came upon a spring. The peaceful trickle sounded like a young child, playfully descending from a cleft in the mountain to the ravine down below and splashing about in the pool, collecting itself around an age-old hollow in the forest floor. He knew that at some point it would join up with a larger stream, and then a larger one, and would somewhere become part of the Great River that fed the jungles before extinguishing itself in the peaceful Caribbean. He dipped his hands into the small pond and splashed his face with the ice-cold water, scaring the tiny fishes. He gasped at the feel of the cold on his skin. A crawdad poked its head out from under a rock, looking to trap an unwary minnow for an early breakfast.

Pancho released his imagination, pondering the time when this same stream was used by the peasant farmers who'd lived only a short distance away. They had come here to draw water, preparing for an early breakfast before the pressing duties of the day. Generation after generation and family after family, these duties had remained constant—the picking, the pruning, the roasting, and the activities that fed the daily lives of colonial poverty.

Suddenly, he grabbed onto the loose earthen floor in fury, his fingers digging deeply into the rich brown. What had before been the desire to free all Venezuelans to their own potential now was a personal vendetta to remove the bastards from power. Not militarily, for Pancho knew he didn't have the strength. *No, we ourselves must remove him. We must expose them for who they really are and then pull them down.*

Pancho thought about the day of Susana's funeral. The poor people, whom he'd always defended as noble, quiet, and oppressed laborers, had jeered. As he, Carlitos, and Benito lifted high the body of his love, heavy in her casket, they had mocked him. El Comandante himself had taken over the airwaves during the funeral to rail against the student movement.

Now the young oligarch students, lackeys of the empire, have seen and lived what the Venezuelan poor must suffer through every day of the week. Maybe now they will be more sensitive to the plight of the poor of this country. Maybe now those sons of mommy and daddy will stop their conspiring and join in our fight to build a new socialist nation. A fight that students should claim as their own instead of serving as the new weapons of the oligarchs.

As they walked through the cemetery, people had thrown vegetables and eggs—her casket had gone into the ground dirty, covered in the final lasting insult from the rabble. The revolutionaries had been incensed even more by Susana's color. El Comandante had said, only a few days before Susana was killed,

How can a black girl, descendent of slaves, allow herself to become again the puppet of those rich, white, racist oligarchs. She is a traitor to her nation and her people, and to the revolution that has given her all her power.

"How special does your princess feel now?" one had said. "Not so powerful as you thought you were …"

Pancho knew, seated on the rock early that morning, that he should not allow hatred to find a place in his soul. But he also recognized that he'd been struggling ever since that day. *And I'm losing.* Pancho took a deep breath. The decaying smells of the forest were no longer pleasant but revolting and—poisoned by anger— seemed to be a metaphor for the unused decay at the core of his country.

"Today," Pancho said out loud, grasping within his own soul, trying to find the power, "I gotta put this behind me. I can't give in. Through hate *they* win."

He got up and walked purposefully up the path to the old chapel. Between the trees he saw the outline of an old green car.

"Okay, now we plan," he said as he burst into the chapel. Everybody was awake, and they were preparing coffee, eggs and toast on the gas range. "What are our assets?" Not even a "good morning." They nodded and got to work, discussing strategy over a hot breakfast and strong black coffee.

First chimed in Juanita from the mountains. "Well, school is in session, thankfully. We have about thirty buses and many more private vehicles. I think I could mobilize a large enough group, at least to show those gringos that this country isn't red from end to end. Our folks are pretty angry about the power shortages, and there are rumors that fuel subsidies will be cut, and we can play on that to get a larger group."

"How long would it take to organize 'em?" asked Pancho.

"Well, maybe if we got word to them by this afternoon, they could drive all night and be ready in the morning."

One by one, they went around the circle. Each answer was similar. Benito the cowboy said, "I could get a bunch of buses here. People are really pissed about the fixed prices on cattle meat. We are all becoming poor. We're tired of the military taking our farms and giving them away as rewards to government officials. Last month they even took my farm. One morning we all woke up early, like we always do, to eat a big breakfast for a long day's work. As we went outside we found fifty National Guard soldiers with AK-103s and an APC waiting for us. Behind them were a few hundred peasant farmers we knew as troublemakers from the community. They grabbed us all, handcuffed us, and escorted us to the other side of the gate to *our* property. There we stood looking through the fence into the farm we'd owned for four generations. We were spectators as the commanding officer said 'Go ahead, shop around,' and the mob flooded into our house. They rifled through our closets, taking my mother's underwear and my sisters' makeup.

They wandered through the kitchen filling their pockets with spices and garlic and expensive cheeses. A group of dirty urchins took off their clothes and jumped, naked, into our pools—two hundred of them, so many that the water actually turned brown. Their parents grabbed bottles of eighteen-year whiskey out of the bar and watched from the poolside chairs."

"I didn't hear about that. When did that happen?" Pancho asked.

"While you were gone, unfortunately, time didn't stand still," Benito said. "We walked, empty handed, to another, smaller property that we have about a hundred kilometers away. They wouldn't even let us take our cars. That theft cost us our livelihood. Now we're living on savings. I don't know what we're going to do. We tried to sue the government, hired a really expensive European lawyer, but El Comandante went on TV and said,

> You people, you large landowners who have more than one farm, why should you alone enjoy the benefits of the land that belongs to the people?

Everybody in the room except Pancho, who was just learning, knew the story well. Benito's dad had run against El Comandante's candidate in the local elections. This had been the payback. "We learned after the dust settled that they split the farm into five hundred tiny pieces. The peasants ripped down our houses to build their miserable huts—and the livestock, what's left anyway, drinks water out of the pool. Even if we got it back, it's already been destroyed …"

After a moment, the young man from the coast then spoke up, returning them to their planning. He explained the fury that the lack of investment at the tin smelting plant was causing. They were dumping toxic chemicals into the sea and causing serious environmental damage. There was a large school of tropical fisheries at the university, and he was studying to be a marine biologist. Each student leader knew the pulse of their university and how to rally the troops for the march.

"But we need to give them word. They all need to leave by midafternoon to get here on time," Carlitos said.

"Before we give the marching orders," Pancho said, "We have something more difficult to discuss. I think we have a problem. We've become very predictable and *extremely* risk averse. I think we're too concerned about being seen as nonviolent."

A pause, then Benito the cowboy spoke up. "Man, what are you insinuating?"

"I think we need to be more provocative," Pancho said.

"What's that going to get us?" asked Juanita. "It will just get more people killed. The idea is to *expose* them, not *provoke* them."

"But we can't seem to expose them without a provocation," Pancho said. "Our marches don't even make news anymore."

"What are we going to do, attack 'em?" Benito said.

"I, for one, don't want to die," said Juanita.

"Maybe that's why we lose. We are too afraid to die."

"That's not fair," Juanita added. "I'm poor, my parents are poor, and we have nothing. I march because I want to be a doctor and all the good jobs are going to the Cubans, *not* because I want to die."

"But to be a doctor, you have to force the regime that is suffocating your profession to change. As it stands, El Comandante will never let you practice. Don't you remember his declarations on this?"

Those of you who want a car or a house shouldn't choose a career to serve the sick.

"Do you think wanting a car or a house is bad?" Pancho asked.

"Of course not," Juanita said. "That's the reason why I study."

"Then we have to make things change."

Benito cut in, "Man, nobody ever talks about regime change here. Our position has always been that we want the government to respect us. *Not* that we want to radically change it. *They* did that. Look what happened. No, we'll get rid of them through the vote."

"The vote?" Pancho said. "The ballot boxes that arrive at the polling places already stuffed full of ballots? The government that throws our popular candidates in jail, or gets the Supreme Court to take their names off the ballots? Or the money they take from the treasury to pay people off at each polling booth? The free beer stands painted red at each station? The revolutionaries with dozens of different voter ID cards? The thugs outside each voting station with weapons? That vote?" Pancho got up and started pacing.

"Pancho's kind of got a point," Juanita said. "We haven't been having success. Maybe it's 'cuz we can't verbalize what we want …"

"Because we don't know what we want," said Pancho.

"We know exactly what we want," said Benito. "We want them to leave us alone. We want them to get out of the way. We want them to let us lead our lives without their ridiculous projects and programs. We want them to let us vote for the leaders that we like. We want them to take their hands out of our wallets, remove their minions from in front of our tractors, and have their military give us our farms back, and we want them to respect us and our opinions and not try to impose their radical ideas that are leaving us in poverty. And we want them to stop telling us what we should think, what we should believe, and how we should act."

Pancho was impressed; this was the most he'd ever heard Benito say in one day. Clearly the last six months had left him a changed man. "Exactly. And how do you think we can get them to do this? They've made it clear that they will refuse all of our demands."

"They only refuse because we are not strong enough to make them change," Carlitos said. "If we could force them to change …"

"But how do we do that? We have no weapons. We have no military. We can't fight them." The beach bum finally spoke up.

"Legitimacy is the sacred shroud upon which all representative governments depend. We know that this government is not legitimate—but nobody else does. We must begin to wrest from them the veneer of legitimacy. Our current strategy doesn't do this; in fact, it does the opposite. As we march, with every step we take we destroy our own message. We must seek a way to show to the world that this is not a government of the people and it surely isn't a government for the people."

Pancho looked around to gauge the response he was getting and saw fear. But he also saw the natural human response to leadership.

"You're right that we need to stick with our nonviolent methods. But we must use our entire arsenal of nonviolent skills, the lessons that we have learned and the experiences that we've had, to directly confront El Comandante, on his territory. We've never done that, and I really think it will cause a change in their response. El Comandante has seen us on television, and he has heard our cries from his helicopter as he hovers above, maneuvering his police and army against us. This time, we will go to where *he* is, at *his* moment, in *his* timing, to tell him that we're not going to take it anymore," Pancho said.

There was a long pause while people thought about the discussion. Finally, the boy from the beach asked, "But how do we do this? What do we use to make the government respond to *us*? They seem pretty content to just let us march up and down."

"Tomorrow," Pancho said, with a dangerous gleam of anarchy. "Tomorrow," he repeated. All eyes looked at him. They waited for his pronunciation. They steadied themselves against the words that made them afraid but that they so longed to hear. "Tomorrow," Pancho said for a third time, "We march on El Comandante himself."

Everybody was dead quiet. Never before had they stood up directly against *him*, in one of *his* events. He was larger than life, the towering figure that occupied the heart, the very core of all Venezuelan life, personal and private. He was untouchable.

"Tomorrow," said Pancho's voice, now a whisper, "At night, El Comandante will be attending his damn socialist student function. He will be arrogantly entertaining those stupid gringos, throwing insults around like he always does. They came, paying their own money, for a revolutionary show."

Pancho looked down. "Tomorrow, we'll give it to 'em. We will show them that the emperor has no clothes; we will show them that we still yearn to be free. Tomorrow we will march for justice, for freedom, and most importantly, for Susana. But by God, we will march."

"Crack." Pancho looked up quickly toward the window. He thought he'd heard something. *Must have been an animal.*

34

✳ ✳ ✳

The little yorkie nudged Doña Esmeralda awake. He needed to go outside. *It's nice that, on a day like today, some things remain normal.* She caressed her tiny terrier, enjoying feeling the silky soft hair. He was so old, outliving all other dogs by decades—as if the spirit of the country or the ghost of Gonzalo knew she needed her companion and allowed him to shake off the chains of time. The dog had been a gift from Gonzalo when he had taken a long business trip through Europe and had to leave Doña Esmeralda behind. During those months she had been suffering from a difficult pregnancy, one that would keep her off her feet for most of the nine months—and that would end in disaster. *He'd always been so thoughtful, even wanting to give me entertainment as I had to be off my feet.*

She had given birth, a few weeks early, to a son. But the birth had been problematic because of her age, and the baby arrived sickly and delicate—and had not lasted out the winter. "I buried him on a fine morning," she told her yorkie, "and with him my hopes of leaving something behind." Only two years later, she buried Gonzalo, one large grave beside one smaller—infinitely smaller.

"After you died, I have nothing left except this, your lasting token," she said to Gonzalo, caressing the terrier. "Not even my family. They abandoned me like everybody else."

Her family was in London, or Madrid—she could never remember. They hadn't spoken since the day she had forced them all out of the family business in a cutthroat move that had netted her billions of Asnos. "It serves me right that they hate me," Esmeralda said, "I had nothing for them when they needed it the most. Now that I am in need, they have nothing for me."

"You did what you had to, my dear, to be strong and keep our businesses running," Gonzalo said, only his face visible sticking through the wall.

"But for what?" Her only consolation was her great-nephew, her sister's grandson, who was still living in San Porfirio.

"If we don't fight for freedom," Carlitos would often say, "Who will?" He had never asked Doña Esmeralda for anything, which was why she found it so strange that morning when he called her on her home phone.

"*Tía*, how are you?" Carlitos' voice sounded distant—as if he was calling from a long distance, or with great emotion that kept him from fully committing his voice to the enterprise of talking.

"I am well, Carlitos. It's good to hear from you. How are you doing?" All of a sudden, Esmeralda felt guilty. It had been too long since they'd spoken. She really didn't know how he was doing, financially, emotionally, or even physically.

"I am doing okay, *tía*." And he hesitated. She waited patiently for him to tell her the reason for the rare contact.

"*Tía*," he said slowly, "You know I haven't ever asked you for anything. I never wanted to abuse family ties, just because you had money. But now, well, I need some help. We are planning something. I don't want to talk over the phone, but we ran out of money. This is not a personal project—we are going to stand up for ourselves, finally."

Doña Esmeralda knew exactly what he was referring to. She had never been very convinced by the marching up and down of these youngsters. She didn't think that it would achieve any real solution to the long-term problems the country was facing. But she admired their courage.

"Go on," Esmeralda said.

"Well, you see, you remember Pancho, right? Pancho Randelli?"

Why did that name sound so familiar to her? She wracked her brain. "Pancho, Pancho, Pancho. Randelli. How do I know him?" she tentatively queried her nephew. "That name rings a bell."

"Sure, you know, the kid who lost his girlfriend? You have to remember him—his father even worked for you when you owned the electric company."

A light bulb went on in her head. Of course, the Randelli family—they had been good, faithful middle managers; she had even met them on various occasions during the annual Christmas parties or the weeks when she would take her managers on retreat. "Of course I remember."

"Well, he's back. And we need money for an event. Just this once, Pancho is good at fund-raising. But he's just back. Will you help us?"

"Yes, I can help you. But I need to meet with you and with Pancho's father," she said cautiously. All night she had been mulling over a particular problem and realized that she'd just had the answer handed to her—so what if it cost her a little bit more money?

"His father?"

"Yes, just bring them by the house later today." They hung up.

Now on to bigger business, she said to herself.

35

* * *

Carlitos returned from outside when he had finished with his telephone call. The students had set aside their bedrolls and spread out a large map of the city on the floor and were marking it up with pencil. "Well, I talked to my great-aunt. This time, our financial problems are solved. She is willing to help us foot the bill. But, Pancho, this is a one-time thing. I am not comfortable getting my aunt involved in this. She is an old lady who has suffered a lot over the years, but although she's mean as an alley cat, she would *never* be involved in anything illegal. I know it was our only option, but we had better start fund-raising pretty quick."

"Thanks," said Pancho. "This gives us what we need for now. Following tomorrow, we'll be able to raise more money."

"One thing," Carlitos said tentatively. "She has one stipulation. She wants to meet face to face, and she wants me to bring your father."

"My father?" Pancho said. "That's strange. I didn't want to bring him into this. He was one of the most insistent that I leave after, well, after Susana was killed. He isn't happy I am involved with you again."

"Well, if we want the money, we have to. That's how my aunt has always been—always strings attached to everything." Carlitos gave a shrug.

And they turned their attention to the large map in front of them. "At eight o'clock," Juanita was saying, "El Comandante will be here at the airport."

She pointed to a spot on the map. "He will be addressing the socialist youth forum. This is an important event, one that he looks forward to 'cuz it gives him a chance to put on a show for foreigners. He won't miss it. Having gringos hanging on his every word inflates his ego."

"The airstrip is here." They marked it with their pencils. "The stage is set up right here." Another mark.

"First, before we plan, we must be clear. Now that we have our strategic objective, what's our tactical goal?" The other students simply looked at him, knowing it was only a matter of time before he answered his own question. Pancho looked around. "Well?" But there was still no answer.

"Our primary goal is to force El Comandante to change his plans, that is, to cancel his appearance at the event. If we can demonstrate that we can make him change, he'll lose face and power, and it would be a fantastic win for us," Pancho said.

"Of course, our fallback position—as I stated previously—is to provoke El Comandante," Pancho said with a flourish. "He has never before been challenged at one of his events, and he will be angry. He will want to make sure that the situation is calm for him to appear and deliver his choice words. So, we start early and strike hard and fast, and if we can't get him to cancel his appearance, we'll at least have the gringos see what is really going on here."

Pancho looked around. Juanita was nodding. Benito the cowboy was still chewing tobacco but seemed to be on board. The boy from the beach had slouched on one of the old, broken-down benches and was squinting her approval. The other students had come into line. Finally, Carlitos interjected, "I think we agree."

"Okay," said Pancho. "Let's get down to business."

36

✳ ✳ ✳

"I have never received so much abuse in my life," Freddy growled as they were coming out of another middle-class building. He was sweaty and dirty from changing light bulbs in strange places under hostile stares, and his pride was hurt. As soon as people figured out that he was American, the insults increased in volume, frequency, and creativity, and he'd been told in very graphic ways what he could do with his light bulbs.

"I wanted to do some of the ground work," he told Geronimo as they caught their breath outside the next building. "But I wasn't expecting to be humiliated. I sort of thought it would feel more heroic."

One old woman had hit him in the forehead with an egg, and her husband had dumped coffee grounds on his head. He was dirty and smelly, and he needed a break.

As he stepped onto the sidewalk, the emissary walked up to him. He had been sitting on a flowerpot beside the building, smoking a cigarette and reading a copy of *La Navaja*. He handed the paper to Freddy. The front title read, "Opposition Politicians Eat Babies for Breakfast." The corresponding pictures and story outlined the cannibal practices of some of the most important opposition leaders.

"Get a load of this," the emissary, Freddy's mentor who had been missing in action since the plane flight, said without greeting.

"Looks like they caught this *hijo de puta* with a baby he had stolen from a barrio. He was about to cook him and put him in a stew."

A smile spread across Freddy's war-weary face. "Hey, good to see you. Where have you been?"

Ignoring the question, the emissary said, "Listen, I need to talk to you. Walk with me." Geronimo shrugged and went down the street to the little pastry shop on the corner to brandish his revolutionary credentials and his little pocket list to see if he couldn't get a free lunch out of the owner—it almost always worked.

The emissary and Freddy walked down the street in the opposite direction, turning right at the street corner. All around them the buildings were thirty or forty stories high. Their façades were old, not colonial-era but built during the previous dictatorship a half-century before, and their middle-class residents assured they were still relatively well maintained. From the buildings came ordinary people walking their dogs, going to and from work, or checking their mail.

The postal system, never very good, had totally collapsed when El Comandante had given the management of it to a commune run by his alcoholic brother. With the impunity afforded by blood, the new postal workers had taken to opening people's mail and delivering only the items that didn't have any value or letters that weren't interesting enough to publish in *La Navaja*. And although people had stopped using the government's mail system, the commune still occupied the plush building in the center of town, and the employees used their paychecks to hold extravagant parties. Upon moving to the city, El Comandante's brother and his minions had occupied the top ten floors of the all-glass building constructed to serve as the nerve center of the greatest postal service on the continent. At night they could be seen through the translucent windows having sex, taking whore's baths using buckets of water carried from their communal bathrooms, or watching pornography on their newly purchased flat-screen TVs.

Since nobody was mailing anything anymore, most of their energy was spent selling pirated movies and other contraband out of the basement using the large warehouses where the mail had been stored and sorted as a makeshift, black-market outlet mall. To nobody's surprise, except perhaps the government, which constantly denounced the treason, private companies had replaced the government in the letter distribution business.

Freddy observed with interest these the last refuges of normality in an increasingly peculiar country. On vacation in Florida with his family, he'd once witnessed firsthand the arrival and passing of a minor hurricane. This neighborhood felt uncannily like it was itself in the eye of a nationwide maelstrom. It was an odd sensation, and one that he didn't like. As he walked down the street, he could feel the malevolence flung at him; at times, it hit him with more force than the eggs and garbage. The message was clear: "You are not welcome here."

The street itself was potholed and crumbling, starved from many years of underinvestment. There were few cars parked in the open, and those that he did see had makeshift metal cages around them for protection. Although some of the buildings had bought generators, the public lighting system no longer worked, and criminals were known to prowl the night looking for cars to steal. Despite the feeling of a community under siege, the atmosphere was peaceful, and Freddy was even guiltily beginning to like this middle-class neighborhood—*I could even fit in here. I'd just have to change my shirt.*

As they walked, the warm sun toasted Freddy's skin, and the wind glancing smoothly on his skin cooled him down. The breeze tickled his cheeks and set the emissary's gray-and-black beard to blowing. Freddy's heart filled to bursting with love for that moment. *It is these simple times*, he thought, *that are the heart of camaraderie and bring me into the collective that is being organized in this beautiful country.*

"Here's why I wanted to see you," the emissary said as they walked. Freddy leaned closer and held his breath. "We are having a problem with shipping some important things to America. The CIA has taken over the parcel services, and all of our packages are being confiscated and searched, with the important stuff seized. This has been happening for a while now. We tried to get our own people to carry the things on the airplane, but they are also being closely watched in Miami and New York through their 'no fly lists.' Every time they show up, the stuff is confiscated and they are turned away at entry. We can't get what we need to into the country. We have it on special inside information that the American government is very worried about revolution."

Freddy sucked in his breath.

"Your special task—your first special task—is to deliver items of great importance to the Venezuelan consulate in Miami. These items are of extreme value, and that is why the gringos are so worried about them."

"But ..." Freddy began to speak.

"Before you ask, I know what you are thinking. I can't tell you exactly what the items are because I haven't even seen them yet myself. But I will tell you that they are special marketing pieces and messaging for an important campaign. We're preparing a media and public relations blitz inside the United States, to start in the big cities of Miami, New York, and even Washington. It's going to be big—huge, in fact. It could change everything. But to get this done, we need to ship in the videos, shirts, brochures, pamphlets, and other items that are essential for our campaign."

"But ..." Freddy tried again.

"I know what you are thinking," the emissary went on. "Why don't we just print and prepare everything we need in America? Well, the CIA is aware of our campaign and is going to every length to stop it. They have their people all over, and every time we use a local printer they take our money and they return to us a product that is either destroyed or that actually displays counter-revolutionary messaging. It is a little game that sometimes the intelligence services play with each other; they let us know that they know so that maybe we will stop. But we won't stop. We *need* to get these items into America."

The corner of Freddy's mouth dipped ever so slightly downward. He had hoped to stay on in Venezuela and maybe even get a job with one of the social initiatives (although hopefully not something that would get him attacked every day).

"If you do this well, and you show us that we can trust you, you will be rewarded with a position in this important campaign. There is nowhere that you can help us more than in your own country, where you know your way around and will be a better advocate for our revolution to your countrymen. It will, of course, mean you coming and going a lot from Venezuela and of course helping with these youth rallies. They are our best ways to get in contact with volunteers that can help our cause when we need them. After the campaign is over, we'll have another project for you."

A glint appeared in Freddy's eyes. "I will do this." Freddy held his head high in what he hoped was nobility. "I will join in your campaign to help win over the American people, my people, to the important cause of revolutionary freedom."

The emissary grinned.

37

✳ ✳ ✳

Doña Esmeralda had planned the timing of her walk with her Yorkshire terrier perfectly. "I need to stretch my legs and get my dog some exercise," she'd told Clarita deliberately. It was a lovely sunny day. She was in good spirits, and the unnatural bulge taped to her thigh gave her a sense of excitement and intrigue but also, more importantly, of purpose. She left her house, pulling her little yorkie with his blue harness up the street.

She lived in an exclusive gated community. The increase in crime had forced the neighbors to band together, paying an exorbitant monthly fee to an armed security group that did round-the-clock patrols. The company was made up of former members of the Venezuelan Special Forces who'd formed their security company after being purged from the military during El Comandante's increasingly frequent bouts of paranoia.

There are those within the military, within Special Forces, who have taken an oath to protect the motherland and me but have instead decided to conspire. I know who you are. I know where you eat your cheese empanadas, and who you talk to. Mark my words, it won't go lightly for the soldier that joins the empire's futile planning to restore the corrupt oligarchs to power and plunge the people back into poverty and misery.

The next day a list had appeared in a gazette expelling several hundred soldiers from the military. They were, coincidentally, soldiers who had received some sort of training from the Americans to participate in peacekeeping missions in Africa. The small group of expelled soldiers had decided to use their skills in a different way.

Access to what they called "the facility" was only granted based upon specific requests written in triplicate by an authorized community member. Esmeralda had just cleared a guest, whom the mercenary had said was named "Ruben Dario," a famous Nicaraguan poet—and, she knew, General Gregorio's favorite author. She walked slowly down the street toward the recreation center where there was a swimming pool, a small café, and a spa. On the hills above and behind "the facility" were the ominous barrios. The security company had installed a large electric fence to keep the unwanted underclass out—but Esmeralda could still see them, a fact that always put her off. Parked beside the curb was a nondescript beige hatchback. As she walked by, the door popped open, and she quickly got in, grabbing her yorkie by the collar and pulling him into the front passenger seat with her, slamming the door too hard in her anxiety.

"*Hola, Esmeraldita.*"

"*Hola, mi General,*" she said with a wink of the kind that passes two old friends who, in a previous life, had also been lovers.

"Esmeralda, I am sorry to have brought you into this. I know it's dangerous. But if we miss this chance, who knows when we will ever get our next opportunity. El Comandante doesn't appear in public very often these days, and his plans are never announced long ahead of time." He looked in his rearview mirror as an armored car from the security firm peeled around the corner on one of its many patrols. The four men clinging to the rear bumper were wielding M-16s purchased from the leftovers when El Comandante rid his army of "gringo hardware," claiming it was being used electronically to spy on the FARS and was controlled by gringo technology that would jam the firing mechanism at the perfect moment in the battle he was sure was coming, thereby causing him to suffer a humiliating defeat.

"I understand, Gregorio. I am an old woman now. I can't wait forever to see my country recuperated from this human waste—this revolutionary riffraff. This may be my last shot to get my companies—my life—back before I die. To return things to the way they were before—that's all I think and dream about. I am alone, Gregorio, up there in that house. There is nothing for me anymore. Anyway, what could they do to me? I have already suffered all the disgrace they can throw; now it's our turn to throw back."

"*Sí,* Esmeralda."

"And anyway, I called you—remember? They want to take my house; I told you that, right? I don't think I could live through that. I am sure I would simply perish from the humiliation. So this is as much my decision as yours. In every life there comes a moment when fate meets destiny—when the path we must walk is no longer our choice. This is my path, and our moment. Before I die, I want to take back what they stole—or destroy them, and myself, trying."

"Do you ever regret us?" The general asked the question haltingly. After years of war games, he was unaccustomed to dealing in affairs of the heart.

Esmeralda thought for a long moment.

"I'm sorry. Never mind," Gregorio said, looking away.

"No, *mi General,* I want to answer." A few more seconds passed. "Those were different, more carefree times. Back when the poor knew their place and left us alone. Remember my *quinceañera,* that elegant party at the equestrian club? That is a night we will always have—even through all of this. You, Gonzalo, and I stealing *papa's* car—he was so angry. Back then I loved the mountains and the solitude; I wasn't afraid of them. Up, up, higher we drove down that beaten-down old colonial road, just to see where it took us. I don't think it had been used in centuries, some remnant from our glorious colonial past. Up into the mountains and higher and higher, the air grew crisp and cool, and we turned the heater on, warming ourselves with that bottle of rum we stole from the party."

"*Sí,* I remember," said Gregorio, but she was no longer talking to him.

"Gonzalo was driving and almost hit that strange animal, and as we got out to see what it was and follow it into the forest we were surrounded by angels, the protectors of Venezuela, just spinning in circles around the blue and silver fire that they had prepared in our honor. The beautiful fairies, just twisting and glistening and chanting that beautiful melody that only they know. I always thought, before then, that they were just stories that my grandmother told me about the times before development, before electricity, when we were closer to the spirits. I haven't heard tell of them in many decades, since our country has started to collapse. They were supposed to watch out for us, to care for us. I wonder where they have gone—why they have ceased their vigil from up on the sacred mountain."

"Your father was so angry he sent out the *Guardia Nacional*," Gregorio chuckled.

"Back when the institutions of state were at *our* service, not our *predators*."

"I do remember those times, Esmeraldita. The expensive dinners with our politicians, discussing affairs of importance to our nation. Hosting the American ambassador and other diplomats …"

"Dancing into the night, not worrying about being robbed or car-jacked. The three of us would go down to the clean, pristine, and lonely beaches and frolic in the warm water. Now they are strewn with beer cans, thousands of screaming urchins, and that insufferable thumping music."

Gregorio chuckled.

"But to answer your question, I regret not having been faithful to Gonzalo," said Esmeralda. "I loved him; I always did. What we did looks petty in the glaring light of time. And compared to weighty moments like the ones today, it seems hollow and pointless."

As she gazed into her past and upon her indiscretions, the brutal hand of time wiped away the once-lovely woman that she had been, leaving in its place the crusty, bitter old hag. "I think I could have loved you too, Gregorio, should moments and decisions have been different. But, such as they are, I save my regrets for my loss of country, for my loss of position, and for my loss of Gonzalo.

Everything else seems just trivialities along the long and labored path of my years," she said with an honest, sad smile.

"I understand." Gregorio did not seem pleased with that answer, but he was not surprised by it either. "Did you bring it?" And they dove into business.

"Yes," Esmeralda pulled a manila envelope out from under her dress. "You can count it, but it's all there. I might as well put it to good use, because it will do me no good where I am going."

"Thank you, Esmeralda."

"But you'd better use it quickly. I went down to the bank this morning to make the withdrawal, and the bank said that in order to withdraw more than the minimum I had to sign an affidavit stating what it was for. I said I was going to buy a store in the mall—a story they say they are going to check into. Sorry, I couldn't think of anything else …" Esmeralda shrugged carelessly.

"No need to apologize. If we pull this off, Esmeralda, we will once again be free. Then, we will be young again." Gregorio smiled a sad smile. "And we will drive down to our beach, free it from the riffraff, and dance all night long to music and champagne—like we did in the old days. And we will prepare a special toast in memory of Gonzalo."

"Maybe." Esmeralda frowned. "Or maybe Pandora 's Box will finally have been opened. As for me, I'm too old to worry. This is what must be, and now is the time."

"Oh, and one more thing," Gregorio said. "Remember what we discussed yesterday? We're gonna need a blackout, immediately at eight o'clock."

"Yes, I remember. I already have a plan. I'll tell you if it worked when we meet."

"Again, the club, this afternoon?"

"Yes," said Esmeralda. "We will have our last meeting."

Esmeralda stepped out of the car and gave Gregorio a sad good-bye. The beige car pulled out of the curb and drove away, leaving Esmeralda walking slowly back to her house, her tiny dog sound asleep in her arms. She entered her house, and immediately the intercom rang. It was Carlitos, her nephew.

"Thank you for coming," Esmeralda said to Carlitos and Pancho's father as they walked into the house. "It's good that you are here."

"Thank you, *tía*, for your help with this. You know I wouldn't ask if it weren't an emergency. I won't tell you what we're up to, but I promise it is totally legal—or would be in a free country."

"*Si, mijito*," Esmeralda said. She handed him the second of her bulging manila envelopes. "I'm happy to help. Now go, I need to talk to Mr. Randelli." And with that, Carlitos was ushered toward the door and out onto the sidewalk.

38

* * *

"I'm back." Carlitos bounded into the old chapel grinning ear to ear. "And the old bag coughed up the money. Amazing. She didn't say as much as two words to me—seemed anxious for me to leave so she could talk to your dad, not sure what about."

Pancho looked up from his position on the floor of the chapel, which resembled an advance field camp for a conquering army. The entire chapel floor was carpeted with maps of the city. They swished as the battery-operated fan pushed them around, swiveling on its axis.

Ignoring Carlitos's majestic entry, Pancho simply said, "Come over here," as if he had not noticed that Carlitos had been gone.

"Okay, here's the highway that cuts across the city, going right in front of the airport." He had marked it in green. "We need to strategically position our marchers to get the best impact." Pancho was glad to be back; this was what he was good at.

Diving right into the planning, Carlitos asked, "Have we informed our people? How many can we count on?"

The four university leaders from San Porfirio responded, almost in unison, "We called our phone tree contacts, and they are sending word down their lines. We have to assume that our students here in the capital are going to be the backbone of this march—and so we have to draw a good crowd. We don't know if the military will let the buses from the interior pass by."

In the past, during the days of heavy marching, the army had stopped buses full of students irrespective of whether they were going to the planned march or not, even buses full of primary school students, and had held them for more than twenty-four hours.

"We figure that between us five universities, we can pull together almost ten thousand students," one of the student leaders said. "We can assume that as soon as the citizens see us marching, they will also join, so our numbers could swell. We figure maybe fifty thousand, maybe more …"

Pancho interjected, "We've called Radio Mega FM. One of my old buddies works there, and starting tomorrow morning he has agreed to broadcast the announcement for the march. He figures he can broadcast for a few hours before he gets shut down. So say we start at eleven o'clock with the broadcasts. By one he's shut down, but by then people have started to assemble. From there, instant messaging can mobilize more people—until the government shuts that down, too." He bit his lip. "But I think we may have a problem with this march. We decided not to request a permit. We figure that they will tell us no anyway, and if we ask obediently it will only give them time to mobilize their troops, their water cannon, and their damn teargas. They'll know tomorrow morning, but at least this buys us almost sixteen hours of prep time."

"Sounds fine," Carlitos said.

"As for us," Juanita said, beaming, her cell phone still in hand, "We have about one hundred buses all set up. We went ahead and pulled the trigger even though we didn't have the gas money, assuming your beloved prune of an aunt would come through, so we have about five thousand people."

"Same with us," said Benito. "Everybody is also getting their banners ready, packing their food, and getting their spray paint and T-shirts ready."

"The symbol we're gonna use," said Pancho, "is the two-handed *V*, the sign of the revolution, but upside down and with a pair of handcuffs between the two fingers."

"One of my people put it together," Juanita said.

"And it's gone out to all the tiny printers in the country. We're gonna have a lot of T-shirts and stickers—thanks to your aunt." And Pancho bowed low to Carlitos.

They walked back over to the center map again. "Okay," said Pancho, "so people should meet here." He pointed to the far end of the highway, a straight shot of about four kilometers from the airport. "There, we will start to gather at about noon. We figure that by two or three we'll start walking, which will bring us to the airstrip maybe at about five or six, in time to upset El Comandante's event." He looked again at the large map.

"Here," he said tapping the large map with his index finger, "We'll have the large moving speaker platform out in front. It'll be draped in the colors of the Venezuelan flag, and on it we'll have some of our local music groups playing. I'll be on this platform, as will some of our other young leaders, including some of the politicians—the young ones. Everybody has already been notified."

He was rattling off details like machine gun fire. "Behind the platform, here and here, we'll have two ambulances. They'll be donated by one of the friendly local governments. Here, at the front, middle, and back, will be large trucks that will have the water. Street vendors will show up to sell snacks—no need to arrange that." He looked around. "Okay, guys, what have we forgotten?"

The team of ten students looked around at each other. They had done this so often that organizing these marches had become second nature.

Pancho stood up on a broken-down bench at the front of the church.

"In the past, we have marched for many reasons." Pancho looked each student in the eye. "We marched when they took our political leaders to jail. We marched when they stole the money out of our bank accounts and when they started putting together their lists."

Pancho's voice filled the old chapel to spill out in golden waves into the forest. "Sometimes, we marched not for any real reason except to convince each other that we still could, and to band together in that simple knowledge. Since the government started imprisoning our dissidents, closing our radios, and 'recuperating' our newspapers—

sending their thugs to beat up and silence any challenge—we found solace in the relative anonymity of the march."

"But this time, it will be different," Pancho said. "This time we don't march for each other. This time we march against *them*. This time we are going to challenge El Comandante himself, on his turf, in front of his guests. This march won't be another act of self-consolation but a true act of defiance."

The students broke into a round of applause, and a cheer went up, stolen from the revolution: "To victory."

Pancho scrutinized each face and found them to be ready. He sat with his juvenile generals in a circle on the floor, passing their magical bottle of local rum from one person to the other like a war pipe. Taking a break from the preparations, they murmured quietly, steeling themselves for the following day and hoping they were ready for what was to come, knowing in their hearts that the most probable outcome of this march would be the violence that they so desperately wanted banished from their exhausted country.

* * *

Across town, Freddy was deeply immersed in his mission. He'd left the emissary, whose parting words had been "I'll find you tomorrow with the bags." Freddy walked the long, solitary road back in the direction of where he had left Geronimo. But things had changed: he was no longer a boy doing 'revolutionary tourism,' crafting a memory he would recount to his children when he got home from work somewhere in Middle America. He was a *participant* now, with a boss and a revolutionary assignment. Alone with his thoughts, the activities of the youth meeting were starting to take on a tragic, comedic quality that was wholly unwelcome. He began to feel more vulnerable, alone in this neighborhood, wearing a red shirt and with a huge red backpack full of light bulbs. The stares and glares took on a more sinister quality, and Freddy wondered if perhaps he wasn't playing at a game before really understanding the rules. But something in him hardened against his own doubts, and he decided he'd had enough abuse and hailed down a cab.

"*Bonjour*," the taxi driver said. "Where can I take you?" His accent was thick with French and creole. He had shoulder-length dreadlocks, a tie-dyed shirt, and flip flops. The biggest cigarette Freddy had ever seen was clenched between the three remaining teeth on the right side of his mouth. The taxi was rusted with age, painted various shades of green, and had multicolored running lights chasing each other around the collapsing car's chassis. Freddy looked the cab over, pretending to know what to look for, and shrugged as he threw his bag into the backseat. Immediately he smelled something sweet and pungent.

Through the rearview mirror, the cab driver gave Freddy a once over and, noticing his red T-shirt and his blond hair, said, "You must be from America, right?" Freddy responded in the affirmative and gave him his destination, the airstrip.

"Ah, sure. You know, *mon ami*, no matter what they are telling you in there, Venezuela has seen better days. I have been robbed seven times this year—each time they took my money, all my day's earnings. The last time they even took my taxi. I tried to explain that it was all I had, the only thing I can use to feed my family and pay for my *rancho* on the hill. That hill over there." And he pointed. "But did they stop? No, just gave me a good bump on my head to teach me to shut up."

He laughed, leaning back dangerously over the seat to show Freddy the mark on his forehead where he had been beaten with the butt of a gun. "Now I gotta drive this thing. But I figure the uglier the better when it comes to my ride—who'd wanna steal this?"

"So, I keep going on—what other options do I have? Don't let the talk about the pretty revolution fool you. This place sucks." Following the nature of taxi drivers the world over, this man was opinionated, boisterous, and dangerously honest.

"Just drive the cab," Freddy said.

"I keep thinking I should have stayed in Haiti," the cab driver went on, ignoring Freddy. "There, at least, I had places to go without worrying about the violence. It was violence I understood, not like this. But, *bon*, what can I do? I too bought into stories. It sounded better than the dirty streets of Port au Prince. Man, was I wrong.

These *fils de pute* are *worse* than the last government—at least those guys let some money get through."

"Would you just drive the car?" Freddy said again, an edge on his voice.

"I went down to get one of their taxis after mine was stolen. You know what they said? They said, 'Are you a member of the revolutionary taxi syndicate?' I said, 'What?' They said, 'The taxi syndicate that signs up to give people from the barrios free rides to the marches.' I said, 'Free rides? What do I look like, a charity service?' They just threw me out of the building. Since then I've been driving this thing," he chuckled again.

They arrived at the airport, where Freddy paid the man his money. He felt a little sorry for being short with him but was unwilling to apologize, instead saying, "Just so you know, I think the revolution is for your own good." He slammed the door and walked away. The cab peeled away in response, almost knocking into a soldier on patrol with a flamethrower spitting small points of fire. For a minute Freddy thought the soldier was going to torch the car, but he simply lifted his middle finger and screamed something incomprehensible to which the cab driver responded with his own epithet.

* * *

"Arghem," said Teniente Machado said into the microphone. All eyes turned immediately to the stage. "Now that we have mostly all returned and have rested from our morning's labors, we'll begin our afternoon's program." He signaled to the soldiers who were assembled at regular intervals along the large, elongated, brightly whitewashed wall that reached across one entire end of the base. Each set of soldiers stood at attention in front of a set of tables covered with camouflaged tarp.

"Voila," Machado yelled, and each soldier pulled back the tarp to reveal buckets of paint and various sizes of paintbrushes. "This afternoon, my revolutionary comrades, you will be painting a mural for El Comandante to see when he comes tomorrow. It will be a mural about the peaceful revolution, and about the downfall of the empire, and about the torture that God will inflict on the oligarchs when they die."

Machado was pleased with the last line; it wasn't in the prepared notes he had received from his predecessor but he'd been adlibbing quite a bit, and it was going well. *I can't believe they fall for this.* Machado chuckled. The protocol was clear: every time visitors came, they would spend the better part of a day doing a mural. Murals, according to the Cuban revolutionary adviser who had come to assist this newest and therefore least experienced of the revolutionary governments of the continent, were an excellent way to keep people busy, build spirit, and allow people a public—and thereby controllable—avenue for artistic expression.

Cuba's government had arrived at this activity after several almost disastrous false starts. First, they'd tried poem writing, but they had discovered that poems could contain irony, and since they could be written anonymously they were sometimes unflattering. One particular poem had described, with Latin flair, a flourishing relationship between Fidel and a talking goat named Esteban. The story line had gone something like this.

One day, Fidel had been walking down a dirt road not far from Havana when he had come across a goat. Looking at his register of the farms adjacent to the road, he saw that there was no reported goat among the meager possessions of the farmers. But the goat was beautiful, and since he was the fearless leader he knew he had the right to anything he saw in his path, especially unregistered goats. He went to pick up the goat and carry it back to the 1950s American-made military jeep that he'd seized from the house of Batista, having watched the former dictator drive the car he really wanted—the fantastic limousine—into a tree beside the presidential mansion. To his dismay, as soon as he picked up the goat, it had asked him, in an intelligent and thoughtful tone, "What in the name of all that is holy do you think you are doing, old man?" Not accustomed to being spoken to in this fashion, he dropped the goat back onto all fours.

"*Gracias.*"

Now the communist was flustered. He couldn't have his authority challenged by goats, especially beautiful unregistered goats he found along one of his roads. But the goat was so lovely, he couldn't bring himself to harm him, and his tongue was so piquant that he was immediately enamored by the animal. So he decided to go about teaching the goat in the ways of revolution. He found that the goat was a willing and eager student. Every day, shirking affairs of state, he would drive out to the village and hold lessons for the goat about poverty, about fighting the empire, and about the evils done by capitalism. "I never knew," the goat would say in awe, "about any of this. I was just a simple goat, going about my duties here in this village, following orders and eating grass. But now that I know, I will be a faithful follower and a willing mentor of other goats."

And the goat went about converting the other goats in the area to the cause until Fidel had a revolutionary army of goats at his beck and call, ready for any imperial invasion or domestic conspiracy. And a strong and lasting love developed between Fidel and Esteban, a love that seemed to both natural and powerful—a true love that would stand the test of time.

Evidently Fidel had been quite upset by the whole affair, finding the story somehow offensive to his honor. Music, which they tried next, had developed a nuanced mechanism for double meaning. A certain song, which Fidel assumed was about himself, had turned out to be about an activist imprisoned for wearing his underwear on the outside of his pants as a sign of protest. The fearless leader was again enraged. Each time his rage crested he would demand the life of the unfortunate bureaucrat who'd envisioned the ideas, making other civil servants more close-lipped about their own ingenious plans. Ah, but murals. Bold, colorful, exciting, and very obvious— the perfect propaganda.

Machado liked this activity and had carefully saved photographs of each increasingly sophisticated presentation. The next day, during his speech, El Comandante would bless the mural, call it the most beautiful thing he had ever seen. "'A representation that will last for a thousand years upon this wall, demonstrating the patriotic revolutionary zeal of the American people to fight with and beside the Venezuelans to destroy injustice, poverty, and hatred,' I believe were his exact words last time," Machado's colonel had told him upon giving him the list of sanctioned activities.

"As soon as the kids go home, you need to paint the wall white for the next group of gringos," were Machado's exact instructions. He was also pleased that the event kept the gringos busy for a long period of time—*problems are starting to crop up like wildfire. And besides, the whole thing is humorous and worth a good laugh.*

"Come retrieve your paints and organize yourselves. A mural is not an easy project; only a truly committed revolutionary can harness the power to make an appropriate representation that has both meaning and life." And he went back upstairs to his office.

39

✳ ✳ ✳

Doña Esmeralda, General Gregorio, and the politician were again having drinks at their club on the edge of the town. "Where is Alejandro?" Esmeralda asked.

"Like I told you, Esmeralda, we brought him to meet you only once. It is much too dangerous for us to be seen together. Every time we meet, we risk detection. And that, as you know, could be catastrophic." Gregorio chastised Esmeralda in a light tone born out of familiarity and confidence. "Rest assured, he knows his role and will carry it out with discipline and honor."

"I *can* tell you," he said as he leaned back in his chair, the same overstuffed foyer chair of the day before, "that he received your support and passed it on to the necessary parties. He is now in possession of the items, and we are moving forward with the plan."

"Can't I know the details?" Doña Esmeralda was accustomed to being in control, and in her experience, putting other people in charge of something always meant that the results were less than satisfactory.

"I shouldn't show you this, but …" and he pushed a folded piece of paper across the end table. Esmeralda picked it up conspiratorially and read it quickly. It was an arrest warrant for El Comandante for misappropriation of funds, abuse of executive authority, political discrimination, and drug trafficking. It was signed by the only

Supreme Court justice whose political position was not written in red on his sleeve.

She passed the warrant back.

"Now, let me ask you, what about the electricity? Were you able to talk to your man?"

"Yes, Mr. Randelli will shut off the power in the whole city at eight o'clock sharp …"

"*Names.*" Gregorio raised his voice but quickly brought it down again. "I told you I don't want any names. Just tell me you arranged it, and I'll believe you."

"Yes."

"Good. By the time the lights come back on, the warrant will be served."

The politician had not said a word. In fact, he seemed lost in his own world.

Unseen by Esmeralda and her coconspirators, the invisible servants were standing all around them, signaling to each other excitedly.

* * *

"Damn it." A large blob of red paint had just fallen into Freddy's eye from the boy three rungs up the ladder. "Be more careful." The boy was apparently trying to paint an American Air Force jet dropping blood bombs, but the result more closely resembling a vulture relieving himself on a group of stick figures. Freddy's hands were hurting from scraping and painting and scraping and painting again. *This is more difficult than I would have thought.* He deflected his frustration by using it as a teaching moment for his team.

"It's with these carefully placed images that we are able to deliver the most powerful messages. You know, like they say, a picture is worth a thousand words. As the revolution has learned, it is not with guns—" the noise of a large tank interrupted him as it careened around the outside of the airstrip in its relentless patrols— "but with the power of ideas that we will have our final advantage, our checkmate against the power of the empire." He leaned back on the ladder, stretching his back from the blistering work.

Mia wiped her hand across her forehead and said, "Dude, shut up already." Freddy threw a nasty glare in the direction of the offending comments and went back to work.

He was in the process of drawing an Uncle Sam stick figure with a little swastika and Hitler mustache, but it wasn't coming out right and looked more like an angry Italian woman with a mustache. He would have to do it again. And back to scraping and painting …

* * *

Teniente Machado walked purposefully into his office, sat down in his leather chair behind the large wooden desk, and started enthusiastically scratching a very nasty case of jock itch. *These damn uniforms. Trust the god-damn Chinese to make material that doesn't breathe,* he thought as he watched an enormous green cockroach crawling up the venetian blinds covering the windows. Machado frowned as he dug into his rash with his nails, trying to ease the agony. As he worked, he realized that all of a sudden the room smelled strongly of earth and rotten coffee. Machado looked up from his task to see the intelligence man standing in the center of the room. "Greetings," he hissed.

"*Jesucristo bendito*, don't do that," Machado said. "You scared the shit out of me." He quickly pulled his hands out of his pants. Now fully visible, the man was wearing civilian clothes and was unshaven and slightly damp. A large owl feather clung to his woolen sweater.

"It is tomorrow. I heard them with my own ears; they are planning to march on the airfield and disrupt the closing of your youth conference. They are hoping to either force El Comandante to cancel his appearance or provoke violence to show the gringuitos that we are thugs."

"Interesting. What time do we think they will arrive?" *Teniente* Machado asked.

"They say between five and six, to create a disturbance just in time for when El Comandante is supposed to arrive at eight."

"Hmm," Machado said, half to himself. "They want violence, do they? They want to stop El Comandante's appearance? Tomorrow, the crowd for El Comandante's speech should be impressively large.

Let's prepare some pre-speech activities for them. Thank you, I'll take care of the rest." The man vanished. All Machado heard was a faint tapping sound as a large cockroach scurried out the door.

"*Señor.*" Miria pounded on the door, and Machado knew that he would have to save his private task for later that evening. Instead, he poured a glass of ice water down the front of his zipper, making a questionable stain but relieving the itch. His secretary ushered in the invisible bartender from the club, and Machado this time had him stand against a large, colorful portrait of the commander of the army. He was followed closely by the tails that Machado had placed on the suspects.

"They are planning to arrest El Comandante," was the combined message. "Tomorrow, at eight o'clock. They have a warrant. They have even organized with the power company—there will be a blackout from eight o'clock for ten minutes."

"We followed Capitan Alejandro Fuentes, the fourth man in those pictures, to an apartment overlooking the airstrip."

"What do we know about Fuentes?" asked Machado.

"Frankly, *mi Teniente*, not much. He is a career military man and a good soldier. Clean record. Consistently promoted. His motivations are unclear." Machado frowned but gave an imperceptible shrug. Things were coming together.

"Fine, fine work, men." Machado was smug, already envisioning his promotion and pay raise. "Nothing need be done tonight—but tomorrow will be a busy day. I need everybody in early." He leaned out the door and said to his Miria, "Get me the *Casa Naranja.*"

Machado rifled around in his desk drawer until he found a half-smoked Cuban cigar. He lit it using a lighter shaped like El Che, the flames spouting from the top of his red beret. It had been a gift from his previous supervisor, the *Capitán* in charge of the armored tank division stationed on the beach. The gringos, having finished their work as the golden twilight rapidly approached, were finding their jeeps for their transport back into the hills. The murals were, this time, worse than ever, and he cringed at the representation of El Comandante that looked like a fat, Indian Santa Claus. He couldn't believe these gringos. *They really will believe anything.* Then came the final rap on the door.

"*Mi Teniente*," said his airport security manager.

"*Si.*"

"I have bad news."

"You always have bad news; I don't know why I haven't fired you yet."

"I'm sorry, sir. We couldn't find any holes. I have no idea how the drugs are making it through." The guardsman cringed, awaiting the explosion.

He wasn't to be disappointed. "I told you not to return until you found the problem." It was worse than an explosion. Machado was speaking in even, cool tones. "You imbecile, what do I pay you for? Okay, listen here. I'm giving you until tomorrow to figure it out. This is what you will do. Starting the following morning, I want you to search every single item going onto *every single* airplane with dogs. I don't care if El Comandante himself is traveling; I want his plane and his baggage checked."

Then he lowered his voice slightly and said slowly, "Of course, that doesn't mean *our* luggage with *our* merchandise, you idiot." The man nodded. "Nothing goes on any airplane—passenger, military, or transport—without going in front of a dog. No exceptions. If anybody has any problem with this, they can come see me."

The man gave a crisp salute. "*Entiendo perfectamente, mi Teniente.*" And he was gone.

Machado threw himself into his large, oversized leather office chair, rolling the cigar around his tongue. He was exhausted. *So much conspiring, so many people. Why don't they just let me do my job and make my small money? Why do they push? I am so sick of people. I wish they would all just go away. We really need to lock this all down; this is getting too difficult to manage. But seems people are afraid to do what it takes.* His rapid-fire, random thoughts were the product of stress and fatigue. He prepared to call it a day. Tomorrow would come early. He went to the closet and pulled out his cot, unfolded it onto the hard tile floor, and grabbed the thin blanket from the shelf. He didn't even take off his uniform but simply turned off the lights and collapsed into the cot, immediately falling asleep.

40

* * *

A nd again the tentacles of night engulfed San Porfirio de la Guacharaca. This musty night was pregnant with the tenseness of expectation, of waiting, like the calm when the Venezuelan Caribbean reflects like a glass surface as the storm clouds roll forward, the sheets of shimmering silver visible in the distance while the fish scuttle through the quiet waters for their hiding places under the rocks of the lagoons. The lieutenant was sleeping comfortably face down on the cot in his office, dreaming the dreams of the increasingly immoral.

* * *

The young students had set up their camp for a second night, seeking solace and protection in each other's company as the fear of tomorrow brought a chill to their bones and made more than one of them shiver imperceptibly. They sought in their camaraderie the harmony that is so important before momentous occasions, the feeling of togetherness building their intercourse so they came to feel as if they were part of each other's thoughts. The cowboy pulled out a *charango*, made from the shell of an armadillo, and they all sang songs of revolution—a new revolution that would in turn set them free of *their* bondage.

* * *

Freddy had gone back to his house with his military escort, where he found Geronimo waiting for him with a few cold beers. Before drinking a beer, he went into the small bathroom—separated from the rest of the house by an old shower curtain covered in American cartoon characters—and tried in vain to wash the paint out of his hair, off his glasses, and out of his skin. Unsuccessful, he went to sleep resplendent in the brilliant colors of the Venezuelan flag.

* * *

Through that shared nervous connection created by conspiracy, Esmeralda and her accomplices did not sleep at all that night. Tomorrow, the sun would inevitably rise and usher in the day—the fateful day—and, ready or not, prepared or unprepared, they would have to move forward. All night long Esmeralda tossed and turned; her tiny yorkie looked on in a silent, nervous vigil, occasionally licking dry a renegade tear that escaped as Esmeralda thought about the decades of suffering and frustration she had lived through.

As she tossed and turned, Esmeralda clutched in her fist a gift from the captain, her vice-like grip causing blood to drip down the chain. A locket, from Alejandro and delivered by the general, was a thank-you from a grateful family—his great-aunt's locket that had been passed down through generations. Inside, newly engraved in bold cursive, the words, "Lest we forget, never again."

41

* * *

Freddy bolted wide awake.

He looked at his wristwatch. It was still in the very earliest hours of the morning, but sleep had fled, chased away by a strange sense of anxiety in anticipation of something unknown. Try as he might to return to his slumber, he could not; his eyes were locked wide open. Still physically tired from his activities, he shrugged and pulled on his pants, a T-shirt, and his ball cap—to cover his long, unruly mane of hair, still painted in a rainbow of colors—and cracked open the door. He immediately heard soft incantations tinkling like a bell in the predawn stillness. As he peered through the crack, he saw the small plastic statue of Maria Liberia moving around in front of the shrine that Geronimo's grandmother had set up. She was collecting some of the coins and food left in front of her the previous evening by the devoted oracle, stuffing the coins deep into her tiny dress, making it bulge as if she were pregnant.

Each night, Geronimo's aging grandmother would take a one-half Asno coin from the old coffee can she kept on top of the refrigerator and crawl in loving submission on her hands and knees across the bare cement living room chanting prayers for Geronimo and for her Comandante. When she arrived at the statue, she would place her wrinkled lips on the small blue-painted feet of the idol and say quiet words, words meant only for herself and her protector. She would then leave the coin and some food, with a soda cap full of local beer, in homage to Maria Liberia's ongoing work to keep Geronimo and her loved ones safe. These practices, the unorthodox expressions of syncretistic Catholicism, brought over at the dawning of Columbian history from the islands and mingled with the animistic beliefs of West Africa to feed the Latin need for mysticism in their dealings with the natural world around them, were called *Santería*. Geronimo's grandmother was a *santera*—in fact, the most famous *santera* in the barrio. If asked, she would trace her beliefs back to a boatload of slaves that had arrived, via Puerto Rico, to be unwilling servants in the rice paddies of the oligarchs at San Onofre, a colonial agricultural village halfway between the important port city of Santo Tomas and the border. There, clinging to each other in terror, knee deep in murky water, toiling bent over the back-breaking labor of harvesting rice, they had found their support. And they had found their power.

It had been a harshly humid Caribbean summer; the sweat had poured off the backs of the slaves as they worked tirelessly in the fields. First a plague of frogs had invaded their paddies from up in the jungles. They were large green monsters who voraciously devoured the delicate seedlings during the night. The slave community had placed fires around the paddies hoping to frighten away the monsters, positioned guards to beat away the frogs, and even dug a moat around the paddies and filled it with piranha brought in from the Great River. Nothing had worked, and the frogs had kept coming until the paddies stood naked for the sun and the rain to mock. They had replanted, pulling deep from springs of money they didn't have to lovingly place each little shoot in the water again. This time, the plants grew well, and the shoots began to thrive. The slaves were happy, and the weekend before the harvest they held a premature celebration, drinking from a vat of *chicha*, a drink of fermented cassava made with their own spit that had been prepared for the postharvest celebration.

The following morning, while they were all still suffering from the *chicha*-induced hangover, a rogue wave, twenty-five feet high, leaped into the air beside their village and drowned the paddies, almost two kilometers inland, dragging their harvest back out to sea. The slaves were dismayed, knowing that the slave masters were even then on their way to collect the harvest and if there was not enough they would seize and sell some of their children to make up for the costs.

"Oh, woe is us, what shall we do?" Distraught, they had gone to the village shaman, an old woman who still only spoke the language of the Dark Continent. The old woman was black as a moonless night; her teeth were brown from the years of incessant smoking her profession required. She was wearing a brown dress sewn from the reeds harvested from the nearby lagoon, and her long, braided hair was held in place with crab pincers. Her house was a cacophony of mystical artifacts: crystals and skulls, jars full of bizarre things, and in the center a fire tinged green and orange. She stood from her cross-legged position by a closed window and selected a gray substance out of a jar to drop into the fire. "Yemanja is angry," she told them, studying the flames, "because you preempted the celebration of the bounty before the harvest was in, and in your impatience you forgot to revere her in thanks for the gift so close to her shores."

That night, the community held a celebration on the shores of the Caribbean. They took five of the prize roosters from the village, chopped their heads off, and sprinkled the blood in the surging tide. They then constructed a raft of bamboo measuring fifteen feet across and placed on it rice shoots, the bodies of the five chickens, and a bottle of the finest local rum. One of the strongest swimmers, a young gangly boy, pulled the raft beyond the cresting waves into the heart of the Caribbean, all the while holding a torch in his mouth. When he made it beyond the tide that threatened to pull their gifts back into shore, he lit the floating offering and swam quickly back. The community, standing on the beach in hopeful anticipation, witnessed the blue-tinged explosion followed by a stunning display of maritime creatures: dolphins jumped, killer whales breached, seals and otters played together, and the people knew their offering had been accepted.

The next morning, the paddies were full of the most bountiful harvest in years. In celebration, the people uncovered a second vat of *chicha* and celebrated all day long, losing themselves in oblivion by midafternoon. Slightly past midnight, they heard through their drunken stupor the pounding of rocks and the sound of a thousand stampeding llamas that is always associated with landslides. The next morning, they found their paddies filled with mud and rocks by a wave that had traveled the impossible distance from the mountains.

Running back to the oracle, they demanded to know what had happened. "The Pachamama is offended at you not offering mother earth thanks for the bounty that most obviously comes only from her," old woman explained. She further clarified the problem, "Yemanja and the Pachamama are, in fact, sisters. At the beginning of time they had a falling out over power and congregation, and they parted ways, one going into the mountains to become the mother of the land and the other wading into the sea to find her home among the kelp and cod as the watery bride of Poseidon. However, each has laid claim over the coastal areas as their domain. Since you are coastal slaves, you must appease both of the angry siblings or risk the wrath of both." And she became quiet, smoking her hand-carved wooden pipe filled with tobacco harvested from the garden behind her small wooden hut, which was built on stilts to protect against the monsoon tides.

"This we shall do." Curious about why the oracle had not mentioned this before, but grateful there was a solution, the slaves prepared a sacrifice. At the foothills of the mountains they found a cave, and they followed it inside until they touched the spine of the mountain itself. There, they beheaded their finest goat and sprinkled the blood around in a circle on the cave floor, which was covered with bat droppings and prehistoric fossils. They laid on top of the blood wreaths of flowers and—of course—a bottle of their finest rum, which their fastest runner set to blazing and fled before the blast destroyed the mouth of the cave and hid their sacrifice forever. In the light of the explosion, they saw cougar and panther frolicking, watched by flamboyant parrots and bats that flew in circles causing the air to become a vortex. They knew their sacrifice had been accepted.

The following morning, the mud had melted into the finest paddies, with full-grown rice plants springing from them twice as high as the previous day. That night they did not celebrate, anxious not to repeat any mistakes, and the next day was filled with the hard work of harvest. The work was done by late afternoon—in time for the slave masters to arrive and confiscate the bountiful harvest.

Complaining that it was not enough, the white men—dressed in fine clothes and riding powerful horses—took with them two small girls as punishment for the laziness of their slaves. The girls would be sold at the slave markets of Cordoba.

Desperately saddened by their fate, the slaves drank themselves to sleep on a third vat of *chicha*, this time not in celebration but consolation. "Woe is our fate" they said to mount and sea, "for we are thrice cursed."

The next morning, to their surprise, another full crop had filled the fields. "We are saved," they shouted, hugging each other and dancing with joy at their good luck. Through a friendly local priest they purchased back their stolen offspring. Every year after that they repeated their gifts to the Pachamama and Yemanja who, over time, had merged into a third and more fantastic deity called Santa Liberia. Ever since, the blacks of Venezuela were stalwartly *santeros*. Geronimo's mother was a direct descendent from the oracle, her black skin diluted by intermarriage but her power remaining strong.

But, for the community, her claim to power and position within the barrio was an event closer to home. It had been a dark night due to the power outages caused by the sabotage of the oligarchs as they tried to disrupt daily life of the poor in retaliation for their unwavering support for El Comandante. The marching had been incessant, and Geronimo had spent most of his time in the valley below organizing and commanding his red army. He would return home only to wash or eat something, or to seek further recruits for the undeclared war that was being waged in the streets and back alleys of the capital. "I have to go, Grandma," he'd said as he gathered clean shirts and drank water. "We are defending our way of life."

The life of the nation had drawn to a standstill. The supermarkets and kiosks were empty of supplies, having been affected by the national strike that sought to shut down the country. Geronimo's grandmother was worried. She was worried about her Comandante and her grandson, who was, according to him, a leader in the defense of the revolution. She would watch on TV—in the brief moments when there was power, and when it was not showing cartoons—as the marchers confronted each other, focusing her sharp gaze on the blood that covered the streets and desperately identifying bodies—hoping that they were not hers.

As the days turned into weeks and Geronimo's appearances became more sporadic, his grandmother turned to Maria Liberia. She gathered together the toenails of her grandson, a picture of El Comandante, three pigeon eggs from the plaza in the center of San Porfirio, and a candle the size of her thigh melted from the fat of the edible rat from the Great Plains. "Oh Maria Liberia," she said to the shrine she had set up on the curb of the barrio, "Deliver us from this time of tribulation and deliver our precious Comandante from the danger he is suffering at the hands of the godless—who do not recognize you as the spirit guardian of Venezuela."

A crowd started to gather, kneeling in prostration before the plastic statue of Maria Liberia. Then, a strange thing happened. As night fell, the statue came to life, illuminated by its own light, and she spoke—reassuring those assembled of the righteousness of their cause and her protection of their precious, peaceful revolution.

Within the hour, the oligarchs had been beaten back, and El Comandante appeared on TV declaring an end to the insurrection. Dozens had been killed, but Geronimo arrived back home— granted, smelling of the street and of tear gas, and eyes bloodshot with lack of sleep, but safe and unhurt. The following day, the entire community arrived at Geronimo's house to say thanks and to offer homage to the savior of the revolution and the most powerful *santera* in the barrio, to whom they owed their endless gratitude.

Freddy crept into the room to investigate further and surprised the figurine come to life. She immediately froze, leaping back up into her nook and returning to plastic, her smile plastered in red on her face and her dress still bulging. He walked quietly into the still and silent living room and sat down on the small love seat. He could hear Geronimo snoring in the room he was sharing with his grandmother. Privacy is infrequently a welcome guest in the poorest households of the world, and Venezuela is no exception. Freddy thought about his large house in the Midwest. *I think we Americans,* he said to himself, speaking out of the wisdom brought by a short stint of travel, *have too much of a sense of individuality and personal space. Look at these people: they are extremely happy sleeping together, eating together, and living one upon the other like bees. That's their support network—we in America could learn something from them.*

He stood and went over to the tiny green plastic table to read, in his limited Spanish, some of the great works he found on the tattered old bookshelf that was leaning up against the wall. "No Clancy here," he said out loud as he thumbed through works of Cervantes, Freire, Marx, Neruda, and important communist authors. He picked up one book called *Discursos del Comandante* and opened to a random page. They seemed to be transcripts of El Comandante's various speeches. One entry caught his eye. It was highlighted in yellow, with exclamation points on both sides in the style of Latin enthusiasm.

There are those that say that the economy is collapsing, and that the revolution is moribund. To that, and to them, I respond that it is the capitalist appendages of our national economy, which I have worked so hard to destroy, for the betterment of our people, which are gangrene and dying. And these poisonous limbs are the parts that we must lop off once and for all, for these are the final vestiges of the selfishness of the *escualidos*, who use their money for personal pleasure through capitalist consumption. And what do we care? They can't import expensive cars? They can't take expensive vacations? They can't have multiple homes? Those are capitalist excesses that are destroying our environment and will end the world if they cannot be stopped.

It was, to Freddy, like a morning devotional that made his mind soar on the wings of inspiration and gratitude; inspiration to the words and what they did as they played in his mind; and gratitude to fate—never God, he didn't believe in God, no good communist believed in God—that had played its part in guiding his steps to this glorious place.

Just at that minute Geronimo stumbled out of the bedroom, and they greeted each other as old friends, as brothers. There was no hot water in this tiny hovel, so they took turns in the cold shower in the small room without a door. After a simple breakfast of day-old beans and rice, salted with that special cheese that Freddy was starting to really enjoy—eaten in the special harmony that only silence can bring—they again returned to the airstrip.

Their ride was quiet, as if everything that needed to be spoken had already been said. Now they were simply waiting for the next few hours for the things to play out. Geronimo looked like he was chewing something over in his mind. He would occasionally take out a card and write down a word or a thought before replacing it in his back pocket. Arriving, Freddy was stunned. Their small troop of Americans was submerged in a flood of humanity.

Freddy followed the trickle up into the hills from the hovels and back alleys of revolutionary power. In his mind's eye, in the early tropical morning it looked like the mountains were bleeding—like a stream of blood from a thousand cuts all across the hillside rushing, pooling itself around him in a lake of anger and power and poverty. Down every stairway, out of every hovel and hole, between every narrow building and upon every irregular roadway, the steady, constant march approached.

"I've never seen anything like this," Freddy told Geronimo, who said proudly, "We the poor of Venezuela are always ready to serve our country."

Every individual member of that torrent of collective humanity was draped in the paraphernalia of the revolution. Red shirts with El Comandante's face on them, red hats blazoned with the communist party logo. Red armbands and the ever-present Venezuelan flag, modified by El Comandante in an act of revolutionary anger to reflect the changing nature of the newly refounded republic. In the center of the national crest, AK-47s had replaced arrows, and the face of El Comandante had been superimposed upon the ever-present Asno. The colors had been changed to include the Cuban flag.

On the highway that made its way east of town, out into the lawless rural areas, was a line of buses as far as the eye could see. They were parked where the highway left San Porfirio, just past the toll booth, where the road narrowed to two lanes and began to snake out across the great lengths of Venezuela to the border and the ocean. The buses were of all makes and sizes. Some were old American school buses painted in colorful murals depicting the scenes Freddy had become used to. Others were buses that belonged to the military, painted drab green with Venezuelan flags on each side. Some small buses were for daily transport of the poor people around the towns and cities of the interior.

The press of humanity was stifling. Even in the cool morning, the heat generated by that many sweaty, unwashed bodies was making Freddy a bit nauseous. "What is going on?" he asked Geronimo.

"You'll see," Geronimo said. He was again silent.

At the very far end of the airstrip, a large group, maybe three or four hundred people, were lounging beside their motorcycles. There was something more brutal in their countenance, a violence more brazen than in the eyes of the mob that surrounded him, an impunity more tactile, a malice more palpable.

The mob itself, packed tightly across the airstrip toward the stage, was composed of many different types of people, and Freddy decided to walk closer to get a better feel for who they were. As he walked through the crowd, snippets of conversation floated up from the crowd. "How much were you paid?" asked one fat man with a long mustache to another. "Up in our barrio we were offered fifty thousand Asnos."

"Same for us," the other replied.

"But we were promised lunch. Probably just the same hot-dogs like usual," the fat man complained. He was wearing a pair of blue jeans and some slip-on loafers. His plump feet almost burst through the stitching. His head was bare, and his greasy hair was sparse and plastered to the top of his rotund head.

As he walked on, Freddy found two very attractive girls and stood beside them, looking away into the distance but staring at them out of the corner of his eye. They had on the red shirts of El Comandante but had cut him off midface to expose the elaborate tattoos painted around their belly buttons. Their pants were faded jeans and so tight that Freddy wondered how they'd managed to squish into them. Their nails were long and intricately painted, and their hair was painted with red streaks—special for the day. "I really hope I'm not pregnant," one was saying. "I can't afford to have another baby right now—I don't know what to do with little Juancho as it is."

The other responded, "Well, that serves you right. I told you that guy was no good." They both looked across the horde to a large, powerful biker who was leering and making obscene gestures in the direction of the girl—after which he slapped a buddy on the back and said something that Freddy was sure was neither polite nor flattering.

Continuing down into the mob, Freddy ran headlong into the emissary. Surprised and pleased, he greeted him. The emissary, however, was nervously looking around and was all business.

"I've been looking for you. I've had the important knapsack delivered to where you are staying. Make sure not to open it; it's rigged so the contents are damaged if it's not opened correctly. We take extra precautions against the gringos getting their hands on our materials before they go public—they'd love to expose our campaign." And he thanked him for his revolutionary spirit. "There is also one other thing."

"Anything."

"I've just been watching the setup of the opposition march, more out of curiosity than anything else …"

"The opposition march?" Freddy asked.

"Ya, you didn't know?"

"Know what?

"There's a large *oligarquia* march on the highway a few kilometers away. They want to ruin El Comandante's speech. You're gonna stop em, that's what all this is for." He gestured around to the mob. "Anyway, the leader's a friend of yours."

"Whadya mean?"

"Your old buddy from school in the Midwest."

"The jerk who pushed me?" Freddy was surprised.

"Yup. This is a bad kid. Rotten to the core. He looks charming and sounds flowery, but he's dangerous, and a liar. If you get a chance, teach him a lesson." The emissary nodded at Freddy, as if foreshadowing what was to come, and said, "I've got some things to do today, more work to prepare for the campaign. But I'll see you tomorrow as we fly back."

"But …" Freddy stumbled around for something to engage the emissary, trying to keep him around for at least a few minutes more. But he had already vanished.

The horde was multiplying faster than Freddy could imagine, filling up the airstrip and spilling out onto the highway beyond. There were fat people, skinny people, old people, young people, black people, white people—it was mesmerizing. Time seemed to either stand still or speed up as the people kept coming.

Somebody in the back of the crowd turned on a stereo, and the pounding music of reggaeton pulsated like waves, making the assembly gyrate in synchronization with the beat. A soccer game broke out among high school students using several trees and a half-empty beer can as goalposts. Filled with fervor, Freddy dove into the celebration. He joined the group that was dancing, shaking his derriere energetically. The music stopped, and everybody applauded him, cheering on as he beamed. He ran over to the high school students. Taking off his shirt, he displayed proudly his unsightly rolls as he huffed and puffed, trying desperately to score a goal and garner the respect of his hosts. He went on to the T-shirt vendor. "*Dame quince*," he said, pointing to several red shirts and hats. He distributed them to the people he saw who were not sporting revolutionary gear.

He climbed a few steps and saw his mural from yesterday afternoon. Instead of the crude stick figures of the day before, revolutionary energy had breathed life into his work. He was stunned at the image of the last supper; the perfectly painted face of Jesus had assumed the perfect semblance of El Comandante. Bleeding out from the head wounds caused by the crown of thorns, red blood—the shimmering bright red of new blood—trickled down the painting and collected in a depression on the sidewalk at the foot of the mural. Out of this glistening, living wetness had sprouted a thick green vine that crawled along the sidewalk and climbed a nearby tree. The vine was almost as thick as Freddy's wrist, and out of it sprang exotic animals and wonderful creatures. Then, just as his head started to spin, the presence of such a multitude started to suck away his oxygen, and he gasped to breathe, feeling as if the sudden claustrophobia would make him collapse—just then, Lieutenant Juan Marco Machado strode boldly onto the stage and seized the microphone.

42

*** * ***

"Good morning." Pancho stretched and stood up, greeting his coconspirators. The corners of the chapel were still filled with darkness. A kinetic energy of collective purpose vibrated through the narrow room. They made their final pot of coffee, black and pungent. "Is everybody well rested? We have a long day today. Today, we're gonna surprise the revolution with a small revolution of our own."

"My people have made it through." Juanita was talking with somebody on her phone. "No military stopped them, although there were a lot on the road."

"My cowboys didn't run into any problems either," said Benito. "Strange, they were just waved through."

Carlitos stretched and went outside to relieve himself. He came back in whistling.

Pancho had taken a seat in front of the window, cradling in both hands his hot metal camping cup filled with coffee. He'd been up very late preparing his speech—the one he'd give at the student march. He was practicing it, adding the final flair for which he was famous.

"How's it coming?" asked Carlitos. All the students knew that Pancho was an excellent speaker.

"I think I've got most of it down."

"When should we get going?" Carlitos asked the group.

"Let's wait a little while," Pancho responded. "At least until the sun comes up and some of our buses are here, so we can start organizing and preparing."

Around him the students slowly began to roll up their sleeping bags and wash out their dishes, packing them in boxes and carrying them out to the cars. Seconds turned into minutes, and the sun leaped from the green jungle, burning out the haze in an explosion of energy. The time had come. They all walked in unison outside, turning and giving quiet thanks to the small chapel for its protection and refuge. The hills were coming alive with the colors of daytime; the deep greens of the canopy and the occasional pinpricks of pastel that were the orchids were now fully visible. They heard a small animal scurry somewhere and the squawking of a flock of large colorful macaws in the trees above the hills. In the distance, a howler monkey sounded like a lion, eager to impress his possible mate. They were silent for quite a while, taking it all in and reflecting on Pancho's words—knowing again it was freedom they wanted.

Then, energy rumbling from his low voice, Pancho said, "Let's go."

And together they marched down to their cars to drive the short distance back into the city, over the ruined roads, to the westernmost part of the highway—where the people were already beginning to assemble.

"We're here." Pancho jumped out of the car and climbed to stand in full height on its roof, yelling greetings to the assembled students. The angry, bitter student of English was gone. Pancho the leader had returned, absent the crippling self-doubt as he embraced again his element. The students congregated around his car, pushing and jockeying for the opportunity to welcome him. A roar of joy and defiance exploded spontaneously from the assemblage. He hopped off the car and shook hands like a returning hero, like a politician, like a star. His suffering, of which they were all well aware, made him more dearly beloved of his followers. "Welcome back. Susana would be proud," they said, and "We are glad you are here—you look good, time has done you well," and even, "Don't worry, in your absence, we were with you."

"Thank you," was all Pancho could say. "Let's set this thing up."

They walked over to the truck platform that had just arrived. The speaker system was set up; they decorated the platform with the colors of the student movement and hung on its sides the flag, the original flag, of their beloved Venezuela. The ambulances were placed, the water set to cool in its trucks. The street vendors began to assume their positions, sprinkled through the crowd to maximize profits. The buses continued to arrive. Slowly, like caterpillars, they inched along the highway and came to a stop at the far west end of the city—the sounds of their brakes hissing in the air, complaining from the long journey, overheated with the weight of their anxious passengers.

"We have come," read the hastily painted letters on the side of one. "Democracy means freedom," said another, and "Stop us, if you dare," was the message delivered by yet another. They had encountered no problems; in fact, only a few of the buses had been held inside their universities by communist students; who had punctured the tires and broken the windows in an attempt to silence dissent.

"Pancho, the radio is here." Carlitos had returned to his role as Pancho's chief of staff. Pancho sat in front of the microphone, inside a van—shielded from the whistles and the excited screams of those outside—and said, "I invite you to join us, friends and lovers of freedom. We are marching. We don't have a permit. We can't pay you. What do we have? At least for now, we still have our freedom. So help us defend that freedom, and come unite with us as we try to preserve our country for ourselves and our children. Now, to the far west end of the *Autopista de la Liberacion*, so aptly named for just this moment—there you will find us, and you will march with us again."

And this message went out far and wide. Into the diners, into the malls, into the homes, and into the churches. And the people responded. Tired from the water shortages, the power shortages, the violence, and the cacophony of incompetence that left them gasping for breath and locked in an epic fight to wade through the overpowering weight of revolutionary bureaucracy to accomplish even the smallest, most insignificant tasks—they came.

And they continued to come. The trickle became a stream and then a torrent.

"I have never seen anything like this," said Pancho to Carlitos.

"Ya, it's been a long time. People are losing hope." Out of the buildings came old women with their little dogs. Invalids in their wheelchairs were pushed by their neighbors. Families, men with their young daughters on their shoulders. Single mothers hand in hand with their children. Priests dressed in their long, black Catholic robes. Evangelicals in their cheap suits and ties holding oversized Bibles. As far as he could see, strollers, dogs on walking chains. Here was a golf cart with four elderly men, their walkers tied to the back. And there, the boy scouts in their uniforms, passing out bottled water to the marchers. A man was pulling his child's red wagon full of water and food, handing it out freely as he went. Another had a backpack full of small Venezuelan flags he was distributing to child and adult alike.

The crowd was pooling in the center of the highway, expanding exponentially in every direction. Old, young, black, white, Indian, immigrant, oligarch, peasant, student, heathen, hedonist, and priest—all marching together as one in a single loud proclamation of defiance. All of a sudden, from the cumulous clouds that were doing somersaults through the heavens above, a heavy rainbow fell. It hit the gathering assembly and exploded, splashing everybody with the glorious colors of freedom. Pancho had to shield his eyes from the Technicolor blessing as Mother Nature herself lent her support to their endeavor. The marchers, daring to stand and march, to be seen, might as well have been marching naked, as vulnerable as they were to all the power of the state rallied against them not far away. Yet they seemed unafraid.

That day, the press of people did not feel like a vacuum, without oxygen, but instead light and airy, like a meadow filled with flowers. From the back somebody started singing songs old and new, hymns that reminded them of their country and their heritage. Many had gathered around a famous comedian who was putting on an impromptu sketch amid loud, raucous laughter. A marching band had come from a local high school to add their talents to the din. Pancho stood back, proud and humbled to lead such a testament to human resilience.

* * *

From his office window Teniente Machado cast his gaze across the red sea of humanity, an evil smirk adorning his face. "So they want a fight, do they?" He snorted. He had always thought that the security services were too easy on the student marchers. If it had been *his* decision, he would have put them in their place long ago. His orders, delivered as always verbally so there was no paper trail as a testament to their actions, had always been "No, we can't be seen to exercise brutality" and "We must not let the tide of world opinion turn against us. Let them march; they will soon tire. It will be summer soon and they will go to America, or the beach, or the mountains, and we'll pick em apart one by one."

Fat lot they knew, Machado thought in disgust. The students had not stopped marching. Sure, the intensity had dropped, but they were still a nuisance. And by the sounds of the intelligence reports he had been receiving all morning, this one looked to be a big one. But finally, at long last, it *was* his decision.

"El Comandante goes on at eight," the interior minister had said the previous night. "You do what you need to to keep those *hijos de la oligarquia* from our event. We won't be bullied." And the phone had clicked off with resolute finality.

Machado had almost licked his lips. He had a plan, a plan to put an end to this once and for all. *So, they want us to show these gringuitos how brutal we can be? Well, as I always say, show someone brutality and they are shy. Ah, but let them crack a skull or two and you've made a friend for life.*

Last night, before falling asleep on his cot, he had made the phone calls that had activated the Network for the Defense of the Revolution, created by El Comandante for a day such as this.

We must have a way to organize ourselves. There will come a time when this peaceful revolution will have to defend itself from the tyranny against which we fight so hard. And we must be ready.

Following that order, the barrios were organized. A revolutionary commander was appointed, always a party member who was faithful and could be counted on to follow orders. They were given a slush fund to keep them honest, were entrusted with harmless secrets to buy their intrigue, and sometimes were even armed and given guerilla warfare training by friendly—*oh, we'll call them nonstate actors.* Machado smirked. This time, he had gone all out. He mobilized not only San Porfirio's pyramid but the entire nation. Early in the morning—El Comandante never slept—Machado had received a large suitcase of Asnos from the interior ministry, every Asno he'd asked for to fund this event and a few for himself for his dedication. It seemed his work that day was important.

Gazing out the window, he took stock of his handiwork. There were tens of thousands, maybe hundreds of thousands of people. It was like a sea of red, like a crimson orgasm. He liked the color; the uniformity in his mind emphasized discipline and the red aggression, anger, and violence. No ambulances, water trucks, or snack food for his marchers. He'd brought in fifteen hot-dog stands and hundreds of street vendors to give away cold beer.

On the side, the military were preparing. There were five hundred military police officers dressed in full riot gear. Beneath their plastic shields, helmets, and bulletproof vests they looked like large insects that had crawled from the depths of the jungle beyond the city—evil creatures that leered and snapped at each other as they awaited their human prey. The whale, a bruised old water cannon that had been so effective so often, had drunk its fill of water and was dragging its belly convulsively toward the front lines. At the ammunition table, cadets were dispensing rubber bullets, tear gas canisters, and stun grenades.

It was approaching eleven. The timing was right. The equatorial sun had heated things up early this day, driving the mob to drink. That was good. He walked outside. Thunder and lightning pounded from far away—ominous sounds that underscored the tone of this march. He went down the stairs and past the Russian helicopters—one recently reassembled and fueling up for his personal use, so he could watch his handiwork from above—and across to the platform where he bounded energetically up the steps.

* * *

"Students, young people, American friends, and defenders of the revolution." The military man Freddy knew as Machado started to speak. The mob pulsated around him. He was finally gonna get his orders. "This is a special day. Tonight, El Comandante will address you all from the exact place where I am standing. You are the few, the privileged; you should find it in your hearts to feel lucky. To hear El Comandante speak in person is a gift. It is to understand the soul of our peaceful revolution and to fall into communion with an unbroken line of revolutionaries going back centuries to names we read about in awe and reverence." Freddy felt the buzz and knew something big was going to happen.

"But before you can listen to the words, you must prove yourselves worthy." Freddy was holding his breath. The lieutenant continued, "Out in front of us along the highway, which was built to facilitate our ability to live and work together in harmony, approaches an angry mob of counter-revolutionaries." He hesitated while the crowd hissed. Freddy joined in enthusiastically.

"Their goal is to force El Comandante to stay home tonight. They wish to deny you, our guests, the opportunity to hear him, and to prove to you that it is they—the coupsters, the oligarchs, and the selfish capitalists—that still run Venezuela. Our task is easy: we will go to them and show them that we will defend our revolution and our glorious Comandante. And we will remind them, once again, that they do not run things here." His flourishing speech ended. The silence of the masses exploded in a crescendo of applause, and the collective oozed itself like a cerise bruise through the gate onto the highway, where it began its advance upon the enemy.

Freddy goose-stepped forward, passing by the side of his mural. The pooled blood was still feeding the strange, black fruit. Lining up beside the vines, each marcher picked a blood-grape, partaking in the bizarre Eucharist as they went forth to do El Comandante's bidding. Biting into the grape, Freddy savored the squishy sweetness, a flavor he'd never experienced before. Into his limbs rushed a new energy, and his mind exploded with a violence like none he'd ever felt. Righteous fury filled his soul. *How could they, these imposters, try to take from us the only thing that has been good in our lives, the only person who has loved us, and the only wonderful project where we are able to participate just as we are?* His mind seethed, and his face contorted. Around him the countenance of his fellow marchers changed. They became an angry underworld army.

He was swept off his feet and toward the highway, floating along as he tried to regain control of his feet and momentum and as he wrestled with the demon in his soul. He struggled for breath and for the opportunity to think about what he was going to do. He was filled with anger and pride. The floor moved below him, and the highway—the battleground—approached relentlessly. *If only my dad could see me now,* he thought as he plunged through the exit.

* * *

Pancho had everything ready, just as he liked it. It was almost eleven o'clock, and people had been milling around for several hours. The timing was right. He climbed onto the back of the truck, the moving stage, and gazed across the crowd. As far as he could see were colorful shirts, flags, banners, signs, and the occasional clown or mime—their only weapons for this battle—one in a long line of battles in the war for the return of their freedoms. Down the narrow streets beside the multitude he could see dozens of police and military officers. They were waiting and watching on their motorcycles and in their armored vehicles. But as of yet, no attempt had been made to stop him—they were going to let him march. *Maybe the revolutionaries are spoiling for a fight too.*

"Everybody," he yelled through the microphone to the throngs.

"Listen," he tried again.

"Hear me." Finally, the crowd grew silent. At the back, everybody turned to face him. A large group of young people who had cleared an area and were playing baseball with a stick and a bottle cap put an end to their game. "We are going to start now. I want to remind you that whatever happens, don't let them provoke you. We can't resort to violence. The flowers of our new freedom will not spring from soil soaked with the blood of our fellow countrymen."

Pancho looked around at the attentive faces. They were the faces of the students, immortal in their youth. But also the faces of the old, wizened with sorrow and experience. And the faces of the bedraggled middle class struggling to survive, and looking to him in hope, in this new world they hadn't asked for and didn't want. He realized that what for him it was about politics, about power dynamics and the advancement of ideas; but this was not the cause of the march's momentum. In fact, it was the opposite; it was an anti-politics march. They, as Benito had said, simply wanted to be left alone. Most moving to Pancho were the innocent children, who, although they couldn't understand the gravity of the moment, were excited nonetheless.

"Let us move peacefully and orderly. While we march, we will listen to our great musicians from the plains as they regale us with the sounds of our freedom." A group of cowboy students stood up to sing. The song, "*Que Viva Los Estudiantes*," was greeted with a roar of applause and cheering and an explosive surge of movement down the highway.

* * *

Doña Esmeralda decided that morning, while listening to Radio Mega over a bowl of bran flakes, which had cost her twenty-five dollars at the supermarket, that she would participate in this young man's march. *Today's the day I'm going all out. I might as well push the envelope. Maybe it will make a difference*—and with that, she started to dress. She put on a brand-new pair of walking shoes, an expensive jogging suit that she had bought on her last trip to Miami, and a sun visor. Over her head she wrapped a kerchief. On her fingers she had only one gold ring, her wedding ring, which she never took off. On her neck she sprayed an expensive perfume, causing the little yorkie to sneeze and glare at her in anger. She then got out the makeup—the waterproof stuff, knowing that she might sweat, at least in the parts of her body that were not made mostly of plastic and that still *could* sweat—and wrapped a Venezuelan flag around her shoulders. She picked up her tiny dog in her arms and headed out to march. He licked her silicone face; smiling up at her in understanding and support, and let out a little yelp.

43

✳ ✳ ✳

The red march was underway. Emboldened with the juice of that fantastic fruit, Freddy was pulsating with excitement and a new, special kind of anger. He put one foot in front of the other, step, step, step right step. He was like a foot soldier marching on an advancing army. *They will never get by me.* He puffed his chest out as far as they would go, sucking in his stomach and imagining himself a warrior of old defending his king. He was, nevertheless, keeping one eye on the bikers, who were scary ... *but probably important for a march like this one*. He was also trying to get ahead of one foul-smelling man who'd already drunk a lot of beer. The man was munching and mumbling in Freddy's direction, making gestures he didn't understand. At one point he flung the last several bites of his hot dog, barely missing Freddy but smudging his pants with ketchup. Freddy decided it was best to keep his distance.

On the back of a large pickup truck was a sound system. It led the way at the front, encouraging people on with snippets from El Comandante's speeches—quick, angry bursts underlaid with deep bass music reaching all corners of the highway and bouncing off the high apartment buildings on either side to echo back into the crowd. Geronimo walked quietly by Freddy's side, immersed in thought.

✳ ✳ ✳

Pancho was like a force of nature. He leaped from the back of the truck to slap a few friends on the back, giving a jovial smile. He hugged an old woman; he took the place of an elderly man pushing his wife in her wheelchair. He took the hand of a small child on the shoulders of her father while listening to an account of the man's struggles. He conversed intensely for several minutes with one of the student leaders who had come from far away, an old friend whom he had not forgotten. They consoled each other over the leader's recent financial problems, and then Pancho was again on the move. He smiled, he laughed, he encouraged, he consoled, he cried, he uplifted, and he emboldened. And he brought people together, uniting the solitary and encouraging the faint of heart. Overhead, the rainbow that hovered over the march was like the pillar of smoke of old that had helped another lost nation also seeking freedom.

Pancho was keenly aware of his gifts.

He climbed back up on the moving stage. Toward the east, he could see the sunlight shimmering off a sea of red dark as thunderclouds rolled above the oncoming hordes, and he realized immediately the government's game. He wasn't surprised. They had marched at the same time as the revolutionaries before. But the marches were never planned to clash. Usually he even held clandestine meetings with the government to make sure that they avoided bloodshed. This time was different: the revolutionaries *were* spoiling for a fight.

"Up ahead of us," Pancho grabbed the microphone and screamed to the crowd, "there is another march; a sea of red is coming our way. They will try to make us withdraw. They will try to stop our advance. But we will not back down, and we will not be intimidated. They will have to move—they will have to let us through."

* * *

Ahead Freddy saw the shimmering explosion of colors. This was them. The enemy. The coupsters. The oligarchs. The people responsible for the poverty of this nation, responsible for its destruction, and those to whom they could not surrender, no matter what.

Geronimo had also seen the other march, and he pushed and elbowed, dragging Freddy with him through the crowd to the truck with the speaker. He grabbed the microphone and yelled with all his energy, "Revolutionary brethren, you will see in the distance the enemy, those who would take our precious Comandante away from us. Make no mistake: no matter what they say, they are the devil. They would have us returned to poverty and misery so they can continue to steal the resources of the nation for their own selfish gains. Walk toward them, do not let them pass, and force them back. *They must never march again*."

* * *

Time to take a closer look, Machado thought, and he rushed to the landing pad, leaping into the Russian helicopter waiting to its instructions. It took him a few minutes to issue his orders to the Slavic pilot, but soon enough the engines coughed to life and the rotors began to twirl faster and faster, gathering force for the massive machine to clutch at the air around it, ponderously inching upward. The noise was deafening, even under the headphones. Outside, the wind whipped the camp into a gale. Through the tempest, leaflets with El Comandante's face on them, anti-Semitic propaganda, pictures of Uncle Sam with blood running down his huge Dracula teeth, and pictures of El Che flew in all directions. One flew up to stick to the front windshield of the massive helicopter before fluttering away into the morning sun.

Teniente Machado smelled the acrid stench of jet fuel heavy in his nostrils, making him gag. All of a sudden, a loud shrill beeping penetrated the din, and the massive craft, only a few inches off the ground, slammed back down to earth.

"Eimm sorry, sir, but thees aircraft nees vork, ve will take another one." The blond pilot shut off the engine, and the rotors came slowly and tragically to a halt. None of the other Russian helicopters were working, either. When he had asked this morning, Machado had been told it was due to some of the parts needed for emergency repairs being stuck in customs—nobody had paid the entry tariffs at the customs house, and the Russians were unwilling to accept payment in black beans.

"Ve vill take this von." They moved past the powerful beasts till they were standing in front of a training helicopter, a tiny two-seater painted bright yellow.

"You're kidding?" But if he was to see his handiwork, it would have to be from this ridiculous little craft. Machado folded himself in half, smashing his gut to fit into the tiny space.

The diminutive yellow fly buzzed as it exploded into the air and zoomed over the marches to hover above the police line separating them. The two marches had almost reached each other. From his vantage point, the lieutenant could see the opposition student march. The marchers, like multicolored insects, were scurrying behind a large truck that had a speaker and some people on top of it. The affair looked like a collage dropped from a celestial paintbrush. Toward the middle was an empty space where a group was dancing to music, music he couldn't hear but that made him angry anyway. There appeared to be at least a hundred thousand people. Using his hands, he instructed the pilot to fly the length of the parade and determined it was at least four or five kilometers long.

His own march was going well. The hordes that were oozing from the barrios and the airfield were a sea of glistening red that inundated the highway as the swell surged toward the enemy. The differences were stark. The pulsating beating of El Comandante's words caused the mob to throb. They slogged forward under their collective impulse, the revolution pulling their feet forward to the inevitable confrontation. They were celebrating too, dancing to the music and spinning as they edged toward their opponents. But the red afforded them a more menacing appearance, of a torrent of blood flowing together from so many sources and turning into a great river—crashing and ebbing now against the thin line of black and green that was holding back the gruesome tide.

Between the two, the black-and-green dyke, impossibly thin, serving as containment to the rushing, flowing, pulsating, surging sea of red, was made up of his National Guard and the military police. In the center squatted the whale. Its massive green-painted frame was supported by huge tires, and the monster was belching black smoke. Machado had deployed it strategically as the anchor of his defense. From its position, the powerful jets of water could reach both sides of the highway and the entire first flank of the oncoming student marchers. At the back of his march was a water tanker—in case the protest was too heated and the whale ran dry. The security forces were lined four deep from guardrail to guardrail. They had belts of stun grenades and tear gas, machine guns on their shoulders, and long bulletproof vests reaching down to their jackboots. Machado smiled down at his handiwork and gave a thumbs-up to the Russian pilot, eager to share his pride with somebody. The Russian pilot nodded.

As Machado buzzed overhead, slowly, slowly, slowly both marches closed the distance. All of a sudden, a tiny figure jumped from the crowd and bounded onto the platform in front of the student march. Machado mouthed the words, "Take me down lower" to the Russian pilot. *I need to see who that is.* They moved lower, slowly and carefully, until the lieutenant was hovering directly over the line of military. The young man, hair whipped into disarray by the helicopter's vortex, grabbed the microphone, and everything seemed to freeze.

* * *

"There you see them," Pancho cried to the crowd from atop his perch, his words reverberating from the microphone and through the speakers, shaking the entire highway. He raised his hand to signal across the draconian line of military police and the ocean of red. "Look at them, and look hard, look long. They are here to stop us from marching."

A scream, the combination of many thousands of individuals raising their voice in united defiance, exploded from the crowd. They cheered and jeered for several full minutes, throwing their voices above Pancho and above the pounding beating of El Comandante's voice to fall like arrows upon the revolutionaries.

"Friends and lovers of freedom, look at them again." He paused. The noise died down until the silence he induced was heavy with expectation and with unfulfilled power. "For it is not against them that we fight. No, our battle is greater still. It's against that which they represent—the old ideas that are meant to return us to a time without laws and rights, under the power of one omnipotent overlord whose authority is not only total but also arbitrary. A political project designed to deny enlightenment."

"And what is enlightenment, except the ushering in of light? And what is light for? It allows us to see. For centuries, culture after culture has embraced the enlightenment that has allowed them to *see* the universal principles that define our humanity. And through that sight, we have been able to act. Slowly and with hard work, we have won battles to protect those principles. We have seen in Europe the universally accepted legitimacy of domination, occupation, and colonization be pushed aside, paving the way for the occupiers' withdrawal and the creation of independent nation-states whose governments by their people are answerable only to their people and the individual, universal, progressive, inalienable, and un-renounceable principles of enlightenment."

"We have seen the plague of wars and violence, the result of darkness, come gradually to an end under the steadfast supervision of the Geneva Convention, protecting the basic rights of nations and people to no longer fear unwarranted invasion from barbarian armies. We established the Universal Declaration of Human Rights, the International Covenant on Civil and Political Rights, the American Declaration on the Rights and Duties of Man, and the Inter-American Democratic Charter, all of them outlining what we as humans believe are the basic protections of individuals within society. Not the social and cultural rights that the communist dictators espouse to keep us in poverty and misery, no. But these fundamental rights that allow us to understand, exercise, and protect the *most* important of our freedoms. These freedoms are ours to use, to enjoy, to share, to promote, and to defend against all others *and at any cost*. Because these are the very gateway to enlightenment. And enlightenment is the backbone of civilization."

Pancho paused to let the people catch up. He squinted in the sunlight and took out a baseball cap to shield him from the powerful sun. "Yet civilization is a fragile thing. We, the residents of civilization, have witnessed the darkness of ignorance, violence, hatred, and slavery as they have, generation after generation, overcome different nations and peoples like a tsunami. One after the other, people who have *refused* to remain vigilant have received as a reward for their slumber the black mark of bondage and have delivered unto their children only the birthright of despair."

"This phenomenon is by no means new. The Romans, after attaining the pinnacle of civilization, receded into the complacency of sloth and gluttony—*and socialism*. Slowly, resident after resident of Rome embraced public subsidies to prop up their bloated lifestyle—assuming, as all parasites do, that there will always be somebody else to pay for *their* indiscretions. Finally, after centuries, the weight was too much, and a weak and lazy empire collapsed. The city, Augustine's famous city upon a hill, was plunged into darkness—a darkness that drew all of Europe into a millennium of obscurity, disease and death."

Pancho had found his voice, "We have seen this more recently in Europe." He was surprised to find how naturally the words flowed. "As the murderous German rabble—enticed by sweet and symphonic words—took a culture that had given us Bach, Handel, and Beethoven and transformed it instead into the society known for Mendel, Goering, and Himmler. Manipulating the unwary, a soothsayer took power—yes, even legitimately. Through casting of blame he found the perfect scapegoat for ills unaddressed. It was the French occupiers, it was the Americans who waged war, it was the homosexuals, it was the gypsies, it was the miscreants, and finally—it must be the Jews. Hiding behind the comfortable ideology of National Socialism to veil the murderous, thieving rampage, this society extinguished the lights of its own civilization in an orgy of murder."

Pancho looked at the crowd around him. They had grown silent, captivated. Children were still on shoulders, elderly had sat down on the asphalt, and the students had lowered their banners. Pancho heard the whir of the rotors of a tiny yellow helicopter as it hovered overhead.

He continued, "While emblematic, these are of course not the only cases. When people across the world are told they are their brother's keeper—and brought into unfree relationships of bondage one with the other through the erroneous principles of social responsibility—slavery is the only end. Like in the now-defunct USSR that energetically promoted those ideas, millions upon millions were forced to work at jobs not of their choosing, for products not of their liking, and in places not of their consent, in constant fear of the absolute power of a corrupt and illegitimate regime over every aspect of their lives."

Somebody in the red march turned up to full volume the fierce words of El Comandante, played in a reel, repeating and repeating and repeating the call to revolution.

Pancho didn't care. "And to make that model work, those nations were converted into the largest prison camps the world has ever seen. This imprisonment was justified through the principle of socialism where, people were told, we must destroy the personal pursuit of happiness in order to advance. This pursuit, they said, is the result of arcane, primitive animal instincts."

"Instead they replaced it with *their* version of enlightenment— illumination through personal misery and perpetual servitude to others. They took acts of individual creation and, denying the source, put the product to the service of the destruction of its creator. But how long can that work? As the obese weight of unthinking society crushes me, I ask, how long can my creativity last? For all creativity stems from *individual* acts of creation. Acts that glorify the individual man as he seeks to make his own mark on this world that he loves."

Pancho paused.

"So, you ask, what do I need *them* for?" And Pancho pointed again to the red mob. "And why, then, would I continue in bondage? Their answer comes from the pounding words you hear, repeated ad nauseam by El Comandante. We continue in bondage because *they need us*. They know this, and so do we. But we do not need them. This, my friends, is the source of the conflict. Understanding the vulnerability of their position, they use the only tools they possess to enforce our intercourse—their guns. 'Your government is the source of all authority,' says El Comandante as he waves in the air his AK-103, newly purchased with *our* tax money for use against us."

Pancho continued, "And that begs the question, fellow Venezuelans, the same question that has always been asked by the enslaved time and again. From where does the legitimacy of governance come? The new dictators of the world would have you believe, stealing the form if not the spirit of democracy, that their authority comes from the majority. They tell us that as long as they can manipulate, cajole, threaten, buy, or beat an enfeebled majority into voting for them, they then obtain the ultimate right to rule as they please. And as they rule they force the victims of this fraud not only to applaud but to actively participate in the construction of their new prisons. But is it so? Is *that* democracy legitimate?"

Pancho yelled this out to the crowd, which screamed *no* in response.

"What did you say? Let's let that helicopter hear you." And again they screamed *no*, this time so loud that the helicopter rose in the air a few meters and the soldiers cocked their shotguns.

"Let us not talk of democratic governance as the right for *those* unwashed mobs to plunge our beloved Venezuela into civil war. Or the right to redistribute what was never theirs in the first place. Let us not see democracy as our opportunity to loot those who are our betters. Let us not see democracy as a means for revenge or a means of social control or social engineering, or an excuse for the violence that is always the last recourse of the hordes when they do not succeed in pulverizing our cities and towns in their endless, tireless leveling processes. For this is not democracy. Democracy, real democracy, starts with freedom and has individual freedom as its only goal."

Pancho took a deep breath. "Therefore, this warped idea is what we have come together today to fight. We are fighting to give ourselves the right to continue in the desperate search for individual competence, integrity, truth, and happiness. For the creation of a world where the reward for firm discipline is granted through personal advancement, where the rules are clearly spelled out, and where unflinching principles are upheld by sacrosanct institutions."

He stopped again, for just a moment, to catch his breath. The heat of the midafternoon equatorial sun, which bounced off the pavement and off the sweaty faces of his followers, was converting the march into a cauldron. He pointed at the military officers. "Look at these men of arms here, armored against the free citizens of the republic. They are the very visible representation of how hard this fight is. Because they are here to defend not those who create—but those who can only *take*."

"And, through their guns, they have found power. The power to put the exceptional to the service of the mediocre. The power to seize what they want without repercussions and then force us to produce even more. And they have invented a lie. That lie, argued eloquently by their guns, says that their *desire* for material equality is justification enough. Not possessing exceptional qualities themselves, they feel justified in harnessing our truths of science and economy and morality to improve their lives—using their only tools, their guns."

"Yet we know they are wrong. We know that instead of leading to the improvement of society, this slavery can only lead to the disintegration of the social fabric and end in war."

He continued, "But take heart. This, *our* story, the story of a free, truly democratic Venezuela, is by no means over. We must now seek a more direct reckoning. The consequences of our failure must be presented with more competence and coherence. And the principles of compassion that they use to justify their theft, must be shown *not* married to their murky doctrines of pity. No, instead they must be *molded* into the competent response of creative and thinking individuals as we seek to find our counterparts and ignite the spark that will light the brilliant fire of ability, which will in turn prove the motor of *our* national development."

"So let us take their words, 'social justice,' and talk about the right of the individual to achieve his maximum potential regardless of the circumstances of his birth. Let us take their word 'compassion' and speak not of the pity toward an unwashed urchin of the jungles or the slums but the ability to see our equal in the figure and the fight and the force of a man seeking to build something *himself* but without the tools. Let us not look at compassion as the pity we feel for the wounded dog that limps to our door or the hungry cat screeching in the night. Instead let us see compassion as a helping hand to our true brothers, who through misfortune due to birthplace find that struggle of the self-made man more difficult."

He pointed again over the police and to the mob. "As you can easily see, in this fight we are outnumbered. So surrounded, like an oasis in the African Sahara or a fortress encircled by cannibal warriors, we can only grasp hold of our final defense—reason. For reason is the only force that can protect us against the overpowering press of human flesh that would devour us, sucking dry our ability, resources, and spirit, and then cast us aside in the hunt for the next human sacrifice to their misbegotten ideas." Pancho threw away a shell he had picked up for effect, brought by one of the students from the beach town.

Pancho paused again.

The helicopter still hovered above, its rotors grasping the unmoving air as it tried to steady itself. The police in line were becoming agitated in the heat and under the constant pressure of the mob. Pancho said, "And you, my fellow Venezuelans, *know* this more than anybody else. Because you have lived it and watched it these many years. You see how the dangerous principles of the unthinking man are peddled in every arena of our society, from our books and movies that sell us collective work for social reasons to the intellectuals who tell us that murder of self is the birthplace of civilization. We are spoon-fed principles of social rights disguised by the nouveau philosophers of our times to enshroud the true end— the angry, vengeful robbery of our ideas, our things, and our very lives. These principles that we work for, to make our lives better and provide more happiness to our families through our own industry and business, are what they would take from us."

Pancho brought his voice to a whisper. He allowed them for a moment to hear the booming of El Comandante's angry calls to revolution. He took a bottle of water out of his back pocket and poured it over his head, feeling the delicious, smooth, soothing coolness trickle down his hair and soak his shirt. "Our Comandante tells us, however, that business is the *root* of all evil. Ignoring the source, he uses our money, stolen from us in the form of taxes or expropriations, to wage war against us. And when the fruits of our hard work are used up and cast aside, leaving the final product of our tireless labor and enlightened mind only a rusting shell, El Comandante then carefully and eloquently explains that only when we return to the days of wax candles and hungry peasants dropping seeds into a hole will we truly be in harmony with one another. As we scurry about fixing the damage caused by his minions at the bidding of his untenable revolutionary ideas, we are told that we must keep serving him. He is, he tells us, the only true intermediary between peoples. He tells us, even as the increasingly useless money devalues in our pockets and our exhausting efforts to keep alive his dream are destroyed by his minions, that it is only *this* service that ennobles and gives legitimacy to our lives. As our families go hungry, remain jobless, or are brutalized, he tells us that these are the only rewards for our hard work—and for them we must be grateful. And more disturbing, he tells us that the perpetuation of his incoherent and destructive policies will lead to the growth of world good, but that we must work harder and must be more dedicated, for the failure is ours, never theirs,—and *always*, above all, we must reject personal happiness to reap the reward of our tireless sacrifice."

Pancho was reaching the climax. "But, as is too apparent by the casinos, the whiskey, and their fantastic houses, this sacrifice is not their sacrifice, *not ever*, but only our own. From their lofty posts, purchased without sweat, they tell us that we should strive for social justice by 'spreading the wealth around,'—the wealth *we* created by our thoughtful discipline and for our own use, and taken from us at the point of a gun, to give to those who could never create it and could never deserve it. This is the revolution."

He had reached the end of his speech. "And this is the path to destruction. When you take away a person's ability to benefit from something he built, then you relegate him to one of a pack of rats, feeding off of whatever he is able to scrounge from the waste bin of the world."

"And this is what the revolution wants—to relegate us all to animals gnawing at each other in a desperate attempt to survive. But we, all of us who are here today, are here to say *no* to El Comandante and his plans. We say we will fight, we will not go away. And this march, your presence here today, is evidence of this."

And Pancho looked around the crowd, the silence again filled with expectation, and lowered his voice again, whispering into the microphone. "Evidence that we will not accept their enslavement. And now, we will push through, we must push through, so El Comandante himself will see our masses and feel our presence— or flee in fear. And when he is gone—or has surrendered to our reason—we will build our democracy, an uncoerced democracy that represents freely the enlightened mind of the civilized individuals, and we will build our own shining light upon this hill—our Venezuelan hill."

The silence lasted, and lasted, as people digested the words. Then, a long way back in the march, someone started clapping. That clapping was echoed by another person off to Pancho's right. And another person, and one by one the entire march—a hundred thousand strong—began to cheer and to yell in support of the words and their freedom. The screams were overwhelming and the energy was palpable. Pancho was taken aback, surprised, and moved. *There is still hope for Venezuela.*

44

* * *

Doña Esmeralda was no fool. She knew quite well that the march was going to get rough. *I'll stay at the back where I can escape.* She was walking slowly, carrying her small dog. He was excited and yipped energetically at the passersby as they rushed to the front of the march. Accustomed to rarely leaving the large house, he was excited to see so many people.

"*Hola*," she heard behind her. She turned and recognized an old friend. Esmeralda couldn't even remember her name.

"Hi," she said.

"Where have you been? It's been so many years."

"It's been difficult since Gonzalo died," Esmeralda said, not answering the question.

"Why don't you march with us?" Now Esmeralda recognized her. She was a manager at the national mining company that Esmeralda had once owned—that now belonged to the government.

"Thank you, I think I will." And she bent over to put her yorkie down onto the hot pavement.

"How are things going?"

"Oh, they're fine. Since the government stole everything from me, I've just been sitting at home. I don't have very much activity anymore." She didn't mean to sound pathetic, but it came out sad, and she almost started to cry.

"Well, I hope this is the day. I called in sick to work. If they figure out I'm here, they'll fire me or worse, but I don't care. I'm sick of everything," the woman said.

"Don't worry," Esmeralda said, a little too loudly. "We're working on the real solution to our problem. Don't put all your faith on this march; we've marched so many times now that it's irrelevant. But, as it turns out, it's a good distraction." She knew she was sharing too much, and too loudly, but unaccustomed to conspiracy and frustrated by her own powerlessness, she was bragging. "We have a plan that's in motion as we speak. We're going to bring this to an end once and for all."

Her marching companions just looked at her sympathetically. Esmeralda realized how she must sound, the delusional words of a booze-addled old woman who'd lost everything. *You'll see,* she thought.

"How are things at the company?" she asked, changing the topic.

"Pretty bad. The machines keep breaking down, so we're not mining very much anymore, except the gold mine—and you know how small that is. When things started going wrong, they blamed the engineers and fired them all. Then these people they brought in ..." the woman shrugged. "Young kids with revolutionary credentials like community organizer or street fighter, graduated from one of their two-month 'universities,' and with the arrogance of the truly ignorant. And some others, very odd foreigners who don't even speak Spanish."

"Where are they from?"

"Who knows? They all have strange beards and talk in mumbles. They don't have personnel files, and they all have Venezuelan IDs. They arrive in buses and go right into closed-door meetings with the senior company managers, and then they take the company helicopters into the jungle for days or weeks on end. In the big choppers they even carried and assembled forward operating bases, you know, like the ones we use when we're prospecting? They seem to be looking for something, but it's all very hush-hush."

"For what?"

"Don't know. We never thought the jungles had much, so never even bothered looking."

Silence for a while.

"More than the great socialist nation, I feel like we've become scavengers, taking parts from one piece of dead machinery to try and give a few more months of life to another. It's all very depressing. It won't be long before there is nothing left." More silence.

As the march went on, Esmeralda could see up ahead, far in the distance, a line of military officers. At one point, the march stopped moving, and they stood milling around until a young man jumped up on the platform. She had seen him a lot on television and assumed that he was her nephew Carlitos' friend. A little yellow chopper hovered overhead, and Esmeralda joined the crowd as they threw it the one-finger salute. The sun bounced on her and a beautiful rainbow descended, making the fantastic colors explode all around them and filling her with hope. *Maybe our plan will be successful. Maybe we'll finally be free.*

Then the young man started speaking. She was dumbfounded. "How does a child know all that?" In his eloquence she found clarity, as if after such a long time in the dark somebody had ripped aside the curtains. She listened as the words formed themselves into thoughts. In those thoughts were nested the hatchlings of a new Venezuela, of a Venezuela she could love again. They were the powerful force of individual freedom, and her heart yearned to believe they were meant for her—that they were a defense of her life. But, now brutally honest as she approached the end, she allowed herself to remember the payoffs, the dark meetings in dank places, and the blood money that had flowed through her now-defunct empire.

While the boy spoke about individual achievement, Esmeralda flashed back to one special, sickening story, an event that had always haunted her and that took place on her *finca*—a *finca* she'd never even visited yet held within the white-knuckled clutch of her domain. The peasants of this *finca*, after generations on the land in conditions that Esmeralda had never even bothered to see, out of desperation petitioned the local government to allow them to buy the land they'd worked for those many years. It had been a legal request, couched in common law dating back to the times of independence. But it would mean losing her farm. She'd instructed her enforcer—what was his name?—to pay off the local magistrates. She'd known it was wrong, but it was the way things were done, and her lasting impunity had left her without the tools for moral deliberation. The farmers had returned that day dejected after the hearing, walking the long, hot road together, returning to their slavery. The farmer with the idea—identified by the enforcer—was cast off his land, family and all. The rest had returned to their brutal, short lives, the only reward for their initiative an increase in the fees collected by Esmeralda's henchman.

No, these words—these wonderful words—are not for me. But so what? They represent a great Venezuela, even I can see that, and while in this new Venezuela I have not earned a place, I will still welcome the change. He finished, and she joined her hands as she celebrated the new generation of young leaders. But then things grew quiet while a lone voice across the police line offered a rebuttal laced with anger and derision. Even though she couldn't hear the words, she could feel the tension brought about by latent violence, and said to her friends, "We'd better get out of here." She rushed off the highway and down a side street, returning rapidly home.

Back home only a few minutes later, she entered the kitchen where Clarita was making a pot of soup. *That's a lot of soup*, thought Esmeralda. "Make me a gin and tonic," she ordered, and she switched the television from the omnipresent *novelas* to the government's station. She pulled up a bar stool, sat down, and drank deeply, preparing to pass the time until all the world would see her handiwork.

45

***

Freddy had heard the whole speech—and a hollow had formed in the pit of his stomach. Around him the beer had flowed more freely, and those beside the truck had turned up the volume on El Comandante's shrill orders and expletives. The same tape played over and over, set in contrast to the young student's words, now sounded more anxious, more nervous, and, more significantly, a little desperate. He was wracked with doubt. More importantly, around him the energy seemed to drain out of the revolutionary march. In an ominous sign, the massive balloon of El Comandante giving the V, which had been hovering over the parade, popped. It sagged down to lie on the ground off to the left. In the air the crows, having flown from the dark areas of the country to participate in the riot against the students, were flying around in circles, squawking in disarray. The tide was turning. The people had stopped advancing and were milling about, murmuring in confusion.

Geronimo left Freddy's side. He looked anxious. At once, the revolution seemed petty and ridiculous. But what could they do? Casting about desperately for leadership, Freddy watched, feet bolted in place, as Geronimo marched resolutely to the truck with the sound system and grabbed the microphone.

"Comrades and revolutionaries," Geronimo screamed, using the sound system to reach out to every corner of the red march, "you have just heard the sickly sweet voice of evil. You have listened to the oligarchs, the lackeys of the empire, as they have defended yet again their right to privilege, to wealth, and to power. They have denigrated our glorious, peaceful revolution. They have dragged the image of our beloved Comandante through the mud. And they have *finally* said what they think about *you*. They have called you rabble, mob, unwashed, mediocre thieves and liars. This is what they believe about us, the *majority*, who has suffered under the weight of their discrimination and corruption for too long. For generations they made deals in back rooms and distributed political positions among themselves, positioning candidates of their *own* choosing and buying votes while we foolishly and impotently went along—hoping for them to throw us a scrap as they emerged from their restaurants, or waiting breathlessly for a piece of metal sheeting in exchange for our vote."

Around the march, people were listening to Geronimo, their looks pleading. "While they took the wealth from *your* natural resources and flew to Miami, to New York, to London, and to Madrid to spend the ill-gotten fruits from their illegitimate theft, we lived on the hills and suffered in violence and hunger."

Geronimo laughed loud and hard. "They call *us* the thieves? We, who have recuperated the goods that belong to all of us and *finally* put them to the service of all the people. As we distribute more evenly what is rightfully ours, recuperated from them who stole it, we still don't come close to reclaiming the fistfuls of cash they took when they had the power."

Geronimo paused. "We have recuperated enough to feed our families; they bought fur coats. We have freed money to pay for schools; they bought airplanes. We have redistributed the goods of the state to provide for you basic health care; they bought third and fourth houses on the beach. And even more importantly, we freed ourselves from the crushing weight of their ideology that told us that we were not equal simply because we could not create. It told us that we were not eligible for the goods that *they* have because we didn't invent something. And they constantly drilled into us that *our* needs were not enough to warrant their money, no, that we had to produce and create and innovate and exchange. But exchange with what? We are poor. They constantly told us we were not entitled to the money that we saw freely moving back and forth between their hands and through their bank accounts—money that rightfully belonged to us and that we could have used to build a better life for ourselves."

Geronimo's words were having the desired effect on the crowd. Freddy and his new companions were captivated and grateful. Geronimo climbed higher on the speakers and brought his voice up a notch to be heard by all. He looked around; there were thousands, in fact hundreds of thousands of them. There *had* to be many more than the other march. "Well, I say enough. I say that it is our *need* that entitles us to what they have. As we have heard, from each according to their ability, to each according to their need. They may hold the powers and resources of creation, but that only increases their responsibility. For who is more responsible, the man who bakes the bread or the man who needs the bread to feed his family? It is the natural order of things that the person who can create *should* be put to work for the benefit of all those in need. For without this, how is it possible for those of us who are poor, who haven't had privileged educations or who haven't inherited businesses and stores—how is it possible for us to have what they have? No, we cannot, for it is already there—and protected by the crushing weight of their ideas. Is it not so?"

And Freddy screamed *yes* with the rest of the crowd, agitated now and steaming at the injustice. "So instead, we must take it and put it to work for the majority—to feed the children who are so very needy. To educate to the down-and-out and the alcoholics. To give the young girl with five children a place to lay her head. As I was walking along today, I talked to a young woman named Julieta. She is unmarried and is pregnant with her second child. Her oligarch employers fired her from her job as a waitress in one of their dozen restaurants because they felt she could not keep up with the strain of the job while pregnant. They didn't even pay her severance, just told her to get her things."

Murmurs of anger rippled through the crowd. "How is this possible? It is for her that the owners must work, not the other way around. For she, and the rest of you, are the true owners of

Venezuela—not the people you see over there." And he pointed over the backs of the National Guard toward the multicolored opposition mob.

"They are who have kept us in bondage for so many years, through their total control of the things that would give us freedom. But now, we have arisen, we have woken up."

Freddy saw that Geronimo, too, was sweating—and his sweat poured down his shirt, soaking it. He looked around for a bottle of water. "We have said to the oligarchs that, finally, we see what they have done to us. We have thrown off their rules, their capitalism, which says that only if you produce are you allowed to consume. We have told them that, in fact, we *will* consume. How will we do this? By finally advancing beyond those prehistoric, uncivilized, and inhuman values that talk of individual rights and the pursuit of individual happiness through private property. We have progressed beyond their understanding, taking that giant leap in our reasoning as we advance systems of *collective* rights and *collective* happiness—through *collective* property. For it is in the collective alleviation of *our* suffering and fulfillment of *our* joint needs that we are truly human. It is in the redistribution from those who have plenty, more than enough, to those who are so desperately needy, that we find our justice and humanity. Those people who you see on the other side of these revolutionary soldiers who protect us and our future are unable to accept this. They prefer to continue to steal the nation's money and mistreat others—and to revel in the shirking of their collective duty. They are the animals here, looking to fulfill their most basic instincts for power, money, and pleasure instead of realizing that they *too* are part of Venezuelan society and need to be part of the solution to the crisis that *their* capitalism has foisted upon us."

He took a breath, pausing to gauge the impact of his words. Freddy nodded up at him, encouraging the rebuttal so eloquently delivered by his friend that was the final response, in his mind, to the terrible, arrogant, agonizing words that still tormented him from across the police cordon. Those words had filled him with fear and insecurity. But in Geronimo's words he was finding comfort and rest.

"But I ask you, my friends," Geronimo said, "What happens in a world where those that have the tools of creation and the mechanisms for advancement refuse to surrender them to the will of the collective and the superiority of the majority? What happens if they are *so* selfish and *so* backward that they don't understand that their very existence is allowed only for the service they can provide to their country and to others? They think the amassing of wealth and power is for their *own* use and their *own* enjoyment? Like you heard our friend across the way say, for the pursuit of their *own* happiness? What about *our* happiness? If nobody has given *us* the items *we* need to pursue it, what will *we* do? *We* weren't born with a factory or with a large bank account. *We* weren't born into a rich family that was able to pay for the best schools and the best health care. My fellow Venezuelans, you know all too well that capital amasses just like gravity. For those who have it, more sticks to them. For us who do not, even what we have is taken from us. This, my friends, is even in the Bible."

Geronimo was getting to his final point. "So I repeat, to you my friends and comrades, what do we do if those across the way—who have everything—refuse to understand that its part of their moral responsibility to help provide for us, who don't have *anything*? Well, the answer is quite simple. It is an answer that is rooted in hundreds of years of enlightened history—from the French revolution to the Cuban, to the teachings of Marx and the words of El Che. We have the right—nay. Not the right, that's a poor choice of words. We have the *responsibility* to take from them who have it and redistribute it to those who don't—to those who are suffering, weak, poor, and hungry. That, my friends, is what power is for, and *that*, my friends, is what government is for."

He let the words sink in as people focused their beer-soaked minds on understanding what he was saying. "They will tell you that government is for their protection and for their safety, or even better, that the government should do nothing at all and simply stand aside. That it exists to allow and empower them with the opportunity to amass more wealth and accumulate more power. They will tell you that their political rights, allowed by their fragile governments, are more important than our rights: our rights to work, to a house, to food, to clean water, and to our cultures. But this is not true—those antiquated political rights have kept us in poverty for many years, and what good were they really? What good is freedom of speech when I can't read? What good is freedom of movement when I don't have a car? What good is freedom of assembly if I don't have a house under which to assemble? And what good is freedom of religion if I don't have food? None of these rights have any meaning, and they have been devised by the capitalists to keep us asleep in eternal poverty."

And Geronimo stopped. He motioned to somebody in the crowd to give him a bottle of water. Freddy realized what his friend wanted and pushed his way through the crowd to throw his water bottle to his parched, powerful friend, allowing Geronimo to renew his voice. "But we have finally woken up. How have we done this? To whom do we owe our salvation? Who has brought us into the light from the darkness? El Comandante is our savior and our benefactor—the source of our light and the center of our universe. He has shown us what is ours, and he has given us the confidence to take it."

At Geronimo's mention of El Comandante, a loud and powerful yell erupted from the crowd. Geronimo went on, "And how has he done this? First, he delivered to us the most important lesson of all—that we are more. We were so trapped in our poverty and so discouraged by our misery that we did not realize that simple and beautiful fact."

Geronimo smirked. "'They talk about democracy,' he told us, 'So let us rise up, let us use their democracy, which is so precious to them, to bring about the fundamental changes in society that we know will allow us to build a better country and world. They say majority rules? We will show them who the majority is. They say that we should put everything to a vote? Let's vote on who should lay claim to the resources they so *efficiently* produce and then hoard. They say they should have the right to denigrate us and our revolution—let's vote on it. They say they should have the right to their private property—let's put it to the people. We'll see what the majority says about all those privileges they so carefully gathered all those years.'" And Freddy smiled at the logic.

"And with these lessons, using these tools," Geronimo went on, "We remade the fundamental systems and mechanisms of our state. We brought change to the way the country was organized. We replaced the antiquated and archaic political rights with our progressive, advanced social and cultural rights. We voted away their damaging 'separation of powers,' another carefully crafted plot to have a government that can't make radical advances. And we voted ourselves for the redistribution of their assets. And did they oppose us? Of course. They conspired to destroy our glorious, peaceful revolution. They tried to kill El Comandante many times. They marched back and forth, up and down, and were the obstacle to the reforms and the changes that were legally being implemented across the country by our new democracy—the *true* democracy instituted by El Comandante."

He took a breath to finish. "And now, we have the most progressive, most advanced country in the world. We are making history and building socialism, our socialism, from the ground up. And we will continue to do so. Because we are more. And we have our new, revolutionary army that understands it is at the service of the revolution and knows that the true enemies of Venezuela are not abroad but are here, across that line, the hundreds of thousands that would still take away our advances and return us to our poverty and our barrios with nothing. And we have our Comandante, the father of our great revolution and the heart and soul of the new Venezuela."

And with that he was finished. "Therefore, my fellow revolutionaries, we must not let them pass. Enough with the marching and the opposing and the conspiring. Let us, once and for all, eliminate this scourge that continues to drain the life out of the country. Let us show them, today, that there is no place for them in the new Venezuela."

And a visceral, animal cheer exploded from the mass. The equatorial heat had combined with the free alcohol, and the ecstasy of the angry words fed upon the fruit of the poisonous vine that so many had partaken of to set the turbulent, violent horde pulsating with a renewed, savage desire to finally, once and for all, put an end to these people whom they hated so much.

"The time has come." Geronimo hopped down off the speaker and returned to stand beside Freddy. He was glowing with power and authority—a changed man. "You will see what will happen now …"

* * *

Hovering above the two marches, Teniente Machado couldn't hear the speeches through the noise of the rotors from the tiny helicopter, but he could see the reaction to the culmination of both speeches. On the one side, the cheering and the uplifting yell of frustration and resistance. On the other side, he had almost felt the pulsing of that living mass of red as it pressed against the military police and the National Guard.

From out of the turbulent redness, *Teniente Machado* saw a lone beer bottle leap into the sky. It flew as if in slow motion over the helmet-crusted heads of the National Guard and over the whale. It reached its zenith close to his helicopter, so close that Machado could almost smell the cold golden liquid and could read plainly the label on the bottle. Then it slowly began its descent into the colorful assortment that was the opposition parade. Everything slowed down again as the bottle finished its course in an explosion of glass and gold and blood upon the head of a young girl. The girl fell slowly to her knees and then onto her back.

Immediately, all hell broke loose.

The pulsing mob breached the dyke made by the National Guard and poured through the cracks between the soldiers to fall upon the students. In the student march, a large group of the elderly and of children instantly turned to flee, looking for a low spot to leap out over the side of the highway, some falling fifteen feet to the streets below. A large contingent of solid young men stood firm, confronting the stream of red that was turning into a river. The whale powered up, and a stream of water burst upon the opposition students, forcing them back. Even over the rotor of his small engine,

Machado could hear the popping sounds from the rubber bullets as the National Guard fired into the student march. He could see in various places the wafting smoke of tear gas as they tried to force students back down the highway and to their fleeing buses. But it was no use: pandemonium and violence were feeding upon themselves, and the drunken orgy was becoming impossible to control. "Let's go," Teniente Machado yelled to his Russian pilot, calling off his bird's-eye observation.

* * *

Standing on the mobile platform draped in the Venezuelan flags, Pancho had listened to every word of Geronimo's speech. He was so close to the National Guard that he could have reached out and touched them. He had yelled down to them. "Get out of the way. We have a right to be seen, to be heard." The military men just smiled as they gripped their weapons more deliberately. The young revolutionary across the picket line was finishing, and Pancho had felt the tide turn against the opposition march.

Pancho leaped off the truck stage and was running back to Carlitos when he saw, flying overhead, the bottle spinning and spinning above the crowd, the green mixed with the golden brew spilling out of it as the drink showered down upon the soldiers and the students. It flew twisting and twirling upon itself as it reached its zenith and started to descend. He looked over and saw Juanita. Dear Juanita. She wasn't looking, engaged intensely with one of the other students at her side.

"Watch out," Pancho screamed, but his voice was swallowed up by the crowd. He started to run, but as if in a nightmare he couldn't move, his legs weighing against the rest of his body. His leaden legs lifted slowly, and he elbowed and pushed people of out his way, trying to get to her, to go to her. "Juanita," he belted out in anguish. And as he ran, he watched frame by frame as the bottle crashed upon her head, exploding in a colorful shower of green and gold and red. She collapsed, unconscious. His desperate run finally brought him to her side.

Behind him, the National Guard hardened their flanks, preparing for battle, and the humming from the water cannon filled the air.

"It's okay, you're okay, we'll get you to the ambulance," he said to the limp, unconscious body as blood flowed freely down the Indian features of her young face. "Somebody get the ambulance," he yelled, and then he turned back to his friend, covered with blood. "Please be okay." Finally the ambulance arrived, chirping its way slowly through the crowd. Pancho laid her gently in the ambulance with a final squeeze of her hand, and it began to move slowly back through the crowd and out toward an exit. The blaring sirens and flashing lights, now fully engaged, were the last he saw of Juanita. Crestfallen, he turned. He was still the leader, and his makeshift army of freedom was losing ground. They had come ready for a fight, but he realized now that he hadn't known what that meant. Susana, now Juanita. What would be the eventual cost of freedom? And was it a price they were willing to pay?

He turned to face the onslaught in time to see a seam in between two national guardsmen burst apart as a group of angry revolutionaries, sweating from the sun and the liquor, beers and sticks in their hands, slashed its way through the hole. They raised their sticks high into the air, and their faces shone with the joy of the merciless. They lifted and let fall their weapons of war with vigor—up, down, up, down, they clubbed their way into the melee. Beer spilled down their faces as they drank, feeding their sense of omnipotence. Each swing of their sticks brought new blood to the pavement, and the sick, tangy smell of carnage pervaded the parade. Bodies were lying unconscious on the ground, haphazardly strewn where they had fallen. A few were moaning—pleading for help. Pancho pushed against the mass of people surging against him in desperate flight. At the edge of the march, several people were pushed over the railing, falling the fifteen feet to the street below in a sickening crunch. Immediately in front of him, one of the cowboys went down, clubbed on top of the head as he was shepherding a child away from the violence. Pancho pushed and shoved until he was approaching the front line and finally stood, squaring his shoulders to face the rushing mob. *This is my fight. I will stand my ground.*

* * *

"Attack!" Geronimo's pounding orders screamed with such energy that they rattled Freddy's brain. Caught between indecision and euphoria, he was losing reason. Geronimo was transformed from the peaceful and playful housemate of yesterday to a wild and rage-ravaged animal. He was wielding in one of his hands a bottle, its bottom broken and the shards of glass serving as an impromptu dagger. His other hand held a large stick from which rusted nails protruding menacingly. He was leading the charge, goading his army on and pushing it forward. "There is room over here," he said to some, and "Push through where you can, don't worry about the military, they won't shoot you" to another group, and "Over there is a break, the students are over there now—go get them."

Pandemonium reigned, and Freddy didn't know what to do. Wild eyed, he flicked his gaze back and forth between Geronimo, the military, the mob, and the students. He looked up and realized that the helicopter was speeding away—*I wonder where it's going and who was in it? I wonder where the birds went. I'm kind of hungry.* His disjointed observations highlighted his confusion.

"Come this way," Geronimo ordered Freddy, grabbing him angrily by the shirt. Freddy followed. Most of the other members of his team had already plunged into the fray. A scarce few were trying to run through the mob in the opposite direction back to the airfield. For a second, he thought about joining them; but Geronimo had grabbed him and thrust him toward a large crack in between the national guardsmen, yelling, "You push right there."

Freddy felt something cold and slippery sliding into his hands. He realized that Geronimo had handed him a bottle. The slick firmness was reassuring as he closed his fingers around the neck. *Hmm, that's a big, heavy beer bottle. They sure drink a lot of beer down here,* he observed.

"Push hard. You can make it through." And then Geronimo was gone looking for more people to inspire into the fight. Still seeming to float above his body, Freddy followed the orders and pushed, hard, between a national guardsman and a military cop. The space between them grew. He was surprised by how easily they were giving way. His eyes were starting to burn from a strange gassy smell—he was starting to cough. He could hear above him the popping and the whizzing of rubber bullets.

"Ouch." Then he was through. Immediately, a big cowboy pushed him. "Hey," he said, and turned to push back when he saw the size of the boy. He felt insulted. Some of the pent-up anger he'd first experienced in his fight in the school returned. *How dare they push me. I'm a visitor here. We're just trying to do what's right. I'm tired of being pushed around. All my life I've been bullied. I'm sick of it.* Justifications flooded his mind as he saw that, here, they were winning—the opposition was fleeing. Here, he was on the right side. He targeted a young student in front of him, giving him a hard push. "Aargh," shouted the teenager as he fell to the ground.

A shudder started in Freddy's feet, crept up his legs to his waist, and moved into his stomach, causing it to cramp up. It continued up his spine and down his arms, now tingling with a powerful emotion. Finally, the pulse moved into his head, making him dizzy and lightheaded. His whole body vibrated as he watched the young man get up, trying to run away on a twisted ankle.

That felt good.

Another man was running away, his daughter held high on his shoulders. Freddy stuck out his foot, tripping him. The man fell to the highway. The little girl went down from that height, banging her head on the pavement. Blood trickled from the scrapes, and she exploded in tears. Another girl, off to his right, concentrated on throwing a rock at the police. He intercepted the act, took the rock from her, and hurled it into the crowd of fleeing protesters. He didn't see where it landed, but his arm tingled at the effort.

I like this.

A medium-framed boy ran in his direction. He was wearing bracelets around his wrists. Freddy was annoyed; he hated boys who wore jewelry. He lifted his bottle and clubbed him in the head, laying him out on the ground.

He grinned.

Expecting guilt, he was surprisingly apathetic. He swung his makeshift club at another, striking him on the side of the head.

Blood spurted across the pavement—a little even got on Freddy's shoes, which annoyed him even more. "Move aside." Freddy was getting into it. He pushed one young student, a girl, as she was running to the side of a fallen friend. She let out a shriek.

"Hey, you," he screamed as he pushed another in the back—she was already running away, and she fell to her knees, ripping her pants and tearing the skin on her knees. She stood up, blood running down her legs, and looked at Freddy quizzically. "Just run," he yelled in English, and she pushed herself onto her feet, limping on her twisted ankle in the opposite direction.

Now Freddy was excited. He hit another girl in the head with the bottle, and she came crashing down. The girls were easier; they didn't fight back. He was a little afraid of those huge cowboys over there. He didn't want to get his ass handed to him.

"Stupid capitalists!" He was in full swing now, his bottle whizzing back and forth. This one he pushed, that one he kicked. He found one fellow on the ground with blood flowing into his eye from a cut on his eyebrow and gave him a savage kick in the stomach. "Oligarch!"

Geronimo again appeared at his side. "How is it?"

Freddy answered, "Teaching them a lesson." And they were swinging their hands and their feet and their bottles in unison, protected by the whizzing of the rubber bullets above their heads and by their red T-shirts. Then out of the corner of his eye Freddy saw the young man he'd fought with in the Midwest—*the leader*, he slurred sarcastically—trying to help another girl to her feet. He remembered the emissary's special request and pushed through the crowd in the boy's direction.

* * *

Pancho had plunged headfirst into the fray, joining the big, sturdy cowboys, strong from their work and their time on the land. They were better organized and were trying to push back a flank of brutal revolutionaries who were using broken bottles—and trying to provide pace for a group of young high-school girls to escape. Pancho picked one girl up off the ground and pushed her in the direction of the cowboys, "Run! Get out of here quickly," he told her, and she was off.

He turned around in time to see a national guardsman point a gun at his face and fire. He jumped aside just in time, hearing the whine and smelling the acrid stench of gunpowder as the rubber bullet whizzed by his eye. The bullet found a different mark, and one of the cowboys doubled over in pain. All around him, the mayhem was increasing. In front of him there were three men and one girl on the ground, holding their heads as blood poured out of their ears. He began to choke, realizing too late that a military policeman had thrown a teargas canister at him. He quickly took out his handkerchief and a little vial of vinegar and breathed through that—the tangy zest of vinegar cut the choking smoke and allowed him to breathe.

"Over here," yelled Carlitos. He turned in time to see a dozen of the motorcyclists dragging a girl away from the march. He sprinted, closing the distance rapidly. Pulling hard, he freed the girl from the band. The motorcyclists jeered maliciously and let them go, giving Pancho a savage kick to the ribs.

"Over there." He saw a group of drunkards with red handkerchiefs around their faces hitting a middle-aged man who had doubled over and was on the ground screaming, curled protectively in the fetal position. Pancho and Carlitos arrived quickly, Pancho pulling him out from under the bruising fists while Carlitos fought back hard. The burly cowboys were serving as a rear guard, positioning themselves in a flanking move between people that needed to escape and the aggressors, their fists flailing and boots kicking to divert the aggressive attention. One by one, they rescued people and set them running back in the direction of the buses.

The whale was in full operation, drowning its targets in a powerful burst of water, forcing them off their feet. But by now, Pancho knew, his march was in full retreat. Beaten back by rubber bullets, by teargas, by little beanbags fired from the shotguns of public servants, and by the whale, he realized that they'd underestimated the revolutionaries thirst for blood. He was crestfallen. *How had he misjudged their potential so badly? How could he have been so naive as to bring his people into another fight like this? Had his time away made him forget the reality of the brutality of the revolution? Why, oh why, had he gotten his people into this?* He knew, instinctively, that from this there would be no return, no recovery, and no peace. They were outmatched on every level.

And in the mayhem, groups of revolutionaries—dangerous ones from deep in the barrios—were falling in impunity upon anybody they could find—old, young, boy, girl. The strongest, most capable students had their hands full rescuing the wounded from the battleground, carrying them back to the ambulances that were by now speeding back and forth between the march and the private clinics—the public hospitals had been told to refuse admittance to anybody not in a red shirt. One group ran interference, pushing a motorcyclist over while the others saved a grandmother in a wheelchair. Across the highway, the cowboys pulled a revolutionary thug off of a young girl and kicked him, allowing the girl—with a torn blouse and her breasts exposed—to run for cover. Yet another group was using a large sign to ward off the powerful stream from the water cannon. They held it high, the water washing off the words "We are all Venezuelans" that had been painted with so much care by an association of disabled students from the mountains. The cardboard offered important protection as they walked an injured Indian away from the melee.

And then Pancho saw him, the fat gringo boy he'd fought before. Pancho recognized him instantly—but he was astonished by the change. He still had the shoulder-length yellow hair, the tubby, dumpy form, and the thick eyeglasses. But his countenance was different. Instead of innocent naiveté, the boy's face was now warped by a mask of hatred and impunity. The look that Pancho had so often seen in the face of the revolution was now the overpowering feature of this gringo. He pushed aside two other people in his way, walking slowly toward Pancho. On his jeans, face, and hair were sweat, dust, and the blood of others. He had a large splatter of blood on his knee. A bottle was clutched tightly in his right hand.

"You bastard," the fat boy said. "You believe what you said up there? I have seen your kind in America as your selfishness and greed destroy my country. Here, you are bringing this peaceful, revolutionary country to its knees through your lies. I've seen your version of 'democracy' and what it has done to the true patriots of this country. You should be ashamed."

"You," Pancho responded. "Don't do this. You don't understand. You are free, living in a free country. Don't do this. This is not your fight; don't so quickly participate in the enslavement of others."

"Enslavement? That's what you call these your countrymen and their fight for equality? You think they are enslaving you? What have you people done to them all these years?"

"What do you know about it, *gringo de mierda*?" Pancho was enraged by the gringo's arrogance. "You buy a passport and an air ticket and pretend to lecture *me* on *my* country? Either join us, the future, or get the hell out of the way. You don't belong here."

"I belong wherever I want. We are free."

"You are free. You will never know what it is like to see your people denied opportunity, expelled from school, fired from work, robbed of their money and their possessions and their future—only because of their beliefs. To you, this whole process is interesting, quaint, and exotic. You will never know our struggles," Pancho said.

Pancho saw rage fill the bloodshot eyes of his enemy and tried to turn, but it was too late. Arm raised, the kid known to Pancho only as Freddy raised his arm and brought the bottle crashing down on Pancho's head. Blood spurted and then flowed, and his body fell to the ground—unconscious.

46

* * *

Teniente Machado was pacing up and down anxiously around his temporary office. He'd returned to the airstrip, leaping out of the little yellow helicopter as soon as it touched gingerly to the earth. Passing the Russian helicopters, he'd seen five mechanics with a thick manual and a Russian/Spanish dictionary. One of them had a large bolt in his hand and was trying to match it with a picture in the manual. "You all are *still* trying to fix that thing?" He walked by them in disgust, not even bothering to salute, and bounded up the stairs.

Up in his office, reports were already starting to come in. "The police lines have been broken," said the first. Then came "Our marchers have pushed back the enemy" and "It is a total rout, with the enemy in full retreat." Machado received his field reports with gravitas and sobriety. This was the closest to managing a battle that he'd ever come, and everything needed to be perfect—the eyes of El Comandante himself were on this endeavor.

"Okay, it's now almost five o'clock. El Comandante will be here in a few hours. We have one more issue to resolve before then," he said to his aide-de-camp. He yelled through the open door, "Bring me the head of the strike unit."

"*Reportando, mi Teniente.* I am here awaiting your orders." Major Quispe appeared immediately at the door and entered the room formally. He stood at attention in front of Machado's desk and saluted with the crisp confidence of one accustomed to violence. Machado was very pleased—he had handpicked this man for his new career and was eminently proud of his choice.

Quispe was a monster. Machado had discovered him in one of the largest, most dangerous prisons in the country. There, Machado had chosen him out of a crowd after he beat to death four cell mates with a cafeteria tray. It was rumored that Quispe was not himself fully human. According to the prisoners he'd interviewed, Quispe was the offspring of a peasant woman who had fallen in love with one of the mountain creatures that lived in a hidden valley in the Andes. These creatures rarely made contact with their human neighbors; they were content to live among their own kind, feeding off the abundant resources of their secret land. Running from an unwanted marriage, Quispe's mother had found herself almost freezing to death in a mountain pass, lost in the heart of the Andes. There, she entrusted her soul to the virgin and passed out, only to awaken in a wonderful valley full of amazing creatures and fantastic beauty. She'd been saved by one of the elders of the tribe and had fallen deeply in love with him despite his horrific appearance. After a time, she'd given birth to a son—but the half human, half monster was unwelcome in either society and had found his place in the brutal underbelly of Venezuela, where he was revered for his strength and his terror.

And he seemed to enjoy the position that Machado offered him in the heart of the revolution. He followed orders, even some of the most controversial orders Machado could think of. Quispe had a crew cut, thick features, a prominent jaw line and cheek bones. His chest stuck out, even under the bulletproof vest, and one of his legs was the thickness of two of Machado's. He was an accidental Venezuelan, or maybe better said he represented the first Venezuelans, his features more Neanderthal than mestizo. On his belt was a large knife—he preferred it to his guns because, in his own words, "It is slower and delivers the message better." He was the perfect enforcer.

"So, the little thing that we talked about yesterday. Are you ready?" Quispe nodded with another crisp salute.

"*Si, mi Teniente*," he said to Machado. "Everything is ready just as we discussed."

"That's fine. Follow me. It's time to execute the warrant. I don't foresee any problems. The plan is incompetently organized and foolishly executed—just another harebrained scheme."

"Yes, sir."

As he was preparing to leave, Machado strapped on his 9 mm, tying the laces around his thigh. Before departing, he received the latest missive from the front lines. "The students are in full flight. The leader has been detained—although he is injured. He is being taken to the military hospital for now. Other students arrested."

He quickly pulled on his olive green flak jacket and grabbed his shotgun, rushing out the door in front of his Neanderthal thug, his mouth broken in a wide grin. Together they pounded down the stairs and mounted an idling APC with a dozen other men all dressed in full combat gear.

Things are going right according to plan.

47

✶ ✶ ✶

It was over, and Freddy was ambling back to the airstrip. His shoulders were slumped over, and he was dragging his feet—placing one foot in front of the other was sapping all his remaining energy. Beside him, Geronimo was glowing. Unable to even walk straight, he alternated skipping, hopping, and running ahead, then falling back and joining Freddy. "Wasn't that *magnifico*? They won't march for a long time. Finally we showed them who runs things here. We stood and measured ourselves, toe to toe, and we beat them. They were ill prepared and cowardly in the face of a fight. It's like I tell you: they are full of lofty words, but when faced with violence they cave. Their ideas are old and tired and no longer inspire emotion, and they don't have the stomach to really defend them. Their time in charge of this country, and this world, is rapidly coming to an end. Their marching and conspiring days are over."

Freddy was nauseated. He was trying not to throw up—breathing deeply to control his stomach. He kept looking back over his shoulder—and back in his mind to what he'd done. He saw in his mind's eye, clearly and frame by frame, his attack. He saw the look of curious confusion in the eye of his adversary. He saw the student leader raise his eyebrows as Freddy raised the bottle and then the sheer, dumbfounded surprise—total shock—as Freddy brought the bottle down on the top of his head. It had shattered. Freddy was still holding a shard of the neck, holding it so tightly that it had cut into his hand, and new, fresh blood was dripping from his vice-like grip and onto the pavement as he walked, a trail of his own guilt answering—his only answer to the cries of victory.

"Revolutions are bloody," he repeated to Geronimo over and over.

"*Así es*," Geronimo said, not realizing his affirmations were a soothing balm to Freddy.

"They cannot be done peacefully. Blood *has* to be shed in order for the revolution to adjust itself and make itself heard. Right?"

"*Correcto*, everybody knows this. It takes some getting used to, but soon you will see the glory in what we did."

"And those people, those students, they wouldn't back off, wouldn't give way, and wouldn't allow us *our* moment ..." Freddy thought back to the people he had seen. There was that old lady who had been pushed onto the floor as a drunk revolutionary had overturned her wheelchair. There was the little fellow, must have been just into secondary school, who had gotten belted in the head by a board. Freddy's mind painted for him the surreal image in vivid colors of the pretty young girl, probably just into her freshmen or sophomore year of college, running bare breasted as she fled from her attackers. He saw the huge kids, dark and tan from their time on the plains. Shoulders broad under their cowboy hats and boots clacking on the asphalt as they moved in unison, in a coordinated dance of resistance—standing boot to boot and taking beatings, and giving them, in unison. And as the tempest reached its crescendo, he remembered having looked at the military.

"They really enjoyed it. They were smiling as they cocked and fired. I saw people go down—I saw them fall." He said this out loud, and Geronimo looked at him sideways. "Geronimo, I even heard the order from the senior commander, 'As long as it doesn't have a red shirt, it's open season, men. Happy hunting.'" Freddy spoke incredulously. Geronimo ignored him.

"Revolution is bloody," he kept repeating to himself, "Marx said so. If I am unwilling to shed blood for the cause then I am an unworthy servant of the revolution." And he began, ever so slowly, to tear up and cry. He wiped the tears away quickly, knowing that

Geronimo would ridicule him. "Man, that's sweaty work," he said, wiping his face and head with his blackened shirt, leaving blood and dirt stains running down his cheeks.

Geronimo's eyes gleamed with pride. "Yes, my friend, today you proved that you are an *hijo de la revolución.*"

"I certainly feel like an *hijo de algo,*" Freddy mumbled.

48

* * *

"Capitán Alejandro Fuentes." Machado marched purposefully through the smoke and wood shards of the exploded door, followed by his Neanderthal enforcer. Behind Machado, dozens of figures in black and green marched into the apartment.

On the table, still unassembled, was the sophisticated communication equipment necessary to take over the airwaves. Purchased only that day with money from the old woman, this was the last piece in the arsenal of subversion. Through the antenna that was being assembled, the captain would be able to interject himself at the height of El Comandante's speech to issue his call. He had only needed a line of sight to the camera trucks that would be covering El Comandante's revolutionary rally. Machado walked to the desk and picked up a piece of paper—an arrest warrant. He read it slowly. Here was the epicenter of a conspiracy that he assumed reached through the student movement, into the military and even the bureaucrats. Proof of their power, the treatise stated, would be the abrupt power outage at eight o'clock exactly. When the power returned, the warrant would be executed.

"You are under arrest for treason and conspiracy to kill El Comandante. Get to your feet." Quispe grabbed the navy captain by his collar, hauling him to a standing position. "You, traitor, aren't even worthy of a military tribunal. You're going to suffer. You're going to tell us everything that you know. And then you are going to die. The only decisions you have left are how painful this process will be and how long it will take. Quispe, here, will be in charge of your confession. And frankly, between officers, he likes his job."

Alejandro simply stood quietly, his jaws clenched and trembling. Either from fear or from anger or defiance—it didn't matter much to Machado. The instruments of persuasion in his toolbox were very powerful, and, in the end, everybody talked.

"Things don't go lightly for traitors in the new Venezuela." Machado lifted his hand high in the air, bringing it down firmly as he backhanded the *capitán* across the face, his gold ring leaving an angry welt on the moribund man's cheek. The blow sent the navy man staggering to the floor, blood dripping from his nose and mouth.

"You just wait to see what we have in store for you," were Quispe's only words, raspily spoken as if from a long distance, coming from someplace deep and dark. And a cynical, evil, mirthless grin crept across the caveman's face.

* * *

Back at the airstrip, Freddy sat in the middle of the group that had formed itself into a circle around him—the misery of the guilty finding a balm in the company of others. "You did well this afternoon," he said in a monotone voice. "Your families would be proud of you."

Around him, the faces cheered up slightly. They were bloody, sweaty, and covered with paint and grime and dirt. One of the girls had vomited on the trip back, some of it spilling on her shirt and smudging the red face of El Che. Another young man had collapsed in a loose pile of bones and cloth at the foot of a small tree, seeking respite from the late afternoon sun. They looked at each other, seeing red eyes, grime-covered faces, and hands cut and bruised.

Freddy knew that at all costs he had to keep talking. Any silence, even short lived, was too laden with malevolent meaning. "Well, my faithful friends," he said, lifting up his chin and trying to pretend that he didn't want to cry, "it's terrible what those oligarchs tried to do."

He was trying his version of the truth on the small troop, honing it to make it believable—he was going to have to use it for the rest of his life. "I can't believe how they just came on like that, just pushing and attacking. You all defended yourselves, and the revolution, quite nobly. You should be proud—there were really dangerous people in that march. Geronimo was saying that sometimes even people are killed." He looked around for Geronimo, for backup, but his friend had disappeared again.

The kids' heads bobbed up and down, grateful at him for the prospect of altering their story. "Nobility is not, necessarily, being totally clean. Nobility instead is being able to defend the dirt under your fingernails." Freddy was trying to wade through the guilt and find a platitude that would stick.

The sun was starting to set; it was now six thirty, only an hour and a half until the arrival of El Comandante. Freddy got up, stretched, and walked over as close to the front of the crowd as he could. He was still a long distance away. The massive crowd had returned from the march and was waiting patiently to hear words of praise from the leader. Freddy held his nose. Engulfed by the crowd of sweaty, fat protesters, he could barely breathe. The deadly concoction of perspiration, cologne, and body odor was overpowering. And mixed with the sweet aroma of stale beer and the occasional hot dog, the stench was unbearable.

Freddy was unhappy.

* * *

At the national electric company, Pancho's dad was sweating bullets. He couldn't believe what he was going to do. He was wheezing with fear, and his eyes were bloodshot—he thought maybe he was going to cry.

He looked up at the clock, watching the seconds tick away slowly, slowly, slowly. Each second was a lifetime and during each lifetime all he could think about was his job, his family—his life. His mouth was totally dry—he hadn't eaten anything for twenty-four hours and was beginning to feel faint.

When the old woman, his former boss, had asked him for help with her plan, he had refused, of course. How could he help? His life, his family. He was not a courageous man; he had never fought for much in his life. But she'd said that he had to, that it was part of the agreement for her support for Pancho, that she was sure it was going to work, and that it was foolproof. Why had he agreed? His stomach seized up again, and he squinted with pain.

At five minutes to seven, the door to the equipment room abruptly opened. Mr. Randelli panicked—he was supposed to be alone.

In walked his boss. His mouth went completely dry.

This was not a friend. She was the person who supervised him at all the marches. The woman placed in her position to spy on everybody. Yet she had demonstrated some charisma and a certain compassion for him.

She looked at Pancho's dad with an almost imperceptible shake of her head. "I'm sorry to say that you are going to have to leave. You know why. You are being fired," she said nonchalantly, writing something on her omnipresent clipboard. "On top of this, you will be blacklisted from any government service. This includes any job, loan, health care, passport, dollars, or anything else that you want from the government. You will not get it. Your little plan was discovered. It was all I could do, I hope you understand, to keep you out of jail. I told them you were harmless, and I even said that you had been threatened. You owe me this—your freedom."

She shook her head again, looked at Pancho's dad with those sad eyes, and let out a slow, mournful whistle. "You are done. Go home. Pray they don't take away your house." And she escorted him from the building.

The first thing Mr. Randelli could remember after that was standing on the street. In his arms he held a box with all his items from decades of work—a red hat, a picture of his family, an old cassette player, and his lunchbox. And with only that, Pancho's dad faced the street. He looked around, up at the buildings lit by the lights he had worked his entire adult life to provide. Light. He had always been proud of his job. He gave light, and light was life. In darkness came danger and death. Now, he was no longer the giver of light. He was, simply, a middle-aged, balding fat man. He sat on the curb, and he started to cry.

* * *

Doña Esmeralda was glued to her TV set, and she was drinking too fast. The waiting was proving interminable. *Why the devil won't eight o'clock come?* She looked at the refrigerator. On the counter in front of her were some empanadas that Clarita had made. There was a whole stack of them—way too many—but she was too nervous to eat. The reporter was at the concentration in front of the empty stage. In the back she could hear the terrible beating, beating, beating of angry music.

"What did you feel about the march?" the reporter was asking a woman—all made up with red lipstick and a red shirt, her hair dyed red and red makeup on her face. "It was glorious. We finally showed those miserable, terrible oligarchs that we exist and are more powerful. We showed them that now, finally, this is our country, and they can go to hell." A smile spread across the woman's face, showing her crooked yellowed teeth.

"And you, what do you have to say about our Comandante now?" The reporter had moved on to a man on a motorcycle whose sole reply was flashing the revolutionary salute and then flipping up his middle finger. "And this is the salute for *them*," he said, and they both laughed.

It's almost eight, Doña Esmeralda thought, looking at the clock. *Where is El Comandante?* She continued staring at the television screen. Occasionally her gaze flashed expectantly to the blue-tinged fluorescent light that some ridiculous youngster had had the nerve to come into her house to install. If the light flickered off, that would mean that the plan in its entirety was working. She drained her glass in frustration and encroaching panic, holding the expensive crystal goblet out in front of her.

The sudden unexpected shriek of the telephone made her lose hold of her glass. It fell in slow motion the interminable distance to the floor, and the room filled with the tiny bells of expensive crystal shattering into thousands of pieces. The little yorkie at her feet fled for safety, yipping and barking in confusion and fear. *It's only the phone*, she chided herself as she went to answer it, trying to slow her rapidly beating heart. But a little voice inside her was telling her that something had gone wrong. She looked at the number on the caller ID—Miami.

"Esmeralda." The voice panting, panicked, on the other end of the line was General Gregorio's. "Esmeralda, listen to me carefully."

Immediately, her heart skipped a beat. The hand holding the telephone broke out in a sweat. "You must get out of there. Alejandro's been arrested. They know everything. Go outside, get in your car, and drive. Just drive, drive, drive, and keep driving until you get to the border, any border. Forget your money, your position—forget it all. It's all over. But you must think about your life now."

"But Gregorio, why are you in Miami?" Esmeralda issued the foolish question; her thoughts were perfunctory and disjointed.

Silence.

"Gregorio." More silence.

"Gregorio." It was now a command.

"Well, you see, I had something to do here. Some discussions with the Drug Enforcement Administration who are keen to get their hands on the kingpins. I was going to come back into the country ..."

She knew him well enough to know that he was lying. "You son of a bitch, you got scared and you ran. And you saved your own ass. *Vete al infierno,* you coward." She slammed down the telephone, her anger instantly morphing into blinding fear. *What will I do now?* She walked to the living room and sat back down, looking out over the city, *her city*.

"Gonzalo, what will I do?" she asked, and the summoned shade immediately appeared. "I can't tell you, sweetie. I don't belong to that world anymore. As *Jesucristo* said, 'let the living take care of the living, and the dead, the dead.'"

"But ..."

"Have strength, *bebe*. You were always so strong. So much stronger than I. So much more sure of yourself. That's what I always loved about you."

"But it's all over, Gonzalo. That was my only hope. There is nothing left but darkness and pain. They are coming for me, sweetheart." Esmeralda sighed. "No, that's not true. They came for me a long time ago. I just didn't have the strength to see it."

"I love you, *mi amor*," Gonzalo's shadow said, a transparent tear running down the cheeks of a ghost who had never had the strength to move on. "And I'll be waiting for you on this side." He slowly faded away like the morning mist of the Venezuelan highlands. She fixed herself another drink, her shoes crunching over the shattered glass. *'Drive,' Gregorio said? Where will I drive to? I haven't driven for three decades. Without my money? Without my status? Without …?* She walked back to the kitchen and sat down on the barstool, paralyzed by fear, indecision, and powerlessness. Clarita was frying more empanadas.

49

✳ ✳ ✳

For Freddy, the evening continued on in relative calm. He was feeling a little better about himself. Through a colossal effort of will, he was effectively deflecting the blame of his encounter to his enemy. *Why did they march today? They knew this was our day,* he thought. And, *nothing would have happened if they had gone home when they were told.* He finished off with, *they didn't have a permit. What they did was illegal.*

Everybody was talking, one eye fixed expectantly on the stage.

Then a hush fell over the assembly. Idle chatter stopped, and everybody turned to the far-off stage. The pounding music stopped. The silence clicked away; either minutes or hours passed. It could have been days. Freddy was filled with an impending sense of the momentous. Something was going to happen. Something was happening.

They waited.

Finally, after an interminable silence in which even the parrots in the trees had stopped squawking, the speaker exploded into the most exciting words Freddy had ever heard. "Friends of the revolution, put your hands together as we welcome our fearless Comandante, savior of the country, freer of nations, the master of our destinies and the reincarnation of the liberator himself."

And, appearing as if from nowhere—Freddy hadn't seen a convoy or a helicopter, *it's as if he just materialized*—at long last

El Comandante arrived, striding confidently onto the stage. Big, dark men fanned out around him and through the crowd, their watchful eyes missing nothing as they spoke to each other in a heavily accented Spanish different from that to which Freddy had become accustomed.

Freddy was immediately filled to overflowing by a sense of awe. After so long waiting, studying, and planning for this moment, he was at last seeing El Comandante in the flesh. All his work, his preparation, and the difficulties he had gone through were finally going to be worth it—he had arrived and was sitting at the foot of the master. Freddy forgot the students, the march, and the violence, focusing everything in him on the moment.

The minister of the interior stepped to the front and took the microphone. The military man Machado was back toward the rear of the stage, a backstop highlighting the main event. "Comrades," the minister said. Freddy held his breath. "Young people from abroad. Revolutionaries. Tonight you will listen to El Comandante. He has come here to recognize your commitment to our peaceful revolution and to thank you for your efforts in defending Venezuela from our enemies. Today, we have made important strides with your help, and these do not go unnoticed, unobserved, or unappreciated. But they are just one battle in a war we have been fighting for years. A war against illiteracy, poverty, misery, injustice, and suffering. But in that war, we have a leader, a general, a comandante." As he said that word, the entire crowd erupted in explosive jubilation. "Without our comandante, we are soulless, wandering aimlessly and desperately in the twilight. With him, we are fulfilled. Now, please give a revolutionary welcome for your Comandante and the messiah of this glorious peaceful revolution."

The screaming, the clapping, the whistling, and the cheering were deafening. They went on for several minutes, with the speakers blazing and people throwing things up into the air. The euphoria was exacerbated by the alcohol and the feeling of impunity they were still enjoying after their afternoon's struggle.

Then he stepped forward, taking the microphone. Freddy's heart fluttered.

Estimados amigos revolucionarios, and my blessed Venezuelans. Welcome tonight to the peaceful revolution. Today, you have succeeded, at long last, in breaking the backs of the oligarchs. Those students won't be bothering us anymore. You have seen to that.

The crowd exploded again in cheers.

You have demonstrated to them that those of us who serve the revolution are peaceful, but we are not afraid. We will not allow them to continue their sabotage indefinitely. That even we, who have been so patient, waiting for decades, no centuries, have finally reached our limits. And when those limits are reached, we have teeth, and by god our peaceful revolution can bite.

The screaming was louder still—the ground Freddy stood on was shaking with the power of it. He waited several full minutes and then quieted the crowd to continue.

I have come here to tell you several important things. The first, and the most important, is that tonight—while you were beating back the brutal selfish hordes that have so desperately tried to destroy our revolution time and again—our military intelligence uncovered an assassination plot. Yes, tonight, here, on this very stage, they were going to kill me.

Silence and a drawing in of breath. Freddy was shocked. *It's real.*

But I will never be eliminated. For I am of the people. I am the people. And they can't kill the people, they can't kill the revolution. I am just one man, and if I go, a thousand will jump up to take my place. Let them know, those coupsters, that their time is coming. Even now, they are being rounded up one by one and will have to answer to the revolution for their barbaric, cowardly conspiring …

El Comandante went on, speaking for many minutes on this subject—using expletives that would make a sailor blush, amusing the crowd with his histrionics and a polished, masterful performance.

Freddy was under the spell of El Comandante's power and magnetism. Then, out of nowhere, the emissary appeared at his side. "Freddy, my son, what do you think?"

Freddy turned. "I have no words," he said, and the emissary only smiled.

"I'm sorry to have missed the march. I've been working on something else, very important, very hush-hush. But I would never have missed this event. I would never have missed the opportunity to hear El Comandante speak to you, my special young people, and to watch your reaction as you come face to face with our savior." And he smiled what was, to Freddy, the smile of an elder and mentor. Freddy was filled with warmth. He turned back to the stage to listen to the Comandante spin his web.

> But enough of that. Tonight, I am here to recognize and commemorate a pivotal moment. For today is an important anniversary—for me and for the glorious revolution that is so much greater than I am. This is the day, the very day, on which so many years ago I walked to the top of a mountain, out there on the Great Plains, and promised to free my country and my people from the brutal chains of capitalism, selfishness, slavery, and colonialism.

A cheer went up among the people, a scream heard around the city, a yell of violence and of repudiation of their common enemy.

"Remember," the emissary said in the moments of silence that followed, "I have dropped off the bags, like we agreed. They are at the house where you are staying. But remember, nobody should open any of it. You will take it with you onto the plane, bypassing our customs. In Miami, you probably won't ever see it. I will have my people pick it up straight out of the airplane—so don't worry about that. This is a tremendous service to the revolution." Freddy just nodded, his attention focused on El Comandante.

I'd like, today, to tell you all a story, a revolutionary story. A revolutionary story from the Great Plains of Venezuela. A long, long time ago, in the heart of those beautiful plains of ours, there was a large *finca*. This *finca* was owned and operated by a *familia oligarquica*. They had ruled this land with feudal brutality for generation after generation, since before we freed ourselves from Imperial Spanish tyranny. But even after independence, the slavery for the peasants working that land continued.

El Comandante took a swig from a small cup of coffee placed strategically on a stool beside him. "Ah, Venezuelan coffee, the best in the world." And he went on,

This huge piece of land was farmed by peasants—a large group of several hundred who should have been the real owners of the land. They worked the land, so why would they not own the land they worked? Because they hadn't bought it? Capitalist ideas. The work was hard. My students, know this: the work is always hard when you work for your masters, not each other. Just like the work of a president is hard if you are working for a foreign empire, like a dog chained to their bedside. Yes, those peasant farmers worked, and they slaved, and they labored. But everything they were able to produce in a good year was handed over to the fat, sweaty white hands of the oligarchs. And in a bad year. Oh, in a bad year. Those same fat oligarchs that forced the people to call them *"Don"* and *"Doña"* would come and take even what the peasants didn't have—their very food, leaving them hungry and miserable. And this criminal behavior was sanctioned by the government of those times and applauded by one rich, corpulent oligarch to another.

He stopped for effect, looked around, and gave a playful wink to somebody in the audience.

They even called the workers *"mis indiecitos."* On Christmas sometimes they gave away cheap dolls from the company store, or allowed *"sus indiecitos"* to keep an extra kilo of the meat they worked hard to produce every day. And life was hard on this plantation. To travel off the land for visits, they had to get permission. And to leave the land permanently, they first had to pay off all the debts they had to the oligarchs. This was impossible—because, just like in the capitalist system we are so desperately trying to destroy here, they were constantly plied with new things and charged exorbitant prices at the company store. If a cigarette costs one Asno in the city, it would cost two in the company store—that's how the oligarchs kept them in slavery. Ah, capitalism. It lined the pockets of that rich family and left our comrades so poor they couldn't plan, dream, or even think. Or care for their sick. Or learn to read. Into this void came a caring, compassionate *comunista*. A Catholic priest. Not like the Catholics that we have here today, right here in San Porfirio de la Guacharaca, who drink expensive whiskey and look for expensive whores. Not the *hijos de la oligarquia* who use the church to keep us feeling poor and guilty—who tell us that our place, the place that their God intends us to be, is in the muck and the mire and the misery. No, a real *revolucionario*, a real brother. His name was Padre Ignacio.

* * *

While El Comandante spoke, *Teniente* Juan Marco Machado eased himself off the stage and began walking through the crowd. He wanted to see and feel for himself the impact that El Comandante was having on these young people. He wanted to judge for himself whether his efforts in organizing these events had merit. He walked in the direction of the fat kid they called Freddy. As he walked, he saw the back of the head of someone talking intensely to the boy. He approached closer and saw that it was an older man who spun on his heels to walk away and barreled directly into him.

* * *

Freddy was filled with El Comandante's story—a real story of poverty and revolution. *What an incredible man.* The emissary turned to walk away and collided shoulder to shoulder with the military man.

"*Hola*," Freddy said cheerfully, greeting the military man he'd become friendly with. He noticed immediately that the emissary had gone white. He started stuttering, mouthing words that Freddy didn't understand. From the suave confidence of a minute before, the emissary had morphed, disintegrated right before Freddy's eyes—he looked as if he were going to faint. He started to turn, looking like he was planning to run. "I have to go."

But the military man grabbed him by the arm and said, slowly, "*Tú.*"

But El Comandante started speaking again, and Freddy turned his attention back to the master, denying any distraction that would steal from his moment and ignoring the power struggle that was starting behind him—and that he didn't understand.

* * *

"Enrique ..." Machado said. That face, even this many years later, Machado would never forget. Enrique, the oligarch's hated enforcer, turned taxi driver, turned diplomat and emissary. How many times had he thought of the man, of what he used to do, of the way he had behaved.

Machado was instantly transported back in time—back decades to the small village in the large *finca* where he, the offspring of a poor peasant family, suffered out his long days with only the dream of advancement and with his only companion in those visions the kind, gentle hand of a Jesuit priest—Father Ignacio.

* * *

Padre Ignacio was a young Jesuit priest. He traveled from village to village teaching the children of peasant farmers. You see, young people, here in Venezuela we understand that the most important thing is education. To read, this is far superior than marching up and down. For with reading, you can build your future and understand your world. To have a house, that is far more important than being able to stand on a street corner and scream obscenities at the revolution. For what am I but the father of the revolution—and what kind of a child screams at their father, who is only trying, through much personal sacrifice, to provide them with their basic needs? And my young people, to have health care, that is so much more important in your lives than the right to vote now and then for the next corrupt oligarch who will lie to you and steal your money. We lived that, for many years, and know the folly and the oppression that it brings. And that was what Padre Ignacio was trying to bring to that small village—that tiny town— using what we all know is the humanizing power of literature. He started with *Don Quijote de la Mancha*, teaching people to think about the transcendental. Then he went on to teach other important books like Paulo Freire, like Schopenhauer, and yes, even Marx and Engels. He was giving the children a platform for evaluating their world and understanding what was about to happen in it. He built relationships with the students and through the students with their families. He helped one special family as the old man was dying of consumption—giving freely of his small Catholic wages for a funeral. He helped another one during harvest day. He would go out and spend Sunday afternoon, the only days that the angry oligarchs allowed 'sus indiecitos' to rest, singing songs and playing with the children, or would minister a kind word of healing to whomever would listen. He was a gentle man—a man of mystery—and a revolutionary.

El Comandante held the hundreds of thousands of marchers in the palm of his hand. They breathed when he did, they felt as he felt.

Freddy had a tear in his eye while thinking about this dedicated young priest. He wanted to be that priest. He felt a connection with El Comandante, as if Freddy himself were sitting at El Comandante's feet and learning, alone. Nobody else was there; the lesson was solely for him. He had forgotten the incidents on the highway—hadn't El Comandante himself said to them that they had done the right thing? He was engrossed in revolutionary rapture.

* * *

Even in her panicked pacing, Doña Esmeralda paused in front of the TV. She had stopped counting how many drinks she'd had. She was paralyzed in despair and indecision. *What will happen to me? What can I do? Where will I go?*

But El Comandante was talking about something that, for some reason, seemed important to her. She stopped and stood, trying to focus, leaning on the bar to reinforce her grasp on reality. *He's talking about my* finca. *The one those damn peasants stole from me.* That stupid, irrelevant event that had seemed to mean so much, that had somehow set in place a chain of events that led in a an unbroken line to this moment …

* * *

"I have looked for you these long years." Oblivious to El Comandante's rapture, Machado was, at long last, confronting his nemesis, Enrique. "Yet you have eluded me. You escaped into nothing, and now I find you here, hiding in full sight, in our revolution? How dare you—this revolution is for the true *hijos de Venezuela*, not for traitors like you, soaked in the blood of *our* martyrs. I have thought of you every day since that day and waited impatiently for this moment."

Enrique was starting to regain a little bit of his composure. He glanced quickly from side to side, eying the military police that seemed to be everywhere. To Machado he seemed to be forming a plan, thinking of escape. Yet he rebutted, "Ah, man." And he fell back to his silken tongue. "You say you thought of me, looked for me, imagined this day? I must tell you, I didn't give you a second thought. I ran to save my skin. But I am a faithful employee, and today I serve the revolution just as faithfully as I served my old employers. I am a survivor, Machado, not an idealist. There is only one way to survive in this world, and that is to make your own place and make your own way."

As he was speaking, he was stepping slowly away. Machado could see him eying the open gates of the airport, only fifty meters away.

* * *

One day, this wonderful young revolutionary Catholic received a special shipment of books from Spain. These books were a compendium, a collage of stories of peasant revolutions, from Russia, to France, Nicaragua, Mexico, and even America. These stories were written not from the point of view of the thinkers and planners of revolution but from the minds and the hearts of the peasants who most suffer under the weight of oppression.

Freddy watched as El Comandante raised high in the air an old, tattered manuscript.

I was even able to get a copy for myself, and I occasionally read some of the stories to remind myself of why it is that we have embarked upon this epic struggle. These books, paid for out of impoverished pocket of Ignacio, went into the hands of his students—as a *real* Christmas gift and a timeless lesson.

He turned around to lay the tattered book carefully on the table behind him, took another drink of coffee, and came back to the microphone.

But in that small *finca* village, there was an evil slave master. An enforcer put there by the oligarch family who couldn't even be bothered to visit '*sus indiecitos*' and find out what their lives were like. No, they were too busy accumulating the infrastructure of the nation under their greedy belt, spending their money in Miami or in Europe without any thought to the poverty of the people who kept them at the pinnacle of their wealth and power. This man was an arrogant, evil man. He took advantage of the farmer's daughters. He stole food, crops, and goods from the company store, charging them off to this or that family. He conspired with one family to attack another that was emerging from poverty. And he always reported back, 'All is well at the *finca*' to the white oligarchs.

El Comandante took a deep breath and slowed his voice, lowering it a decibel for effect. Freddy leaned forward, consumed by the story.

"Well, all was not well at the farm."

Freddy was trapped inside El Comandante's story. He'd forgotten the power struggle that was going on behind him.

One day, this slave master approached a weak child—an abused little girl who feared him more than anything in the world. And he asked her, that fateful day, "What is that dirty priest teaching you?" Shaking and trembling, she could not speak but only handed up to the enforcer the book—this book.

And El Comandante picked up again the tattered manuscript.

The slave master was enraged. "This is what you are learning?" he screamed. And he smacked the girl across the mouth, spilling her blood across the grass.

El Comandante looked at his followers. Freddy immediately thought of the blood that had been shed only hours before, but he quickly put the image out of his mind. El Comandante continued,

You see, violence is the only recourse of the weak. Well, that evening, the enforcer stayed up late. He watched and waited as Padre Ignacio finished up in the small school at the center of town, locking the door and going out back to his tiny one-room shack to make his humble dinner. Just as he crossed to the back and was enveloped in darkness, he saw the slave master's eyes gleaming white and yellow in the night, and he felt the blade slip in between his ribs, piercing his lungs so he couldn't even cry out for help. He died that night drowning in his own blood, another sacrifice to appease the *oligarquia* and their lust for power and control.

El Comandante was silent.

* * *

"And that was the day." Without even realizing it, Machado and Enrique had been frozen in time, listening to the story from El Comandante and reliving that moment, decades in their past, when so many things had changed for both of them. "That was the day, *hijo de puta*," Machado said, "When I promised I would not spend my life like that. When I knew that there would be a better way, and when I decided that I, too, would make revolution. Just like in those books that Ignacio gave us."

* * *

Led by one bold student, one true student.

El Comandante was whispering into the microphone. The entire mob leaned forward as if sharing a special secret with their leader.

> Not like the students you saw out there this afternoon, no, but a revolutionary student. Led by him, the townspeople started to organize. They knew who had killed Ignacio—it was obvious. And their hatred for the slave master was deep and broad. They chose the moment, the perfect moment. It would be at the burial of Ignacio—they would undo what had been done and throw off the chains forever.

* * *

"Right after the funeral," Machado said to Enrique, "We knew where to find you. You see, it was Sunday; you'd be drinking with your buddies down at the tavern. We knew the only way to finally free ourselves from the slavery was to free ourselves from *you*."

"Yes." Enrique was edging closer to the door, Machado following him in his rage, blind now to Enrique's plan of escape. "But you underestimate fear, my friend. I was tipped off—I knew you were coming."

"And you fled like a dog in the night, like a coward, like a thief. But here you are now. Again, after all these years, and today it is *I* with the power."

* * *

For Freddy only the story existed.

> That day, the ripples of revolution started to spread out from that small, lost *finca* of slavery and brutality to engulf the entire country in flames. That day, the farmers stormed the town, putting to death the employees of the enforcer, the owner of the company store who had kept them in poverty for so long. The slave master, however, was not to be found. Like all cowards, he had fled and vanished into the night. That day, the crowds bathed in the oligarchs' pool, ate what they would from the restaurants, drank their fill of beer from the tavern, and pissed upon the bodies of those who had kept them in slavery.

El Comandante had reached the climax of his story.

> And that day was the day that I, a young private in the military, learned that the oligarchs' hold on power is tenuous. I saw that a steadfast and stalwart effort of a meek, thoughtful communist can remove them in a day. That day, my young American friends, the revolution started. Spreading like wildfire, it reached our ears, so far away, tucked inside a barracks on the other side of those plains, under the watchful eyes of our mountains. And that was the day we walked to the top of the hill and vowed to overthrow the government.

* * *

Enrique tried a different tactic. "I am a faithful and obedient employee. That should make the revolution proud. I have seen the folly of my ways and have changed." He was seeking to buy some time as he edged closer to the large gate.

"Not this time." Machado had regained composure. A steely, sickly grin spread across his face, and he said to the military police officers within earshot, "Seize this man." Enrique tried to sprint to the gate, but he was too late. He was grabbed around the ankles by the police. He went down hard, hitting his head on the pavement. They flipped him over, and six pairs of hands reached down to grab him.

* * *

Doña Esmeralda was dumbfounded, stuck to the TV set in her kitchen. *So that's what happened?* She had never understood why that vile, ungrateful mob had risen up against her. She never knew, except that when she reported the takeover of her farm to the police, they had told her, "We are dealing with these things all over—they seem to have spread like wildfire. We just don't have the manpower, and we had really better not push the envelope just now."

She had even gone to the military—her *friend* Gregorio, she thought angrily—who at that time was a colonel and had his ear on the pulse of the nation. "Listen, *querida*, we can't deal with your particular problem right now. We've got a full-scale revolt in some of the bases in the interior. We are trying to fix the issue. Don't worry, we'll get your farm back, but for now we must settle this down."

Before he'd vanished, she even remembered getting reports from her man in charge—a man named Enrique, she seemed to recall. He had always said that things were going well and according to plan, and he had always seemed so professional, which is why the revolt had taken her so much by surprise.

If I had only known, she said to herself. *If I had only known* …

And just then the door exploded inward. A dozen soldiers rushed into her house, followed by a massive, terrifying monster. "Come with us," the Neanderthal ordered. She robotically put down her drink and walked slowly with them out the door, not even questioning or fighting, just bending over to give her tiny yorkie one quick scratch behind his left ear. Her small dog's confused, mournful yipping was the last thing Esmeralda heard as she left the house. Walking up the driveway were two bedraggled women with two and three children respectively, all their earthly goods piled high in a wheelbarrow pushed by the youngest boy. "Enjoy my house," Esmeralda said to them acidly as she was hustled into the military jeep. As they drove off, she saw Clarita come out and embrace the two women, leading them into her and Gonzalo's castle.

* * *

The story finished, El Comandante's speech went on and on. Late into the night, he spoke. He spoke about the revolution. He spoke about history, geopolitics, and government. He talked angrily about the oligarchs, about the white people, about the students, and about the Americans.

Geronimo, who had reappeared at Freddy's side, said, "Do you understand better now?" Freddy simply nodded, lost deep in thought. The night began to draw to a close. There were some songs from a local band. Some awards were given out. El Comandante finished his speech, immediately vanishing as mysteriously as he had arrived.

Freddy looked around. Teniente Machado was nowhere to be seen, and the emissary had also left. *It's over. But it's really just beginning.* Yes, tomorrow he was headed home—with a special and important delivery. But, as he had already convinced himself, he would be back quickly. *I will be spending a great deal of time in Venezuela.* And he smiled, not understanding the truth in his words.

50

* * *

"So." *Teniente* Machado arrived bright and early at the Air Force academy. It was here, in the basement, that the most valuable prisoners of the revolution were always held. There were no jailers here; there were no pesky human rights groups or family associations that demanded access to their loved ones. There weren't even any lists, since this place didn't exist. Here, there was just pain—and atonement.

"You thought you could finish with our revolution that easily? Did you think we were stupid? Did you think we weren't on to you? Foolish man." The prisoner Alejandro simply stared back at the *Teniente*. One of his eyes was swollen shut, and he was naked and covered with blood and scars.

"You and your kind will never be back—this country is ours now. I will see to that. I give you my solemn oath. You have spent your last days as a free man."

There was something about Alejandro's demeanor. Machado knew from months of experience that he was hiding something. But try as they might, they'd been unable to get him to confess. The process had been hard work, work Machado hated but that seemed to give the beast Quispe renewed energy. He'd been working all night and still did not show any signs of fatigue. As he looked down, the *capitán* turned his head upward and looked at Machado directly and unflinchingly through bloodied and swollen eyes. Then suddenly he raised the corners of his lips, cracked from abuse and dry from lack of water, into an awful, peaceful smile. Mirroring his shoulders, Machado's soul slumped. He was suddenly immensely tired. *How did it ever come to this?*

He turned to Major Quispe. "We have all we need from him. He has told us everything. Finish him off. Do it quickly, please." And he turned to leave the room.

* * *

Morning arrived early for Freddy. True to his word, the emissary had left the bright red duffel bag sitting on his bed. Emerging from his room, Freddy took his last breakfast with Geronimo and his family.

"Thank you so much," he said to Geronimo. "I have learned a lot. I'll never forget this week—it's changed my life. I have some things to do in America, but I promise I'll be back. There are too many important things going on here that I don't want to miss out on." He gave a hug to Geronimo's grandmother, accompanied by a little peck on the cheek, and went outside.

There, the waiting jeep took him down to the city where, sitting in the bus on the airstrip, the rest of his team was ready to go to the international airport down by the beach.

They made their slow, agonizing way down to the airport. Stuck in traffic, Freddy read the news from a newspaper stand that was selling special editions of *La Navaja*."

"Seventeen Killed in Student March—Murdered by Their Own People to Sully the Name of El Comandante."

The other paper, the one that Geronimo said was owned by the oligarchs and published antigovernment lies, read, "Bodies of Military Man and Student Leader Found—Families Denounce Torture" and, below, "Supreme Court Justice Killed in Apparent Mugging Attempt."

Freddy was pensive and quiet, not wanting to talk, but he did notice that four other young people carried big duffel bags. If asked, he had been instructed to say, "Gifts from El Comandante, some shirts to distribute at my school." He imagined that was the same order the others had been given. He was a little disappointed. *I thought it was my special bond with the emissary.* To think that the emissary had been as friendly and kind to other people made his man-crush ache.

Even more, he didn't feel like talking. They arrived at the airport to leave, and he expected to see the emissary. But he was nowhere to be found. The airplane, a large Boeing 727, was waiting on the runway. They bypassed customs, just as his friend had said he would, and parked within walking distance of the aircraft. Emerging from the bus first, he grabbed his duffel bag and his luggage and started to walk to the airplane. He would check his baggage in at the bottom of the stairs—there was a person waiting specially for them. *Here I go.* And he walked forward.

Standing by the side of the airplane, by the luggage, were four national guardsmen with drug-sniffing dogs. Freddy didn't think anything of this. The driver of the bus, who was escorting them to the airplane, said to the guardsmen, "These are special guests of the revolution. They are not to be searched."

The guardsmen answered, "We have it on the highest authority that everybody is to be searched. If you don't like it, take it up with military intelligence." Freddy didn't care; he was deep in thought and just dropped his bag on the runway and started to board the airplane. He had just taken his first step onto the roll-out stairs when the drug dog started barking and snarling at his bag. He hesitated. One of the guardsman ordered him, "Come here and open this bag."

Freddy stepped down off the stairs and onto the tarmac. Returning to Venezuelan soil sent a jolt through his body—a jolt of foreboding. "But, *señor*," Freddy responded, "These are special documents for the revolution, going to Miami." In his fear Freddy, had forgotten his cover story. "They are not to be opened."

"I don't care," snarled the guardsman. "Open it."

"*No*," Freddy attempted to say firmly, but his voice broke.

Disgusted, the national guardsman unsheathed a large hunting knife from his belt and sliced open the bag. "What do you think you are doing?" Freddy yelled. But his yell was cut off in midsentence as the guardsman reached into his bag and removed brick after brick after brick of tightly packed, cellophane-wrapped cocaine.

"Special documents for the revolution, you say?" said the guardsman.

Freddy was dumbfounded. Immediately, his insides seized with fear and he doubled over, vomiting on the runway. He looked around. Not knowing what to do, he made a futile attempt to run up the stairs into the airplane. The guardsman reached out as he fled, grabbing him by the lapel and pulling him hard onto his back, splayed out in his own vomit. "*Gringo de mierda*, give me your passport."

"Well, sir, my passport was stolen," Freddy said as he stood up, the pain shooting through his back from where he had hit it on the side of the stairs. He withdrew his travel letter from his pocket. "The embassy gave me this." And he handed the document to the military man, his hand shaking.

"This? What the hell is this? You mean you are *indocumentado*? You mean that you are not really a gringo after all?" A smile spread across the man's face.

"That's an official document." Freddy sucked in his chest and tried to sound commanding.

"I've never seen this before, *carajito*," the man said. "Since you have no papers, there is no way to tell anybody who or where you are." Then the man yelled to his subordinates, "Get him out of here."

Freddy was dragged kicking and screaming across the tarmac to a waiting truck. He never saw whether, behind him, the other four students with their duffel bags made it through.

51

* * *

Pancho woke up, his head pounding. He tried to open his eyes, noticing immediately that one wouldn't open. He raised his hand to his eye—it was swollen shut. The memories were starting to return sporadically. He vaguely recalled having been in a hospital. He reached up to his head to find it bandaged and neatly wrapped. *But I'm not in a hospital now.* He looked around the small room. The walls were cement, the floor was cement, there was no window, and in the corner was a small toilet—with an empty bucket beside it. His heart skipped a beat. He looked toward the other side of the room to iron bars, and his stomach seized. There were benches along all the walls. Pancho realized immediately that he was cold and felt below to the bench. His hands caressed rugged cement. There was a single forty-watt light bulb hanging from the ceiling—it was one of the social initiative variety, casting a sickly pall around the room. The place reeked of sweat and death.

He heard a scream from down the poorly lit cement corridor, followed by a sick whimpering sound.

He had been thrown like a rag doll into the corner and left there. His clothes were still bloody from the previous day, and he badly needed a shower.

The memories were returning faster and with force. *It was that young gringo. He hit me.* The situation was sorting itself out. *There were the military hands—the ambulance.*

The door of the cell just opposite him opened, and a pair of rough hands threw a decrepit old woman in. She fell hard on her hands, and her wig fell off her head. Pancho looked at her with startled curiosity. She was made up as if she were going to a party, although the makeup was running down her face from the tears. She had no jewelry, and other than the look of terror on her face she looked unharmed.

Pancho looked closely at her. "Don't I know you?"

Her head snapped up, and she squinted through the bars, responding dryly, "Maybe not, but I know you. You needed the money, sent my nephew to get it. So I exchanged money for your father. Just like everybody else, you wanted my money. Just like everybody else, I bought you." The room returned to silence.

And the silence continued. They stared at each other, at the walls, and at the floor. Occasionally they would glare into each other's eyes—unwilling accomplices in joint subjugation. The time went on; the silence grew thick like a fog that they could cut through only using the dirty knives that were thrown on the floor in front of them with their clear soup and hard, day-old bread. Then they heard the sound of jackboots approaching, followed by a scraping sound as another door slid open. A guard yelled, *"Gringo narco de mierda"* and threw a boy into a third, adjacent cell.

He was white, fat, with long stringy blond hair. His eyeglasses were still on his face, but one of the lenses had been shattered. His shirt was soiled, and there was blood dripping down the side of his head from where he had received a smack from some nameless soldier. Pancho immediately recognized the boy, although his face was swollen from crying. In Pancho's mind, the most startling change—notwithstanding the blood, and the dirt, and the fear—was the change in demeanor. Yesterday—in fact, the last thing he remembered from yesterday—was this face. This face—angry and arrogant, filled with malice of impunity and naive insolence. *This kid with that bottle ...* And Pancho touched his hand to his head, fondling the tender lump that had formed, all the while staring at the young man in hatred.

So much had happened, Pancho recalled, since he had first seen the gringo, in that stupid social studies class that seemed so long ago and so far away from this place.

"You," Pancho hissed with venom and incredulity.

Freddy wrapped his fingers around the cold iron bars and looked, immediately recognizing Pancho's face. He turned his gaze to the bandage on Pancho's head and the blood on his shirt, and then he simply put his head down and began to cry again. "I was questioned, and questioned, and slapped, and slapped again," Freddy said. He heaved huge, dry, wracking sobs.

"If only El Comandante knew that I was set up." Freddy looked up at Pancho and the old lady. "He would free me. Just yesterday, he was talking about how important we were to the revolution. I'm important. I was tricked ..." and his voice drifted away.

"Boy," Esmeralda said through her own bars. "Young, foolish gringo. El Comandante doesn't care about you or me. And he especially hates him." She pointed to Pancho.

"I am here," Pancho said to Freddy, his voice slow and deliberate with anger and fear, "Because I dared to march. Because I dared to have my voice heard above that of El Comandante. And because I challenged him."

Not to be outdone, Freddy sucked in his wracking sobs and fought back. He repeated the only statements and phrases that eased his conscience. "You are here because you refused to follow the law and apply for a permit. You marched illegally, and people were killed."

"Be honest to yourself for once," Pancho said to Freddy. "Do you *really* think that's it? Do you *really* think that they would have simply given us a permit, just like that? Do you think we haven't tried? We wanted to march right to El Comandante so he could see us and hear us. Since when is it a crime to want to be heard by our leaders?" Pancho was speaking slowly; his head was pounding, and he didn't want to get too agitated.

Freddy was silent. He turned to Doña Esmeralda, desperately struggling despite his situation to regain the feeling of comfortable superiority of only last night.

"You." He pointed at her. "I know who you are and what you represent. It is because of you that the revolutionaries have to be strict. You never allowed them to have rights when you had the power. When you were in charge, they were refused jobs and houses and money. You kept them in poverty for generations. And you are surprised that they rise up? And you are surprised that it gets messy?" His voice was angry but quiet. For a moment he had forgotten where he was.

Esmeralda said, "Young man, I don't claim to be fair. I don't claim to have worked for others. I was born who I am, and lived my life in the pursuit of my own happiness. Are we not allowed this pursuit, so valued by Americans, just because there are many poor people in our countries?"

Freddy whispered, "Not when it keeps them in poverty."

Pancho interjected, "But don't you see the danger? You're angry at this old lady—fine, she hasn't done anything for me either. She lived in luxury with the money my dad made managing her business. But he worked—and the rules were fair, and our humble, middle-class discipline allowed us to start to build. I go to school—at least, I *went* to school. Soon enough, I could have graduated and continued to build, using the principles we understood. Principles that protected us, that kept the way forward clear, and that shone a light in front of our feet as we walked down the path. But what about the rules that these thieves follow—what happens if *those* values win? Mediocrity, hatred, revenge, pillage. With those ideals, how will any of us be protected? How can anybody advance?"

Pancho drove the nail home.

"Ask me, once, if I believe that you are a drug trafficker? Look at you. You are not the type. You were duped and fooled."

Freddy looked down. He was embarrassed, angry, but more than anything scared. Being reminded of his own circumstances filled him with terror.

"You were fooled by El Comandante into thinking that you serve some purpose here. You were fooled into thinking that the ridiculous projects they had you work on were somehow advancing *socialism*. They never told you what they really are: schemes they've come up with to cement their control and their power. And you were conned by whomever gave you those drugs."

Freddy was silent.

"Now let me ask you, honestly," Pancho said. "Do you think you will get a fair trial here? Do you think the fact that you were fooled matters? Do you think that the lawyers, the law, and the facts will save you? Do you think there is a judge in this country who will see your case for what it is, not through the lens of politics, or racism, or revenge—or worse, who is not simply taking his orders from El Comandante? No, you yourself said so when you first spoke. You expect El Comandante to swing open that huge steel door and lift you to your feet. Let me tell you, my friend, he won't." And Pancho saw Freddy starting to shake. "You are here, with us. I will not be judged lightly, this lady here will be condemned, and you will be lucky if the American embassy even finds out you are here to get you out, letting you serve your long sentence in an American jail."

Esmeralda repeated, again, words that neither young person understood, like a broken record. "If I'd only known. I didn't realize what was happening. I paid honest people for an honest job. I tried to be kind. I even sent Christmas presents ..." and she quieted.

The three prisoners stared at each other through their bars. The sounds of screaming had stopped, replaced by the sounds of whimpering. The stench of suffering and death was powerful in their nostrils. The floors and walls were cold and clammy to the touch. As they were silent and pensive, the realization hit home for each of them. There was no salvation, no hope, and no tomorrow. Each had been searching in their own way for freedom and for meaning. All in different places and by different means. But in the Revolutionary Socialist Republic of Venezuela, all such searches find their natural end in places like this. The silence extended—it was a deep silence filled with remorse and with despair. They looked down, and the teardrops that fell pooled together, running down through the hidden jail and into the sewers of San Porfirio, joining with the countless tears of an oppressed nation as they fed the floodwaters of the Great River.

52

* * *

"El Comandante wants to see you," the messenger from the Casa Naranja told *Teniente Machado*. Machado was sitting in his spartan office in the Air Force academy, to which he'd fled as soon as Quispe had finished the deed. He jumped anxiously to his feet. It would be the first time he had met El Comandante face to face—alone. He was nervous, but at the same time excited and proud, and he started to get himself ready for his important meeting. His week had been a good one. He'd controlled the students, disrupted an assassination—*at least, that's what I'm telling people*—and, more importantly, he'd found the hole in his airport security. His drug network was intact. "Thank you," he said and swallowed the last of his scotch, a stiff drink to purge his memory of the *capitán's* last moments.

He went to see El Comandante.

"*Mi Comandante.*" He stood straight in front of the gilt, wooden desk. Famous original paintings were hung elegantly on the walls of the Palacio Naranja, and the chairs were of the finest Italian leather. El Comandante was leaning back in his seat behind the desk, one booted foot resting on an ornate ivory stool with images of elephants and African hunters with spears etched into its sides. He took out a bottle of expensive whiskey from a desk drawer and, slowly, poured doubles into two hand-carved crystal glasses—purchased from an ancient European estate by the foreign minister and brought over to meet the exquisite tastes of the dictator.

"Sit down, *Teniente*. Have a drink." Machado sat obediently in the straight-backed chair, his medals and his dress uniform—donned specially for this occasion—digging into his large stomach.

"It's been a good week, *Teniente*." El Comandante tasted the whiskey. "I have been watching you. You've done well. With the gringo students, that was masterful. That ridiculous arrest warrant, fantastic. We rooted out, again, another source of discontent. How much did we have to pay that politician?"

"Only fifty thousand dollars," said *Teniente* Machado with pride.

"A fine investment." And El Comandante lifted the glass and drained it to the ice, listening to the clink of the cold rocks on the side of the crystal.

"There's one other thing, sir," said Machado. "He's asked to have his name taken off the blacklist. Seems he wants to be a politician again."

"I think that's fine. He will come in handy in the future."

"*Si, mi Comandante.*"

"You are a good and faithful soldier. Now, I have another problem. As you know, we have an election coming up—and it would be a pity if the revolution were to suffer any setbacks."

Machado leaned back, rolling his whiskey around his mouth before swallowing, and said in a low voice, "*Mi Comandante*, the revolution must go on."

Printed in the United States
By Bookmasters